ON
COLD
GROUND

ALSO BY
D. S. BUTLER

Lost Child
Her Missing Daughter

DS Karen Hart Series:

Bring Them Home
Where Secrets Lie
Don't Turn Back
House of Lies

DS Jack Mackinnon Crime Series:

Deadly Obsession
Deadly Motive
Deadly Revenge
Deadly Justice
Deadly Ritual
Deadly Payback
Deadly Game
Deadly Intent

East End Series:

East End Trouble
East End Diamond
East End Retribution

Harper Grant Mystery Series:

A Witchy Business
A Witchy Mystery
A Witchy Christmas
A Witchy Valentine
Harper Grant and the Poisoned Pumpkin Pie

ON COLD GROUND

DETECTIVE KAREN HART SERIES

D.S. BUTLER

THOMAS & MERCER

Published by Thomas & Mercer, Seattle

www.apub.com

Amazon, the Amazon logo, and Thomas & Mercer are trademarks of Amazon.com, Inc., or its affiliates.

ISBN-13: 9781542017596
ISBN-10: 1542017599

Cover design by @blacksheep-uk.com

Printed in the United States of America

ON COLD GROUND

PROLOGUE

They had no idea he was watching. He'd been trailing them for three hours, and they still didn't have a clue.

He'd watched them eat dinner, then spent what felt like hours at the Lincoln Christmas Market, following them as they perused the stalls, admiring the lights and decorations. But finally, they'd had enough of the fake, gaudy celebrations, and were heading away from the castle.

The couple kept gazing at each other in a lovey-dovey way. Nauseating. That was why they hadn't noticed him. They only had eyes for each other. He smirked. Very careless.

Leaning against the black railings in front of the Judges Lodgings, he watched people stream past him. The temporary market, in and around the grounds of Lincoln Castle, drew large crowds. This year more than most, after the event had been cancelled last year.

From his vantage point, it looked as though the historic building were hunched over, embarrassed by the meaningless festivities. People here had no respect for the past. Earlier, he'd watched in disgust as an elderly man walked past the entrance to the dungeons, wearing a Father Christmas hat and a scarf with flashing blue lights, slurping from a cup of mulled wine and munching on a gingerbread biscuit. So much for the true meaning of Christmas.

He didn't understand the appeal. It was noisy. There were too many people in the area. And it was freezing. He cupped his hands and held them against his mouth, his breath hot against his numb fingers. He wasn't exactly dressed for a stroll around the Christmas market. His dark jacket had proved too lightweight once the temperature began to steadily drop as the afternoon headed into the evening. The baseball cap he wore helped to shield his face from the many CCTV cameras but did little to keep him warm.

Irritated, he looked at his watch. Things were not going to plan. He'd played his part to perfection, but hadn't counted on this development. He felt a sharp pain behind his eyes and took a deep breath of icy air. He needed to relax. It would all work out. Events had just unfolded differently than expected, that was all. He'd done everything right. No one could accuse him of not achieving his objective.

Earlier he'd been ready to go home, but his hands had been shaking so violently he'd needed something to calm his nerves. He'd gone to the nearest pub and ordered a whiskey to take the edge off. The warm, soothing effect of the alcohol had just started to kick in when the couple walked into the pub.

What were the chances? Were they on to him? Did they know?

Now, after traipsing around behind them for three long hours, he was sure they didn't. Well, almost sure. It had been a coincidence they'd walked into the same pub. But he didn't like coincidences. They made him nervous.

Of course, he knew who *she* was straightaway. *The problem*, as his boss referred to her.

He grinned. When his boss was feeling less polite, it was *the thorn in my backside* and a few other choice words.

He was still grinning when a tall, thin woman wearing a pair of fluffy pink earmuffs gave him a stern look as she walked by. 'Weirdo,' she muttered.

He stared after her. He was the weirdo? He wasn't the one wearing pink earmuffs, was he?

He grunted in disgust and turned back to his targets. They were passing the Magna Carta now, laughing together. She was quite easy on the eye, but he looked like a bloke you really wouldn't want to cross. Still, appearances could be deceptive. The information he had on her suggested she was the more dangerous one. The one he had to watch.

He walked slowly after them. Despite the cold, it was nice to be outside doing something physical for a change.

He glowered up at the dark sky as snow started to fall. He sniffed. The cold air was making his nose run.

Two children walked by, their plump faces smeared with sugary goo, holding toffee apples. That wasn't a Christmas thing, was it? But it didn't seem to matter. Whatever was on sale, the daft tourists lapped it up.

He slowed as the couple stopped to gaze at each other, chatting away, smiling like they were the only two people in the world.

He wanted to step between them and warn them not to get too happy because it wouldn't last. It never did.

A shove from behind made him stagger forward. The culprit was a large, squat man with a bald head who continued on his way, not bothering to say sorry.

He clenched his fists, but it wasn't the time or place to make a scene. He couldn't draw attention to himself, but muttering some obscene words under his breath in the man's direction made him feel a little better.

The crowds weren't there to celebrate the true meaning of Christmas. They just wanted cheap ornaments for their Christmas trees and to gaze at the twinkling lights like gormless fools.

A teenage girl walked past holding a paper cup. The smell of hot chocolate made him look closer. The cup was filled to the brim with cream and topped with marshmallows. Where had she got that? It was the only thing in the entire market he'd like to buy. He had a sweet tooth, and the thought of wrapping his cold fingers around a cup of hot chocolate was very tempting.

He turned back, only to see the couple he'd been following weren't there. He straightened, craning his neck, trying to see over the heads of a group of German tourists who were strolling past and having an animated conversation.

Why were there so many people here?

He couldn't have lost them. He'd only taken his eyes off them for a few seconds.

Walking on, he searched the crowds.

Three women, dressed in skintight jeans and skimpy tops, tottered past on sky-high heels. They'd obviously had quite a bit to drink. Maybe the alcohol was keeping them warm because none of them wore coats. The tallest one, with curly brown hair, was tunelessly singing a Christmas song at the top of her lungs.

He shook his head and walked on.

This was not good. Losing track of them for a few seconds was one thing, but they'd been out of sight for over a minute now. He paused. They couldn't have vanished. *Think*. Where would they have gone?

Then he saw them, quite some way off, and exhaled in relief. They'd been walking fast and were heading towards the cathedral. It stood majestically at the top of Lincoln, a perfect pairing with the historic castle, and quite a contrast to the gaudy market.

He followed, walking quickly, keeping his head down as the snow began to fall harder. A snowflake landed on his nose, and he brushed it away.

The cathedral was illuminated, a beautiful sight after so much false cheer. Would they go inside? Despite the cold, sweat coated his skin. He shouldn't still be here. It was too risky.

He'd closed the distance between them, but in his hurry, he'd been careless. The crowds were thinner here, and when the woman turned, he had nowhere to hide.

He wrenched his gaze away, pretending to look for something in his pocket as his pulse spiked.

It's okay, he reassured himself as her gaze skimmed over him. *She doesn't know you're following. To her, you're another Christmas shopper. Just act naturally.*

The couple were talking more intently now. He had his arm around her shoulders, and they seemed relaxed.

Everything is fine.

The thundering in his chest calmed.

His phone buzzed in his pocket. Usually, he'd ignore it, but being on the phone was a good cover. It looked normal, natural. He pulled the mobile out of his pocket, tapped to answer and then pressed the cold screen against his ear.

'Progress report, Sparrow,' said a clipped voice, instantly recognisable as that of his boss.

They had code names and disposable phones for this operation. He'd been offended by his codename at first. Sparrow – a tiny, drab, insignificant bird. But later, he'd decided it was fitting. No one noticed small birds. They got on with things without drawing attention to themselves.

It was all to protect the boss, of course. Not that he needed it. The man was so slippery nothing would stick to him. His code name should have been a type of snake. Of course, it wasn't. He'd picked *Eagle*. Predictable.

'Fine, boss,' he replied. 'It was a false alarm. A coincidence. I'm following them now. I'm keeping a close watch. You have nothing to worry about.'

'You'd better be right. You know what will happen if you're not.'

His lip curled in disgust. Oh, he was well aware of the stakes. He didn't need reminding.

'I'm hardly likely to forget,' he said, not bothering to keep the scathing tone from his voice.

'Make sure you keep me updated regularly, Sparrow. I don't like to sit around waiting.'

'As I'm following them now, it's not the ideal time to make a phone call.'

'Now listen here—'

'I'm going to have to go. They're moving.' He hung up and felt a thrill of pleasure at his defiance, even though he knew the action would come back to haunt him.

Eagle would find a way to turn the screws. People like him always did.

He slipped his phone back into his pocket, his eyes never leaving Detective Sergeant Karen Hart for a second. He wouldn't lose her again.

Eagle didn't have to worry. DS Hart was oblivious. She hadn't noticed anything.

In Sparrow's opinion, his boss had overestimated her. She wasn't all that sharp. It looked like this job would be easy.

CHAPTER ONE

DS Karen Hart had a full stomach and a pleasant, warm sensation buzzing through her body, thanks to the glass of wine she'd had with dinner.

She smiled against the soft wool of her scarf. She'd been seeing Mike Harrington for the past three months, and despite her initial trepidation, as they'd met during a case in which he'd been a suspect, their relationship had been going well – *really* well. Except for one thing.

She glanced at him and noticed the slight tension in his face. He was going to bring it up again, wasn't he? She could tell. She hadn't known him for long, but she knew when he was building up to something.

Looking away, she tried to think of something to distract him.

'The lights are beautiful. They've really gone all out this year, haven't they?' She pointed at the decorations and strands of tiny white lights that criss-crossed the street above their heads.

Mike nodded his agreement. He was preoccupied, and she was sure he was working out how to casually bring the subject up again.

The Christmas decorations were pretty but understated, and complemented the historic streets in the Cathedral Quarter. Walking up Steep Hill earlier, Karen had let herself be caught up in the Christmas spirit for the first time in years.

She turned back to Mike. He had snowflakes in his dark hair and was frowning. It hadn't worked. She hadn't distracted him.

He pointed to the cathedral, just ahead of them. 'That's where I attended the grief counselling group. Near the refectory.'

'I know,' Karen said. 'You've mentioned it.'

She heard the coldness in her voice and bit her lip. He was trying to help. He'd been devastated by the death of his son, and the counselling group had helped him. Now, he was trying to help her.

He grimaced. 'Is that a cue for me to stop bringing it up?'

Yes, Karen thought.

In the past three months, her life had changed dramatically, and she felt she was coping. She still had sad days, and days when she was furiously angry, but considering she'd lost her husband and daughter and confronted the man who'd used his car to force their vehicle off the road, she thought her anger and sadness were understandable.

But Mike seemed to think he knew what was best for Karen, and that was starting to get very irritating.

'It's not that you can't mention it, Mike,' Karen said slowly. 'But I know myself, and while I don't have anything against counselling in theory, group therapy is not for me.'

'But—'

Karen held up a gloved hand. 'I saw a therapist after Josh and Tilly died.'

It was still hard for her to talk about them. The pain hadn't gone away, and she'd think about them every day for the rest of her life. Mike seemed to think it wasn't healthy. He wanted her to talk, to share her grief, but her stomach twisted with anxiety and her chest felt heavy with guilt when she tried.

'It's a good group,' Mike said earnestly. 'I found it helped to talk to people from all different walks of life, and realise that we all experience grief in our own way.'

Karen shrugged. 'I'm not really a sharer, and sitting around drinking tea and eating biscuits while dissecting my personal life with a group of strangers isn't my idea of fun.'

'It wasn't . . . fun,' Mike admitted. 'But it helped. I thought you might—'

Karen shook her head, cutting him off. 'No. It wouldn't suit me. I handle things differently, and I have to do what's right for me.'

Mike nodded. 'Absolutely.'

'So you agree?'

'Sure,' Mike said.

Well, that was easier than she'd expected.

Mike kept telling Karen she needed help with her 'trust issues'. But was it any wonder she was reluctant to trust people after discovering DI Freeman had lied to her face?

Freeman had been a close colleague, someone she'd worked alongside for years. He'd often offered her a shoulder to cry on, when actually he'd known all along who had been responsible for the death of her family. He'd covered it up because he'd been on the payroll of a local crime family. Officers working in traffic had taken bribes to alter the accident report, and two officers from the Thames Valley police service were also found to be associated with the same criminal gang. And Karen was convinced they'd only just scratched the surface. The corruption went deeper than Freeman. Until it was rooted out, Karen felt she was entitled to 'trust issues'.

She pulled on her scarf to tighten it. The evening had turned very cold.

'Although, to be absolutely sure it's not for you, you'd actually have to attend at least one meeting.'

Karen sighed. She should have known he wouldn't give up that easily.

She sensed a movement behind them and turned, but saw nobody close by except a man digging around in his pockets.

'Do you fancy a hot chocolate?' Mike asked, nodding in the direction of a stall set up a short distance from the cathedral.

Karen frowned. That was out of the designated area, wasn't it? She wondered if they had a permit, but then decided to take off her police officer's hat for the evening.

'I don't think I could eat or drink another thing,' she said, patting her stomach. 'I'm stuffed. Dinner was delicious, and the portion sizes were huge.'

They started walking towards the cathedral again. Mike's apartment was close by, in one of the row of terraced houses that encircled the cathedral. Most of the buildings were owned by the church but some were private, and somehow Mike had managed to snag one.

She assumed he was a tenant rather than the owner, though the rent must be costing him a fortune and he couldn't be earning a great deal from his job at the dog shelter.

But that was her detective's instinct causing her to question everything. It was none of her business. He'd tell her about the property if and when he wanted to confide in her. Karen didn't want him to think she was interested in his financial position or eyeing up what he was worth.

She looked up at the sky. A flurry of snowflakes swirled in the air above them. 'I think this snow is getting heavier,' Karen said. 'Do you think it'll settle?'

'I'm not sure. It feels a bit too warm,' Mike said, looking at the slush on the cobbles. 'Shall we go back to mine?'

'Actually, I'm going to head home,' Karen said. She'd stayed at Mike's for the last three nights, and she really needed to get home and do some washing.

'Is that because I pushed you too hard on the grief counselling thing?'

Karen went up on her tiptoes and kissed Mike's cheek. 'No, I've just got stuff to do at home, and I'm back to work tomorrow.'

He put an arm around her shoulders, and they started to walk to her car.

Karen leaned into him and couldn't help thinking that, if he'd only stop bringing up the grief counselling, things could very well be perfect.

◆ ◆ ◆

They were walking by the west front of the cathedral, passing the barriers at the renovation works, when they heard the scream.

They stopped short and turned to look. A middle-aged woman stood just outside the arched entrance. She raked one hand through her shoulder-length grey hair and used the other to cover her mouth. As the woman turned, Karen realised she'd met her before, just a few weeks earlier. What was her name again?

Panic contorted the woman's face as she took rapid, jerky breaths.

'Eunice?' Mike said, his arm slipping from Karen's shoulders.

Of course. *Eunice.* That was her name. Karen smoothly slid into work mode, moving away from Mike and striding up to Eunice.

'Is everything all right?' Karen asked, though it clearly wasn't.

Eunice was shivering. She wore a long green cardigan but no coat, and had a lanyard around her neck with a symbol and her name printed on the card.

Eunice grabbed Karen's arm, opened and shut her mouth a few times without any noise coming out, and then finally managed to say, 'He's dead.'

Karen put her hand over the woman's. 'Who's dead, Eunice?'

'He's inside.' Eunice pointed to the cathedral entrance. 'In the chapel. I nearly t . . . trod on him. I think he's been murdered.'

Karen turned. 'Mike, would you mind standing here and making sure no one enters or leaves until I get back?'

He took up a sentry position by the door. Karen tried to persuade Eunice to go back inside.

'I can't go back in there!'

'Just into the entrance,' Karen suggested. 'It'll be warmer. You don't have to go into the chapel. I just need you to point the way.'

Eunice swallowed and raised a hand to her throat. 'I don't know. I think we should wait for the police.'

Karen rummaged around in her handbag for her ID. 'I am a police officer, Eunice. Detective Sergeant Karen Hart of the Lincolnshire Police. We met a few weeks ago.' She held up her ID. 'If you show me where you found him, then I'll call it in.'

'Oh, yes.' Eunice blinked, recognition dawning. 'I remember. You're Mike's partner. It was lucky you were passing,' she said, glancing at Mike then peering at Karen's ID. She took a deep breath, trying to gather herself.

'Are you working today?' Karen asked, as the woman slowly edged inside.

'Yes. There aren't any group meetings at the weekends, but I'm taking the donations today. It used to be a voluntary contribution, but now if people want to see all areas of the cathedral open to the p . . . public, we ask them to pay. H . . . helps with the upkeep.' Eunice spoke quickly, gulping shallow breaths between sentences.

'I imagine it does,' Karen said, as they walked across the large stone slabs of the entrance and into the main cathedral. Two huge Christmas trees stood either side of the vast space. It was an impressive sight.

'I sit at that desk there.' Eunice pointed at a small desk, set back against the wall. There was a till on the counter and stacks of leaflets, as well as a pile of large glossy guides to the cathedral.

Eunice led Karen to a small arched entrance close to the desk. The woman's breathing had become ragged, and she was gripping Karen's arm.

'He's in there,' she whispered. 'Between the pews.'

It was warmer inside than out, but Eunice was still shivering.

'Okay. Are you all right to wait here for a minute while I go in?' Karen asked, gently disentangling herself from the woman's hold.

Eunice nodded but kept her wide eyes fixed on the entrance to the chapel.

Karen didn't want to disturb a possible crime scene, but she needed to know there really was a victim before she called it in. She grabbed a pair of gloves from her handbag. It paid to be prepared.

'Can you look after my bag?'

Eunice blinked and, with trembling hands, took the handbag from Karen.

Karen stepped inside the chapel, taking a moment for her eyes to adjust to the dim light. A yellow cleaning sign had collapsed by the entrance. She stepped over it. The chapel was small, with pews running either side of a central walkway. The floor was made of stone slabs, worn smooth by the footfalls of centuries of worshippers.

At the back of the chapel, candles had been pressed into sand-boxes. A prayer request station had been set up in a dark corner. Under other circumstances, the darkness could have been soothing, even meditative, but now Karen wished for some powerful crime-scene lights.

There was no body visible immediately, but as she moved further forward, she saw a man's shoe between the first and second pews on the right side.

She stood at the end of the pews and looked down. The body of a man with brown hair, greying at the temples, lay between the benches. His forehead was a bloody mess. Karen peered closer.

What looked like a ligature mark snaked across the front of his neck.

Had he been strangled? Tried to commit suicide? She looked up to see if there were any cords attached to the rafters or the ceiling. If he'd tried to hang himself and the rope had broken, he could have fallen to the floor and hit his head. That would explain both injuries, but there was no sign of any rope or cord.

Karen manoeuvred herself around the first pew, trying not to lean on anything, and reached down to press her gloved fingers against his neck.

It was possible he was still alive. If she detected a pulse, then she'd need to start CPR and call for an ambulance. The space was tight and uncomfortable, but she waited, hoping to detect his heart beating.

He was freezing cold, though his body wasn't stiff.

She felt no pulse and shifted her fingers, hoping for a different result in the new position. She took her time, making sure, following her training, methodically checking for any sign of life.

But the man was dead, and going by how cold he was, likely had been for over an hour.

Eventually, with a sigh, Karen straightened and left the chapel. She ripped off her gloves and then grabbed her phone from her pocket to call it in.

She smiled sympathetically at Eunice. 'Why don't you go and sit at your desk? You've had a bit of a shock.'

'He was murdered?' Eunice asked as she gave Karen her bag back. 'I don't know when it could have happened. I've been at the desk most of the day.'

'Once I've spoken to my colleagues, I'll come and have a chat.'

'Was he killed here?'

'I'm not sure yet.'

'What an awful thing to happen just before Christmas, and here of all places,' Eunice said grimly. 'It's sucked the Christmas joy right out of me.'

Karen turned away as her call was answered. As she gave the control team the details, she couldn't help agreeing with Eunice. Her Christmas spirit had vanished too.

She'd had a few days' respite, but crime didn't stop for Christmas.

CHAPTER TWO

The scenes of crime officers had set up in the chapel by the time the pathologist arrived. Karen was glad to see Raj was the attending pathologist.

'Had a promotion, Karen? Are you the SIO on this?' he asked, smiling broadly so his large moustache tilted up at the edges.

'No, but I was passing when the body was discovered.'

His eyebrows lifted. 'Off-duty?'

'Yes.' She nodded towards the chapel – though there was little need, as the location of the body was evident from the number of police staff milling about and the extra lights being wheeled towards the scene. 'Not sure how long he's been there. A cathedral employee found him, and I went in to check for a pulse. I tried not to disturb the scene any more than necessary.'

While Raj went to look at the body, Karen decided to go back to the reception desk to talk to Eunice Greene again. She hadn't managed to get much information from the woman earlier. The shock had taken hold, and she'd grown less and less talkative as the minutes passed.

Before Karen reached Eunice, she was stopped by a uniformed officer. Young, tall and fair-haired, with cheeks rosy from the cold, he looked inexperienced. He cleared his throat nervously.

'DS Hart?'

Karen turned to him. 'Yes.'

'I'm PC Ray Watts.'

Karen waited for him to continue.

'Sorry. I just wanted to ask if you need anything. Coffee perhaps? That lady looks like she could do with something warm.' He glanced at Eunice, who was shivering.

'Thank you, PC Watts. That's a good idea.'

Eunice sat hunched over, clutching her cardigan around her body, as Karen approached.

They'd first met under very different circumstances. Eunice helped to organise the counselling meetings at the cathedral, and Mike had engineered an encounter between her and Karen at a coffee shop.

It had been presented as an accident, but Mike was not a natural liar and Eunice was as transparent as glass. After a few exclamations of disbelief from Mike, and comments from Eunice about what a small world it was, Mike had invited Eunice to join them for coffee. At first, Karen had been amused. Mike scheming to introduce Eunice so that Karen would suddenly decide the counselling group was a good idea after all was hardly an evil master plan. But when neither of them backed down after Karen's polite but firm refusal to reconsider her aversion to group therapy, she'd lost her temper, leading to her first proper row with Mike.

They'd called an uneasy truce that evening, but even days later, Mike had refused to drop the subject.

'Can you tell me what happened when you found him, Eunice?' Karen asked gently when she reached the woman.

Eunice looked up and blinked at her. 'I was going to light a candle in the Morning Chapel. I do that once a week for my friend, Sally. She's not been well. I noticed someone had left a "Cleaning in Progress" sign at the entrance, which was odd because it's usually cleaned in the mornings. I looked in, and at first I thought the chapel was empty, but then I saw him. The light's not very good in there. But I saw his shoe sticking out of the end of a pew. I thought he'd had a fall and hit his head.' She raised a hand to her forehead. 'You know, all the blood.'

Karen nodded.

Eunice took a deep breath and swallowed. 'Well, when I got closer, I saw he had marks on his neck.'

'Did you touch the body?'

'I checked for a pulse but couldn't find one. I touched the side of his neck, but that was all.'

'And did you touch anything else in the chapel?' Karen asked, thinking that Forensics was not going to have an easy job with this one. The Morning Chapel probably had a steady stream of visitors all day, every day. There would be a mass of fingerprints and a tangle of forensic evidence to decipher.

Eunice frowned and looked up. 'I leaned against the pew to steady myself. I might have touched the floor with my hand as well when I knelt beside him, and I knocked the cleaning sign over as I rushed out, but I don't think I touched anything else.'

Her teeth were chattering now.

'Eunice, do you have a coat with you?' Karen asked.

'It's out the back.'

'Okay, why don't you get it.'

'Do you think the carol service will be able to go ahead tomorrow?' Eunice asked, getting to her feet.

'I'm not sure, Eunice. Possibly not. It depends on how long the crime scene team need access to the cathedral.'

'I see.'

'And we should probably speak to who's in charge, so that would be the dean?'

'Yes, the dean. I'll telephone her and tell her what's happened.'

'Thank you.'

'Two coffees.' Karen turned to see PC Ray Watts proudly holding two Costa Coffee cups. 'Oh, where's she going?'

'Just to get her coat. She'll be back. Thanks,' Karen said as she took the coffees from him.

She put Eunice's on the desk. It felt wrong to drink inside the cathedral, so she carried her cup outside. PC Watts stuck to her like a limpet, talking about his hopes of becoming a detective.

'It's been my dream since I was a little kid,' he said. 'Any advice for me?'

She smiled as she approached Mike, and then took a sip of her coffee and frowned.

'What's wrong?' PC Watts's gaze dropped to the takeaway cup, then back up to Karen's face.

'Milk, no sugar,' Karen said.

PC Watts's face fell. 'Isn't that how you take it?'

'It is, but how did you know that?'

'I asked this gentleman.' PC Watts nodded at Mike. 'I found out from one of the other officers that he was your partner and asked him.'

'A bit of detective work, then?' Karen smiled.

He blushed and shrugged.

'I'm impressed. My advice would be to carry on as you are, PC Watts. I'm sure you'll make a good detective.'

He beamed.

'Can you start taking statements and contact details from the tourists and staff inside the cathedral? Ask them if they saw or heard anything.'

'Absolutely,' PC Watts said, with such enthusiasm that Karen almost expected him to salute.

She turned to Mike. 'Sorry, I'm going to have to stay. It looks like a murder.'

'You okay? You look a bit pale.' Mike hunched his shoulders and turned his back against the wind as snowflakes drifted towards the cathedral entrance.

'I'm fine. I'm the most senior officer until the SIO gets here.'

'Who's the duty SIO?'

'Morgan.'

Mike's face settled into a frown. 'I'll stick around until he gets here.'

Karen gave the rest of her coffee to Mike and then headed back to find Eunice, who was now sitting at the reception desk wrapped in a brown padded jacket.

'That coffee is for you, Eunice,' Karen said, sitting beside the shivering woman.

'Thank you,' Eunice said, but didn't touch the cup.

'I know you've had a terrible shock, but I need to ask you a few questions. Is that okay?'

Eunice nodded.

'Did you know the victim?'

'Yes, his name is . . . was . . . Lloyd. Lloyd Nelson. He's a member of my amateur choir group.'

'Do you have any idea who could have wanted to hurt Lloyd?'

'No, none at all. He was a lovely man.'

'Were you expecting him here today? Was he here for choir practice?'

'No, we practise on Tuesday evenings. He did say he would pop by to collect the new sheets of music. I print them out for everyone, you see, and then Lloyd drops them off.'

'So you knew he was coming to the cathedral? Did anyone else?'

'No, I didn't know he'd come today. He just said he'd be by to collect the music at some point this weekend.'

'Does the cleaning sign that you knocked over belong to the cathedral?'

'I think so. They're kept in storage near the cloisters. They're often used near the refectory as that area gets cleaned regularly when the building is open.' She frowned. 'Do you think the killer put the sign there to stop people going into the chapel and discovering the body?'

The shock hadn't dulled Eunice's brain. She'd put into words exactly what Karen suspected.

She asked Eunice a few more routine questions, then gave her some privacy while she telephoned the dean.

Karen walked back to the entrance. She wanted to keep out of Raj's way until he was ready to talk. There was nothing worse than someone peering over your shoulder, demanding updates, while you were trying to concentrate.

She looked up at the Christmas trees – real trees giving off a strong scent of pine. Decorated with tiny bright white lights, the twin trees were a welcoming sight for visitors. Quite a contrast to the scene in the chapel right now.

She remembered the carving on the man's forehead, scarlet against the white of his skin. It had looked like a cross, but it was hard to be sure. Maybe Raj could clean up the wound, and they'd have a better idea. Was it gouge marks that just happened to look like a cross, or was it intentional? Was the victim *marked*? A cross made sense in a religious environment like this.

Karen shivered as a draught ran through the cathedral, and she put her hands in her pockets. Morgan should be here soon.

She looked across at the gift shop to the right of the entrance. The manager was packing up for the night as had been requested, and PC Ray Watts was asking him questions.

The shop was opposite the Morning Chapel. There was a chance he might have seen something. Plus, the shop might have

CCTV. She'd have to ask the dean about cameras *inside* the cathedral. She hadn't spotted any. Perhaps the invasion of worshippers' privacy would be frowned upon?

She heard footsteps on the stone floor and turned to see DI Morgan. He was frowning, and a shadow flickered over his expression as he saw Mike standing sentry at the door. He hadn't said as much, but she knew Morgan didn't consider Mike Harrington a good choice. Not that it was any of his concern, Karen thought.

'Surprised to see you here,' Morgan said to Mike.

'Karen asked me to stand on the door and make sure no new visitors came in.'

'Right,' Morgan said. 'Well, we'll handle it now, thanks. I'll put a uniform on the door.'

Mike glanced at Karen.

'Thanks, Mike,' she said. 'I'll give you a call later?'

Mike gave a sharp nod and turned away, striding past the safety barriers – put up while the restoration work was ongoing – and heading in the direction of his apartment as the snow drifted down.

'So, what have we got?' Morgan asked, bringing her back to the scene.

'A body in the Morning Chapel,' Karen said. 'Male, mid-forties. Lloyd Nelson. He has marks on his neck consistent with strangulation. Raj is in there with him now.'

'Strangulation or hanging?' Morgan asked, clearly thinking along the same lines as Karen when she'd first seen the body.

'My money would be on strangulation,' Karen said. 'There was no cord above him to indicate he tried to hang himself. Plus, there are markings on his forehead. It looks like he has a symbol carved into his skin.'

Morgan's eyes widened slightly. 'A *symbol?*'

'I think so,' Karen said. 'It looks like a cross to me, but it's hard to tell with all the blood on his forehead.'

'I don't like the sound of that,' DI Morgan muttered.

'No.'

'Have you spoken to the dean?'

'Not yet. Eunice Greene, the lady who found the body, is getting in touch with her. I've met Eunice before. Mike knows her. She helps to run a counselling group at the cathedral.'

They walked slowly towards the hub of activity.

'The body was found in this chapel. It's open to the public. No charge,' Karen said, pausing as they came close to the doorway. 'There was a cleaning sign at the entrance, possibly placed deliberately to stop people entering the chapel and discovering the body.'

The yellow sign was flat against the floor, and the chapel looked very different now with the crime scene technicians' lights set up and illuminating every corner of the room. The smooth stone floor and historic stonework and carvings were exposed to the startling light. It seemed invasive and unnatural in the setting.

'I happened to be passing when Eunice found the body,' Karen said.

'So you were first on the scene?'

She nodded.

'And you were out with Mike?'

'Yes,' Karen said slowly, not wanting to get into a conversation about Mike. 'Eunice ID'd the body. He's in her choir group, apparently. I've spoken to a few of the tourists who were making their way around the cathedral. I didn't pick up on anything suspicious there, but PC Watts is taking their details just in case we need to get in touch with them.'

'A bit of a shock to the end of your evening,' Morgan said, his tone softening.

Karen gave a wry smile. 'You could say that. You took a while to get here tonight.'

'Yes, the traffic was terrible.'

23

'It always is with the Christmas market.'

Karen introduced Morgan to Eunice, who told them the dean was on her way in. 'It shouldn't be more than ten minutes,' Eunice explained, and she went again through the description of how she'd found the body, for Morgan's benefit.

It seemed cruel to have a witness repeat themselves, to go over it multiple times, describing what must have been a very distressing experience. But Karen had learned early on in her career that it was vital. Each time, the story changed just slightly, and there was a chance more information would be revealed.

Not long after they'd finished talking to Eunice, Raj exited the chapel. His dark hair gleamed, and he smiled at them. The smile lifted his carefully styled moustache. 'DI Morgan. Hello!'

'Hello, Raj,' Morgan said. 'Does it look like murder?'

'Yes,' Raj said. 'I'd say strangulation. I might be able to give you an idea about the ligature used once I get him back to the lab. There was ID on the body.' Raj held out a wallet in an evidence bag.

'Thanks.' Karen pulled on gloves and went through the wallet. 'His cards confirm it's Lloyd Nelson,' she said. 'We've got bank cards, gym ID, store cards, but no driver's licence.'

Morgan asked, 'Anything else you can tell us, Raj?'

'Yes. It's difficult to say for sure, but I think he was probably killed here. The marks on his forehead were made soon after death. There was still some bleeding. I'll give you a more precise estimate for the time of death when I get him back, but I'd guess he was killed only a couple of hours ago.'

'A couple of hours?' Karen repeated, surprised. 'He felt cold.'

Raj nodded. 'It's cold in the chapel. The ambient temperature does make a difference, and he's lying on the stone-cold floor.'

'What do you think is carved into his forehead?' Karen asked. 'I thought it looked like a cross.'

'I agree,' Raj said. 'Maybe not a deliberate carving, though. Once I clear the blood away from the wound, we'll have a better idea. I'll take more photographs.'

'Any idea what was used to carve his skin?' Morgan asked.

'Not yet, no. No weapon has been found at the scene, at least not so far.' Raj looked over his shoulder at the busy comings and goings in the chapel, as the crime scene techs went about their work. 'I'd say probably a little knife. Something very sharp with a small blade, anyway.'

Karen left Raj and Morgan talking and stepped closer to the chapel. Above the door was the carved face of a cherub. It must have seen some sights in its time, but surely it hadn't witnessed many events as gruesome as this.

CHAPTER THREE

Karen left Morgan to speak to the dean. He had the simple job. She had the unenviable task of informing Lloyd Nelson's family. It was never easy telling a family that a loved one had passed. But if anyone could shed light on who killed Lloyd Nelson, his family were a good bet.

She called ahead before picking DC Sophie Jones up on the way. After her family liaison training, Sophie had been hoping for her first FLO job for a few months now, and Karen decided this would be a good case to start with.

Sophie slid into the passenger seat of Karen's Honda Civic. 'Evening, Sarge. We've got a death message to deliver?'

'Yes. A man called Lloyd Nelson. He was found in a small chapel within the cathedral. Looks to me like he's been strangled. He also had something carved into his forehead.'

Sophie twisted in her seat so she was fully facing Karen. 'Something was carved into his forehead? That's sick!'

Karen indicated to turn off towards Coleby. 'It is,' she agreed.

'And his body was left in the cathedral,' Sophie mused. 'Sounds to me like some kind of symbolic murder. Maybe a ritual killing. What was carved into his forehead?'

Sophie spent her nights reading FBI manuals on serial killers and true crime accounts of unusual cases, so her immediate assumption that this was a ritualistic killing didn't surprise Karen.

'Well, let's not get ahead of ourselves,' Karen said. 'We're not really sure what's on his forehead. It's all a bit of a mess. We'll have a better idea when Raj has cleaned up the body and wiped away the blood.'

She didn't add that she thought it had looked like a cross. That would add fuel to Sophie's speculations, and as it had been dark in the chapel, she could have been mistaken. In her experience, murders were usually motivated by love, hate or greed. Ritual murders were few and far between.

'Are there symbols anywhere else on his body?'

Karen shook her head. 'No. At least, Raj didn't mention any. He might find more when he does a fuller examination at post-mortem.'

'I went to lunch at The Bell with my parents a few weeks ago,' Sophie said, pointing out the sign. 'It was really nice.'

Karen turned on to Coleby High Street. Houses lined both sides of the street. Terraces on one side, bungalows on the other. 'Is this where the Nelsons live?'

'Yes, number 32. If you feel up to it, you can take the lead on this.'

Sophie looked surprised but pleased. 'Absolutely, Sarge.'

'Remember to give them some time to process the news. Be compassionate. Don't rush into questions right away,' Karen warned as she parked outside the Nelsons' home – a small house, constructed from light bricks with a grey tile roof.

It was more convenient for the senior officer to take the lead, but that didn't help inexperienced officers learn. Observing wasn't the same as doing. There was a different skill set involved.

Karen had to admit it was unnerving letting Sophie handle a sensitive job. Families were unpredictable, and reactions to learning about the death of a loved one could vary. Stunned silence was a typical response. But at times, she'd witnessed hysterical ranting, sometimes even physical rage. You never knew what to expect.

When two officers had turned up at her house with pity written all over their faces and delivered Karen's own death message, her first response had been shock and disbelief. How could her husband and daughter be dead? It seemed impossible.

Knowing how it felt to be on the receiving end didn't make delivering the news any easier.

After they rang the bell, the door was opened by a boy in his early teens. His hair was long and fell over his eyes.

'About time,' he said as the door was opening. 'We've ordered pizza because . . .' He trailed off. 'Oh.'

He'd been expecting to see someone else. His father?

Karen and Sophie showed their ID. 'DC Sophie Jones and DS Karen Hart of the Lincolnshire Police. Is your mum home?'

He nodded but said nothing, stepping back and opening the door wide. Then he turned. 'Mum, the police are here!'

A woman entered the hallway, clutching a tea towel, a strange half-smile frozen on her face as though she were caught between wanting to be polite and wanting to tell them to go away. 'Okay, Sebastian. Go back into the living room.'

The boy pouted, looked at Karen and Sophie, then did as he was told.

The drone of the TV got louder as he opened the door to the living room and slipped inside. The woman closed the door with a shaky hand.

'It's Mrs Nelson, isn't it? Is it okay if we come in?' Sophie asked.

The woman nodded. 'Yes, Beverley Nelson. Is everything all right?'

They entered the hall, and as Karen shut the front door behind them, Sophie said, 'Is there somewhere we could sit down, Mrs Nelson? I'm afraid we've got some bad news.'

The woman reached out to brace herself against the wall, as though she were afraid her legs might buckle. 'Bad news. What sort of bad news?'

It always went like this. They hardly ever sat down before getting the news. Who could blame them? Karen certainly hadn't wanted to. She'd wanted to know immediately what bad news they were there to deliver.

'Is your husband Lloyd Nelson?' Sophie asked.

The woman raised a hand to her mouth and nodded.

'Then I'm very sorry to tell you we believe Lloyd is dead. A body was found at Lincoln Cathedral this evening.'

'No.' She looked from Sophie to Karen and back again. 'That can't be right. I spoke to Lloyd a few hours ago. He was fine.'

'Is it all right if we sit down, Mrs Nelson?' Sophie said.

Beverley headed into the kitchen at the back of the house. 'You'll have to come in here. I don't want to upset the children.'

'They'll have to know eventually,' Karen said softly.

'I can't just spring it on them.' Beverley slumped into a chair at the kitchen table. 'I'll have to think of a way to make it easier—' She stopped abruptly, as though suddenly realising there was nothing she could do to make the news easier.

'I'm very sorry, Mrs Nelson,' Karen said. She sat down opposite the woman.

Beverley gripped the edge of the kitchen table, shaking her head. 'Are you absolutely sure it's him?'

'He had his wallet on him, and his gym membership ID was inside,' Sophie said gently. 'We believe it is Lloyd. Though you will be able to identify his body.'

Beverley swallowed hard and pressed her hands against her face. 'Is this really happening? What was he doing at the cathedral?' she muttered. She spoke to a spot on the ceiling rather than directly addressing Sophie or Karen.

The doorbell rang before Sophie could answer, but Mrs Nelson sat still, staring blankly at the Artex pattern above.

Karen got up and saw Sebastian at the front door. He grabbed money from the telephone table to pay a delivery driver. 'Mum,' he yelled. 'Pizza's here.'

He brought it into the kitchen. He took one look at his mother's face and asked, 'What's going on?'

'You'd better get Caitlin, Sebastian.'

He slid the pizza on to the counter and went to get his sister.

Caitlin was younger than Sebastian; Karen guessed her age to be around ten. She entered the kitchen nervously, sticking close to her brother's side.

When Beverley Nelson said nothing, Sophie frowned and looked perplexed. It was evident to Karen she was wondering whether Beverley wanted to tell the children herself or expected Sophie to do it. Karen almost took charge but held herself back. Sophie could handle it.

'Would you like me to tell the children what's happened, Mrs Nelson?' Sophie asked.

Beverley's face crumpled. Her eyes brimmed with tears as she nodded.

Sophie turned to Caitlin and Sebastian, and leaned down to their level. 'I'm very sorry to tell you that your father has passed away. I know this must come as a terrible shock and—'

Beverley interrupted. 'He isn't their father. I mean, Lloyd treated them as though he was. He loved them like they were his own, but he's not their biological dad.'

'Oh, I see.'

The boy put his arm around his little sister's shoulders when she began to cry. Then Beverley opened up her arms and Caitlin ran into them, sobbing as her mother wrapped her in a tight embrace. The boy moved closer to his mother and stood awkwardly beside her. He was at that age where he wanted to cry but was trying to act tough.

'Are you okay, Sebastian? Do you want to sit down?' Karen asked.

He shook his head and blinked away his tears furiously. Then he grabbed the pizza, opened the box and started taking out slices and putting them on plates. Acting on autopilot, Karen thought. Trying not to think about what was happening.

'Do the children still see their biological dad?'

'Why do you want to know that?'

'It helps us to understand the family history. Saves us time when we're investigating.'

'They see him now and then. When it suits him,' Beverley said darkly. 'Lloyd was more of a father to my kids than he ever was.'

'Can I take your ex-husband's details?' Sophie prepared to make a note on her tablet.

'Brett Wharton. He lives near Gainsborough. I've got his address on my phone. Sebastian, can you get it for me?'

He left the kitchen to retrieve his mother's phone. His shoulders were slumped, and he was clearly trying very hard not to cry.

'How long have you and Lloyd been married?'

'Almost a year. We got married in January. I thought that was it. I thought we would grow old together.'

'I'm sorry.'

Beverley sniffed, and Sophie handed her a tissue and gave the family time to comfort each other, leaving a pause for the news to sink in before she began asking more questions. It was difficult. The family needed time to grieve, but the police required answers

31

if they were to find out what had happened to Lloyd Nelson. Karen thought Sophie was handling the situation well.

'Do you have any idea why Lloyd was at the cathedral this evening?' Sophie asked, after she made a note of Brett Wharton's address and asked a few warm-up questions.

'No. He said he'd gone out to do a bit of shopping, but he wouldn't be long. We were expecting him back hours ago. He was supposed to be picking up a takeaway on his way home. The kids were hungry and didn't want to wait. That's why I said they could order pizza. I sent him a text. He didn't reply . . . How did he die? Was it a heart attack?'

Sebastian handed his sister a plate with a slice of pizza.

'Thanks, love,' Beverley said.

The girl slid off her mother's lap and took her plate to the other side of the table, and sat beside Karen. She picked the pizza apart with her fingers but didn't eat it.

'We don't think it was a heart attack. Lloyd will need to have a post-mortem.' Sophie glanced at the young girl, who was concentrating on ripping apart her pizza but was still clearly listening to every word.

'Was Lloyd a religious man?' Karen asked.

'He goes to church occasionally. I mean, he's a Christian, and he's part of a choir who sing hymns and things, but he doesn't always make it to church on Sundays.'

'I know this is a tough question,' Sophie said tentatively. 'But is there anyone who might have wanted to hurt Lloyd?'

Beverley looked up, her eyes wide. 'No – nobody,' she said with force. 'He was a great man. He was kind, loving, sweet.' She looked at Sebastian. 'Wasn't he?'

The boy nodded obediently.

'He was marvellous with the kids. Couldn't do enough for them, and me. He was the loveliest man imaginable, and there's no

32

way anyone would have wanted to hurt him. I don't understand how this could have happened.'

Sophie made a note on her tablet, while Karen asked about Lloyd's medical history. She suspected he'd had a cardiac problem, seeing as Beverley had assumed he'd died of a heart attack. Beverley confirmed he'd suffered from angina.

'He was an amazing man, never moaned about his medical condition, though it left him breathless at times. He never said a bad word about anyone. Everyone loved him.'

After answering a few more questions, Beverley pinched the bridge of her nose.

'But I still don't understand. If he didn't have a heart attack, then how did he die?'

'We don't know yet,' Sophie replied honestly.

'How can you not know?'

'His body was found in the cathedral. After the post-mortem, we'll be able to tell you more.'

'Was it an accident?'

'I really can't say at this stage.'

'You think he was murdered, don't you? That's why you asked if anyone wanted to hurt him.'

Both children looked up, their sad, worried eyes fixed on Sophie, who hesitated before saying, 'We're not sure. The post-mortem will tell us more.' She slid her card across the table. 'This has come as a terrible shock, and I'm sorry we can't give you the answers you need yet. We'll keep you updated on any developments. You can call me if you have questions. I'm your personal liaison officer. I can stay with you this evening, if that would help?'

'No. We're fine on our own.'

'Is there anyone you want us to contact? Somebody to stay with you for a little while – a relative perhaps?'

'No, we'll be all right.' Beverley lifted her head. 'I just thought of something . . . Lloyd did have a falling-out with someone recently. His boss tried to pass Lloyd's work off as his own. His boss was furious because Lloyd stood up for himself and told everyone in the office.'

'When did this happen?' Sophie asked.

'About a week ago. I'm not sure of the exact date, but they had a big row in the middle of the office, lots of witnesses.'

'Where did Lloyd work?'

'A small software development company called Sparks. The office is in Lincoln, near the university. I can't remember the address offhand, but I could look it up.'

'No need,' Karen said, looking up from her tablet. 'I've found it online. What's his boss's name?'

'Ross Blundell, a youngster who thinks he knows everything, according to Lloyd. No one likes him. He's a terrible boss.'

'Did you ever get to meet him?' Sophie asked.

Beverley shook her head.

They made some tea and let Beverley talk about the man she'd recently married, extolling his virtues. She was very open with them, letting them look through the desk Lloyd used, and his computer. She even allowed them to take a pile of recent bank statements. It was late when Karen finally indicated to Sophie it was time to wrap things up.

'I'm very sorry for your loss, Mrs Nelson,' Karen said as they prepared to leave. 'We'll be in touch tomorrow, but if you have questions in the meantime, please contact DC Jones.'

Sophie pointed to the card. 'If you think of anything that might help us in the investigation, or you have questions, you can call me on either of those numbers,' Sophie said, indicating her work number and her mobile. 'And we can put you in touch with organisations who offer help to bereaved families.'

'Right.' Beverley got slowly to her feet. She looked a decade older and moved stiffly, as though her body had seized up.

They said goodbye to the children, who were now staring blankly at the TV, then left the devastated Nelson family and returned to Karen's car.

When they were safely inside and couldn't be overheard, Sophie said, 'Well, that was interesting.'

Karen pulled away from the kerb. 'Yes. We'll get on to the biological father as soon as possible. Tempers run high in custody disputes. The boss definitely needs a follow-up too.'

'Beverley was very keen to drum home what a nice man Lloyd Nelson was, wasn't she? Don't you think that was odd?' Sophie tucked her curly hair behind her ears and looked at Karen.

'Maybe she was a bit full-on in her praise, but her emotions are all over the place. It's likely that's how she wants to remember him.'

'I don't know,' Sophie muttered. 'It didn't feel right. It was as though she was trying too hard to convince us he was a good man.'

'You could be right. But don't rely too heavily on your first instinct,' Karen said, immediately realising she sounded exactly like DI Morgan. She wondered if Sophie found the advice as irritating as she did. 'It's good to have hunches,' Karen continued, 'but they're useless without evidence.'

'I know, Sarge,' Sophie said. 'I'm just pointing out her desire to portray him as a good person seemed extreme, and that's often a sign to watch out for. Last night I read another two chapters of the FBI book I told you about. It said witnesses often try very hard to persuade the investigator the opposite is true when they're hiding the facts.'

Karen waited for a gap in the traffic and then turned on to the main road. She didn't need a book to tell her that Beverley's behaviour indicated she was holding something back. The question was – what?

CHAPTER FOUR

Karen and Sophie walked into the open-plan office area, and Karen veered right, heading straight for the coffee machine. She needed caffeine.

Fortunately, she'd only had one glass of wine with her meal, and the effects had long worn off. She'd expected to be curled up in bed by now. Instead, it looked like she and the team had a long night in front of them.

She programmed the machine, and as it buzzed to life, she pulled out her phone to check her messages. She had an email from Rick. He was at City Hall, trawling through the central CCTV recordings. He'd sent a clip along with his message. As expected, he confirmed that analysing the video footage wouldn't be easy. The Cathedral Quarter had been packed with tourists, even more so than usual at this time of year.

She tapped on the video file. It was from a camera angled towards the cathedral's west entrance.

People passed by, some with smiles, some with their heads down moving fast. A tall man wearing a bobble hat and long black coat sidestepped a woman struggling over the cobbles with a pushchair. Just behind her, Karen caught sight of the victim, Lloyd Nelson. He was moving with purpose towards the cathedral. He stopped beside one of the blue barriers to allow two women laden with shopping bags to go by. Then he walked quickly again, striding up to the entrance and disappearing inside.

Why was he moving so fast? Simply to get out of the cold? Or was he rushing for another reason? Meeting someone?

Karen cursed under her breath as the video clip froze. The timeline at the bottom showed that the video hadn't finished. It was her phone playing up again.

'Useless piece of—'

'What's up, Sarge?' Sophie asked, wandering up to the coffee machine, mug in hand.

'My phone is on the blink. Three times today it's frozen.'

'Have you tried turning it off and on again?'

'Yes, and it hasn't helped.' Karen glared at the phone. 'I'm going to have to get a new one.' She removed her coffee from the machine.

Sophie put her mug in its place and pressed the button. Then she squinted at Karen's phone. 'Looks quite old, anyway. When did you last apply for an update?'

'It's only three years old,' Karen said defensively. 'My first mobile was a Nokia that lasted for years. They don't make phones like that anymore.'

'But you couldn't do anything on those old-style phones except call people. Speak to Resources, they'll get you a replacement. What were you looking at?' Sophie looked at the frozen screen.

'CCTV from Rick. It shows our victim entering the cathedral. If the timestamp is correct, he went in at four p.m.'

'And never came back out,' Sophie said, picking up her coffee and blowing over the top before taking a sip. 'Did anyone follow him in?'

'Thanks to my phone, I have no idea. I'll have to watch the video on the computer.'

Sophie followed Karen over to her desk.

As she waited for the machine to boot up, Karen pressed the volume and the on/off button on her phone to force a restart.

The video was more comfortable to view on the large computer screen, anyway. As it began to play, Karen sipped her coffee and concentrated on the faces of the pedestrians around the cathedral.

'It's so busy,' Sophie complained, pulling over a chair and sitting beside Karen. 'How are we ever going to pick out the killer? Are there no cameras inside?'

'Unfortunately not in the chapel. A small one near the gift shop, but I don't think that will give us what we need.'

A group of tourists posed for a picture in front of the cathedral. A couple with three kids trailing behind them breezed past, followed by another family and an elderly couple. A man in a red baseball cap wandered by, eating a burger. They all looked innocent enough; ordinary people visiting the market. Karen just wished there weren't so many of them.

A man wearing a bomber jacket, black scarf and baseball cap went into the cathedral. *He could be interesting*, Karen thought, and made a note of the time from the video.

There were many other ways into the large building, and all could be potential entrance and exit points for the killer. Morgan would make sure he'd discovered all routes in and out, and if they were lucky, most aspects would be covered by cameras.

Sophie smothered a yawn. 'Sorry, Sarge. The coffee hasn't kicked in yet. Should I make a start on his financials?'

Karen checked the time. 'Yes, that's a good idea. Make a start on all the background checks on the victim. We need to know everything about him. Put in a request for his phone records too.'

'Do you think we should call on the ex-husband or Nelson's boss tonight?'

'I'll see what Morgan says, but I think it's too late. We'd be better off paying them a visit tomorrow, once we've dug into their backgrounds too. It's better to be prepared.'

Sophie nodded and headed to her own desk.

Karen drained her coffee and then replayed the video. She scanned the crowds, looking for anyone out of place. Connections were usually vital in murder investigations. Both Lloyd's boss and Beverley's ex-husband were high on Karen's suspect list. Both had potential motives. On the other hand, if those markings on Lloyd's forehead indicated a ritual murder, then they could be looking for a stranger – in which case, this investigation could be challenging. How would you solve a case without connections?

Karen blew out a breath and then stared at the screen as the man in the baseball cap entered the cathedral. He seemed different, out of place among the Christmas shoppers. She'd like to see footage of him leaving and wondered if any other cameras had got a shot of his face. She typed a quick reply to Rick's email, asking him to follow up.

She reached for her mobile phone, which had now decided to cooperate, and scrolled through her contacts before selecting DI Morgan's number. She paused with her finger just above the call button as Morgan walked into the office.

Karen headed over to him. 'Any news?'

'The dean was very cooperative – we have a list of staff and a layout map of the cathedral.'

'What about witnesses?'

'Not much luck there.' He held up a thick file. 'We've got plenty of statements from tourists and staff who were inside the cathedral when the body was discovered, but no one seems to have heard or witnessed anything.'

Morgan held open the door to his office, and Karen followed him in and sat down.

'Did you see the CCTV Rick sent over?'

Morgan shrugged off his coat. 'Yes, it looks like our victim entered the cathedral at four p.m. Raj thinks that's probably close to the time of death too.'

'Someone went into the cathedral after him. Most likely a male, medium height and build, wearing a black jacket and a baseball cap.'

'Yes. I spotted him, and asked Rick if he can source better footage from any of the other cameras.'

Karen smiled. 'I asked him to do that too.'

She filled Morgan in on the visit to Nelson's family and then asked, 'Do you think it's worth visiting the ex-husband or boss tonight? I thought it might be better to get to them tomorrow after we've gathered some more information.'

'I agree. Let's see what we can find out about our victim, try to get a good picture of him tonight, then pay our two suspects a visit tomorrow.'

She left Morgan and headed back to her own workstation, then logged into the system, preparing to dig into Lloyd Nelson's background.

An hour and a half later, Karen pushed back from her desk and stretched her arms over her head to release the tension in her back. She went over her findings. Lloyd Nelson, aged forty-six. His marriage to Beverley was his first. No children of his own. No criminal record. Not even a speeding ticket. She found a website for the choir he attended. It was sparse, with few helpful details, but it did have a photo of the choir during a practice session, with their names underneath. They looked like an eclectic bunch, and Karen had noted down the names of all the members in case they needed to follow up later, though she was still betting on either the ex-husband or the boss at this stage.

The boss, Ross Blundell, was unmarried, twenty-eight, and the sole owner of Sparks Software Design. He'd done well for himself, and the smug smile he wore in the photograph on the company's website told Karen he knew it. He had two degrees. One in mathematics and the other in computer science. Clever. No criminal record, but three points on his licence for speeding. He lived uphill, a nice area. Expensive, but then he could probably afford it if Sparks Software Design was successful. Their client list was varied, from a bespoke accounting system for a dog food manufacturer to app development.

Had Nelson angered him by refusing to let his boss take credit for his work, as Beverley had suggested? Or had there been more behind the row? Karen mused over the questions she wanted to ask Ross Blundell tomorrow, then turned her attention to their other person of interest.

Brett Wharton, Beverley's ex-husband, father to Sebastian and Caitlin. One arrest for vandalism two years ago, and another for drunk and disorderly behaviour eighteen months prior. She checked out his social media to find lots of shared posts about animal welfare, and photographs of him and his children. In the photos, Sebastian and Caitlin were young. There were no more recent photographs of the children that she could see, at least not without sending him a friend request.

Karen wished it wasn't so late. She had a long list of questions for Brett Wharton. He had to miss those children.

Office arguments could spill into violence, but custody disputes unearthed a primal viciousness. Ordinary people could be driven to do terrible things if they believed their children were going to be taken from them. Judging from the information she had, Karen believed Brett Wharton had a stronger motive. She stood and rubbed the ache from the back of her neck. She'd have to wait until tomorrow to find out if she was right.

She checked her messages, but there were no updates. Every time she opened her emails, she hoped to see a message from the officer in charge of the corruption investigation, DS Grace, who'd promised to let Karen know as soon as she had evidence to put Freeman behind bars. Karen thought they had enough, but those in charge didn't agree. They wanted physical evidence, witness statements, proof of payments. They had Charlie Cook's statement, but his previous record meant he was an unreliable witness.

They'd said the same about Alice Price, an ex-police officer who'd first raised the alarm regarding possible corruption in the force. When her allegations were dismissed, so was Alice. Her career went down in flames. No one took her seriously. When Karen first met her, she'd appeared nervous and flighty. It was hard to imagine she had ever been anything other than a timid woman, seemingly scared of her own shadow. Karen was determined not to end up like Alice. She would be patient, but she would never give up.

She glanced at the time and was shocked at how late it was. She'd said she'd call Mike, but he'd understand. He'd worked cases himself. As an ex-officer, he knew how it was.

Karen reached for her phone. He might not answer, but she owed him a call. Morgan had been cold when he saw Mike at the cathedral, but Mike had only been trying to help keep gaping tourists away from a murder scene, at her request.

Morgan didn't approve of their relationship. Not that he'd actually come out and said as much, but Karen knew he thought getting together with Mike was a bad idea. He was entitled to his opinion, even if he was wrong.

Mike answered on the third ring, his voice groggy. 'Hello.'

'Sorry, I woke you. I meant to call earlier.'

'Don't worry about it. I guessed you'd got caught up. Was it a murder?'

'Sadly, yes.'

'Are you heading home now? You're welcome to come back here.'

She was tempted. To forget about the case and curl up in bed beside Mike was an inviting prospect, but she said, 'I'll be here another hour or so, and then I'll go back to mine. Early start tomorrow.'

'Make sure you eat something. You can't run on coffee alone.'

Karen eyed her empty mug. 'I ate enough at dinner to last me forty-eight hours!'

He chuckled. 'That's no excuse. Don't skip breakfast.'

'Yeah. Yeah,' she said, grinning. 'I'll give you a call tomorrow.'

She hung up, or at least tried to, but her phone screen had frozen again. The call had ended when Mike had shut it down at his end, but her phone was unresponsive.

'I'm warning you, this is your last chance,' she said, jabbing at the screen without success.

'Are you talking to your phone?'

She looked up to see Morgan wearing a puzzled frown.

'Stupid thing keeps freezing.'

'Here, let me take a look.'

With a frustrated sigh, she handed him the phone. 'I'm going to request a new one.'

A couple of seconds later, he handed it back, smiling. 'It's working fine.'

And it was. She swiped through the app screens, shaking her head. 'What did you do?'

'Just pressed the home button twice.'

'I tried that.'

He shrugged. 'Well, it seems to be okay now. Must have been a temporary glitch. Have you tried turning it off and on again?'

'Yes!' Karen said, exasperated. 'That was the first thing I tried.' She glared at the traitorous phone.

He set down two files on her desk. 'Bedtime reading if you get a chance. Witness statements. I've been through them all, but it's always a good idea to have a second pair of eyes.'

Karen reached for the files and thumbed through them, filling him in on what she'd discovered during the background searches. She finished up by saying, 'So, I think talking to Brett Wharton, the ex-husband, should be our first priority tomorrow.'

'All right, but come into the station first. I want to have a briefing first-thing, then you can take Sophie or Rick with you to see the ex while I update the superintendent.'

'Have you spoken to her about the case?'

Morgan nodded. 'Yes, she was a bit concerned we might have too much on our plates at the moment with the Sam Pickett hit-and-run.'

Karen had been off work for a few days but had heard about the case. A twelve-year-old boy had been cycling home when he was hit by a car and killed. But the driver had fled the scene.

'How's that going?'

'Slowly. No witnesses. No leads. I'm hoping whoever hit the kid has a change of heart and turns themselves in.'

'Did you mention the markings on Lloyd Nelson's forehead to the superintendent?' Karen asked.

'Yes. She shared our concerns.'

'But we're still treating this like a typical murder, looking at friends, family and colleagues first?'

'I think we have to,' Morgan said. 'It could be the killer was angry and wanted to deface the victim. It might not be a symbolic marking.'

Karen hoped Morgan was right. A hit-and-run and a murder were quite enough for one week in the lead-up to Christmas, but the possibility this killing was ritual in nature worried her. If the real motive behind Lloyd Nelson's murder was ritualistic, would the killer be satisfied with one victim?

CHAPTER FIVE

At seven a.m. the following morning, Karen was already at her desk at Nettleham headquarters. She was going over the information she'd collected on the ex-husband, Brett Wharton, when her mobile rang. She eyed it suspiciously.

Yesterday, she'd put in a request for a new phone, but it wouldn't be delivered until tomorrow at the earliest.

'If you freeze again, you're going in the bin,' she muttered, and then answered the call.

'DS Hart?'

'Speaking,' Karen replied warily. She'd recognised Eunice Green's voice. Surely the woman wasn't calling to persuade her to go to a counselling session? That would be verging on harassment.

'It's Eunice, Eunice Green.'

'How can I help you, Eunice?'

'Can I come and see you?'

'This isn't to do with counselling, is it?'

'Counselling? Oh, no, nothing to do with that.'

Karen checked the time. Eunice had been understandably shocked yesterday. Maybe she'd forgotten a detail that had come back to her since. 'I've got a briefing this morning and a couple of appointments. I could come to you, say, mid-morning – unless you can tell me whatever it is over the phone?'

'No, I . . . I have to come to the station.' Eunice's voice wavered.

Karen leaned back in her chair and frowned. 'Are you okay, Eunice? You sound distressed.'

'I am.' Karen thought she heard a muffled sob. 'I need to make a confession.'

'A confession?'

'Yes, I did something terrible.'

Karen's grip tightened on the phone. *Something terrible?* 'Is this concerning Lloyd Nelson's murder?' Karen tried and failed to imagine how the petite, mild-mannered woman could be involved in such a violent act. She volunteered at the cathedral and was someone who went out of their way to help others; Karen couldn't think of a less likely suspect. But she'd learned never to rule anything out. 'Can you come now? I could pick you up.'

'Yes. No need, I'll drive myself.' Eunice hung up.

Karen stared at the phone, tempted to call the woman back and get more information. *There's no way Eunice could have killed Lloyd*, Karen thought. It would've taken strength to tighten the ligature around his neck, and Eunice was half a foot shorter and fifty pounds lighter than the victim.

Morgan entered the open-plan office area. 'Morning.'

'Morning. I've just taken an extraordinary call from Eunice Green. She said she's coming to the station to make a confession.'

Morgan stopped walking. 'What about?'

'I don't know – she hung up before I could get much out of her. She said she'd done something terrible and needed to make a confession. I asked if it was about Lloyd Nelson's murder, and she said yes . . . At least, I *think* she did. I asked her a couple of questions to which she replied *yes*.'

'Call her back.'

Karen reached for the landline phone on her desk rather than her mobile. It had worked for the previous call, but she didn't want to push her luck.

The call rang and rang until it cut out. 'No answer. Maybe she's already on her way.'

Morgan leaned on Karen's desk. 'I can't see Eunice killing him alone. She would've needed an accomplice, someone strong, probably a man.'

'I can't see her killing anyone. I don't think she has it in her.'

'I thought you had only met her once before?'

'I know but . . .' Karen trailed off, shaking her head. 'It might be a cliché, but she just doesn't seem the type.'

'She's heading to the station now?'

'That's what she said.'

'Then we'd better get an interview room booked.'

Karen booked the room, then went to get a coffee. Morgan was right – she'd only spent less than two hours in Eunice's company – but she still didn't believe that Eunice could have played a part in Lloyd Nelson's murder and then called for help and lied to Karen so convincingly. She would have to be a first-class actress to pull that off, and she knew from the staged meeting Mike had arranged that Eunice was no actress.

She was walking back to her desk with a mug of coffee when Rick arrived. Dark circles under his eyes, his tanned skin looking a little paler than usual. With his black hair slicked back, he still looked young and handsome, but less vibrant than usual.

'Morning, Rick. Tough night?'

Rick's mother suffered from dementia, and although he employed a carer, he looked after his mother overnight, and that took its toll on him.

He yawned. 'Morning, Sarge. I didn't get home till gone two after going through the camera footage.'

'Is your mum all right?'

'Yes, she had a good night, thanks.'

Karen told Rick about the odd call from Eunice Green.

'Do you think she saw something? Was she covering for someone else, perhaps?' he asked.

'Could be. I've booked out interview room two. Do you want to question her with me?'

'Sure. I'll be fine once I get a cup of coffee.'

When Eunice arrived at the station, the desk sergeant brought her up to interview room two. Karen had set up the recording equipment and put three bottles of mineral water on the table.

Eunice entered the room nervously, clutching her hands together. She wore a long cardigan again, but today she'd opted for beige.

'Good morning, Eunice. This is my colleague, DC Rick Cooper. He'll be sitting in on the interview this morning. Can we get you something to drink? Coffee?'

Eunice looked at the plastic bottles on the table. 'Thank you. Water is fine.'

They sat down, Rick and Karen on one side of the table, Eunice on the other.

Karen started the recording, announcing the time, date and those present, before she turned to Eunice and smiled encouragingly. 'Go ahead, Eunice. You said you had a confession to make.'

Eunice bowed her head. 'Yes.' Her voice was quiet.

'Is this about Lloyd Nelson's murder yesterday?' Karen asked.

Eunice gave a small nod and held a tissue to her mouth.

'You'll feel better when you tell us, Eunice,' Rick said. 'Take your time, tell us in your own words what happened.'

'I was supposed to be working, keeping my mind on the job, staying alert. But at about three o'clock, I . . . I decided to listen to the choir music. My daughter bought me these little earbuds that can connect with my phone without a cable. The music is on my phone, and I hadn't had a chance to go through the pieces yet. I didn't think there was any harm in it . . .'

'Then what happened?' Rick prompted when Eunice fell silent.

But Karen leaned forward, resting her forearms on the table, and studied Eunice. She knew *this* was Eunice's confession. She'd been listening to music while she was supposed to be working.

'You're not allowed to listen to music at work?' Karen asked.

'Well, it's never been said in so many words, but I was distracted. Enjoying myself while poor Lloyd . . .' She held the tissue to her mouth again.

Karen gritted her teeth. They'd delayed the briefing for *this*. She looked at Rick, who rolled his eyes.

'Just so I've got this straight, you're confessing to listening to music while being at work.' Rick's eyebrows lifted.

'If I hadn't been, I might have heard something, been able to help him . . .'

'Okay, Eunice. Thanks for telling us.' Karen stood. She wasn't wasting any more time on this. They should be working on genuine leads.

Eunice looked up, blinking at her. 'Aren't you going to arrest me? Charge me with something?'

'Charge you for listening to music?' Rick asked with irritation.

'You made a mistake, Eunice,' Karen said, her voice cold as Rick left the interview room. She was only just managing to keep her temper in check.

'I know, but it's my fault he's dead. I could have stopped it.'

'No, I don't think you could,' Karen said. Eunice's confession was a hold-up they could have done without, but the woman was genuinely upset. 'If you'd heard something and tried to intervene, you could have been badly hurt. Perhaps you should think of those earbuds from your daughter as a blessing?'

Eunice dissolved into tears. 'I didn't get a wink of sleep last night.'

Karen swallowed her irritation and put a hand on the woman's arm. 'Come on, let's get you a cup of tea. Is there someone I can call for you? You could do with a bit of support from a friend right now.'

She led the woman from the interview room, and they passed Sophie in the corridor.

'Briefing is in five, Sarge.'

'I'll be right there.'

◆　◆　◆

They kept the briefing short, wanting to get out and interview the potential suspects as soon as possible. Eunice's confession had caused an unfortunate delay.

Morgan told the team he had spoken to Raj, who'd confirmed a definite cross had been carved into Lloyd Nelson's forehead.

Karen tensed. She'd been hoping that wasn't the case. 'He's sure it was deliberate? Not caused by hitting his head?'

Morgan looked up from his notes. 'He considers that very unlikely.'

'Does he have any idea what the killer used to carve the cross? We didn't find anything at the scene.'

'Likely a knife, small and sharp. Non-serrated. Probably something that would've fitted in the killer's pocket, allowing them to flee the scene and take it with them.'

Morgan turned to Sophie. 'Anything with his phone records or financials back yet?'

'Not officially, but I did get a copy of their joint account statement from Beverley Nelson. One thing that stood out to me was that Lloyd was a betting man. Payments are going to a variety of betting apps. Also, multiple withdrawals of cash over the last few months, two hundred pounds at a time.'

'So our victim enjoyed a flutter,' Rick said. 'Perhaps he owed money to the wrong person.'

'It's a lead,' Morgan said. 'Follow that up when the records are released, Sophie.'

Then Rick reported back on the CCTV. Unfortunately, he hadn't been able to get a better view of the suspect in the baseball cap who'd followed Lloyd Nelson into the cathedral.

'What about CCTV from private residences and businesses in the area?' Morgan asked.

'I'll follow that up this morning,' Rick replied.

'Right, I think that's it for now.' Morgan checked the time. 'The superintendent will be in shortly, expecting an update. Karen, Sophie, you'll go to speak to Brett Wharton this morning?'

'Yes, we'll head there now,' Karen said, as Sophie directed a smug smile at Rick, who looked fed up. Karen couldn't blame him. A Sunday morning spent staring at security footage was nobody's idea of fun.

Superintendent Michelle Murray liked to be involved in more serious cases. Even if that meant coming in to the station on a Sunday. She could and did delegate, but considered it her duty to give her teams the support they needed. A straightforward domestic murder wouldn't warrant her involvement at this stage, but Karen suspected the fact the victim had been marked had set off alarm bells.

Karen had to admit she was unnerved. The marking of flesh suggested savagery. All murder was abhorrent, but there was something especially sinister about a killer who carved symbols into the flesh of their victim.

CHAPTER SIX

Brett Wharton lived in a small village just outside Gainsborough called Morton. His house was in a row of Georgian terraces, right on the bank of the River Trent.

'Bet he's got a nice view,' Sophie said as they got out of the car.

Karen agreed. The terraces had been painted recently and looked smart and well kept. The small, frost-covered front gardens had no room for parking, so the street was full of vehicles parked up on the kerbs. Karen had managed to squeeze her own car in between a Volvo and a Hyundai.

She searched for the doorbell, ignoring the brass lion-head knocker in the middle of the glossy black door. That was just there for show, wasn't it?

'Can you see the bell?' Karen took a step back to take a full-length look at the door.

'I don't think there is one.'

Karen gave up the search for the doorbell and knocked.

The door was opened by a beautiful young woman with long red hair. She pressed her palms together. 'Welcome.'

Sophie blinked and looked to Karen.

'We'd like to speak to Mr Brett Wharton,' Karen said, holding up her ID.

The woman's hands fell to her sides. 'Oh, you'd better come in.'

She closed the door behind them, and they followed her along a narrow hallway to the back of the house. The woman was bare-foot, her hair was so long it reached her waist, and she wore a white tunic and three-quarter-length white trousers. Not really typical clothes for a cold December day.

They entered a large light-filled kitchen at the back of the house. Wind chimes were hung by the window. Chunks of crystal lined the windowsill, and the sound of panpipe music filled the room.

'Brett, the police are here.'

A slim man with dark curly hair sat crosslegged on a pale blue mat with his eyes closed, humming.

'Brett!' she repeated.

He blinked, and looked startled to see the three of them standing in front of him.

'Sorry, I wasn't expecting visitors.' He was wearing the same odd white outfit as the woman. He was unshaven and hadn't had a haircut for a while.

'Brett Wharton?' Karen held out her hand and waited for the man to get to his feet. 'I'm DS Karen Hart, and this is my colleague, DC Sophie Jones. We'd like to ask you a few questions.'

'I see. Please, sit down.' He waved them over to the kitchen table, in front of the patio doors.

Karen sat down and saw, as Sophie had predicted, that they did have a beautiful view of the River Trent. The grass along the riverbank was still covered with patchy frost, sparkling in the weak December sun.

'Should I make coffee? Tea?' the woman asked, looking uncertain.

'That would be lovely, Jacqui,' Brett said.

'Is Jacqui your partner?' Sophie asked.

'Yes, Jacqui Peck. Look, I don't want to be rude, but can I ask why you're here?'

'Of course,' Karen said. 'We're here because Lloyd Nelson was murdered yesterday.'

'Lloyd?' Brett paled and raised his hands to cover his face.

'Who's that?' Jacqui asked.

After a pause, Brett collected himself. 'Bev's new bloke. They were married this year.'

'Your ex-wife?'

Brett nodded.

'Oh. That's awful.' Jacqui grimaced. 'I'll make the drinks. What can I get you?' She looked at Sophie and Karen questioningly.

They both asked for coffee, but Karen didn't take her eyes from Brett. Watching his reactions could provide a wealth of information.

'You didn't hear about his murder yesterday, Mr Wharton?' Karen asked.

'No, I didn't. Bev should have told me, since I'm the kids' father, but that's probably too much to ask.'

Definite bitterness there, Karen thought. 'I imagine the news gave her quite a shock. She's got a lot to deal with at the moment.'

He raised his head, eyes sharp. 'Yes, of course. I wasn't thinking. She's probably beside herself. I'm sure she would've got in touch eventually.'

Jacqui called from the kitchen, 'She never bothers to tell you what's going on in the kids' lives. I don't know why this would be any different.'

Brett flushed and shot a look at Jacqui. He was willing her to shut up.

'You don't get on with your ex-wife, Mr Wharton?' Karen asked.

'I wouldn't say that. We have our moments. But we're no different from any other divorced couple. I don't know many people who have split and still get on.'

'What did you think of Lloyd?'

He shrugged. 'Didn't really know him.'

'But you must've had an opinion. After all, he was living with your children.'

Brett clenched his teeth. 'All right. I didn't think much of him. But it was Bev keeping me from the kids, not him. She's the one I have an issue with.'

'Any arguments? Disputes with Lloyd?'

He paused before he shook his head.

'It's easier if you tell us now,' Karen said. 'If we later find out you were hiding things, it looks bad.'

He stayed quiet, thinking. He was deciding whether to let the skeletons out or to keep quiet and hope they never came to light.

'Where were you yesterday, Mr Wharton?' Sophie asked.

'I was here.'

'All day?'

'Yes.'

Jacqui brought the coffee over to the table. 'You don't seriously think Brett was involved?'

'Of course they do. Why else do you think they're here?' he snapped. 'I'm probably top of their list. Jealous ex-husband. That's what you're thinking, isn't it?'

'That's ridiculous,' Jacqui said before Karen or Sophie could answer. She slid into the seat beside Brett. 'He was here with me all day.'

'Did you go out at all?' Sophie asked.

'We went for a walk along the river in the afternoon.' He swore, a vein pulsing at his temple.

'What time?'

Jacqui put a hand on Brett's arm. 'Keep calm. Remember your breathing.'

'I don't know exactly. About three o'clock.' Brett put his hands flat on the table and took a deep breath.

'But you were together all day?' Karen asked.

'Yes, we were,' Jacqui said firmly, and she pushed two mugs of coffee towards Karen and Sophie.

'When was the last time either of you saw Lloyd Nelson?' Karen asked.

'I've never met him,' Jacqui said.

Brett sighed. 'A couple of weeks ago, I guess. I'd gone to pick up the kids. Bev told me I couldn't see them because I was late. Five minutes! I couldn't help the traffic. She was being thoroughly unreasonable. Lloyd came outside to stick his oar in, as usual.'

'Was there an altercation?' Karen asked.

'A fight, you mean?' Brett's cheeks were pink.

'You've attended an anger management course, haven't you?'

'I hardly think it's fair to hold that against him.' Jacqui sniffed and reached for her coffee. 'He went on that course because he was trying to control his temper.'

'He went on that course because he was asked to do so by the family court, in order to see his children,' Karen clarified.

Jacqui blinked and then looked at Brett. She hadn't known about that, then. Karen wondered what else Brett hadn't told his new partner.

'There was no fight – at least, not physical. We exchanged a few heated words, and I left. Came back here. I don't think I'm the unreasonable one. I haven't seen Seb and Caitlin for weeks.' He let out a deep sigh. 'I'm sure you have preconceived notions about me. And I probably deserve them. I've been hot-headed in the past and made poor decisions, but I'm working on improving myself. Since I've started meditating, I feel a sense of inner calm.'

The music shifted from panpipes to a light tinkling tune.

'He really has made big changes,' Jacqui said earnestly.

'Don't bother, Jacqui, love. They've already made up their minds about me.'

'Pretty crystals,' Sophie said, nodding at the multifaceted stones on the windowsill, shifting away from the main conversation to defuse the tension.

Jacqui smiled. 'They help process negative energy. The amethysts are healing stones.'

'How interesting. You're both into this New Age stuff then?'

'It's mainly me,' Jacqui said, as Brett took a sip of his coffee. 'But Brett has been getting more involved, haven't you?'

Brett was still glowering at Karen and Sophie. 'There's got to be something in it. The ideas are ancient. The philosophy still makes sense.' He sounded defensive.

'What philosophy is that?' Karen asked.

'Being at one with the earth. Allowing energy to flow through you instead of fighting it. Some things are meant to be, and you have to accept them.'

'Interesting,' Sophie said. 'Is there a religious aspect? A deity?'

'We're not really following any religion,' Jacqui said. 'It's more about being in tune with your feelings and at one with the earth.'

'And how exactly do you do that?' Karen asked.

'Meditation.' Jacqui smiled. 'We use candles and incense to help us relax as we try to access a higher plane, so we can look back on our earthly bodies and see how small everyday problems really are in the scheme of things, you know?'

Sophie made notes as Karen asked more questions. Jacqui seemed open and transparent, but Brett was guarded. Perhaps that was understandable. He knew they were looking at him as a suspect.

'Any other rituals?' Sophie asked.

Karen sent her a meaningful look. She knew what Sophie was edging towards in her questioning, but they hadn't disclosed how Lloyd had died yet, and she certainly didn't want Brett to know about the mark on Lloyd Nelson's forehead.

'I do a cleansing ritual,' Jacqui said, warming to what was clearly a favourite subject. 'We use sage and incense to clear the space of any negative forces before we start meditating. You should give it a try – meditating, I mean. It might help release the tension.' Jacqui focused on Karen.

'Maybe,' Karen said, and finished the last of her coffee.

'How did he die?' Brett asked suddenly.

'We're awaiting the results of the post-mortem,' Karen said.

Brett exhaled slowly. 'Right. I'd better call the kids, see how they're handling it.' He lifted his gaze. 'Did you see them? How did they seem to you?'

'They were shocked by the news, and upset,' Karen said.

Brett rubbed a hand over his face. 'Yeah, I'd better give them a ring. That's if Bev lets me talk to them.'

'Do they have their own phones?' Karen asked, expecting Sebastian would, at least. She didn't meet many teens without their own mobile these days.

'They do. But Bev doesn't like me calling them. She likes to know when I'm speaking to them.'

'She's so unreasonable,' Jacqui said, flicking her long red hair.

Karen didn't comment. 'We'll be in touch. If you think of anything that could be relevant to Lloyd's murder, you can call me direct.' She handed Brett her card.

He took it and turned it over in his fingers thoughtfully, then he looked up. 'You don't think the kids could be in any danger, do you?'

'I think it's unlikely.'

'But it's possible? Maybe I should try for temporary custody?' He was talking to Karen, but his gaze roamed the room. He was thinking, planning.

'That would add extra pressure to an already stressful situation, Mr Wharton. I'd advise against it.'

Brett pushed up from the table and crossed the room to pick up his phone from the kitchen counter. 'No offence, but I'd prefer to take advice from my lawyer rather than you.'

CHAPTER SEVEN

'Do you think we've inadvertently started a custody battle, Sarge?' Sophie asked as she buckled her seatbelt.

'I think Brett Wharton was just looking for an excuse. Let's hope his solicitor talks him out of it. What did you think of Brett and Jacqui?'

'Bit odd,' Sophie mused. 'I thought Jacqui was harmless enough, but Brett . . . I wouldn't be surprised if he still has anger issues.'

'I agree,' Karen said. 'He was struggling to keep his temper in check. Whether that's because he's upset over his children—'

'Or because he's a killer?' Sophie suggested, finishing Karen's sentence.

'From his point of view, Beverley is keeping him from his children. That has to be difficult for any father,' Karen said as she drove away from Wharton's house. 'It doesn't mean he'd be driven to kill Lloyd.'

'Unless Lloyd stepped in to protect Bev when they were arguing, and tempers ran high . . .' Sophie trailed off.

'But we think Lloyd was killed in the cathedral. It wasn't during an argument over custody. And you saw how Bev reacted when we gave her the death message. She was horrified, genuinely shocked by the news.'

'She was. What if Brett Wharton had been so infuriated by Lloyd sticking his oar in, as he described it, that he followed him to the cathedral and killed him when Bev and the kids weren't around?'

'Then that would have been a cold-blooded murder. He'd have planned it. Two weeks between the argument and Lloyd's murder. Brett would've had time to calm down and think things through.'

'Unless Brett was lying,' Sophie suggested. 'Maybe they met up again, had another argument?'

'Possible.'

'And that New Age stuff was weird. Suspicious.'

'Lots of people meditate these days. Makes sense if he's trying to keep his anger in check.'

'But the symbol, Sarge. Maybe it's part of a ritual. Brett and Jacqui could be members of a wacky cult. Lloyd could have been a sacrifice.'

'Going from meditation to human sacrifice is a bit of a jump, Sophie.'

Sophie deflated with a sigh. 'I suppose. Though I do think there's a ritual aspect to this killing.'

Karen hoped Sophie was wrong. If the killing was ritual in nature then it was unlikely Brett was the killer. Why pick someone you knew for a sacrifice when it was bound to lead the police straight to your door?

Karen drove out of Morton and headed towards Lincoln on the A156, planning to call in on Ross Blundell's home in Saxilby.

'Oh, I forgot to tell you,' Sophie said, searching through her handbag. 'I've got a surprise for you.'

'You have?' Karen asked with a certain amount of trepidation.

'Yes.' Sophie produced two paper tickets from the bag. 'Ta-da!'

'What are those?'

'Tickets to see Dr Michaels on Thursday night! For you and me. My treat.'

'Oh.'

Sophie's face fell. 'I mean, I know it's late notice. If you've got other plans, I'd understand.'

'Dr Michaels is the author of the book you've been reading?'

'Yes, he's come over from America for a book tour. He's amazing.'

'He's a doctor, then? I thought he was a police officer.'

'He's both. He has a doctorate in criminology. There's not much he doesn't know about ritual murders. Consider it research.'

Karen searched for the words to let her down gently. She could make something up, tell Sophie she had plans with Mike that evening, but when she looked at the younger officer's hopeful face, she found herself smiling and saying, 'It sounds interesting.'

'Oh, I'm so glad you think so. I know you're sceptical, but once you see him in person and listen to him talk, you'll be blown away.'

◆ ◆ ◆

Karen parked up outside Ross Blundell's residence, a bungalow on Willow Close that backed on to the primary school. It was a pleasant area. All the homes had neat and tidy frontages, but Karen was surprised. She'd expected Blundell to have a flashier place, with his background.

She reached over to grab her handbag from the back seat, then pulled out her mobile phone. 'I'm going to call the DI and let him know we're about to speak to Blundell. Morgan might have some specific questions for him.'

But once again, Karen's phone was frozen. 'I don't believe this,' she muttered. 'You'll have to ring him, Sophie.'

As Sophie placed the call, Karen got out of the car and took a look around.

It was a quiet, residential area. The weak sunlight had managed to melt the frost. The bungalows all looked very similar, though some – Blundell's included – had been extended by converting the garages. The driveways were all alike too, tarmac rather than paved, but unlike most of the other bungalows, there were no cars parked outside Blundell's home.

Karen felt a spike of alarm. Had he done a runner? Maybe they should have questioned him last night. She ran a hand through her short, spiky hair as Sophie climbed out of the car.

'Doesn't look like anyone's home,' Karen said, and she walked towards the bungalow.

The door was white uPVC, and the house number was on an oval picture of a cheeky-looking squirrel beside the doorbell. It was something Karen might expect her mum to buy, not a geeky tech wizard.

She rang the bell, but as she'd feared, there was no answer.

Sophie waited beside her. 'Maybe he's gone shopping?'

'It's Sunday morning. Nothing's open yet.'

Sophie shrugged. 'Maybe the gym.'

Karen hadn't considered that. Why anyone would want to spend a Sunday morning at the gym was beyond her. 'As long as he hasn't tried to leg it.'

Sophie looked up sharply. 'Do you think he would?'

A shrill voice behind them called, 'He's not in!'

'We'd noticed,' Sophie murmured sarcastically, as they turned to see an elderly woman poking her head out of a window of the bungalow opposite. The net curtains covered half her face, like a veil.

They walked across the road. 'I don't suppose you know where he is?' Karen asked, smiling.

'Friends of his, are you?' the woman asked doubtfully.

'That's right,' Karen said, before Sophie could say any different.

'I expect he'll be at work. He's there all hours.'

Karen thanked the woman, and turned to Sophie as they walked back to the car.

'Let's hope she's right.'

CHAPTER EIGHT

Sparks Software Design was located in a building just off Brayford Wharf, so they parked at Lucy Tower Street. Karen jammed her hands in her pockets as they walked along the wharf, which was busy now as the shops and restaurants were opening. She'd left her gloves in the car. The sun sparkled on the water, but it was bitterly cold.

Sophie pressed the intercom button, and as they waited, they looked at the outside of the building, which had been done up in white cladding with gold-coloured blockwork. The exterior gave it a modern appearance that didn't quite fit with the buildings around it.

'Shall I try again, Sarge?' Sophie asked, after they'd been waiting for a minute without an answer.

Karen nodded, but before Sophie could press the button again, the door opened.

They both stepped back in surprise, as they'd been expecting a response from the intercom.

'Can I help you?'

Karen recognised Ross Blundell from the photograph on his website. He didn't look quite as smug today, more irritated.

'Ross Blundell?' Karen asked, holding out her ID. 'We'd like a quick chat with you about one of your employees.'

Blundell took Karen's ID and studied it. His eyes narrowed.

'Who?' He crossed his arms over his chest, looking at Karen with suspicion.

He stood blocking the doorway, clearly not willing to invite them into the office. 'Lloyd Nelson,' Sophie said.

Blundell huffed out a laugh. 'Seriously? I don't believe this. You should be out there working on real crimes.'

Karen raised an eyebrow. 'Perhaps we could come in, sir? So we can discuss the matter privately.'

'Fine,' he said, standing aside for them to enter. 'But I want it on record that I consider this a complete waste of police time – and mine, for that matter. I'm a busy man. I don't spend my days working on Sundays for fun, you know.'

'Neither do we, sir,' Karen replied dryly.

Karen and Sophie exchanged a look as he marched ahead of them along the corridor, then he opened another door that led to a stairwell.

They followed him upstairs. He was young, tall, good-looking and had a definite touch of arrogance, Karen thought.

The floor, ceilings and walls were all white. Very slick, modern and cold. The whiteness was disorientating after a while. All the doors looked the same.

He had no idea why they were really there. Karen decided not to deliver the news too early. He might be more talkative if he didn't realise he was a suspect in a murder enquiry.

He led them into an open-plan office, which had a large kitchen with a comfortable seating area on one side. It was nicely done, even if everything – from the kettle to the armchairs – was white. It was nicer than their office back at the station. A fancy white-and-chrome coffee machine gleamed on the kitchen counter. Sophie eyed it hopefully, but Ross Blundell didn't offer them a drink.

'We can sit here,' he said, motioning to the plush white armchairs set around the coffee table beside the kitchen.

'We understand Lloyd Nelson worked for you, Mr Blundell,' Karen said as they sat down.

Ross gave a weary sigh. 'Yes, he's worked with me for five years. The stupid man.'

'Why do you say that, Mr Blundell?'

'Well, that's why you're here, isn't it? Look, everything is above board. It was in his contract. I can go into the admin files and dig it out for you, if you like?'

When neither Karen nor Sophie replied, he continued. 'Every part of the software that Lloyd designed was legally owned by me. My company. It's all there in black and white. He signed it, for goodness' sake. I can't believe he actually went to the police over this. I thought he was kidding when he said he'd sue me. It's just unbelievable.'

'Lloyd Nelson was going to sue you, sir?' Sophie said, pulling out her tablet and balancing it on her knee.

'Yes. He claimed I was passing off his designs as my own. Ridiculous. The software design belongs to the company. I own the company, so the software is mine, no matter who designed it.'

This was the argument that Beverley Nelson had mentioned. 'I'm afraid we're not here about that, sir.'

Blundell blinked. 'You're not? Then why are you here?'

Karen didn't answer his direct question straightaway. Instead, she asked a question of her own. 'Was that the only disagreement you had with Mr Nelson while he was working for you?'

Blundell's forehead creased in a frown. 'Um, I think so. I don't recall us having any other issues.' He shifted in his seat. He was no longer righteously indignant. He was starting to get nervous.

Sophie glanced at Karen. She was wondering when they were going to put Blundell out of his misery, but Karen wasn't quite ready yet.

'Would you say you run a company with a pleasant working environment?'

'Yes, I would. Why? Who's been saying otherwise?' He ran a hand through his hair. 'If it was the admin assistant I let go . . . She was terrible. She was employed for one month on a trial basis. Her dismissal was perfectly legal.'

'As I said, sir, we're here about Lloyd Nelson,' Karen said.

'Yes, I know, but why? If it's not to do with the software, then what?'

'Did any of your arguments turn physical?'

He folded his arms over his chest and shook his head warily. 'No. I am not a violent man, and neither is Lloyd.'

Karen leaned forward, forearms resting on her knees, watching Blundell closely as she said, 'Lloyd Nelson was murdered yesterday.'

'Murdered? Good grief. Was it a mugging or . . .' He trailed off, his assessing gaze on Karen. 'No, it can't have been a random killing. That's why you're here. You think he was killed by someone he knew. You think I was involved.'

'Were you?'

'No!'

'Where were you yesterday?' Karen asked.

'I was here at work. All day. Until about nine p.m. We've got a security system. You can check the cameras. I was logged into the network here too.' He put his head in his hands. 'I can't believe this. Who would want to kill Lloyd?'

'Can you tell us about him?' Sophie asked.

Blundell looked up. 'You'd be better off talking to his wife. We work together, but we weren't exactly mates.'

'We've spoken to his wife,' Sophie said. 'But we'd like another perspective, if you wouldn't mind.'

'Right, well, he was generally rather quiet. Not exactly Mr Popular around here, but he got on okay with most people. An inoffensive kind of bloke, really. A bit geeky. Really into software, and he was good at his job. I have to give him that.' Blundell looked down at the floor, his face pale. 'I really can't believe it.'

He did seem shocked. Karen watched him closely, looking for signs he was acting. He was tall, muscular – easily strong enough to tighten a cord around Lloyd Nelson's throat and hold it there until his employee's life drained away. But what motive would he have for doing so? They'd had a disagreement over the rights to some software, but as he'd said, he held the rights – and if it was all in the signed contract, then he had nothing to worry about. He had no reason to kill Lloyd. Unless there was something they'd missed. Another reason Blundell wanted Lloyd out of the way.

'Thank you for your time, Mr Blundell,' Karen said. 'We would like to take copies of your security footage and Lloyd's personnel files.'

He looked up, his eyes sharp again. 'Do you have a warrant?'

'We can get one if needed. It will save on paperwork if you cooperate without one.'

Blundell hesitated for a moment, focusing on Karen with his cold, assessing gaze again, and then nodded. 'All right. I'll get what you need.' He stood up and gestured to the kitchen area. 'Feel free to help yourselves to tea or coffee.'

After he left them, Sophie walked up to the shiny coffee machine. 'Want one, Sarge?'

'No, I'm fine, thanks.' Karen stood up and wandered around the office, looking at the workstations. No family photos, no plants. Every desk was the same.

'How on earth does this work?' Sophie said, frowning as she grabbed a chrome handle.

The machine let out a hissing puff of steam, and she quickly let go. Glancing over at Karen, she said, 'I don't think I'm thirsty, after all.'

Blundell didn't keep them waiting long. He returned with copies of Lloyd Nelson's contract, as well as a memory stick containing security footage.

Karen took them from him and wondered whether the footage could have been doctored. He'd probably have the skills to do so himself. But there were other security cameras along the street and the wharf, so she'd be able to look at those as well, to make sure his alibi checked out.

He gave them a tight smile and a nod. 'Is that all?'

'For now,' Karen said. 'Thank you for your cooperation. We'll be in touch.'

'I'll show you out.'

Karen thought he led them out of the building by a different route to the way they'd entered, but she couldn't be sure as all the white corridors looked the same. 'We may need to speak to other members of your staff this week. I take it that won't be a problem.'

He didn't look happy, but his response was polite. 'I'm sure we could arrange that.'

'Was there anyone at Sparks who Lloyd was particularly close to? Someone who might be able to give us a bit more background?'

Blundell shook his head. 'Like I said, he wasn't really popular. He didn't mix with anyone outside of work, as far as I know.'

They reached the main entrance, and he pressed the green button to release the door.

He watched them leave, standing in the doorway, and they walked back towards Lucy Tower Street.

'What was with all the white?' Sophie said once they were out of earshot. 'It made my eyes go funny with all the LED lights.'

'Mine too,' Karen said. 'It felt sterile in there. Like a laboratory.'

'Do you think he did it?' Sophie asked.

Karen shrugged, crossing her arms and tucking her hands in to keep them warm. 'To be honest, I'm not sure what to make of Mr Blundell yet.'

'He looked shocked when you told him Nelson was murdered.'

'He did. Quite convincing.'

'So what's next? Check out Blundell and Wharton's alibis?'

'Yes, I'll do that this afternoon and look at the security footage. You'd better call in on Beverley Nelson this afternoon. We need to keep her updated on progress.'

'We've not made much yet,' Sophie said. 'What can I tell her?'

'Tell her we're working hard to track down Lloyd's killer. While you're there, try to get her talking. She might give us more to go on.'

'So you do think she was holding something back yesterday?'

'Yes, I do. Perhaps not intentionally, and it might not be relevant to Lloyd's murder.'

'I'll do my best to get her to open up. Can we tell her how Lloyd was killed?'

'As the post-mortem hasn't been completed, we can't say for certain, but you can tell Beverley we believe he was strangled. Don't mention the cross on his forehead.'

They got into the car, and Sophie began to type some notes on her phone. As Karen reversed out of the parking spot, she thought about the two suspects.

Both claimed to have alibis. Blundell's should be easy to check, but Wharton had claimed to be home with his girlfriend, Jacqui. There were no cameras to confirm his whereabouts. He had Jacqui to corroborate, but it wouldn't be the first time a woman had lied to give her partner an alibi.

Karen stopped behind a silver Volvo as she joined the queue to exit the car park, and drummed her fingers on the wheel. She'd wanted a quick resolution to this case so they could help Morgan with the hit-and-run investigation, but it was starting to look like this murder case wasn't as straightforward as she'd hoped.

Maybe Sophie would get something more from Beverley Nelson this afternoon.

Karen made a mental checklist of things she needed to get done. She had to follow up on the choir members, check Rick's work on the CCTV, and maybe run through the witness statements again to make sure she hadn't missed anything. But her first task would be looking into the alibis Wharton and Blundell had provided. She needed to make sure they were telling the truth.

CHAPTER NINE

DI Morgan got out of bed at five a.m. on Monday morning. The heating had only been on for half an hour, and the house was cold. He turned the shower on, twisting the thermostat to extra-hot, trying to get warm. He felt sluggish and slow. No surprise really, when he'd gone to bed after midnight.

He had multiple cases on the go. A robbery, an assault in the city centre, a boy knocked off his bike in Waddington, and now Lloyd Nelson's murder.

The Nelson murder was an intriguing case, and Morgan didn't want to let it go, but his team was stretched thin at the moment. He could get up at five a.m. every morning and put the hours in, but eventually something would have to give. The paperwork was piling up, and as a perfectionist, Morgan hated that. He couldn't stand disorder.

He'd been putting it off, but he'd have to talk to the superintendent today and admit it was too much. They'd have to pass some of the workload to another team – maybe the robbery. That was almost complete. A few final statements to sign off and a meeting with the CPS – and, of course, a multitude of forms to fill in.

They'd been short-staffed since Freeman had been removed from duty. Despite the substantial evidence against the disgraced detective inspector, he was still on paid leave and hadn't been fired.

As such, that meant technically there wasn't a vacancy to fill, so his work had to be spread over the other teams.

Morgan got out of the shower and rubbed the steam from the mirror. His reflection made him cringe. He looked awful, with dark circles under his eyes and pale skin. He picked up his toothbrush and ignored his reflection. He didn't have time to be tired.

At twenty past five, he went downstairs to get a coffee, but paused in the hallway by the front door. There was an envelope, face down, on the doormat. Morgan looked through the circular window in his front door. It was still dark outside and far too early for the post. He was sure it hadn't been there when he went to bed last night. So at some point between midnight and now, this letter had landed on the mat. Odd time to hand-deliver a letter.

He crouched down and flicked the envelope over. His name and address were written in block capitals on the front, but there was no postmark or stamp.

If he hadn't been a police officer, he would have simply opened the envelope and read the contents. But his years as a detective made him cautious.

He went into the kitchen, pulled out a box of gloves from under the sink, and put a pair on before returning to open the letter.

The envelope was normal enough. White, rectangular. Morgan slid his finger along the seal, opening it, and quickly scanned the contents. He'd been right to be cautious.

With the letter still clutched in his right hand, he opened the door and moved swiftly across the driveway and into the street, looking left and right, searching for whoever had delivered the letter. But the road was empty and quiet. The messenger must have visited in the early hours and was now long gone.

He went back inside and stared at the handwritten letter for a long time before slipping it back into the envelope and searching for a plastic bag to put it in. It was evidence.

He thought for a moment, wondering whether to call it in straightaway. But instead, he switched on the kettle, and as it boiled, he stared out at the garden. It was too dark to see more than the shadowy outlines of bare branches and stumpy shrubs. But he wasn't looking at the plants. He was thinking, weighing up the options.

His first instinct was to call Karen and talk it through with her, but it was very early. She'd still be asleep. Maybe she'd be with Mike Harrington. He frowned.

After making the coffee, he put the gloves back on and reread the letter.

Detective Inspector Morgan,
How did you like my tribute in the cathedral?
I wouldn't try too hard to solve this case if I were you. The man was no innocent.
Lloyd Nelson had lots of dirty secrets, but now he's cleansed of his sins. What do you think about that, detective? Would you like to be cleansed of your sins?
Lloyd was a thief. He stole from his employer. He embezzled money from the company for years.
He beat his wife too.
But if you were any good at your job, you'd know that by now.
The Cleanser.

Morgan put the letter back in the bag, removed his gloves and then took a sip of his coffee. His hand shook as he put the cup back on the counter. The letter addressed him directly. How did they have his name? Was it from the killer, or someone unstable who just wanted a bit of attention?

A press release and police statement had been issued to the public on Sunday, but there had been no mention of Morgan's name as lead on the investigation.

Though they'd received letters and phone calls from individuals wanting to take the credit and fame for someone else's gruesome crimes in the past, Morgan's gut instinct told him that this was a genuine letter from the killer. A sick individual who'd picked out their own nickname. The Cleanser.

He took another sip of coffee and then set the mug down on the counter. It tasted bitter.

What did it mean by *Would you like to be cleansed of your sins?* It sounded like a threat. But why target him? *Sins?* Was The Cleanser someone he'd crossed in the past? Or a friend or family member of someone he'd put away?

Was the cross on Lloyd Nelson's forehead some sort of symbol that he'd been cleansed?

Morgan emptied his mug in the sink and reached for his jacket. He had started the day planning to talk to the superintendent, to try to simplify his caseload. But things had just got a great deal more complicated.

He didn't have time to dissect this now, alone. He needed to go to the station, get the team on board and get their feedback. This was a significant piece of evidence. Perhaps the killer thought they were being clever by taunting the police, but Morgan hoped the boasting would reveal clues to the killer's identity. The need to gloat could be the killer's weakness.

◆ ◆ ◆

DI Morgan was already sitting behind his desk when Karen walked into the open-plan office. She felt a nip of guilt, then pushed it away. It was only just after seven. She'd worked late last night, fruitlessly trying to find a hole in one of the alibis. And then she'd helped Rick go through the recent contacts on Lloyd Nelson's phone, trying to find a new lead.

She crossed over and waved through the large glass door to Morgan's office.

He looked up but didn't smile.

She opened the door a crack. 'Do you want a cup of coffee?'

He didn't respond to her question, but instead asked, 'Would you mind coming into my office for a minute? Shut the door behind you.'

Karen raised an eyebrow at that. 'Sure.'

After she shut the door, she took a seat in front of his desk. 'What's up? I'm warning you I haven't had coffee yet, so if it's something that requires concentration, I'm going to be useless.' She smiled, but Morgan's face remained stony.

He pushed a sheet of paper in a plastic evidence bag across the desk. 'I found this on my doormat this morning.'

Karen picked it up, scanned it and then looked up sharply at Morgan. 'This was delivered to your house?'

He nodded.

'They mention you by name. They know where you live.' Karen ran a hand through her hair. 'This is bad, Morgan. It's really bad.'

'I don't think I'm in immediate danger.'

'I disagree.'

'I think Nelson's killer is trying to taunt me with how clever they are.'

Karen put the letter down on the desk and rubbed her hands over her face. '*The Cleanser?*' She shivered. 'What does it mean, *cleansed of his sins*? It seems to be implying Lloyd Nelson deserved to die because of something he did.'

'Yes, I read it that way too.'

Karen pressed her fingertips against her temples, trying to process this new information. It was shocking, and her immediate reaction was one of fear – fear for Morgan.

She read the note again, trying to decipher any hidden meanings. 'It doesn't make sense. They claim Lloyd was beating his wife. Beverley Nelson said nothing about that . . .' Karen broke off, thinking hard. She'd had the impression the woman had been holding something back when they'd spoken, but Beverley hadn't given them any indication Lloyd had been violent. Was she trying to protect his memory?

'Nothing came up on the background searches, Morgan. We were thorough. There were no hospital visits by Bev, no complaints against Lloyd from any previous partners.'

Morgan leaned forward and turned the letter around to face him again. Looking down at it, he asked, 'What about the embezzlement? Did anything Ross Blundell say suggest Lloyd was stealing from the company?'

'No. If anything, it was the other way round. Lloyd accused his boss of stealing his ideas.'

'Do you think the so-called *sins* in the letter are incorrect, then?'

Karen lifted her hands, palms up. 'I really don't know. We can go back and ask, make sure we haven't missed anything.'

'Yes. I think that should be first on the list of tasks today. Find out if he was violent. If he hit Beverley and her ex-husband found out, that gives him another motive. If he discovered Lloyd was hitting his ex-wife around his children . . .'

Morgan didn't need to finish his sentence. Karen knew exactly what he was implying.

'I'll speak to Beverley again this morning. Then I'll get on to Lloyd's boss again, ask him about the possible embezzlement and get him to check the company accounts.' Karen frowned. 'What I don't understand is how does the killer know this stuff? If it's true, then they must be quite close to Lloyd, don't you think?'

'If they are, that would be a good thing. It'll make him or her easier to track down,' Morgan said.

'Do you have any idea what time the letter was delivered?'

'Between midnight and five twenty, which is when I went downstairs this morning and discovered it on the doormat.'

Karen wrapped her arms around her middle and shivered. 'It's horrible to think someone was lurking outside your house. You don't have cameras, do you?'

Morgan shook his head.

'You should get some,' Karen said. 'At least one. They're not expensive.'

'I wasn't expecting the killer to deliver me a personal note, Karen.'

'You and Anthony both nagged me to get a camera. Besides, no one *expects* crime. We've both been around long enough to know that.'

'Hindsight's a wonderful thing.' His eyebrows dipped, a little dent forming between them. That always happened when he was irritated. It wasn't the time to make a big deal out of his failure to install a camera.

'What about your neighbours?' Karen asked. 'There are some big houses along your street. Some of them must have cameras or video doorbells, that sort of thing.'

'They probably do. I'll ask them if any cameras were triggered last night.'

'Good. What are you going to do tonight?' Karen asked.

He looked puzzled.

'I mean, you can't stay there tonight. It's not safe.'

'I'll be fine.'

'I'm serious, Morgan. We don't know what kind of nutcase we're dealing with here. You can stay at mine.'

Morgan started to say, 'I don't think—'

'No arguments. I've got plenty of room.'

'What if the killer delivers another note? I should be there. Might be our only chance to catch them.'

'We'll install a camera. If you insist on staying there, fine, but one of us will be with you. You won't be alone.'

'I'll see what the superintendent says,' Morgan said eventually, evidently realising he wasn't going to change Karen's mind.

The idea that the same killer who'd strangled Lloyd Nelson in cold blood and then mutilated his face had been lurking outside Morgan's house last night made Karen's stomach churn. She felt sick.

She took a deep breath and got up, planning to go back over all the background searches they'd put together, to see if they'd missed something.

Halfway to the door, she stopped and turned. 'What are you going to do about the letter? You're going to have to tell the super.'

Morgan nodded.

'She'll take you off the case,' Karen said. 'There's no way she'll let us continue working on the investigation now you've been named.'

Morgan leaned back in his chair, staring at the letter.

'Whoever wrote that note is threatening you,' Karen said, pointing at the plastic bag, driving the point home.

'I think you're right,' Morgan said eventually. 'She'll likely take me off the case.'

Karen swore in frustration.

'I feel the same. But I can't avoid telling the super about this.'

'I know,' Karen said as she left his office.

He was right, of course, she thought as she headed to the coffee machine. The super would be forced to take the team off the case. Karen didn't need a risk assessment to tell her that.

She reached for a mug and realised her hands were shaking. Anything could have happened last night. The killer had been right outside as Morgan slept, unaware and vulnerable.

She tightened her grip on the mug. It didn't matter how much Morgan protested; he was not staying there alone tonight.

CHAPTER TEN

At eight thirty, Morgan stopped by Karen's desk. 'I've just spoken to Pamela. The superintendent is in her office. I'm heading up there now.'

Karen grabbed her mobile and stood up. 'I'll come with you.'

Morgan raised an eyebrow. 'To make sure I don't volunteer to stay at home alone?'

'Yes,' Karen said, not bothering to deny it.

'You think I'd use myself as bait?'

'I wouldn't put it past you.'

She grinned, but he didn't smile.

'I have full confidence in the superintendent,' Karen said as they entered the stairwell. 'I'm sure she won't let you do anything stupid, but just in case you get any crazy ideas, I'd like to be there.'

'I'm not really the crazy-idea type.'

No, he wasn't, she thought. Morgan was the dependable, sensible, do-things-by-the-book type. She knew that, but she still couldn't stop worrying. It was creepy. The letter writer knew where Morgan lived, and that bit about asking him if he'd like to be cleansed of sin . . . She shivered again.

As they walked up the stairs, Karen shot a surreptitious glance at Morgan. He hadn't smiled once this morning, and though he wasn't as quick to smile as other members of the team, he wasn't usually this stony-faced.

His movements were calm and measured. Unlike Karen, there was no sign of his hands shaking, no sign of fear. But he was more worried than he was letting on. He looked tired.

'You know, Sophie is going to want to stay on the Nelson case. This is her first job as family liaison officer.'

'Understandable. And it's good for the family if we maintain continuity.'

Karen was unsure how to tell Morgan she wanted to stay on the case too. Would he see it as a betrayal? She was his detective sergeant. They worked cases together. How would she feel if she was booted off an investigation while the rest of the team stuck with it?

She was attached to the case. She'd been first on the scene and had put hours into interviewing suspects and researching the victim's background. It would be hard to let that go. Karen glanced at Morgan again. How should she broach the subject? She could come right out and say she wanted to stay on the Nelson case, but Morgan was hard to read. Would she be able to tell if he was offended, hurt?

'Why are you looking at me like I've grown two heads?' Morgan said, frowning as they reached the landing. He tugged the door open.

'I'm not,' Karen said as she walked through the open doorway. 'I'm just concerned.'

'You want to stay on the investigation too, don't you?'

She might have trouble reading Morgan, but apparently he had no such trouble reading her.

'I do,' Karen said slowly. 'But if you don't want me to, then I'll step down as well. I'm part of your team.'

'I appreciate the offer, but as I said, continuity is important. You've already built up a good level of information. Let's see what the superintendent says, but I don't see any reason why you shouldn't continue.'

They reached the superintendent's outer office and saw Pamela at her desk. She waved them in. 'She's expecting you.'

The superintendent's door stood open, and Morgan rapped against it before they entered.

'Good morning.' Superintendent Michelle Murray was still looking at her computer screen. 'I won't keep you long. Just have to send this email.'

Karen and Morgan sat down.

Murray's gaze lifted from the screen to them and back again. 'You both look very serious. I know the work is piling up. I might have good news for you on that score. Temporary funding for a new team. I've just authorised a request to transfer an entire team from Boston.'

'We're not here about the workload, ma'am,' Morgan said, placing the evidence bag containing the letter on the superintendent's desk.

Murray picked it up and scanned it in silence.

She looked up. 'When did you get this?'

'I found it on my doormat this morning at five twenty,' Morgan said.

The superintendent's eyes were sharp. 'This was delivered to your home address?'

Morgan nodded.

Murray pushed up from her desk, paced away and looked out of the large windows, towards the fields and farmland surrounding the station.

'You know I'm going to have to take you off the case, DI Morgan?'

'I expected as much, ma'am.'

'You're not going to argue against it?'

'That wouldn't be sensible.'

The superintendent turned back to him. Her face softened. 'No. It wouldn't. Do you have any idea who sent it?'

'I suspect the person who killed Lloyd Nelson,' Morgan said. 'But unfortunately I have no idea who that is yet.'

'We don't know for sure if it's from the killer,' Karen said. 'It could be someone who's learned of the murder and is using the case for some kind of notoriety.' She hoped that was true, but she didn't really believe it. Even as she made the suggestion, the words rang false.

'We can't take the chance,' the superintendent said, putting her hands on her hips and walking back to her desk. 'We're getting a new team, as I mentioned. I'll have to assign them to the Nelson murder.' She glanced at Karen and gave an apologetic smile.

'You know I have every confidence in you, Karen, but I need a DI to head up this case. Especially now . . .' She gestured to the letter in the evidence bag.

'I understand, ma'am, but I would like to keep working on the case if possible. I think it will help to keep Sophie as FLO, and we can work with the new team.'

The superintendent considered Karen's request for a moment, then turned to Morgan. 'What do you think?'

'It makes sense,' Morgan said. 'Karen and Sophie have spoken with the family and suspects. We'd be setting ourselves back if the whole team was taken off the investigation.'

'All right. You and Sophie can stay with the Nelson case for now,' she said to Karen, and then looked at the letter again. '*The Cleanser. Cleansed of sin*,' she murmured. 'It sounds more and more like a ritual killing. Have you got the post-mortem results back yet?'

'Not yet, ma'am,' Karen said. 'I'll phone Raj later today, to chase it up.'

'And are we any closer to identifying the killer?'

'Our main suspects have alibis, but I'll talk to Nelson's wife, Beverley, again, and ask her about the claim in the letter that he was violent.'

'She didn't mention that?'

'No.'

'Do you think her ex found out about Lloyd hitting her?'

'It's possible,' Karen agreed.

The superintendent sat down and leaned her elbows on the desk. 'Or he could have been targeted by a stranger?'

The vast majority of murders were committed by someone known to the victim. In those cases, there were always threads between the killer and the person they'd killed, which made it easier to investigate. A stranger murder, on the other hand, meant they had little to go on. They'd need to rely on CCTV and physical evidence. In this case, the CCTV so far had not been helpful. The amount of DNA in a public place like the chapel meant getting a clean sample or a match that would stand up in court was doubtful. Fingerprints would be difficult too.

'I can't say for sure at this stage, ma'am.'

'Let's hope Beverley Nelson can give you some more information. And . . .' The superintendent pointed at the letter. 'I take it you're going to speak to Lloyd Nelson's boss again about the embezzlement.'

'Yes, ma'am. He didn't mention anything about that when Sophie and I visited him yesterday.'

The superintendent opened the top drawer of her desk and pulled out a file. She flipped through it. 'The new team will be here this afternoon. I'd hoped to give them a few hours to get settled in, but it looks like they're going to have to hit the ground running. The new SIO on the Nelson case will be DCI Churchill, and he's got two detective sergeants in his team: DS Arnie Hodgson and DC Leo Clinton.'

Karen and Morgan exchanged a look.

Churchill? It had to be the same Churchill, didn't it? Karen's mind was reeling. The last time she'd heard that name she'd been talking to Alice Price about officers suspected of taking bribes. Alice had later retracted her claim that Churchill was corrupt, but the idea Karen would be working closely with him made her nervous.

When Karen had discovered there were corrupt officers in the force, she'd been determined to root them out. She'd spoken to Alice Price after her old boss, DCI Anthony Shaw, suggested it, but Alice wasn't a reliable witness. She'd had a breakdown a few years ago and had to leave Lincolnshire Police.

The superintendent noticed the look that passed between Morgan and Karen. She looked at them both in turn. 'Something I should know?'

'No, ma'am,' Karen said quickly. 'I just recognised one of the names.'

'Which one?'

'Churchill.'

That seemed to satisfy Murray. 'His file looks good. Experienced officer. Have you worked with him before?' Karen shook her head. 'Well, when the new team get here, bring them up to speed.'

'Yes, ma'am,' Karen said. 'I'm going to ask Harinder about installing a camera at the front of Morgan's property today. Just in case DI Morgan gets another night-time visit.'

'Good.' The superintendent looked at Morgan. 'Any movement on the hit-and-run case?'

'Sam Pickett,' Morgan said. 'We've not managed to trace the vehicle that hit him yet. There were no cameras in the vicinity, and lighting is pretty poor too. His parents, Will and Lisa, are understandably devastated. He was their only child.'

'What about traffic cameras on routes heading towards the road?'

'We're going through the footage, but it adds up to a huge number of vehicles. A lot of work. There was paint transferred to Sam's bike, and we're waiting for analysis on that. If we're lucky, and it's from the vehicle that hit him, we could get the make and model of the car.'

'Definitely a car rather than a van?'

'Yes, according to the analysis.'

'All right. Keep me updated on both cases.' She nodded, dismissing them both.

They headed back downstairs to the main office.

'I doubt installing a camera at mine will be much use now,' Morgan said. 'The killer's unlikely to hand-deliver another letter. They'll know we'll be on the lookout.'

'It depends how cocky they are, I suppose,' Karen said. 'They were taking a big risk delivering the letter in the first place. Why not just put it in the post?'

'They like the thrill. The chance they might get caught makes it exciting.'

'In that case, it's definitely worth putting a camera in. I'll ask Harry. He'll know the best make and model to use.'

'Can't I just use the same one as you?'

'We might need one with better resolution. Especially if we need to use the recording later for a conviction. And Harry will know how to disguise the camera. We'll need something low-profile. If they notice the camera, it might spook them and scare them off.'

'So I stay up all night, watching the video feed?'

'No. We can set up an alert. If the camera is triggered, it'll make the app beep and wake us up.'

'Us?'

'Yes, *us*. I told you. You're not staying there alone.'

Morgan pulled a face that made Karen grin. 'My company isn't that bad.'

For the first time that morning, he smiled.

They paused by the door to the office and saw Rick and Sophie at their desks.

'I'll give Sophie the good news. She'd have been very upset at the thought she'd be taken off a possible ritual murder case.'

Morgan cocked his head. 'Do you ever think Sophie might be a bit too keen on all that true crime, FBI and serial killer stuff?'

'Frequently. Did I tell you she's bought tickets to a Dr Michaels talk on Thursday night at the university?'

'Who's Dr Michaels?'

'One of the serial killer experts she follows. An American chap.'

'Never heard of him.'

'I'll let you know what he's like,' Karen said, leaving Morgan at the door. 'She's got me a ticket too.'

CHAPTER ELEVEN

Karen found Harinder in his basement lab. She couldn't remember when it started, but everyone at the station now called him Harry, in reference to his technical wizardry.

Harry didn't take much persuading to help Morgan get set up with a camera. He agreed to source a system and then come over to Morgan's to install it that evening.

'Cheers, Harry,' Karen said. 'I knew we could rely on you.'

'No problem. DI Morgan must have been seriously spooked. I would have been.'

Karen shrugged. 'You know Morgan, he's . . . not one for showing his feelings, but yes, I think he's concerned.'

Harinder was a tech genius. There was no one better when it came to this stuff, as far as Karen was concerned.

She returned to her desk, picked up the landline and dialled the number for the pathologist. She knew Raj was busy at the moment, but she hoped he'd manage to fit in Lloyd Nelson's postmortem today. Who knew what secrets the body was hiding? And they needed all the help they could get with solving his murder.

The call was answered by Raj's assistant, Tim Fellows.

'I'm sorry, Karen, but Raj is in the lab at the moment, and you know he doesn't like to be disturbed. Unless it's urgent?'

'No, not urgent. I hoped he could give me some idea of how long we'll have to wait for the post-mortem results.'

'He'll do his best to get to the post-mortem today. But I can't promise anything.'

'As far as you know, are we still looking at strangulation as the cause of death?'

She heard papers shuffling and imagined Tim going through a file. 'Yes.' He paused, then said, 'Since it's you, I suppose I can tell you what else we've got so far. The blood tests came back negative for drugs and alcohol, so toxicology was all clear. And you know about the markings on his forehead?'

'Yes. When I saw the body, the area was a bloody mess, but it looked like a cross had been carved into the victim's skin?'

'Yes,' Tim said. 'Quite a deep cut through the epidermis and into the fat and muscle layers beneath. I can't tell you much more than that.'

'The cut was made after death?'

'From the amount of blood, probably very soon after death.'

'All right. Thanks, Tim. If you could ask Raj to give me a ring when he has a chance, I'd appreciate it.'

'Will do.'

Karen hung up and pushed back from the desk. By keeping herself busy, she was avoiding dwelling on the fact that DCI Churchill would be here in a matter of hours.

How could she work with him after what Alice had said? How could she trust him?

But she didn't have a choice. Besides, Alice was disturbed. She could have her facts confused. She'd admitted as much herself when Karen had asked more questions about the DCI.

She glanced at the time. DCI Churchill and his team wouldn't be here until lunchtime, and Karen didn't want to sit around waiting for instructions for the next few hours. Not when she knew exactly what should be done.

They needed to pay another visit to Beverley Nelson and ask about the domestic violence claim in the letter.

Karen grabbed her handbag and jacket and walked over to Sophie, who had her head bent over her desk, scanning witness statements.

'I was just checking for something we might have missed,' Sophie said, lifting one of the sheets as Karen stopped beside her desk.

'Get your coat,' Karen said. 'We're going to talk to Beverley Nelson again.'

Sophie's mouth formed a small *o*, but she didn't say anything for a moment. 'But aren't we supposed to wait for the new DCI?'

'He won't be here for a couple of hours yet. There's no point sitting around twiddling our thumbs.'

'But DI Morgan said—'

'Right. I know Morgan technically is no longer in charge, DCI Churchill is, but we know we need to speak to Beverley Nelson about the letter. We don't need a new DCI to tell us that, do we? I've got a copy of the note. DI Morgan has entered it into the evidence database. We need to find out if Lloyd Nelson was violent towards Beverley or the children.'

Sophie nodded but didn't seem convinced.

'Look at it this way – by the time DCI Churchill arrives, we'll have seen Beverley, and we'll be able to tell him what we've found out. You want to impress the new DCI, don't you?'

Sophie brightened. 'Good idea,' she said, shutting down her computer and then snatching up her coat.

As they were walking to the car, Karen told Sophie she'd been to see Harinder, and he'd offered to install a camera at Morgan's house.

'Oh, you should have told me,' Sophie said. 'I could have asked him.'

'Well, it's done now. Why did you want to ask him?'

Sophie's usually pink cheeks turned even pinker, and she busied herself doing up the buttons of her red coat. 'I just thought it would save you a job. I don't mind going to see him. I find him interesting.'

'So do I. I don't understand most of what he says when he gets going on his favourite tech subjects though.'

Sophie smiled shyly. 'He's nice.'

'He is,' Karen agreed, pressing the fob and unlocking the car. 'You sound like you've got a crush on him.'

Sophie looked down, avoiding Karen's gaze, and gave a little shrug. 'Maybe a bit. Just like most of the female staff at the station.'

'Probably some of the men as well,' Karen said, as she got behind the wheel. Sophie sighed as she got in and buckled up. 'Seriously, though, if you like him, I don't think he's seeing anyone. Why don't you ask him out?'

'A date?' Sophie looked horrified.

'Well, yes, why not?'

'Like he'd say yes,' she scoffed.

'He might. You'll never know if you don't try.'

'I do know.'

'How?'

Sophie gestured at herself. 'Because I'm *me* and he's *him*.'

'That doesn't make sense.'

Sophie shifted to face Karen. 'Harry's clever, talented, and everyone likes him. I know what people think of me, Sarge. I'm annoying, a goody two shoes, the station swot.'

Karen felt a pang of pity. 'No one thinks that.'

'They do,' Sophie said as Karen reversed out of the parking spot. 'Rick tells me so, frequently.'

'That's just Rick,' Karen said gently. 'He likes to tease. He doesn't mean to hurt your feelings.'

'I know. He just says what everyone else is thinking.' Sophie stared forlornly out of the window.

Karen wished they hadn't drifted on to this topic, but Sophie needed reassurance. She worked hard and was eager to take on new tasks, but in many ways, she was still young and hadn't yet developed the confidence she'd need to progress in her career.

'We all have faults. Things that annoy other people. You have plenty of positive traits in your favour.'

Sophie looked at her expectantly.

Great. Now she was going to have to list them.

'You're one of the hardest workers I know. When it comes down to it, you're loyal. They're the two best traits a police officer can have.'

Sophie glowed. 'Thanks, Sarge.'

◆ ◆ ◆

Beverley Nelson opened the door. She wore no make-up, and her skin was blotchy, her eyes red.

She didn't speak when she saw them, just nodded and stood aside to let them enter.

Like last time, she led them into the kitchen, and they sat at the table. After a few words of sympathy, Karen asked Beverley if she'd thought of anything that could help their investigation.

'No. I would have called if I had.' Beverley stared glumly down at the tabletop, picking at the skin around her nails.

'We received some new information,' Karen said carefully, not wanting to give Beverley false hope. Though at the moment, the woman didn't seem concerned. She was lethargic, weary. It was almost as though she'd switched off the emotional part of her brain. Karen wondered if she had taken a sedative. 'It's information regarding you and Lloyd.'

Beverley lifted her red-eyed gaze from the table. 'What?'

'A claim that Lloyd was violent towards you. Is that true?' Karen asked.

Beverley stared at her. 'No, it is not.' The lethargy was replaced by a sudden fit of anger. 'Who told you that?'

'It was an anonymous tip-off.'

'What a cowardly and despicable thing to say. Denigrating Lloyd's memory in that way. He wasn't violent *ever*.'

'We understand it could be difficult to talk about,' Sophie said. 'It might not be something you want people to know.'

Beverley's eyes widened. 'I am telling you, he never once raised his hand against me.'

Karen took a deep breath before asking the next question. 'What about the children?'

Beverley looked at Sophie and then back at Karen, shaking her head. 'I don't believe this. You're supposed to be catching Lloyd's killer, and instead you're spreading lies. Horrible lies. He's a lovely man and would never hurt the children or me.' She clenched her fists.

'Are the children at school today?' Karen asked, noticing that the house was quiet and there was no drone coming from the television in the living room, as it had been the last time she'd visited.

'No, they're upstairs. They've never seen me like this. I know it's scaring them, but I can't help it.'

'They haven't seen their father, Brett?' Karen asked.

'No – why? Do you think it's a good idea to get them out of the house, away from this?' She gestured around the kitchen and then at herself. 'They don't deserve this. Maybe I should call him.'

The last thing Karen wanted was for Beverley to pack the kids off to Brett's for a week and then not be able to get them back. The woman had been through enough. 'It's possible Brett might try to gain temporary custody.'

It was hard to see children pushed and pulled between parents. Even normal, level-headed people could go crazy during custody disputes. The person they'd once cared about enough to have children with was suddenly seen as the enemy.

Beverley's face paled. She swore under her breath. 'He wouldn't.'

'He might not, but I thought you should know,' Karen said.

Beverley dissolved into tears. 'It's been awful since we divorced. We've constantly been arguing, always over the kids. And they don't deserve it.'

Sophie handed her a tissue, and Beverley dabbed away her tears.

'I know this is incredibly difficult, and I'm going to do my best to protect your privacy,' Karen said, though she knew if the press got hold of the fact a murder victim had been mutilated in the cathedral it would be splashed all over the local and national news. So far, she'd seen the death reported in one of the local papers, but it didn't name the victim and suggested the cause of death was a heart attack. But things had a way of getting out. They wouldn't be able to keep the press away for long.

'I am going to ask again, and I know that you're going to find it insulting, but it's my job to ask.'

Beverley held the tissue to her cheek. 'All right.'

'I need you to be completely honest with me,' Karen said, meeting Beverley's tearful gaze. 'Was Lloyd ever abusive to you or your children, or anyone else?'

Beverley's lips pursed in a thin line, and she shook her head firmly. 'No. Never. He was a gentleman. I promise you, I am telling you the truth. I'm not sure why anyone would say such a thing, but it's not true.'

'Thank you for being honest, and I'm sorry I have to ask these difficult questions. Unfortunately, I do have one more to ask. Was Lloyd in financial trouble? I specifically want to know if he'd taken any money from his employer?'

Beverley looked blindsided by the question. She stared blankly at Karen for a moment and then said, 'No. I mean, we did have a few money troubles. Nothing we couldn't handle, but to be honest, it did cause a bit of tension between us.' She began to pick at the raw red skin around her fingernails again. 'Lloyd enjoyed betting. He wasn't as bad as some. He didn't place thousands on a bet in one go or anything like that, but it did put a dent in our monthly income. You probably saw the payments to the betting apps on the bank statements I gave you.'

Bev looked at Sophie, who nodded.

'Well, I didn't like it, of course,' Beverley continued. 'And we did have words. But he wasn't a thief. He wouldn't have stolen money. If he had, I would have seen it going to the bank account. We were barely covering the mortgage and our bills.' She looked beseechingly at Karen. 'You have to believe me. He didn't steal any money. He wouldn't.'

'Okay. When did you first realise Lloyd had a betting problem?' Karen asked.

'It was just after we got married,' Beverley said. 'It came as a bit of a shock. I thought he was Mr Perfect, but the gambling was an addiction. We talked about him going into a programme, but he would always back out and say he didn't have a real problem, that it was all just a bit of fun.'

She hesitated, and Karen got the sense she wanted to say more.

Karen leaned forward and reached out to put a hand over Beverley's. 'I know this is really hard. But it's helpful. It could help us find the person who killed Lloyd.'

'You think he owed money to someone, don't you? Some kind of violent loan shark?'

'Did he?'

Beverley's eyes filled with tears again. 'I don't know. I don't think so.' She sniffed. 'We argued on Friday. He wanted to go and place a bet, and I was furious. He took my car to drive to a betting shop in Hykeham. If the kids hadn't been here . . . I think I would have dragged him from the car.' She pressed the tissue to her eyes. 'I was so angry with him. I wouldn't talk to him when he got home. Or the following morning when he said he was going into Lincoln, shopping. I ignored him. I wasn't ready to forgive him yet. So we didn't talk. And then you came to the door and . . . I knew he died thinking I was still angry . . .'

She broke off and dissolved into more tears.

CHAPTER TWELVE

By the time Karen and Sophie got back to the station, Churchill and his team had arrived. Sophie had stopped off at the canteen to grab a sandwich, so Karen walked into the open-plan office alone. She immediately noticed the new arrivals standing near her desk. Rather than step up and introduce herself, she stopped and observed.

The three new detectives were talking to Morgan. She read their body language – all four were tense, though she was probably the only one who'd notice Morgan's discomfort.

She recognised DCI Churchill from his picture on the Boston Police website. Charles Churchill, aged thirty-nine, never married, no kids. He had dark hair and a sulky face. Perhaps that was unnecessarily harsh. Karen could be projecting her feelings on to him. A bit unfair, perhaps.

He was tall, as tall as Morgan, and had his hair styled in a way that probably meant he spent a lot of money on styling products. She imagined him preening in front of the bathroom mirror every morning to make sure his hair looked just right.

His navy suit fit his slim build well, and his shirt was so brilliantly white it had to be brand new. Obviously a man who cared about his appearance.

The man standing on his left clearly didn't. His brown suit was so crumpled it looked like he'd slept in it. The jacket didn't quite close over his ample stomach, so he'd left it open. His trousers were an inch or so too short, exposing his scuffed brown shoes. He smiled at something Morgan said and pushed back his thinning grey hair.

The third man was younger, fresh-faced. Short, tousled mousy-brown hair, and quieter than the other two. He wasn't part of the conversation but was listening attentively. His grey suit was smart but looked lived-in.

She approached them, smiling. 'Hello.'

'Ah, Karen, this is DCI Churchill,' Morgan said, then turned to the old man in the scruffy suit. 'This is DS Arnie Hodgson, and this,' he said, turning to the youngest detective, 'is DC Leo Clinton.'

Churchill turned to Karen. 'Nice to meet you, DS Hart.' His smile didn't reach his eyes. 'Weren't you told when we'd be arriving?'

Ah, so it's going to be like this, is it? Karen thought. The passive-aggressive approach. He wouldn't just come out and ask why she hadn't waited around for him.

'We knew you'd be a couple of hours and didn't think it would be a good idea to pause the investigation for that long.' Karen matched his false smile.

Churchill arched an eyebrow. 'We should get the briefing underway. I take it you at least booked us a meeting room?'

'Yes,' Karen said. 'Meeting room three. It's just along the corridor. This way.'

When Morgan went to follow them, Churchill stopped him. 'I'm sure DS Hart can handle the handover. No need to take you from your work. Superintendent Murray said you were very busy.'

Morgan glanced at Karen.

'No problem,' she said. 'Can you send Sophie along when you see her?'

Karen grabbed some paperwork from her desk, and they left Morgan behind and headed to the meeting room.

When they were seated around the huge table, Churchill looked at Karen. 'Why don't you fill us in on what you know so far?'

Karen did so. She told them about the murder, the markings on the victim's forehead. She briefly described the suspects and their interviews, and then told them about the letter that had been pushed through Morgan's letterbox that morning. The atmosphere changed when Karen mentioned the letter. One of their own had been singled out.

After a brief pause, Churchill voiced the question they were all wondering about. 'Why DI Morgan?'

'We don't know.'

'He really has no idea?'

Karen shook her head.

Churchill tugged at his collar and leaned back in his chair. 'I don't like it.'

'We thought going through his old files might provide some clues,' Karen suggested. 'Probably the best way forward.' Then she said, 'DC Jones and I went to visit Beverley Nelson again this morning, and asked her about the claims of domestic violence in the letter. She vehemently denied Lloyd was ever violent to her or her children or anyone else she knows.'

Churchill nodded thoughtfully, but before he could say anything, there was a knock.

Sophie poked her head around the door.

'Sorry I'm late.' She slid into the chair beside Karen.

'DC Sophie Jones?' Churchill asked, fixing her with an unfriendly stare.

Sophie nodded and put the file she'd brought with her on the table.

'We haven't worked together before, so I'll give you a pass this time,' he continued. 'I do not appreciate lateness. And while you're working in my team, you'll be on time, understood?'

Sophie's cheeks flamed red. 'But I didn't even know you were having a meeting.'

'You were late,' Churchill said simply. 'Don't let it happen again.'

'But technically I wasn't late because I didn't know—'

'You apologised for being late. It was the first thing you said.'

'Well, yes, but—'

Churchill put up his hand. 'Don't make it worse, DC Jones.' He turned back to Karen. 'Please continue.'

Sophie's face was scarlet. She wanted to be liked, to impress her bosses. She was humiliated. Karen tried to swallow her anger and move on, but Sophie's bowed head and her dejected expression made Karen say, 'It wasn't Sophie's fault. Perhaps, in future, you should send a memo and make sure everyone is aware of the place and time of the meeting.'

There was silence in the room. Yes, she was goading him. Yes, it would have been easier to let it go, but he was being unfair.

'I'm not an admin assistant,' Churchill said coldly. He turned to DC Clinton. 'Leo, you'll be in charge of arranging meetings in the future.'

'Of course,' Leo said smoothly.

DS Arnie Hodgson looked very amused by the whole exchange.

'I've told you everything we know so far,' Karen said. She glanced at the clock on the wall. Time was ticking away. 'I was planning to speak with Ross Blundell again and ask him whether the embezzlement claims against Lloyd were true. Perhaps you could go over the files and get up to date while DC Jones and I visit him.'

'No,' Churchill said.

Karen looked at him. What did he mean, *no*? That was the next logical step in the investigation. 'Can I ask why not?'

He turned to Arnie. 'You and Leo will visit Ross Blundell. Arnie can read over the notes in the car while Leo drives.'

'But we're familiar with the suspect. We've spoken to him already. It makes sense if we talk to him.'

Churchill arched an eyebrow.

This was a power play. Great. Now she'd have to grovel.

'I'm not questioning your leadership, but—'

'Actually, DS Hart, that's exactly what you're doing.' He waved a hand at Leo and Arnie. 'Go.'

'Righto, boss.' Arnie stood and hitched his trousers up. 'Nice to meet you, DS Hart, DC Jones.'

Leo followed him out of the room, leaving Sophie and Karen alone with Churchill.

'I'd like you two to produce a clear two-page summary of the case, please. The current case file is a mess.' He stood up.

Karen clenched her teeth. He hadn't even looked at the case file properly yet. He was being obnoxious for the sake of it.

He left the room.

Sophie quietly swore at his departing back.

'DC Jones!' Karen said, shocked, though secretly she'd have liked to do the same.

Sophie scowled. 'He's an utter pig.'

'He's not very likeable,' Karen agreed. 'But we have to work with him, so we'd better make the best of it.'

'Makes you realise what a good team leader DI Morgan is, doesn't it?'

Karen scooped up the paperwork. 'Yes, it really does.'

Sophie saw Churchill as a difficult boss, but Karen wondered if he was far worse than that. He was prepared to put them behind on a case simply to teach them that he was in charge. Arrogant, yes, but was he part of the network of corrupt officers? She didn't know yet, but she intended to find out.

◆ ◆ ◆

Morgan looked up from the paperwork on his desk. Karen and Sophie were sitting together, working on the report Churchill had requested.

He'd asked them what they thought of Churchill, and almost wished he hadn't when they told him.

His suspicions had been correct.

When the superintendent had come to welcome Churchill and his team, he couldn't have been more polite and ingratiating. As soon as the superintendent disappeared, his demeanour changed. Morgan had worked with officers like him before.

DS Hodgson seemed solid, from Morgan's initial impression. A bit scruffy, but an old-school detective, focusing on the case at hand without trying to scale the greasy pole to climb the ranks. He was old enough and had enough experience to handle Churchill. The younger officer, Leo Clinton, was quieter, probably a bit over-whelmed by the forceful personality of his DI.

It was a shame. A good team leader could help with career development and build confidence.

Morgan thought about Rick and Sophie. He should try harder with them. The little chats didn't come easy to him, but he should make an effort for their sakes. Sophie hopped on to any course going – she was hungry for career advancement – but Rick held back. Could be lack of confidence, or maybe the troubles at home stopped him from making further commitments. That was understandable.

Morgan glanced through the window at Rick, who was staring at his computer screen, working his way through routes to the road where the hit-and-run had occurred, making sure they hadn't missed any cameras. Maybe he'd ask Rick to go for a drink later. See how he was getting on and ask if he could help in any way.

Morgan glanced at his watch. It was time. He wasn't looking forward to this. He shrugged on his coat and left his office.

'Where are you off to, boss?' Rick asked.

'To visit the Picketts.'

Rick grimaced. 'Oh. Difficult one that. Especially as we have no news for them.'

Morgan nodded. 'Yes. Fancy a drink later, after work?'

Rick looked surprised. 'All right. Mum's carer knocks off at six, but my sister will be there this evening.'

'Won't take long.'

'Have I done something wrong?'

'No, nothing like that. Just thought we could have a chat about your continuing professional development.'

Rick didn't look very enthusiastic at the prospect but pretended to wipe his brow. 'Phew.'

Outside, Morgan strode across the car park, wanting to quickly get into his car and out of the biting wind. He sat behind the wheel and glanced in his rear-view mirror at the station building. He had the distinct feeling someone was watching him.

Sparrow was smiling while watching Morgan walk across the car park. Things were working out very well.

Divide and conquer. Wasn't that the best strategy? It was a quote from Julius Caesar or someone similar. He'd hated history at school, thought it a waste of time. But here he was thinking of an actual quote and applying it to his plans! Who'd have believed it? Not his history teacher, that was for sure. She'd written him off by year nine.

He'd put no effort into his academic pursuits, according to one school report. That had got him a beating from his father when his parents came home from an open evening. He scowled now, looking down at Morgan's car and wondering why he hadn't driven off yet.

DI Morgan was an interesting character. Quiet, controlled and calculating. Yes, calculating – that was the perfect word to describe him. And a potential problem that had needed to be removed.

Sparrow considered calling up the boss to boast, but thought better of it. He hated talking to that man, even if there was positive news to deliver. He'd find some way to twist it into a threat.

You know what's at stake, Sparrow.

As if he could forget.

Just for once, he'd like to be the one in charge, the one calling the shots.

His phone rang. Glancing at the screen, he sighed; his absence had been noted.

Morgan reversed out of the parking bay, and Sparrow walked away from the window, whistling.

CHAPTER THIRTEEN

It wouldn't take them long to finish the case summary. The information was all there in the reports and statements, if Churchill had only taken the time to look.

'I can do this, Sarge,' Sophie said. 'When I've finished, I'll give it to you to look over. Seems a waste of time, both of us focusing on this.'

Karen agreed. She could go back over the witness statements, perhaps contact members of the choir Lloyd Nelson had attended. It was hard to imagine that one of his fellow singers would attack Lloyd in such a violent way. None had criminal records or discernible motives, and they were all in their sixties and seventies. But she needed to be thorough, and that meant checking out every possibility.

Sophie was more than capable of finishing the report herself.

Karen rubbed her stomach, which was growling, protesting missing lunch. 'All right. I'll look into the choir while you're finishing the report, but first I'm going to get something to eat.'

As she approached the canteen, she saw DC Leo Clinton and DS Arnie Hodgson walking towards her. Arnie was eating what looked like a sausage sandwich. A large dollop of sauce dropped on to his tie, and he wiped it off with a napkin, then spotted Karen.

'DS Hart,' he said cheerfully. 'There's not much left in the canteen. Just a few sandwiches.'

'That will do me.' She frowned. 'I thought you'd already left to go and talk to Russ Blundell.'

'We're going now,' Arnie said.

'Churchill seemed—'

'I know what you're going to say,' Arnie said, dabbing his chin with a napkin. 'He likes to put his foot down at the start. Best to agree with a smile and let him get on with it. He's not all bad, just takes a bit of time to get used to him, that's all.'

You pretend *to agree*, Karen thought, *then waltz off to lunch instead of interviewing Ross Blundell.*

Karen and Sophie would have been there by now, talking to Blundell, getting the answers they needed. She swallowed her irritation. She shouldn't begrudge them having lunch. Everyone needed to eat, but Arnie's carefree, relaxed attitude was grating.

'Do you want help with the questions you need to ask him?' Karen asked, then held up her hands. 'No offence intended. I'm not casting doubt on your interview abilities; it's just that we've already spoken to him.'

'No offence taken, DS Hart,' Arnie said with a grin.

Karen was starting to think that nothing got under Arnie's skin. It was certainly one way of dealing with a boss like DCI Churchill, she supposed.

'I think we've got it under control,' Arnie said. 'Did Lloyd steal money from the company? Are there any discrepancies in the accounts? Blah blah.'

He was right. That *was* the general gist of things, but she couldn't help thinking he wasn't taking it terribly seriously.

'Don't worry, Karen.' Leo smiled, his eyes warm. 'Arnie and I are leaving now, and when we get back, you'll be the first to know what Ross Blundell said.'

Arnie stuffed the last of his sandwich in his mouth and then looked down at his greasy fingers. 'Back in a tic. Just need to wash my hands.'

As Arnie wandered off in the direction of the men's toilets, Leo said, 'I know the DCI wanted us to go to Sparks Software straightaway, but we hadn't eaten, and Arnie is like a bear with a sore head when he's hungry. Trust me, it was better we got him a sandwich now.' He paused for a moment, then said in a lower voice, 'He's a good detective, despite appearances.'

'How long have you been working together?'

'Almost eight years.'

'And you've always worked under Churchill?'

'Yes. He's all right, too. Just tends to throw his weight around a bit at the start – with new people, I mean.'

'Likes to exert control?' Karen suggested.

Leo looked over his shoulder guiltily. 'Well, yes, he does. But you learn how to deal with him.'

Arnie came back from the toilets, wiping his wet hands against his trousers. 'Right then, young Leo. Let's go.'

◆　◆　◆

Karen walked back to her desk with the ham roll she'd purchased from the canteen, but her mind wasn't focused on eating. She was thinking about Churchill. If she wanted to play a full role in this investigation and not be sidelined, perhaps she should take a leaf out of Arnie Hodgson's book. Nod, go along with Churchill's ideas – or at least *appear* to do so.

She sat at her desk, leafing through the information they'd gathered on the choir as she ate her lunch. She couldn't see any angles; nothing jumped out at her. The members of the choir seemed boringly normal.

She glanced at her mobile. Should she call Alice Price again to ask about Churchill? They'd spoken in the past, but it had gone nowhere. Alice hadn't been able to provide any facts, and finally had said she'd been mistaken about Churchill. Worse, Alice's husband seemed to believe Karen was now harassing his wife.

The last thing she wanted was to make Alice's condition worse when the woman was so mentally fragile.

But there was someone she could call, talk things over with. One person who would be interested, and hopefully wouldn't think Karen was paranoid.

She polished off the last of her lunch, reached for her mobile and called DS Grace's number.

DS Grace was the officer in charge of gathering information for the corruption enquiry. Karen liked her. She was blunt, down to earth and worked hard. Karen didn't have any evidence against Churchill, other than the knowledge he was an annoying, arrogant so-and-so, but she could tell Grace that Churchill was here.

'Karen, good to hear from you. Everything okay?'

'Fine.' Karen stood up, walking to the other side of the office and standing by the window. There weren't many people in the open-plan area at the moment, but she didn't want to risk being overheard. 'There's been a bit of a personnel shuffle here. DCI Churchill and his team have come over from Boston to help out.'

'To fill the gap left by DI Freeman?' Grace asked. 'Oh, hang on, you said *Churchill*?'

'Yes, I mentioned him to you before.'

'I remember. I spoke to him. And that friend of yours, Alice Price.'

'She's not really a friend. She used to work with my old boss. He was the one who suggested I talk to Alice. Look, I don't actually have anything more to share on Churchill,' Karen admitted. 'I just thought you should know he'd been transferred here.'

'I appreciate that, Karen. If anything does come up, any alarm bells start ringing, then let me know.'

'I will,' Karen said, hoping she hadn't come across as paranoid.

'Are you still on for the meeting?'

Karen suddenly remembered that there was a corruption briefing meant to take place later this afternoon. She glanced at the time on her computer screen. 'Three o'clock, isn't it?'

'That's right. You'll be there?'

'Yes.'

'I'll see you at three.' DS Grace hung up.

Karen headed back to her desk and saw Sophie walking towards her, frowning down at a printout.

'Sarge, I have a question.'

'Fire away.'

'Lloyd Nelson. Did we find a driver's licence on him when his body was found?'

Karen thought back. 'No, he didn't have one on him. He had a gym card, and various bank, store and credit cards, but no driver's licence. Why?'

'There's no record of him at the DVLA.'

'Right. Maybe he never passed a test or registered a vehicle.'

'I thought that, but Beverley said—'

Karen cut her off, suddenly remembering. 'Beverley said Lloyd had taken her car.'

'Exactly. And if he didn't have a licence, he shouldn't have been driving. I mean, I'm sure it's not related to his murder. It's unlikely someone killed him because he drove without a driving licence.'

'Sophie, you're brilliant.'

'I am?' Sophie looked confused as she leaned on the edge of Karen's desk. 'Why?'

Karen didn't answer straightaway; she was thinking. Putting the pieces of the puzzle together. 'What day did Beverley say Lloyd took her car?'

'Um, Friday.'

'Right, and what else do we know happened on Friday?'

Sophie shook her head and shrugged.

'The hit-and-run. Samuel Pickett.'

Sophie's jaw dropped. 'You think Lloyd hit the boy?'

'It's a possibility,' Karen said. 'Think about it. Lloyd drives to place a bet. On his way back, he hits the kid on his bike. He doesn't stop because he knows he's driving illegally.'

Sophie nodded slowly. 'And if Sam Pickett's parents found out, they'd have been angry enough to . . .'

'Maybe,' Karen said. 'It's a motive, definitely worth looking into.'

'Do you want me to tell DCI Churchill about this?' Sophie said reluctantly.

'I can do it if you'd prefer?'

'I would, Sarge. Thanks.'

When Sophie went back to her desk, Karen reached for her mobile and tried to ring Morgan. It went straight to his voicemail. He would be with them now, offering sympathy to the Picketts. Updating them, though she knew he didn't have much information to share with them.

Karen typed out a quick text message to Morgan and pressed send.

The phone screen was unresponsive. Karen glared at it, muttering. Had the message sent before the phone froze?

Her new mobile should be arriving tomorrow. She switched the phone off, shoved it in her pocket, and then went in search of DCI Churchill. He'd been given an office on the floor above them.

She knocked on the door and waited for Churchill to say 'Enter.' When she went inside, she saw one of the men from technical support tapping away on a keyboard and frowning at the computer screen.

'I'm still not on the system,' Churchill said by way of an explanation. 'What can I do for you, DS Hart? Have you come to give me the summary report?'

'Actually no, it's about a possible development on the case.' She glanced at the civilian support worker.

He looked up and smiled. 'Don't worry about me. I'm done here. Your username and password should work now, sir.'

Churchill thanked him, and the man left the office.

'Sit down,' Churchill said. 'Have you finished the report yet?'

Karen was almost positive Sophie would have finished it by now. 'DC Jones is just making a few finishing touches. I wanted to tell you—'

'That's very disappointing.'

Karen frowned. 'What is?'

'I asked you and DC Jones to work on the report. It's now clear to me that you passed off your work to a junior officer.'

Technically, he was right. Though Karen didn't think she was in the wrong by doing so. It had been a pointless duplication of work. She bit her tongue, took a deep breath and thought, *What would Arnie Hodgson do?*

Tell him he's right, stroke his ego, apologise.

'You're right. I did ask Sophie to finish off, and I shouldn't have done. I'm sorry.'

He blinked in surprise. 'Okay, well, finish the report and get it back to me asap.'

'Of course, I'll send it to you as soon as it's finished,' Karen said. 'But there's one other thing I need to tell you.'

Churchill rested his hands on the desk and interlaced his fingers. 'Go on.'

'Sophie discovered that Lloyd Nelson didn't have a driver's licence.'

'Why is that important?'

'Because we know Lloyd was driving his wife's car on Friday evening. We also know there was a local hit-and-run around the same time. A twelve-year-old boy was knocked off his bike and killed.'

'You think Lloyd was responsible?'

'It's possible. I think we need to ask Forensics to examine his wife's car.'

'And you think Lloyd Nelson's murder is linked to the hit-and-run in some way?'

'Of course, we can't know that for sure, but Samuel Pickett's death could be a motive?'

'It's a stretch, but I suppose we can't ignore it,' Churchill said grudgingly.

'So should I organise a warrant for Beverley Nelson's car?'

'No.'

Karen felt a familiar spark of temper. 'Why not?'

His eyes narrowed, and he gave her a cold smile. He was well aware he was getting under her skin. He enjoyed it.

'I'll ask Arnie to get on it when he gets back.'

'I'm perfectly capable of organising the warrant,' Karen said, trying and failing to keep the irritation from her voice.

'I'm still waiting for your report, DS Hart.'

It was ridiculous. For one thing, Arnie and Leo had only set off about half an hour ago, so they wouldn't be back for a while yet. The wasted time was infuriating.

But how could she say that, without dropping Arnie and Leo in it, telling tales?

'Sophie will finish the report. It's almost done. I can apply for the warrant before Arnie and Leo get back.'

'Are you hard of hearing, DS Hart?'

She clenched her teeth. 'No, I just don't like pointlessly wasting time.'

Churchill leaned back in his chair and swivelled round on it. 'I know I can trust my team to do a good job. I need officers I can rely on. Until I know you are one of those officers, I'll give the important jobs to Arnie and Leo. Understood?'

Karen looked at him in disbelief.

Arnie would probably say to nod and go along with it, but it wasn't that easy. It wasn't in Karen's nature to bow and scrape to a jumped-up idiot who wanted to be the cock of the walk.

'Fine, but I think you're making a mistake,' Karen said. 'We're wasting needless time.'

'Your point is noted, DS Hart. Please close the door on your way out.'

CHAPTER FOURTEEN

DI Morgan sat on a faded green velvet sofa facing the Picketts. He balanced a cup and saucer on his knee. He'd turned down the offer of a cup of tea from Lisa Pickett's mother, but she'd made him one anyway – and so he'd taken it, not wanting to offend. Sam's grand-mother was on autopilot, keeping busy, trying to help in any way she could, even if that was just making tea.

They'd turned the family liaison officer away from the door yesterday, sending them off with a few angry words. *What's the point in you turning up when you've got nothing new to say?* Will Pickett had asked angrily.

He had a point, and Morgan hoped Mr Pickett wouldn't react the same way today, because there was no fresh news for the family now either.

Some cases affected Morgan more than others. He found the ones involving children especially hard. Samuel Pickett had been twelve years old. Sam had loved riding his bike and playing on his PlayStation. He was good at drawing and wanted to be a comic book artist when he grew up. The pictures that plastered his bed-room wall showed he'd had talent. Sam should have had his whole life ahead of him.

Today, Lisa – Sam's mother – sat opposite Morgan, looking out of the window, zoning out of the conversation. She looked tired, her face pale, her unwashed brown hair dragged back into a low ponytail. Lethargy and hopelessness had sunk in.

Will Pickett wasn't as angry today. When Morgan had first met the man, he'd seemed full of pent-up energy, furious, determined to find out what had happened to his boy. But now he was still, almost unnaturally so. He sat in an armchair on one side of Morgan, leaning forward in his chair, his elbows resting on his knees, gaze fixed on the floor.

There was no interaction between husband and wife. Neither one reached out to reassure the other. They were alone in their grief.

'Can I get anyone else a cup of tea?' Lisa's mother got half to her feet, looking hopefully around the room.

She wanted desperately to help. To stop the pain. But there was nothing she could do.

Morgan couldn't blame her for wanting to escape to the kitchen and leave the oppressive sadness in the room.

'No, thank you,' Morgan said.

Neither Lisa nor Will replied.

'So, you have nothing?' Will's voice was barely a whisper. 'Nothing to go on. Nothing to lead you to the person who killed Sam. The person who left him to die in a ditch like an animal.'

Before Morgan could formulate a response, Lisa said, 'He didn't die like that, did he?' She looked at her mother. 'I thought he died instantly, from the impact. He *didn't* suffer.' She turned to Morgan. 'Didn't you say he died instantly?'

A flash of pain crossed Will's face.

Morgan hadn't said that. Perhaps the family liaison officer had said something to ease their grief, though they shouldn't have. Not if it wasn't true.

It was tempting to say something to lessen their pain, even if only a small amount. But he wouldn't lie.

'We can't say for sure.'

'In your experience, though,' Lisa said, leaning towards him. 'Do you think Sam suffered?'

How could he answer that?

Morgan paused a beat, then said, 'Even if he'd survived the impact for a short time, I'd guess he would've been unconscious.'

'So he wouldn't have been hurting, calling for us?' Tears were rolling down Lisa's cheeks, but she didn't seem to notice. Her mother perched on the side of her chair and put her arm around her daughter's shoulders, pulling her close.

'He doesn't know,' Will snapped. 'He doesn't know anything.'

Will's eyes burned. There was the anger Morgan had seen last time.

Morgan had needed to come, to show they were still trying to get answers, that Sam hadn't been forgotten, but now his presence was causing the family more pain.

He stood. 'I'll be in touch. You can call me if you need to.'

Will scoffed and looked away. 'Don't come back unless you have some answers.'

Lisa's mother led Morgan to the door.

'Thank you,' she said. 'I know you're doing your best for Sam.'

'We are. We're checking all traffic cameras that line the roads that lead to the accident spot. It means checking a lot of vehicles, but we should have news soon.'

She put her hand on his forearm and squeezed. 'Thank you.'

Morgan walked to his car, wondering what was worse: being the target of a bereaved father's anger or being thanked by Sam's grandmother. Logically he knew the situation wasn't his fault, that he was trying his best to find the driver who'd killed Sam, but somehow Will's anger was easier to absorb.

So far he'd failed to get justice for Sam. Being thanked made him feel like a fraud.

DS Hodgson and DC Clinton still weren't back by three p.m., when Karen headed upstairs to attend the corruption briefing. She'd sent Churchill a copy of the case report summary via email, not trusting herself to deliver it in person. She wasn't sure she'd be able to be civil if she spoke to him again about the report.

The briefing was to be held in a room on the top floor, near the superintendent's office. Karen hadn't attended a meeting up there before. The room was very different from the ones downstairs they used for their own meetings.

It was huge, for a start. Windows lined a third of the room, making it feel open and airy, despite the fact the December sky was already darkening. The table was solid, though it didn't look like real wood. She put her hand on the tabletop. At least it didn't wobble when she applied the slightest pressure, like the ones downstairs. Even the chairs were different. Impressed, Karen eyed the plush, well-padded swivel chairs on wheels.

DS Grace was at the front of the room, connecting her laptop to a projector.

'Am I early?' Karen asked, smiling.

'No, I think the others are late.' DS Grace shrugged. 'Suits me, though, because I'm struggling to get this thing working.' She pointed to the projector. It was the only thing in the room that didn't look brand new.

Karen helped to get it set up, readjusting the cables from the laptop.

As the first slide appeared on the white screen behind them, DS Grace grinned. 'Cheers.'

'Who's coming to the meeting?' Karen asked, noticing that there were a lot of chairs set out.

'It's usually headed up by Assistant Chief Constable Fry, but today we're being blessed with the chief constable's presence, then you, me and DI Freeman's old boss, DCI Moorland. We have the meetings up here, away from prying eyes.'

Karen had pulled a face at the mention of ACC Fry's name.

Grace noticed. 'If I were you, I'd try to keep a low profile today.'

'Why's that?'

'I know you and Fry don't exactly get on like a house on fire.'

'That's not my fault.'

'He doesn't get on well with most people, as far as I can tell,' Grace said, glancing across to the door, making sure they were still alone. 'But he's in a particularly bad mood today. Apparently, his car was stolen over the weekend, and he's blaming every single officer in the Lincolnshire force.'

'Sounds like Fry,' Karen said. 'Has it been found?'

'Not yet, as far as I know. I wouldn't advise you asking about it, though.' DS Grace chuckled.

'I don't have a death wish,' Karen muttered as DI Freeman's old boss entered the room.

He smiled at them both as he sat down. 'Sorry I'm running late.'

'No problem,' DS Grace said. 'I've only just got the projector set up. And the big bosses aren't here yet.' She winked at him.

Karen sank into one of the comfortable seats beside DCI Moorland. 'How the other half live, eh?'

'Quite a difference to the chairs we have downstairs.' DCI Moorland leaned back, making himself comfortable.

'Yes. I could get used to this.'

Grace straightened, the smile slipping from her face, and Karen turned to see Chief Constable Grayson and Assistant Chief Constable Fry walk into the room.

'Ah, Karen, good to see you again,' Grayson said with a smile. 'Glad you could make the meeting.'

'Thank you, sir. I hope you and your son are well.'

'Yes, well, Ethan hasn't given me *too* much trouble lately.'

Karen nodded at ACC Fry. 'Sir.'

'I didn't expect to see you here today,' Fry said. 'I heard your department was very busy at the moment.'

'That's true, sir, but as you know, I have a personal interest in this investigation.'

He didn't reply, but took a seat beside Grayson.

DCI Moorland met Karen's gaze and offered a small smile.

'Superintendent Murray won't be joining us today,' Grayson said. 'She had to go and pick up her son from school. He's come down with a stomach bug.' He turned to DS Grace with a smile. 'Why don't we make a start?'

DS Grace began the briefing update.

As the minutes passed, Karen grew more and more disillusioned. She had no doubt that DS Grace was an accomplished officer. She'd covered every angle, researched every lead, but still she'd found no link from Freeman to more senior officers.

At the end of the briefing, DS Grace concluded, 'It seems likely Freeman was the officer at the top. We know he was the one who paid bribes to officers in traffic, and we have Charlie Cook's statement that suggests Freeman was their only point of contact.'

'Excellent work, DS Grace,' Fry said, then turned to Grayson. 'As I'd suspected, this whole thing stopped at Freeman's level. Thanks to DS Grace's thorough work, I think we can put this investigation to bed.'

Karen's stomach twisted. He was right. There was no evidence to suggest other officers were involved. Maybe Freeman had masterminded the whole thing. But Karen wasn't ready to let go yet. She sent a desperate glance to Grayson.

But the chief constable didn't notice; he was deep in thought. After a moment, he said, 'I agree it certainly looks that way. DS Grace, do you feel there is any potential in digging deeper?'

Grace glanced at Karen, who was trying very hard to keep her emotions in check. 'There are one or two more things I'd like to check out, sir. But it shouldn't take much longer.'

'Would you care to share what those things are, DS Grace?' Fry asked.

'Alice Price, in particular. I think—'

'Alice Price was an unfortunate case,' Fry said with a sigh. 'I'm afraid anything she says probably won't be trustworthy.'

DS Grace nodded. 'I'll bear that in mind, but I'd still like to follow up.'

'Very well,' Grayson said. 'Keep ACC Fry updated.'

And just like that, the meeting was over and they filed out – all except Karen and DS Grace, who was struggling to disconnect the projector.

'I'm sorry, Karen,' Grace said. 'I wish I could have given you more.'

'No,' Karen said. 'You've done an excellent job. I just expected someone else to be involved.'

'You're still thinking of Churchill, because of what Alice Price said?'

'I know she took it back and insisted she'd been confused, but I'd still like to know why she suspected him in the first place.'

Grace finally managed to pull out the cable. 'I'll talk to them both again. If there's any dirt to be found, I'll find it.'

CHAPTER FIFTEEN

Karen left the meeting room and was surprised to see a tall uniformed officer step out from the office next door. He froze in the doorway, eyes wide, as though she'd caught him somewhere he shouldn't be.

'Ray?' It was the PC who'd been at the cathedral after Lloyd Nelson's body had been discovered. He'd brought her coffee. Karen didn't often forget a face, especially if it belonged to someone who brought her coffee.

He gave a nervous smile. 'Yes, DS Hart.'

'What are you doing up here?' She looked behind him into the office he'd just left. It was empty, and the lights were off.

'I was looking for DCI Churchill's office.' A red flush crept up his neck.

'That's two floors down.'

'No wonder I couldn't find it then.' His nervous smile changed to a goofy grin.

'I'll show you, if you like.'

'Oh, I don't want to put you out. You must be busy.'

'It'll only take a minute.' They walked to the stairwell, and Karen tried to figure out what he'd been doing in the empty office. Did she really believe he'd wandered in there looking for DCI Churchill?

It was a bit of a coincidence that he just happened to be in the office next door from where they were holding the corruption meeting. Maybe she'd tell Grace to be more careful in future – to hold the meetings off-site.

Karen gave him a sideways glance. Ray looked young, fresh-faced and innocent. When Karen had first spoken to him, he'd seemed really enthusiastic about his career path, excitedly asking her questions about the best route to becoming a detective. He didn't look like a spy. But the question remained, why was he there? And why had he looked so guilty when Karen spotted him?

'What do you need DCI Churchill for? Anything I can do?' Karen asked.

'Oh, he said to pop by sometime. He offered to give me career advice.'

When they arrived at Churchill's office, he was on the phone. The door was slightly ajar, and through the gap, Karen saw Churchill scowling and talking in a whisper.

'Oh, he's busy,' Ray said with a shrug. 'I'll come back another time.'

He walked off quickly, leaving Karen watching after him, puzzled.

She lingered outside. Churchill spoke too quietly for her to get the gist of the conversation or determine who he was talking to.

She edged closer, desperate to hear something incriminating. But the movement drew Churchill's attention.

'I have to go.' He ended the call. 'Can I help you, DS Hart?'

She moved forward, stepping into the room, and felt his eyes boring into her. 'I just wanted to check you received the report I emailed.'

Churchill paused. He didn't believe her.

'Yes, I replied to your email.'

'Oh, right.' She flushed. 'PC Watts was just here to see you. He left when he saw you were busy.'

'But you didn't?' Churchill raised an eyebrow. He knew she'd been listening at the door. He wasn't stupid.

'I thought I'd wait until you'd finished your call. I didn't want to interrupt.'

'PC Watts.' Churchill shrugged. 'I don't know who that is.'

'Ray Watts.'

'Never heard of him.'

'He said you'd offered him career advice.'

'Doesn't ring a bell. Now, DS Hart, if that's all, can you close the door on your way out.'

Churchill and PC Ray Watts. Was there a connection between the two men? Was Watts spying on Churchill's behalf? Did he plan on telling Churchill that DS Grace would be paying him another visit?

Karen walked slowly down the stairs. Other than spotting him coming out of the office next to the meeting room, she had no reason to believe Watts was involved. No proof Churchill was corrupt either. Just because she didn't like Churchill, it didn't mean he was a crooked cop.

When Karen got back to the open-plan office, she saw Arnie and Leo had returned. They'd been assigned desks near the coffee machine.

Karen wandered over. 'Any news?'

'Lloyd Nelson's boss insists there was no embezzlement,' Arnie said, scratching his neck.

'How would he know for sure? Lloyd could have been very careful to cover his tracks.'

'Apparently Lloyd didn't have access to the accounts. There's no money missing as far as the boss is concerned.' Arnie shrugged. 'He did promise to have his accountant go back over the books with a fine-tooth comb to make sure. He'll let us know if they find anything.'

Karen wheeled over a chair and sat down beside Leo. 'Do you think that's good enough? If money was embezzled, it could be Ross Blundell's motive for killing Lloyd. Maybe he'd try to hide the missing money from us because it makes him look guilty.'

Leo said, 'You're right. We should get a warrant, go over the accounts ourselves.'

'Think yourself an accountant now, do you?' Arnie said, looking Leo up and down.

Leo blushed. 'No, of course not. I just meant we could get a specialised team to go over it, a forensic accountant.'

'I think that's a good idea,' Karen said, and Leo smiled at her gratefully.

'I suppose,' Arnie said grudgingly. 'I'll ask the boss about it.'

Karen filled them in on what she'd discovered in their absence. She told them Lloyd Nelson had probably been driving on Friday night without a driver's licence, and that Sam Pickett had been knocked from his bike in Waddington and killed that same night.

'So you think Lloyd killed the kid, and then Lloyd himself was killed in some kind of revenge act?' Arnie fiddled with his sauce-stained tie. 'Interesting.'

'It's worth checking out,' Karen said. 'We need to test the theory. If Beverley Nelson's vehicle hit Samuel Pickett as he was cycling home, there should be some trace evidence. Paint transfer. Blood . . .'

'Sounds sensible. Have you got the car?'

'No, apparently I'm not trustworthy enough. Your boss wants you two to do it.'

Arnie gave a long drawn-out sigh. 'I told you how to handle him. It's not difficult.'

'For you maybe,' Karen muttered.

'Great.' Arnie folded his arms and huffed. 'Looks like you and I are going to have to do all the work on this case, Leo.'

'We're perfectly willing to help,' Karen said testily. 'We don't want to be excluded. Your boss is unreasonable.'

'That's one word for it.' Leo grinned. 'Come on, Arnie. You've got to admit it took you a while to get a handle on Churchill. It's not like you had him eating out of the palm of your hand from day one.'

Arnie cocked his head to one side, thought for a moment and then shrugged. 'I suppose you're right.' He turned to Karen. 'I'll tell you what, why don't I go and see Beverley Nelson with DC Jones? It makes sense. She's the FLO. Beverley is familiar with her; there's a level of trust there. We'll ask for the car, but get a warrant in case she's not cooperative.'

'I'm not sure Churchill would like that,' Karen said. 'He was quite insistent he didn't want us on the job. Do you want to clear it with him first?'

'Not really,' Arnie said. He winked at Karen. 'I always find it easier to ask for forgiveness than permission.'

'If you're sure,' Karen said. She imagined Churchill finding out and becoming apoplectic with rage. She had to admit the idea gave her some pleasure.

'I'll sort the warrant,' Leo said, getting to his feet and stretching. 'When was the last time you saw the boss?' he asked Karen.

'She was lingering outside my office just a few minutes ago.' Churchill's cold voice came from behind them, and they all turned.

'I came to ask you if you'd received the case summary I'd sent,' Karen replied. That was her story, and she was sticking to it even if it wasn't very convincing.

He gave her a look that said he wasn't born yesterday. 'I've just spoken to Assistant Chief Constable Fry,' he said, his eyes still fixed on Karen. 'Apparently DS Hart had the time to attend another meeting this afternoon.'

'I did,' Karen admitted, willing him to ask what the meeting was about so she could tell him it was above his pay grade. She'd like to remove the satisfied smirk from his face.

But he didn't ask.

'And if you were needed? Did any of us know where you were? Did you bother to tell the team? Perhaps you sent an email?'

From his smug expression and his sarcastic tone, Karen could tell he knew she hadn't sent an email. 'I wasn't needed. I'd offered to organise the warrant for Beverley Nelson's car; you turned down my offer.'

Karen glared back at him. Why was he talking to Assistant Chief Constable Fry anyway? Why had Fry mentioned Karen's name? The meeting was confidential, for obvious reasons. The fact Fry had been discussing it with Churchill made Karen uncomfortable, especially as Churchill had been specifically referenced during the meeting.

'Did Assistant Chief Constable Fry tell you what the meeting was about?' Karen asked.

Churchill bristled. He picked a piece of lint from his otherwise-pristine white shirt. 'No reason why he should. I just know you weren't working on our case.'

Because I couldn't. Because you told me I couldn't, Karen wanted to shout.

'You're supposed to add any meetings to the diary,' Churchill said. 'You don't just disappear for an hour. Without permission.'

'That's my fault, boss,' Leo said quickly. 'I haven't told them all about the diary system yet. I'll get them added today.'

'No harm was done,' Arnie said cheerfully, ignoring Churchill's scowl. 'We're going to need an expert to go over the accounts for Sparks Software. Lloyd Nelson's boss says there's no missing money, but we should probably check ourselves to make sure. Don't you think, boss?'

Arnie was trying to distract him, change the subject, and Karen appreciated his efforts.

Finally, Churchill turned away from Karen. 'Yes, we have a financial and fraud investigation team. We can pass the details over to them.'

'They're on the system, are they? Shall I look them up?' Arnie suggested.

Churchill said, 'Leave it with me. I know the head of the team.'

'Right you are, boss. We're about to head out and try to get access to Beverley Nelson's car.'

Karen noticed he said *we're*, rather than *me and DC Jones*, so Churchill would assume Arnie was referring to him and Leo.

'Good,' Churchill said. Then he turned back to Karen, 'Don't forget, DS Hart, I expect all your little excursions to be included in the diary from now on.'

Little excursions? Karen fumed, but managed to keep her temper under control. 'Fine.'

Leo and Arnie waited until Churchill had left the office and was out of earshot before turning to Karen and looking at her questioningly.

Leo said, 'He does seem to have it in for you.'

'Not just my imagination then?' Karen said dryly.

Arnie leaned back in his seat, resting his hands on his ample stomach. 'No, the DCI has got a bee in his bonnet about something. What did you do?'

'Nothing. He's not like this with everyone?'

Arnie shook his head. 'He can be a difficult so-and-so at times, but not normally this bad, no.'

'Is it because I'm a female officer?'

Leo replied, 'No. He's got lots of faults, but I've never noticed him to have a problem with women in general. There has to be something specific about you. Have you worked with him before?'

'No. Probably just a personality clash,' she suggested, though really she thought it was more than that.

She suspected Churchill knew she'd spoken to Alice Price about him. Perhaps Churchill's behaviour was defensive.

Perhaps he suspected Karen was on to him.

CHAPTER SIXTEEN

Sophie sat in the passenger seat of the pool car. She kept glancing over at DS Arnie Hodgson, who was driving.

She was glad to still be on the case. The idea she'd be taken off her first case as family liaison officer had been depressing. But she wasn't sure about working for DCI Churchill, or with his team. Leo seemed okay. Pretty normal, actually. But Arnie . . . Well, she'd never worked with anyone quite like him before.

He had a large circular stain on his tie. She wondered what it was. Coffee? No, some kind of food, she suspected. Did he know? Should she mention it? If she were walking around with stained clothes, she'd like somebody to point it out. But Sophie knew she was different from most people. Rick would say she was fussy. But she liked to think that she simply took pride in her smart appearance.

She ran a hand over her pinstriped suit, smoothing the creases, tucked her brown curly hair behind her ears. Then she frowned at the blob of colour on his tie again.

Arnie turned, and Sophie realised he'd noticed her staring at the stain on his tie. She blushed.

'Anything wrong, Sophie?' He raised his bushy eyebrows before turning his attention back to the road.

'No, sorry. I mean, did you know you've got a mark on your tie?'

He glanced down and then chuckled. 'It's only a tiny smudge, barely noticeable.' He grinned at her. 'Adds a bit of extra interest to the pattern, don't you think?'

Sophie looked at the loud, swirling pattern and gave him what she hoped was a polite smile.

Then she turned away and looked out of the passenger window. She had seen Harinder earlier. He'd smiled when she'd passed him in the corridor. He'd actually looked like he was pleased to see her. For a nerve-wracking moment, she'd considered asking him out for a drink that evening, but bottled it at the last second. If he said no, she'd never be able to face him at work again. And despite what Karen had said, she couldn't shake the idea that it was unprofessional to date a colleague. Sophie prided herself on doing everything by the book.

That was what she liked about DI Morgan. He was easy to understand. He followed the rules, he was fair, and Sophie always knew where she stood.

Karen was easier to talk to, though. If she messed up, Karen was the one she turned to. She hated making a mistake, but even worse was making a mistake and DI Morgan finding out and being disappointed in her.

'It's just up here, isn't it?' Arnie asked, leaning forward over the wheel.

'Yes. The next turning.'

Arnie parked outside the Nelsons' house. He turned off the engine and took a moment to look around.

Sophie paused with her hand on the door handle. 'Ready to go in?'

Arnie's large watery eyes scanned the surroundings once more, then he nodded.

Beverley opened the door. Sebastian was behind his mother, clutching a carton of chocolate milk. He eyed Sophie and Arnie warily.

Beverley blinked, focusing on Arnie, trying to place him.

'Hello again, Beverley,' Sophie said. 'This is DS Hodgson. He's part of the team investigating your husband's death.'

'You'd better come in.'

She led them into the kitchen, and they sat down at the table. Beverley seemed a fraction brighter. 'Can I get you a coffee?'

'That would be lovely, thanks,' Arnie said, leaning back and making himself comfortable.

Sophie declined and watched Beverley move about the kitchen, opening cupboards and switching on the kettle.

Sebastian lingered in the doorway. He took a long gulp of chocolate milk, which left a smear around his mouth.

'Go into the lounge, love,' Beverley said to her son.

'I want to hear what they're going to say,' he protested, then wiped his mouth with the back of his hand.

Beverley shook her head. 'Go. I'll tell you later.'

Sebastian sighed and left the kitchen.

'Have you found the person responsible yet?' Beverley asked as she shut the kitchen door.

'We think we're getting close,' Arnie said. 'But we're here today to ask you for a favour.'

'What?' Beverley's eyes were guarded.

'We'd like to take a look at your car, take it away for a few days so our forensics people can give it a once-over.'

'My car?'

'Yes, we won't keep it long.'

She turned her back on them, shoulders and spine rigid.

'I know it probably sounds like an odd request—' Sophie began.

'It does,' Beverley said, cutting her off and placing a mug of coffee in front of Arnie. 'Why do you want my car?'

Sophie felt they should be honest with Beverley. She deserved that much. And the warrant was organised, so if Beverley refused, they could tell her she had no choice – and take it before she had time to get rid of any incriminating evidence.

Sophie clasped her hands together, resting them on the table. 'You said Lloyd used your car on Friday night.'

Beverley sank into a chair. 'That's right. I told you we argued because he wanted to place a bet.'

'But we've found out Lloyd doesn't have a licence.'

Beverley looked at Sophie. 'Doesn't have a licence,' she repeated dully.

'He's not registered with the DVLA,' Arnie explained. 'He didn't have a licence, so he shouldn't have been driving.'

A cold smile spread across Beverley's face. She made a sound that was a cross between a scoff and a laugh. 'He's dead! You can hardly prosecute him for that now.'

'Did you know he didn't have a licence?' Sophie asked.

'No, of course I didn't. Why? Are you going to try and pin that on me?' She was becoming agitated. Sophie tried to remember her training. She needed to be supportive and firm, but understanding. *Show her you're on her side.*

But Arnie got in first.

'You've got us all wrong, Beverley,' he said, leaning forward and looking at her earnestly. 'We're trying to help.'

'By going after a dead man for driving without a licence?'

'We think it might have something to do with his murder,' Arnie said in a low voice as he dipped his head towards Beverley, as though he was confiding in her.

'I don't understand. How?'

'That's why we need the car. We think there might be evidence on it that will give us a lead.'

'What evidence? You're not making any sense.'

'Did Lloyd act strangely on Friday night after he got back?' Sophie asked.

Beverley's head whipped around. 'I told you. We'd had a row. We weren't talking, so . . . I don't know really. You think something happened when he was out?'

'That's exactly what we think,' Arnie said gently. 'There's only so much I'm allowed to tell you without evidence. But I feel like we have to put all our cards on the table here. I can tell you're an honest woman. You adored your husband.'

'I did.' Beverley sniffed and pulled a tissue from the pocket of her jeans.

Sophie shot a look at Arnie. She wasn't sure about the way he was handling this. It seemed a bit manipulative.

'And of course you want us to find his killer as quickly as possible,' Arnie said, patting her hand.

Beverley nodded, dabbing her eyes.

'Then we need to check if the car was in an accident on Friday night. We'll have the folks in Forensics go over it. They can do all sorts of clever stuff. They'll be able to tell us if the vehicle was involved in a collision.'

Beverley blinked. 'You think Lloyd had a crash?' she said slowly, and looked down at the table, thinking. 'You think there was some kind of altercation, maybe a road rage incident. And then the other person involved followed Lloyd, killed him?'

Arnie smiled sympathetically. 'That's exactly the sort of thing we want to find out. I knew you'd understand.'

Beverley nodded, eyes wide as she processed the information.

Sophie sat in silence, unsure of how to proceed. On the one hand, Arnie had been kind to Beverley, and she was cooperating, so the interview was a success, but he hadn't been strictly honest. They believed Lloyd could have knocked a twelve-year-old boy off his bike and left him to die. But that wasn't the sort of thing you could say to a grieving widow without evidence.

Arnie glanced at Sophie and gave her a smile that said: *Job done. We're home and dry.*

'Have you used the car since Friday evening?' Sophie asked.

'No, it's been in the garage since then.'

'Do you mind if we take a look?'

Beverley pushed up from the table and moved to find the car keys. She plucked them from an empty fruit bowl near the fridge.

She held them out to Arnie. 'I'll unlock the garage for you.'

When Beverley opened the garage, they looked over the car, searching for obvious damage. There was nothing major, but then how much damage could a twelve-year-old and a bicycle do to a hefty Volvo? It wasn't a fair contest.

There was a slight scrape on the bumper, light scratches against black. Sophie pointed out the spot to Arnie.

Beverley looked over his shoulder. 'Oh, that was me in Sainsbury's car park. They've put new bollards in the most ridiculous places.'

'Well, if it's all right with you,' Arnie said, straightening, 'I'll put a call in and get the forensics team to come and take the car away. Will you be all right without it for a couple of days?'

Beverley shrugged. 'I suppose I'll have to be.'

'We could organise an alternative,' Sophie suggested. 'Perhaps a hire car?'

'That's all right. The kids walk to school, and I'm not back at work yet. Haven't felt ready.'

'Perfectly understandable,' Arnie said, meeting her gaze. 'Thank you again, Mrs Nelson. I know this has been incredibly difficult for you.'

Beverley gave a small nod, and dabbed at her eyes again with the tissue.

Sophie felt a pang of guilt. Beverley had no idea the forensics team were already on their way. It didn't matter whether she'd agreed or not, though Sophie had to admit it was easier this way.

She watched Arnie talk to Beverley, handing her a new packet of tissues he just happened to have in his pocket. He knew the right things to say. They hadn't been strictly honest, but maybe that was a kindness.

CHAPTER SEVENTEEN

It was the end of a long day, and Karen needed a drink. She'd heard Leo say something about Churchill wanting them all to go out for a team dinner to get to know each other, and she'd bolted. Cowardly? Perhaps, but she'd had enough of the man for one day. And she had plans this evening.

She'd driven home, grabbed an overnight bag, left her car on the driveway and walked down the road, heading to the pub.

She waited until a noisy tractor chugged past, then pulled out her mobile and called Mike.

'Hi.' His voice was warm. 'Still on for dinner?'

'Actually . . .' Karen said.

'Don't tell me. You've got to work late.'

She felt a pang of guilt. 'It's not that – well, I suppose it is in a way. The case is a weird one. I'm going to stay at Morgan's house tonight.' Mike was silent on the other end of the phone, so Karen babbled on. 'He got a threatening letter delivered to his house early this morning. A colleague is installing cameras at the house this evening, and we're both going to stay there just in case.'

'Is that safe?'

'We'll have a unit on standby. But it's unlikely whoever delivered the letter will come back.'

She heard Mike blow out a long breath. 'Right.'

'Dinner on Wednesday?' she suggested, trying to read his mood.

'Yeah, that'll be great. But about tonight—'

'It'll be fine. Really.'

'You'll call me if anything happens?'

'Sure, though I doubt it will.'

'Are you heading to Morgan's now?' Mike asked.

'I'm seeing Anthony for a quick drink first.'

'Your old boss?'

'Yes, I haven't seen him for a while, and something happened at work today that made me think we should have a chat.'

'All right then. Well, take care. Don't do anything stupid tonight.'

'I won't.'

When Karen hung up, she realised she hadn't even asked Mike about his day. How could she be so self-involved? She shoved her mobile back in her pocket, shaking her head. Once she'd spoken to Anthony, she'd call Mike back and have a proper chat.

She pushed open the doors to the pub and saw Anthony was already there, perching on a stool next to the bar.

He waved when he saw her. 'What are you drinking?'

'Glass of red, thanks.'

After they were served, they took their drinks to a table by a window, opposite the glowing fire. Karen put her overnight bag under the table.

Anthony carefully put his pint on a beer mat, then smiled at Karen. 'Is everything all right? You look tired.'

Karen didn't know where to start. Should she tell him about the letter threatening DI Morgan? Mike harping on about grief counselling? Or the trouble with Churchill? She looked at her old boss and felt herself relax. Even now, he was there for her. Listening to her problems, giving her advice. Just for once, she'd like to repay that kindness.

'I'm on a difficult case,' she said. 'Haven't been sleeping much. But how are you? We always talk about me.'

'That's because you live a much more exciting life than a boring old codger like me.' Anthony smiled and took a sip of his pint. 'Things are fine. A bit tedious, but fine.'

'I thought you were enjoying the freedom of retirement.'

'I am most days, but sometimes I miss the routine of getting up in the morning and going to an actual job. Seeing real people.'

'You see your family though, don't you?'

'My sister, occasionally, but she's got a big brood, and they keep her busy.' He removed his glasses.

Karen looked at him as he rubbed his eyes. He was lonely, and she hadn't noticed. 'What are you doing for Christmas?'

'I expect my sister will send me an invitation.'

Karen raised her eyebrows. 'She hasn't invited you yet?'

He shrugged. 'She's busy.'

'Then why don't you spend Christmas with me? Mum and Dad will be there, and my sister, her husband and their little girl, Mallory. You know them all. We'll have a great time.'

Anthony smiled. 'That's very kind of you, Karen, but you don't have to—'

'I know I don't have to, boss. But I'd like you to be there.'

He lifted his pint, clinked it against Karen's wine glass. 'In that case, I'd be very happy to accept your kind invitation.' His smile widened. 'I'll bring the wine and port.' He brightened. 'And the cheese. I've recently discovered the most delightful blue cheese called Cropwell Bishop. I know your dad will love it.'

'Perfect.'

'Now, I've told you about my boring life, why don't you update me on your exciting one?'

Karen started with a less heavy topic. 'Things are going well with Mike.'

'That's good.' He hesitated. 'Isn't it?'

'It is. Really good.'

'There's a *but* coming, isn't there?'

Karen leaned forward, propping her elbows on the table, and sighed. 'There is. You know Mike lost his son?'

Anthony nodded. 'He drowned in an accident?'

'Yes, so he understands. Mike gets me, in the way other people can't.'

'That doesn't sound like a negative point.'

'No, usually it isn't.' She fiddled with a beermat, twirling it around in her fingers. 'A few months ago, he attended a counselling group in Lincoln, which helped him. It was full of other people who'd lost loved ones. They get together and talk about their grief. Share their sad stories.' Karen looked up. Anthony was listening intently and didn't interrupt, so she continued. 'Mike's decided it's a good idea for me to attend one of these groups.'

'Ah,' Anthony said, nodding. 'And you don't agree?'

'It's not me, is it? Sharing personal stuff with a side of tea and sympathy.'

'You've told him you're not keen on the idea?'

'Yes, but he seems fixated on it. Keeps bringing it up.' She bit her lip. 'Do you think I'm unreasonable?'

Anthony quickly shook his head. 'Not at all. You know your own mind. He shouldn't push you to do something you don't want to, but I can see his suggestion is coming from a good place. He wants to help you.'

'He does.' Karen lifted her drink and took a sip. 'I suppose there are worse problems to have.'

'Maybe he'd understand if you explain.'

'I tried. I thought he understood. But then he said I should try one session just to make sure it's not for me.'

'Did you?'

Karen took another sip of her wine. 'No. I've been busy.'

Anthony smiled, lifted his pint. 'And the more he pushes, the less inclined you are to go?' He arched an eyebrow.

Karen couldn't help smiling. 'You know me well, boss.' Then the smile slid from her face, and her tone became serious. 'Do you think I should go?'

'I think you should make up your own mind.' He smiled to take the edge off his words. 'Only you know what you need.'

'You're right.' She leaned back against the upholstered bench.

'And what about this case you're working on? What's the trouble there? Have pity on a bored ex-copper.'

This was safer ground. Not emotional, easier to talk about. Karen rested her forearms on the table. 'It's a weird one.'

'I'm all ears.'

'There was a murder in the cathedral on Saturday. A bit grisly. The victim had markings on his forehead.' Karen spoke softly, so Anthony had to lean close to hear. 'Then Morgan received a letter at home. It was threatening in tone and talked about being cleansed of sin. And the fact it was delivered to his home address has made us all pretty nervous.'

'Yes, I imagine it would,' Anthony said, nodding. 'Is Morgan still working the case?'

'No, the super took him straight off after he told her about the letter, but we're having cameras installed at his house tonight, just in case whoever delivered the note comes back.'

Anthony looked thoughtful. He put his hand on his glass but didn't pick it up. Instead, he ran a finger along the condensation on the outside of the glass. 'Did the letter provide any clues to the killer's motive or identity?'

'No, but it contained allegations against the victim. Allegations that we are as yet unable to prove.' It was on the tip of her tongue to share the theory about the hit-and-run accident, but they had no evidence for that yet. Although he was her old boss, he wasn't a current member of the police service, and she shouldn't technically be sharing any details about an active case.

She lifted her glass of wine. 'Anyway, as you can imagine, it's all been quite stressful. And the cherry on top is that DCI Churchill has been brought over from Boston to take over the case.'

Anthony looked up from his pint sharply. 'Churchill?'

'Yes. It was . . . unexpected.'

Anthony stroked his chin thoughtfully. 'You're working with him?'

'Yes, more's the pity. We've not had a great working relationship so far.'

Anthony reached over and put his hand on Karen's. He wasn't a tactile person, and Karen looked down at his large hand over her own, surprised.

'Be careful,' Anthony said, concern etched on his face.

'With Churchill? Why? What do you know about him?'

Anthony moved his hand to encircle Karen's wrist. 'You've asked me before. And I've got no evidence against him, but he was one of the men Alice Price accused of taking bribes and ignoring crimes carried out by certain criminal groups before she left the force.'

'I know, but Alice withdrew those allegations. She said she was mistaken.'

'And do you believe that?'

'I don't know, boss.' Karen searched his face. 'What do you think? You worked with her. Each time I've visited her, she's been . . . fragile, an emotional wreck.'

'I thought her claims were believable at the time,' Anthony said quietly.

'So what do you think I should do? Go to the super, tell her I think Churchill is on the take?'

'No,' Anthony said hurriedly, tightening his hold on Karen's wrist. 'He could be dangerous. Keep away from him.'

Karen didn't say anything for a moment. How could she stay away from Churchill? She was currently on his team. Besides, was she just supposed to ignore the fact he might be corrupt?

'I can't do that,' Karen said softly. 'You know I can't. I've spoken to DS Grace about him. She's going to follow up.'

Anthony released Karen's wrist and rubbed his hands over his face. 'I don't like this. Can't you get a transfer? Just a temporary one?'

'Why?'

'Because you could be at risk! If Alice was right, then you could be working with a monster.'

'Then staying on his team is the best way forward, because I can get the evidence to bring him down.'

Anthony paled. 'We know what they're capable of, Karen. You need to be careful.'

◆ ◆ ◆

Sparrow sat in the car park outside the pub, the windscreen steaming up. He would have preferred to go inside, but there was no way he could without DS Hart noticing him. He wiped away some of the condensation with an old napkin he found in the footwell.

Luckily they had obliged him by taking a table by a window. Sparrow pulled his tablet from beneath the seat and tapped a few buttons, activating the microphone on Karen's phone. Then he settled back to listen.

Their voices came through clear and sharp. It took him a few minutes to place the man Karen referred to as Anthony, but he made the link eventually and checked on Google to make sure he was right.

The search produced lots of pictures of various Anthony Shaws. But the one Sparrow was interested in was the third hit.

DCI Anthony Shaw stood proudly in his uniform. Must have been taken at some awards ceremony, Sparrow mused, as he clicked and enlarged the image.

Yes, it was definitely him. Why was he meeting DS Hart?

He drummed his fingers on the steering wheel. This was an unexpected development, and Sparrow didn't like those. He didn't like being in the dark. He listened to their conversation with interest, and when Karen finally left in a taxi, Sparrow was tempted to follow her, but instead he got out of his car. He needed more information on DCI Shaw.

He was about to walk into the pub when Shaw walked outside. Sparrow hesitated, then leaned down, pretending to tie his shoelace. But he needn't have bothered. Shaw hadn't noticed him. He was too preoccupied. *Been out of the force for too long*, Sparrow thought.

Shaw pulled out his mobile, dialled a number and then clamped the phone to his ear.

After a moment he said, 'Alice? Oh, sorry, I was hoping to speak to Alice Price . . . Yes . . . It's DCI Shaw. I used to work with your wife.'

Sparrow's pulse spiked at the mention of Alice Price's name.

Shaw grimaced. 'I understand that . . . I promise this won't take long . . . Please, I really do need to speak to her.' Another pause, and then, 'Alice? Is that you? This is DCI Anthony Shaw.' He was quiet for a moment, looking up at the dark sky. Then he tensed and said, 'I'm sorry to trouble you, Alice, but we need to meet.'

Well, that was curious, Sparrow thought as he walked back to the car after listening to the one-sided conversation. Alice Price. A blast from the past. This could be a very interesting turn of events.

He waited until DCI Shaw walked back into the pub, and then Sparrow picked up his burner phone and placed a call of his own.

CHAPTER EIGHTEEN

Karen had smiled and tried to convince Anthony he was worrying over nothing. 'You know me, boss. I'm always careful.'

But he'd looked so troubled that, after Karen left, his words kept echoing in her mind.

She took a taxi to Morgan's, who'd just got home after having a drink with Rick, and when she got there, Harinder was out the front, working on the cameras and installing a new alarm system.

'Hi, Harry. Thanks again,' she said, and rapped on Morgan's front door.

'No problem. Almost finished. Just got to fix the connections inside and hook it up to the Wi-Fi,' Harinder said as Morgan opened the front door and they all went inside.

'Dinner's on me,' Morgan said, holding up an array of take-away menus. 'What's it to be? Chinese, Indian?'

'Pizza?' Harinder suggested, lifting his eyebrows.

'I suppose it's only fair you get to choose, as you're doing all the work,' Morgan said, reaching for the phone. 'What do you want?'

Harinder asked for double pepperoni, and Karen opted for Hawaiian.

'Pineapple on pizza?' Morgan grimaced. 'No accounting for taste.'

Karen chatted to Harinder as he checked the system was working. 'How did you get Morgan to agree to the alarm system as well as the cameras?'

'He didn't have much choice.' Harinder grinned. 'The superintendent insisted. She's also authorised a squad car to drive past the property every half an hour.' Harinder pointed to a small rectangle on the edge of the window frame. 'And all the windows and doors have contact magnetics. If they're opened when the alarm is activated, the siren will sound and send an alert to the station.'

'Great,' Morgan muttered. 'Now I'll be afraid to open a window in my own home, in case I trigger mass panic.'

'It's winter, and it's freezing,' Karen said. 'You can keep the windows closed until we find The Cleanser.'

Harinder then pointed out the motion sensors installed in the corner of every room, and showed them how to set the alarm using an app on Morgan's phone. They'd just finished a practice run when the delivery driver arrived, and they polished off the three medium pizzas in no time. Karen hadn't realised how hungry she was.

After Harinder left, Morgan lifted his glass. 'Shall I open another bottle?'

'Not for me,' Karen said. 'I want to stay sharp, just in case.'

Morgan put down the glass. 'I suppose you're right.' He sank on to the sofa next to Karen. 'So, how are things going with you and Mike?'

Karen heard the change of tone in Morgan's voice when he said Mike's name. He didn't approve of him. He'd made that clear, but it was none of his business.

'Great.' She paused. 'Although he did seem a little worried I was staying here tonight.'

'I'm not surprised. Staying in a strange man's house.'

'Yes, you are a little strange.' Karen grinned.

Morgan frowned. 'Very funny.'

'What have you got against him?'

'Nothing.'

'Don't give me that. Every time he's mentioned you get a look on your face.'

'A look?'

'Yes, like this.' Karen gave an exaggerated sneer.

Morgan chuckled and shook his head. 'I do not.'

'You do have a problem with him though.'

'It's not personal. He was a suspect in a case—'

'He was a bystander. Wrong place, wrong time. He didn't do anything.'

Morgan let out a heavy sigh. 'Okay. I just don't want you to get hurt. You've been through a lot.'

'So has he.'

'I know. That's why I'm worried. You need someone stable.'

'He is stable. He's a good man.'

Morgan said nothing.

'How's Jill?' Karen asked, changing the subject. 'Haven't seen her lately.'

'She's fine. Well, I think she's fine . . .'

'What does that mean?'

'I don't see her much when we have a big caseload. And it's hard for her to understand the demands of the job, you know?'

Karen had been lucky in that sense. Josh had understood. They'd shared childcare, and he'd accepted the times she had to work late with little notice. He'd worried about her, of course, but they hadn't rowed about her absences, like some couples. And now, with Mike, she had someone who had been in the police service himself.

'It can't be easy for her,' Karen said, tucking a cushion under her arm and getting comfortable. She smothered a yawn. 'Are you sure you're okay with this security app?'

'Yes, I'm not a complete technophobe.'

'Why don't you test the camera again?'

With a sigh, Morgan got to his feet. He walked out into the hallway and Karen heard him open the front door. A moment later, the alarm alert sounded on the phone. She called out, 'It's working fine.'

He came back into the room, rubbing his arms. 'It's freezing out there.'

Karen twisted around to face him. 'What do you think the chances are of Sam Pickett's father taking the law into his own hands?'

She'd only managed to speak briefly to Morgan at the station about the possible link between the hit-and-run and Lloyd Nelson's murder.

Morgan sank back down on to the sofa. 'Will Pickett is angry. Very angry, and he's beside himself with grief.'

'Angry enough to kill the man who knocked Sam off his bike?'

'Perhaps, but Will Pickett would have had to find out Lloyd was behind the accident, track him down and then brutally murder him in the cathedral. And why would he have cut Lloyd's forehead?'

'Murder is the ultimate sin?' Karen suggested. 'Are the Picketts religious?'

Morgan exhaled a long breath and looked up at the ceiling. 'I don't know.'

'But they seemed like a normal enough family?'

'Yes, though it's hard to tell when you meet them under cir-cumstances like this.' He ran a hand through his hair. 'I don't want it to be him. I'd like to find Lloyd's killer, but I don't want it to be Will. They've been through enough.'

'Hopefully we'll have some answers tomorrow. The forensics team are pulling a late one tonight, going over Beverley Nelson's vehicle.'

Morgan nodded thoughtfully. They were both quiet for a few minutes, then he said, 'Will is angry. But the accident happened on Friday night. Lloyd was killed Saturday afternoon. How did he track Lloyd down so fast? How did he find Sam's killer so quickly when we couldn't?'

'Maybe Lloyd confessed?'

'Rick's been through Lloyd Nelson's phone records, and there's no record of communication between him and the Picketts. At least, not over the phone.'

'Maybe there was a witness? Instead of coming to us, they told Sam's father?'

'It's possible . . .'

'Or maybe they knew each other already. We could ask Beverley?'

Morgan sat forward, resting his elbows on his knees, linked his fingers and looked down at the floor. 'No, I think we should wait to see what we get back from the car. We don't want to tip Beverley off yet. If she thinks Will killed her husband, it could lead to an altercation, and if we're wrong, we're just adding to the Picketts' and Nelsons' misery for no reason.'

'You're right.' Karen took the plates to the kitchen and started washing up.

Morgan dried up and stacked the plates in a cupboard. 'You don't have to stay here tonight, you know. I could order you a taxi.'

'I know I don't have to, Morgan. But I'm going to.' She twisted round to face him. 'You'd do the same for me, wouldn't you?'

He nodded. 'Fair enough. I've set the heating to come on at five. Early enough?'

'Yes. I'll set my alarm for six.'

They left the kitchen, and Morgan switched off the light. 'Let's just hope the sound of your alarm going off at six is the only thing that wakes you up tonight.'

They climbed the stairs, and she paused at the top. 'Well, goodnight.'

'Night. You can use the bathroom first. It's right next to your room. See you in the morning.'

Karen was looking forward to falling on to Morgan's spare bed and slipping into a dreamless sleep. She grabbed her toothbrush and cleansing wipes from her overnight bag, and used the bathroom.

When she returned to the spare room, she wandered over to the window. There was a small gap between the curtains. She looked out on to the dark street. Nothing moved. The lights were off in the house opposite.

Was someone out there? Watching? Had they seen Harinder fit the cameras?

She caught a movement and turned her head. A small tabby cat crept around Morgan's car. Karen released her breath. Nothing to worry about. Just a cat.

◆ ◆ ◆

When Karen woke, she grabbed her mobile from the nightstand and blinked at the screen. It was just before six, so she turned her alarm off. There were no notifications from the security app. Nothing had triggered the cameras last night.

She put her phone down and stood up, opening the curtains and looking out. It was still dark. She could hear Morgan moving about downstairs.

After calling out good morning, she told him she was heading for a shower. She washed and dressed and then made her way downstairs. The smell of coffee drew her straight to the kitchen.

Morgan's hair was still wet from the shower. He was topping up his mug from a pot of filter coffee. He smiled. 'Want one?'

'Yes, please.'

He poured another coffee, added milk, and then handed her the mug. Karen inhaled the rich, delicious scent, then took a sip.

'Do you want me to drop you at yours on the way in, so you can pick up your car?'

'If you don't mind. I'm not sure what Churchill will have me doing today. I might need it.'

'How's it going with him?'

Karen pulled a face.

'That bad?'

'Sophie said, and I quote, *he's an utter pig.*'

Morgan tried to hide his smile, but didn't quite succeed.

'And you'll be glad to know it's made us appreciate you, as team leader, far more.'

'Glad to hear it,' he said, keeping his face serious. 'I've always been underappreciated.'

Karen laughed.

They finished their coffee in companionable silence and then set off. Morgan took Karen home, where she dropped off her overnight bag and picked up her car, and then they drove separately to Nettleham station.

When Karen arrived, there was no sign of Churchill, Arnie or Leo, and Rick and Sophie's desks were empty. She made herself another cup of coffee and then settled down in front of her computer to check whether they had the results back from Forensics yet. There was nothing on the system. She checked the time. It was unlikely that there was anyone in the lab at the moment. So she pulled up the file on the Sam Pickett case and scrolled through the data to see if she could detect any links between the hit-and-run and Lloyd Nelson.

She was still lost in the exercise when the others arrived.

'Morning, Sarge,' Sophie said, covering her mouth mid-yawn at the end of the sentence. 'Coffee?'

'I've already had one, thanks.'

'One coffee is never enough,' Arnie said, shuffling in, looking like he'd slept in his suit and had just rolled out of bed. Karen doubted his grey hair had seen a comb that morning.

'I had another earlier, at Morgan's.'

Arnie waggled his eyebrows. 'Did you indeed?'

Even Leo looked up from his desk, surprised and alert for gossip.

Karen sighed. 'I stayed there last night in case he had another letter delivered.'

Arnie wandered over to Karen's desk and perched his ample backside next to her computer. 'And was there another letter?'

Karen shook her head. 'No. Nothing. Harinder installed a security system last night, but it wasn't triggered.'

'Maybe they know Morgan isn't on the case anymore,' Leo suggested.

The idea the killer knew that much about their investigative team made Karen nervous.

Leo checked his watch. 'Nearly time for the morning briefing. I've booked meeting room three. We'd better head there now. Churchill doesn't appreciate tardiness.' He rolled his eyes.

Karen logged out of the computer system and then reached for her empty mug. 'If we're having a briefing with Churchill, then I was wrong about the coffee. I do need another one.'

◆　◆　◆

Churchill was already in the meeting room when they all filed in. He was smiling, very unusual for him, which made Karen alert for trouble.

'Good morning, team,' Churchill said, looking very pleased with himself. 'Leo, perhaps you could kick us off regarding Nelson's financial situation.'

'Okay,' Leo said as they all took seats around the large table. He pulled out papers from the file he was carrying. 'As we know already, thanks to the bank statements Sophie got from Mrs Nelson, Lloyd had a gambling habit. They were in considerable debt. He had several credit cards, all at their limit. And they went into their overdraft every month.

'Lloyd was on a good salary, but he was spending it faster than it came in. He had a joint account with Beverley for bills and one of his own, which was mainly used for various online betting websites. There were also some large cash withdrawals.'

'Perhaps he was having a flutter through an unregulated gambling system? Or a betting shop?' Arnie suggested.

'We know he was travelling to place a bet on Friday night,' Karen said. 'Beverley told us he used a betting shop in Hykeham.'

'Yes, and he did visit on Friday night,' Arnie confirmed. 'We have him on CCTV, on traffic cameras and also on Hykeham Road. I've spoken to the betting shop manager, and a member of staff remembers seeing him. Of course, being a betting shop, there are security cameras inside, and I've asked for the footage – but even without that, I think we can say with relative confidence that Lloyd did pay them a visit on Friday night.'

It was good to have it confirmed. Karen leaned forward, looking at Arnie and turning away from Churchill. 'That strengthens the theory that Lloyd was the one to knock Sam Pickett off his bike in Waddington. One route from the betting shop to the Nelsons' house would take him via that lane.'

'I'll have to stop you there, DS Hart.'

Churchill was looking particularly smug. Was he going to reprimand her for talking without asking for permission?

She smiled and looked at him expectantly. She was determined not to let him get under her skin today.

'It's a bit of a stretch,' Churchill continued. 'We don't know the route Lloyd took when he travelled home from the betting shop.'

'No, but we can find out easily enough. We just have to check the traffic cameras coming out of Hykeham and follow his route. Leo could check to see if—'

'Oh, you're assigning the work now, are you?' Karen took a deep breath as Churchill cut in. 'Please, tell us what you'd like Leo to do.'

Leo sank lower in his seat. Sophie glowered at Churchill, and Karen could feel her body tense. *Ignore him. He's just trying to get a rise out of you.*

The only person who seemed completely oblivious to the undercurrent in the room was Arnie, who was leaning back in his chair, looking perfectly at ease.

'Perhaps Leo could check the traffic camera data to check the route. Or I could do it.' She turned to Leo. 'I wasn't singling you out. You just mentioned the traffic camera footage yesterday.'

Leo looked like he wanted the ground to swallow him up. 'It's fine,' he said quietly. 'I don't mind doing it.'

'Pointless,' Churchill said, his gaze fixed on Karen.

She paused, determined not to give him the satisfaction of her raising her voice or losing her temper, then asked, 'Why?'

'Because I've had the preliminary report back from Forensics on the car.'

All eyes in the room turned to Churchill.

'There's a small scrape on the bumper, but they believe it's unrelated. Highly unlikely to be caused by a collision with a bicycle. There's no paint transfer. In fact, no evidence of a serious accident at all.'

Karen felt the energy and enthusiasm she'd had for the case drain away. It had been such a good link. She'd been almost certain there was a connection between the hit-and-run and Lloyd's murder. But she couldn't argue with forensics.

'So Forensics said there's no way the Nelson vehicle was involved in the hit-and-run?' Leo asked timidly.

'They are ninety-nine point nine per cent certain the vehicle was not the one that hit Sam Pickett.'

'It was a possibility, though,' Leo said, shooting Karen a small smile. 'We had to look into it.'

'Right, it's a setback, but now we need to focus on what to do next,' Churchill said, and began assigning tasks.

As they trailed out of the briefing room, Karen was deflated.

She felt a hand on her shoulder. It was Leo. 'Don't let him get to you. It was a strong theory.'

'But the wrong one,' Karen said, folding her arms over her chest and sighing.

'Keep your chin up. We'll get there,' Arnie said. 'Now, who wants a sausage sandwich?'

Karen smiled, despite her miserable mood. 'Not for me, thanks.'

'I'll have one,' Sophie said, and Karen watched as she wandered off with Arnie. They were working well together, but they made a mismatched pair. Sophie, young and fastidious; and Arnie, older and far scruffier.

'Are you okay?' Leo asked, looking genuinely concerned.

'I'm fine. Just disappointed the lead was a dead end, I suppose.'

'Arnie's right,' Leo said with a kind smile. 'We'll get there. It's just a setback.'

Karen followed him into the open-plan office, and he looked over his shoulder and said, 'The theory was sound, but I suppose sometimes a coincidence really is just that.'

CHAPTER NINETEEN

Nina Brown parked outside the smart apartment block and looked up through the windscreen. There was no light on in her sister's apartment. Maybe not that unusual for anyone else, but Laurel hated dim light. She always had. Their father used to go angrily around the house they grew up in, switching off all the lights. *It isn't even dark yet*, he used to say.

Of course, they'd shared the blame, even though it was Laurel who turned them on.

The fact the window was a grey square rather than beaming out bright light made Nina pause. She had been angry on the drive here, fuming that she'd had to cut short her week away with her fiancé. It had been a make-or-break holiday, too. They were trying to get their relationship back on track, not that her sister cared.

Laurel knew how important this holiday was, and yet on Friday night, when they'd been eating dinner, she'd called.

Nina had known from the expression on Terry's face that if she answered the call, she wouldn't hear the end of it for hours. So she'd pressed the red button, directing the call to the answering service. Laurel had left a garbled message. Blathering on about how she'd done something wrong and how she needed to make it right. She sounded wrecked. Probably too much white wine.

At the time, Nina had been irritated rather than worried. Laurel had always been a bit of a drama queen.

Nina got out of the car and slammed the door. She scanned the car park for her sister's car and saw it in the corner, a white Audi, so she was likely to be home.

Good. Because if Nina had made a wasted journey, she was not going to be happy. Terry's face had looked like he'd swallowed a wasp when she told him she needed to leave the hotel for a few hours to see her sister. The hotel was in Norfolk, too, so it had taken her an hour and a half to get here.

Of course, she'd tried to call Laurel before leaving. Laurel had left the message on Friday evening, and over the weekend Nina had tried multiple times to return her call, but she hadn't picked up. She'd almost driven over yesterday but had decided to give her sister one more day to respond. She'd left messages. Laurel had to know how worried she was, but she hadn't called her back. *Selfish.*

Nina had told her fiancé why she'd been so distracted yesterday, expecting him to be understanding. That was a joke. He'd thrown his hands up and said, 'Do what you want. Go and see your sister. I don't care.'

And there was the rub of it. He didn't care, and so there really wasn't much point in carrying on with the relationship. So, this morning, with tears running down her cheeks, she'd packed her bag and said goodbye as he sat stony-faced on the bed.

It would be nice if, just for once, Laurel was the one to take care of her. To make sure *she* was all right. To hug her and ply her with white wine and ice cream until she felt better.

Nina sighed. That wouldn't happen. She was always the one who did the looking-after part. Her younger sister would expect Nina to clean up whatever mess she'd managed to get herself into, and comfort her at the same time. It wasn't that Laurel wasn't intelligent and successful. She had a degree in economics and had worked for an investment bank in London for a few years, built up a nice little nest egg, but she didn't have the staying power. She'd left that job under a cloud, and taken up a position in Lincoln at a financial services company.

Still, it paid well. Better than Nina's job, anyway.

Nina pressed the buzzer next to Laurel's apartment number and then rubbed her arms, feeling the chill of the December air.

Come on. Just open the door already.

Gripping her keys tightly in her left hand, she pressed the buzzer again.

No reply.

Where could she be? Her car was here. Perhaps she was in the shower? Nina had a spare key to Laurel's apartment, but not one for the main entrance door.

Just as she was considering going back to her car to wait, the glass door swung open, and a man dressed in a tracksuit and trainers came out. He smiled at her and held the door open.

Nina returned his smile. 'Thank you. I'm just visiting my sister,' she said. 'Laurel Monroe, number 22,' she added, in case he needed an explanation, but he'd already set off, jogging across the car park.

Nina took the stairs to the second floor and knocked on the white door of number 22. She waited, then knocked again. After two minutes, she sighed and selected the spare key, and let herself in.

Immediately, she knew something was wrong.

The smell. Like something had gone bad, rotting.

It was boiling in the flat, too. The heating was going like the clappers.

Nina shut the door and fanned her face as she walked into the open-plan living area. She set her keys and handbag on the kitchen island and then walked over to the window, using the small key on the sill to unlock it, and opened it wide.

The radiator beneath the window was boiling. What a waste of money!

She sucked in a breath of fresh air and listened, expecting to hear the sound of the shower. But it was very quiet in the apartment, and only the tiny *plink-plink* of water dripping steadily into the kitchen sink broke the silence. Nina pushed up her sleeves and tightened the tap.

What *was* that smell? She wrinkled her nose and looked around the kitchen. Did Laurel have a problem with her fridge? Maybe the power supply had cut out, and the food had gone bad?

She opened the fridge, and the light came on. There was a new bottle of Chardonnay inside, some butter, a shrivelled lettuce and a carton of UHT milk. The smell didn't seem to be coming from the fridge.

She scanned the kitchen. Four empty wine bottles were lined up on the kitchen counter beside the sink, but other than that, it was tidy.

It was a lovely flat, with a high-spec kitchen, fancy light fittings, huge windows and cream walls and carpets. Nina felt a pang of jealousy, comparing it to her small rented house in Lincoln city centre, which was in a terrible state compared to her sister's apartment – filled with second-hand furniture and horrible multicoloured carpets that must have been decades old. No matter how much air freshener she sprayed, or how many perfume diffusers she set in different areas around the house, she couldn't get rid of the persistent musty smell, and suspected the cause was damp.

But the smell in her sister's flat wasn't caused by damp. It was a peculiar, sweet, stomach-churning scent.

'Laurel?'

No answer.

'Laurel!' She shouted this time. 'It's Nina. Are you home?'

Still nothing. With a sigh, she headed out of the open-plan area to the back of the apartment, towards the bedroom. As she walked along the corridor, the smell got stronger, and for the first time, Nina felt a bubble of fear build in her chest. She pressed a hand against her stomach.

'Laurel?' Her voice was quiet now, tentative.

She paused beside the bedroom door and put a hand on the wood panelling. Her heart was thudding. She pushed it open and then froze in horror at the sight in front of her.

Her sister was sprawled on the cream carpet beside the bed. Had she fallen? The bed was neatly made, but a half-empty wine glass sat on the nightstand. She must have been so drunk she fell before getting into bed and injured herself badly. The blood . . .

She needed help. An ambulance. CPR.

Nina tried to process what was happening, what she needed to do. But deep down she knew Laurel was beyond help. Her skin was mottled, and her face was covered in blood.

There were dark red stains on the cream carpet. Nina staggered forward and raised her hands to her face. 'Laurel . . .'

Oh no. Had she taken her own life? And Nina hadn't taken her seriously. She'd carried on with that stupid mini-break when her sister . . . Physical pain made her bend over, her arms wrapped tight around her middle.

Nina looked around for an empty bottle of pills. Maybe she'd downed them with the wine, then – groggy from the alcohol and drugs – fallen and hit her head? But there was no pill bottle.

'Please,' she whispered. 'Please don't be dead. I'm sorry. I should have come before . . .'

Nina sank to her knees beside her sister's body, and the smell caught in the back of her throat. She felt her stomach protest, churn, and she clamped a hand over her mouth. She couldn't be sick. Not now.

She must have fallen. That was surely how she'd bloodied her forehead. But then Nina saw the livid red line at the base of Laurel's throat. Her body stilled as she stared. There was no sign of whatever had been wrapped around her sister's neck. Which meant this was no suicide.

She crawled towards the door and used the handle to yank herself up.

She needed to get to a phone. To call for help. The police. Someone had done this to her sister.

And that someone could still be here.

◆ ◆ ◆

Karen stood over the body. The victim, Laurel Monroe, was twenty-seven years old, slim, with long brown hair. She wore a set of gold rings on her right hand. One was inset with a tiny turquoise stone. A thin gold chain encircled her neck.

Blood had trickled from her forehead, coating her brown hair at the temples. Now the blood was dry. She wore a thin white T-shirt and grey yoga pants. Casual, dressed for a day at home. There was a bruise on her left forearm, but the injuries that concerned Karen were the bright red line around her throat and the gashes on her forehead.

'Any guesses on how long she's been dead?' Karen asked Raj, who had walked to her side.

'A couple of days at least.'

'She looks the same, doesn't she?'

'You mean the same as Lloyd Nelson?'

Karen nodded. There had to be a connection between the two victims. Laurel Monroe had been strangled, and her forehead had been mutilated just like Lloyd's.

'Could she have been killed the same day as Lloyd Nelson?' Karen asked.

'Hard to say exactly. But yes, I'd guess she died on Saturday, or maybe Sunday.'

Laurel's eyes were closed, but her head was tilted in a way that made it look like she was trying to communicate with them.

Karen looked around the room but saw nothing. No notes. No name written in blood on the floor. Nothing like the movies. Just a vicious, bloody murder.

'Cause of death?' Karen asked.

'Most likely strangulation,' Raj said, his face grim. 'No evidence of sexual assault.'

'And it doesn't look like a burglary,' Karen said, pointing to the rings on the victim's hand. 'She's still wearing her jewellery, and there's cash in the nightstand. First place a burglar would look.'

The smell of death was overwhelming in the small, hot bedroom. 'Has anyone managed to turn the heating off?' Karen asked, addressing the officers searching the room.

'Yes, it's off,' said the officer closest to her. 'Trouble is, the insulation is a bit too good in these new buildings, if you know what I mean. It keeps the heat in, and the *smell*.'

'DS Hart!' Karen heard the clipped tones of Churchill's voice and groaned. She shot an apologetic glance at Raj and walked out of the bedroom.

Churchill was in the kitchen. 'Oh, there you are. Leo said you think this murder is related to Lloyd Nelson's.'

'I'm convinced it is. She's been strangled, and there's a cross carved into her forehead.'

Churchill looked around, his eyes scanning the other people in the room. He leaned towards Karen. 'Definitely a cross?'

'Yes, and there's no other carvings or knife marks on her body, just like Lloyd.'

163

Churchill swore.

'They haven't taken Laurel's body away yet if you want to—' Karen gestured in the direction of the bedroom.

Churchill shook his head. 'The crime scene photographs will be good enough for me. Who found the body?'

'The victim's sister, Nina Brown. She received a garbled message from Laurel on Friday evening and hadn't heard from her since. She was worried, so she let herself into the flat today with her spare key.'

Churchill's features softened. 'It must have come as a shock.'

'Yes, I've sent her home. I'll go and talk to her and get a full statement after we finish up here.'

Churchill's eyes narrowed. 'I take it you at least asked her some preliminary questions before sending her home?'

'I did. She has no idea who killed her sister. Said her sister was happy generally, had a good job. No current boyfriend.'

'Found something,' one of the technicians called from the bedroom.

Churchill wrinkled his nose at the smell and covered his face with a handkerchief as they entered the room.

The technician held up his gloved hand, holding a small clear bag of white powder.

'Drugs,' Churchill said. 'Maybe she was killed by her dealer? Maybe she hadn't paid?'

'There's no evidence Lloyd was on drugs,' Karen said. 'Nothing on the tox screen.'

'No, but we didn't search his house.'

'He was killed in the cathedral, and we didn't find anything on him.'

'What better place to supply a client with drugs? No cameras. A nice quiet chapel with no witnesses.' Churchill shrugged.

It didn't make sense. Lloyd had a gambling addiction. There was no evidence he had a drug problem.

'Perhaps this killer is doing what he said in the letter,' Karen suggested. 'Cleansing people of their sins. Lloyd was a gambler. Laurel took drugs.'

Churchill looked around sharply. 'Don't talk nonsense.'

'It's not *nonsense*. It's a legitimate theory.'

Churchill leaned forward so abruptly that Karen flinched. He hissed in her ear. 'Stop! We're not in the station now, DS Hart. Walls have ears. We can't have your theory leaked to the media, understand?'

Karen stepped back, creating space between them. 'Understood.'

Churchill gave her a cold smile. 'Good. I'm glad we're on the same page.'

CHAPTER TWENTY

Nina Brown lived in a bay-window-fronted terraced house on Horton Street. The street was on a hill, and there was no parking outside and no driveways or gardens. The front doors of the terraced houses opened directly on to the pavement.

Karen and Leo parked around the corner and then walked up the hill towards Nina's house.

'It's had a bit of work done. Windows have been replaced,' Leo noted as they approached the property.

A white diesel van passed them, chugging up the road. Karen couldn't help thinking that even with good windows and sound insulation, the noise from traffic would be constant during the day.

They knocked on the grey front door.

Nina answered, looking pale. 'Come in. Can I get you a drink?'

Leo and Karen declined the offer as they entered the dark hallway. Nina led them to a square lounge at the front of the property. The door to the kitchen was open, and Karen got a glimpse of the kitchen units, which were a faded yellow colour and old – but everything was spotlessly clean.

'Sorry about the smell,' Nina said, gesturing around. 'I think it's damp. I've been on to the landlord, but he hasn't done anything.' She sank into an armchair beside the fireplace, which looked to be original but obviously wasn't used, as there was a display of dried flowers behind the grate.

Karen could only detect the smell of a floral air freshener and the chlorine scent of bleach.

'Landlords, eh?' Leo said. 'Mine is just the same. It takes him forever to do basic maintenance.'

Nina managed a smile and then gestured at the other chair and sofa, indicating they should sit down.

Leo took the chair, and Karen sat on the sofa, which had wooden arms and looked like it belonged in a conservatory.

'I'm very sorry we have to trouble you again so soon, Nina,' Karen said. 'But it's important we find out everything we can about your sister, so we have the best possible chance of catching the person responsible.'

'She was murdered then? I suppose I knew that really, but I've been trying to convince myself she could have got those injuries on her own,' Nina said.

'We believe she was strangled,' Leo said gently. 'Once we get the post-mortem results we'll be able to tell you more.'

There was a noise from the kitchen. A small tabby cat stopped in the doorway, inspecting them, then rushed through the room and disappeared.

Nina's cheeks coloured. 'My cat, Tommy. I'm not supposed to have pets. The house is rented.'

'Shy, is he?' Leo asked.

'A bit, with people he doesn't know.'

Leo chuckled. 'He was probably quite annoyed to find us in his living room.'

Nina managed a smile.

Leo leaned forward, forearms resting on his knees. 'We need to ask you some sensitive questions. Do you feel up to answering them?'

167

'You want to know if I can think of anyone who would want to hurt Laurel . . . And I've been racking my brains, but I can't think of anyone.'

'She didn't have any new relationships, or a relationship that ended recently?' Leo asked.

'No.' Nina looked at Karen. 'I told DS Hart earlier. As far as I know, Laurel wasn't in a relationship with anyone at the moment, and none of her previous boyfriends had been violent or threatening.'

She smoothed her hand along her cream-coloured trousers, methodically pressing out the creases. 'I just can't believe it's happened. I should have come sooner. I should have checked out of the hotel on Friday when she left the message. Maybe I could have done something to stop it happening.' She looked up. 'Do you know when she died? Was it on Friday?'

'We're not sure. The post-mortem will give us a better idea,' Karen said. 'But we believe she had been dead for a couple of days before you found her.'

Nina wrapped her arms around herself. Her lower lip trembled. 'I was away when she needed me. I was staying in Norfolk, and I didn't want to leave.' She shook her head and closed her eyes. 'But I wish I had.'

'Can you tell us more about the answerphone message?' Karen said. She'd asked about it when she'd first spoken to Nina, but the woman had said her battery was flat.

'Oh, right, yes. I put my phone on charge. You can listen to it if you want?'

'That would be very helpful, thank you.'

Nina disappeared from the lounge, and they heard her footsteps on the stairs.

Leo and Karen didn't speak until she returned.

'Here it is.' Nina entered the room, looking down at her mobile phone. She tapped on the screen a couple of times and then held it out for Karen. 'You press 1 to hear the message again.'

Karen took the phone from her. 'Thank you.'

She listened carefully to Laurel's shaky voice. It was an odd sensation to be hearing Laurel talk on what could have been her final day alive.

'*Nina, I need your help. I've done something really stupid. Really, really stupid this time, and I don't know what to do.*' She broke off and sobbed. Then her voice came back, quieter. '*No, that's not true. I do know what I have to do, but I don't want to. I'm scared, Nina. Please pick up.*' Laurel didn't say anything else for a long time, but Karen could hear her ragged breathing on the recording. Then finally she said, '*I think I've made a decision. I know what I have to do, but I need to talk to you about it. I need to talk to someone. I can't do this on my own. Nina, please. Call me back as soon as you can.*'

That was the end of the message.

Karen lowered the phone. 'Thank you for letting me listen, Nina. Is it okay if DC Clinton listens now, too?'

She nodded, and Karen handed Leo the phone.

'When did you listen to the message?'

'Friday evening.'

'Did you call her back?'

'Not right away. You must think I'm an awful person,' Nina whispered, shaking her head. 'You're thinking how could she hear that message and not rush to her sister's side? I get it. But you don't know what she was like. It wasn't the first time I got a message like that. After she lost her last job, I had panicked phone calls and messages day and night, expecting me to drop everything and help her.' She covered her face with her hands. 'I sound like such a complete cow.'

Karen said nothing, and waited for Nina to continue. When she didn't, Karen said, 'No one is judging you, Nina.'

The woman took a shaky breath and pressed her palms flat on the arms of her chair. 'The thing is, I had no idea it was so serious. If I'd known her life was in danger, of course I would have rushed back, checked she was okay.'

'Did your sister often have crises in her personal life?'

'Yes, but she was never in danger like this. She'd done something wrong at her previous job, not that she'd admit it. I'm not even sure what she did. She wasn't prosecuted, but they let her go. If you listened to Laurel describe what happened . . .' Nina shrugged. 'She made it sound like the world was out to get her.

'I always tried to help. But in many ways, she was far more successful than me. I mean, she still had money. She practically fell into the next job and was only unemployed for a few weeks. Her previous employer gave her a great reference despite the falling-out. But with Laurel, there was always drama. Sometimes I just wanted to look out for me for a change. To put myself first.' She pushed her hair back from her face and took a deep breath. 'Things haven't been going too well for me. I'd gone to Norfolk with Terry to try to patch things up and make a go of our relationship. I didn't feel like I could just leave him at the hotel and go running after Laurel.'

'That's understandable. Laurel's death wasn't your fault,' Leo said, lowering the phone from his ear.

'I could have done more.'

'You didn't know.' Leo's voice was low but firm.

Nina started to cry.

'Can we call anyone for you?' Karen asked. 'A relative or a friend?'

She sniffed. 'No, thank you. I'm fine.'

Leo handed the phone back to Nina. 'With your permission, we'd like to take a copy of the message.'

'Of course.'

Nina leaned back in her chair, wiped the tears from her cheeks and turned her head to stare at the flowers in the grate.

'We need to ask a couple of difficult questions now, Nina,' Karen said.

Nina twisted back around to face them. 'Okay.'

'Did Laurel take drugs?'

Nina's cheeks flushed, and she hesitated before replying. 'You mean illegal drugs . . . ?'

Karen nodded.

'She had done in the past. Cocaine. I think it started when she was working in London. She told me everyone was doing it.' Nina's gaze slid between Karen and Leo. 'Do you think her death was down to a drug habit? A dealer or . . . ?' Nina broke off, staring at Leo.

'It's early days, Nina,' Leo said. 'We don't know anything for sure yet, but that's certainly something we're looking into.'

'As far as I know, she wasn't taking anything now. Maybe this was someone from the past – her old job?'

'Do you think her drug habit could be why she lost her previous job?' Karen asked.

Nina's features tightened. 'It could be. She didn't tell me that, though. She said it was an unfair dismissal and they were lucky she didn't sue them.'

Nina was unaware that they'd already found a bag of white powder in her sister's flat. Karen considered it unlikely Laurel had quit her drug habit when she left London.

She watched Leo as he asked Nina more questions. He was good, Karen thought – competent and kind. Nina opened up to him, talking more about her relationship with her sister. It hadn't been an easy one. Sibling rivalry – and perhaps a bit of selfishness on Laurel's part – had led to a difficult relationship. Despite that,

171

Nina's grief was real, and it was clear she desperately regretted not coming to her sister's aid the one time she really needed her.

◆ ◆ ◆

Afterwards, as they walked back to the car, Leo asked, 'What did you make of her?'

'I think Nina is the type of person who's honest to a fault.' They'd only been inside for a minute when Nina had confessed to having a cat even though her landlord didn't allow pets. 'If she knew who was responsible for her sister's murder, she'd tell us.'

'I agree,' Leo said as he shifted aside for a woman pulling a shopping trolley. 'They obviously had a difficult relationship, but there was love there too. What did you make of the drug angle?'

'If this were a new case, completely unrelated to anything else, then I'd consider that the major lead,' Karen said, putting her hands in her pockets as the wind picked up.

Sleet began to fall from the heavy grey clouds.

'But you think it's related to the Lloyd Nelson case?'

'Don't you?' Karen turned to look at Leo.

He nodded sombrely, rubbing his chin. 'There are several coincidences.'

Karen thought back to what he'd said earlier. *Sometimes a coincidence really is just that.* But in this case, there were far too many of them.

'Both victims were strangled, leaving almost identical markings. I wouldn't be surprised if Raj tells us they were made by the same type of ligature. And both victims had crosses carved into their foreheads. How many times have you seen that before on a murder victim? Because I never have.'

'I think you're right,' Leo said. 'But the question now is what do Lloyd and Laurel have in common? Because from where I'm standing, I can't see a link at all.'

And that was the problem. There seemed to be nothing connecting the two victims apart from the mode of death. It looked random. And that scared Karen.

She hunched her shoulders up against the cold as she dug around in her bag for the car keys.

She couldn't think that way. She couldn't even contemplate them not finding this twisted killer, because that would be a terrible failure. It might look random, but there had to be a link. If they worked hard enough, they'd find it.

CHAPTER TWENTY-ONE

On Wednesday morning, Karen woke early. It had been another quiet night at Morgan's. The security system hadn't been activated.

She opened the curtains and looked out at the dark street. They'd worked late last night. Finally leaving the station after midnight.

She showered, dressed and worked out how to use Morgan's coffee machine before he came downstairs.

'You're up early.'

Karen got up from the chair by the window and stretched. 'Couldn't sleep. I was thinking about the case, trying to figure out the link between our murder victims.'

'Is there one?' Morgan asked, holding out his hand for Karen's empty coffee mug. 'Another?'

'Please.' She followed him into the kitchen. 'If there is, I haven't found it yet. Beverley Nelson doesn't know Laurel. Nina Brown said she doesn't know anyone called Lloyd. They have no crossover contacts on social media.'

Morgan poured the coffee. 'It's difficult to see what they have in common.'

'Exactly. The only thing I can think of is that they probably both owed money.'

'The drugs and gambling?' He handed Karen her mug.

'Right.' She took a sip. 'But they were unlikely to owe money to the same person.'

'It's not unheard of for drugs and gambling to be overseen by a criminal group.'

'No, but it's not common. And I can't imagine the top dog in a powerful crime syndicate going after two people for a few hundred quid.'

'How much cocaine did you find at the flat? Owing her dealer is one thing, but if she was dealing herself, encroaching on another dealer's turf?'

'We haven't found any evidence she was dealing and only found a tiny amount of cocaine at the flat. I spoke to her previous employer yesterday. He said they'd suspected she'd been taking drugs at work for a while, and after she was caught on one of the internal cameras snorting drugs at an office party, they let her go.'

Morgan thought for a moment. 'And you're sure they were killed by the same person.'

'Yes, I'm convinced they were.' Karen sighed. Her mind was going around in circles. She felt like a dog chasing its tail.

Something was off about the letter to Morgan too. He'd gone through his past cases, to see if the note was from an angry criminal he'd dealt with in the past, but had come up blank.

'Any new theories as to why you received the letter?' Karen asked.

'My past sins, you mean?'

'There has to be a reason it was sent to you.' She smiled. 'Are you sure you don't have skeletons lurking in the closet?'

Morgan shook his head. 'I've been thinking about it non-stop, but there's nothing, unless it's a past case . . . And even then, I can't think of anyone who'd go to these lengths . . .'

Karen took another sip of her coffee. Drugs, gambling . . . were they red herrings? Was there something else that linked the victims? Something they'd missed so far?

'Okay, so the link is the killer. He or she knew them both,' Morgan said.

'Or it's random. The Cleanser is selecting victims they believe are sinners.'

'Which would make them far harder to catch.'

Karen nodded miserably.

'But not impossible,' Morgan said. 'You'll get there.'

'I wish I had your confidence. How's the Pickett case progressing?'

Morgan grimaced. 'About as well as yours. The parents are devastated, but I have nothing new to tell them. I'm only grateful I didn't haul Will Pickett in for questioning. That would have made things a hundred times worse.'

Karen tensed and put her mug down on the counter. 'I'm sorry. That was my fault. I was so sure Lloyd travelled that way home. It was the right time, and he didn't have a licence so could have panicked and driven off rather than stopping to call for help . . . It all seemed to make perfect sense until we got the forensics back and his car was clean.'

'No harm was done. Will Pickett will never know how close we were to bringing him in.'

Dawn light gave the sky a pinkish glow. Karen leaned on the counter, looking out of the frosted window. Despite the cold, a robin was singing in the back garden, impatient for the sun to come up and the day to start. Karen shared the bird's impatience.

They left Morgan's and made the journey to Nettleham in their separate cars.

They hadn't been at work long when Leo approached Karen's desk. He still had his padded jacket on but wore gloves. Not woolly, cold-weather gloves, but blue nitrile gloves, the type they wore when handling evidence. He had something clutched in his right hand.

'Everything all right, Leo?'

'Not really, no.' His hands were trembling. 'I woke up to find this on my doormat.'

'What is it?' Karen asked, but she didn't need to. The white envelope in the evidence bag provided the answer. 'Another letter.'

Leo nodded. 'Scared me half to death when I found it.'

'Does it mention you by name?'

Leo shook his head. 'No, but it mentions the second victim, Laurel Monroe. I took a photo of it on my phone and sent it to the team email.'

Karen reached for her phone, but the screen wouldn't respond. Muttering under her breath, she logged on to her email on the computer. While it was loading, she glanced up at Leo. He was leaning against her desk and didn't look steady on his feet. She pulled over a chair. 'Sit.'

'Thanks.' He sank into it and held the letter out from his body, as though he were expecting it to catch alight.

'Have you filed it in the evidence log?'

'Not yet. I was . . . well . . . I just came straight here.' He reached up and cupped a hand over his mouth, breathing into it. 'Didn't even clean my teeth. Just threw on some clothes and headed to the station.'

Karen opened the email Leo had sent, and the note appeared on the screen.

By now, you'll have discovered my second sacrifice. It took you long enough. I'm sure Laurel Monroe would have been disappointed no one looked for her earlier. But then she didn't deserve anyone to care, did she? She was a sinner. She spent her nights behind a sex cam to earn enough dirty money to spend on her disgusting drug habit.

But now she is clean. I have cleansed her of sin.

Laurel died on the same day as Lloyd, but it took you days to find her. I wonder how long it will take you to find the next one. Perhaps I should give you a clue to level the playing field?

The next one will be much closer to home.

The Cleanser.

Karen swallowed hard and reread the text.

Everything seemed to fade around her, except the bright computer screen. The words stood out, black on white. It was all she could see. The world started to spin. She put her hands over her eyes, taking a moment, trying to think straight.

Closer to home?

That was a threat. Did it mean one of the team would be next? Morgan?

'You okay, Sarge?' Rick's voice made Karen turn. He walked over to stand beside Leo.

She managed to nod. 'Yeah. It's . . .' She searched for the words but came up blank.

'You look exactly how I felt when I found the letter,' Leo said. 'Do you think I'm a target?' he added as Rick read the note over Karen's shoulder.

Rick let out a low whistle.

Karen wanted to reassure Leo. He looked at her with fear in his eyes. He was willing her to say it was all phoney bluster, an empty threat, but she couldn't lie. She couldn't play this down. It was too serious.

'I think we're all at risk, Leo.' She pushed herself up from the desk. 'Is Churchill in yet?'

'No.'

'Then we need to file this in evidence and go straight to the super.'

◆ ◆ ◆

Leo's colour had come back by the time they got upstairs; his cheeks were pink. They'd left the letter in the evidence locker and printed out a copy of Leo's photograph of the contents. Karen thought Superintendent Murray would be satisfied to see the photo of the note. When they reached Pamela's desk, the superintendent's assistant looked up. 'Good morning.'

'Morning, Pamela. We need to see the superintendent.'

'She's on a call.'

'It's very urgent.'

'All right. Just a moment.' Pamela pressed the white flashing light on her telephone and put a call through to the office. 'DS Hart's outside. She says it's urgent.'

A moment later, Pamela waved them in.

Superintendent Murray hung up the phone as they entered the office. 'DS Hart, DC Clinton, what's the problem?'

'There's been another letter, ma'am. Delivered to DC Clinton's house.'

The super frowned as Karen placed the printed copy of the note on her desk. She quickly read the letter.

'No mention of Morgan this time,' she mused. 'And no mention of DC Clinton, even though it was sent to his house?'

'No, ma'am, but I have to say, I'm rattled,' Leo said. 'They must have put the note through the letterbox while I was sleeping.'

She nodded. 'I understand. It's horrible. Do you have someone you can stay with for a few days?'

'I do,' Leo said slowly. 'But to be honest, I think my presence would put them at risk, and I'm not prepared to do that. I couldn't live with myself if . . .'

'A hotel then? We can cover expenses. Vary your routine. Don't be predictable.' She glanced at Karen. 'That goes for you too, and all members of the team. Be alert.'

'Yes, ma'am,' Karen said.

'Are the allegations in the letter true?'

'We believe Laurel Monroe regularly took cocaine, but the sex-cam stuff came as a surprise,' Karen said. 'We have her phone and laptop, so if it's true, we'll find evidence on there.'

'It could be a client?' Leo suggested. 'Someone who watched her on the internet?'

'Did Lloyd Nelson use any of the sex-cam sites?' the super asked.

'No,' Karen said. 'At least, his laptop and phone were clean. I suppose it's possible he could have had a spare phone or tablet we haven't found. Perhaps he had it on him when he died, and The Cleanser took it with them.'

'Well, those sites aren't free,' Leo said. 'We should have seen evidence on his bank or credit card statements if he made payments.'

The super and Karen both turned to look at Leo, who flushed pink. 'I mean, not that I know that much about it . . .'

'That's your priority then,' the super said. 'Find out Laurel's secrets. They could lead us to the killer. And send DCI Churchill up to my office as soon as he gets in.'

When they got back down to the open-plan office, they found Sophie at her desk and told her about the second letter. Karen gave her a moment as she struggled with the news. She was caught between excitement at working on a case with her first potential serial killer and terror at the idea that one of the team could be targeted.

'I'll get on to the tech team, tell them specifically what we're interested in, so they can prioritise,' Sophie offered, processing the development. 'This is pretty scary, Sarge. Maybe we could ask Dr Michaels if he has any ideas.'

Karen frowned, then remembered Dr Michaels was the self-proclaimed serial killer expert from America. 'I think we should keep things in-house for now.'

'But he'd be able to help. He's worked on cases like this before.'

'I'll mention it to the superintendent, but we need to concentrate on the basics. Thorough police work. Treat this like any other case. Focus on the details, and the big picture will become clear. I'm going to give Laurel's sister a call. I'm sure Nina would have mentioned it if she'd known her sister was working as a sex-cam girl, but we have to make sure.'

Churchill swaggered in, his coat still buttoned up to his chin. The tips of his ears and nose were red from the cold.

'Nice to see you have time for a chat,' he said, looking at the three of them and shaking his head. 'I suppose you've already solved the murders. Because you wouldn't be wasting time otherwise, would you?'

He had a nerve. They'd been here early, ready to put the work in. *He* was the one strolling in after everyone else. Karen was tempted to point that out and order him up to the superintendent's office, but they didn't have time for disagreements. Their lives could be in real danger if they didn't solve this case, and she didn't have the energy for petty disputes with Churchill.

Karen glanced at Leo. 'You'd better tell him.'

Churchill put his bag on an empty desk and began unbuttoning his coat.

As Leo filled him in, Karen walked back to her desk. She had work to do.

CHAPTER TWENTY-TWO

Karen sat down at her desk and reviewed the note again. There was no doubt the letter was threatening. She scanned the contents, looking for clues. If the staff in the tech department managed to trace Laurel's sex-cam footage back to a site with registered viewers, then they could get a list of customers and start from there.

She opened the top file on her desk, containing the background on Lloyd Nelson. They could ask Beverley Nelson if she knew if her husband had watched Laurel Monroe strip off over the internet, but that would be an awkward conversation. It was better to wait and see what information they gleaned from Laurel's computer. Going off a half-baked theory could be hurtful to the Nelson family, and unnecessary if they were wrong.

Karen had been quick to seize on the potential link between Lloyd Nelson driving without a licence and the hit-and-run that killed twelve-year-old Sam Pickett. That had been a lesson. She couldn't leap to conclusions. She'd been sure there was a connection, but the forensic evidence had discredited that theory.

She'd only flicked through the first few pages when the phone on her desk rang.

'DS Karen Hart.'

'Karen, it's Todd. I'm on the desk today. Can you come down? You've got a delivery.'

'I'll be right there.' Karen pushed to her feet. It had to be her new mobile phone. Finally. It was supposed to have been delivered yesterday.

But when she reached the reception area, she saw Todd, the desk sergeant, grinning at her. She looked over to the desk but couldn't see a parcel. He pointed to the other side of the reception area, where a familiar figure stood by the door.

'Mike? Is everything all right?' She immediately imagined there was a problem. Since the sudden deaths of her husband and daughter, she'd felt like bad news was always just around the corner. Surprises unnerved her.

He held a large coffee in a red takeaway paper cup with a white lid, and a small brown paper bag. 'Everything's fine. Just brought you a coffee and your favourite pastry.'

'A chocolate twist?' Karen's stomach rumbled in anticipation as she took the paper bag and looked inside, then inhaled the scent of the sweet buttery pastry and melted chocolate. 'About a million calories and worth every one. Thank you.'

'I was just passing.' He shrugged. He was wearing his huge, padded black coat, making him look larger than normal, and he smelled of the cold outdoors.

'Passing the station?'

'I'm doing some private training, just down the road. A new dog, severe behavioural problems.'

'Sounds like a challenge.'

'They're always the most rewarding.' He smiled. 'Still on for dinner tonight?'

'I'm not sure. I wouldn't be the best company, to be honest.'

'I'm a good listener.'

'Maybe later in the week?'

'All right.'

'There aren't any other surprises in here, are there?' Karen asked, lifting the paper bag.

Mike's forehead creased in confusion. 'Like what?'

'I half expected you to have hidden a leaflet about that grief counselling group behind the chocolate twist.'

He smiled, shaking his head. 'I'm not that devious. If you don't want to go, that's fine. I'll not mention it again.' He made a zipping motion across his mouth. 'I'd better not keep my new client waiting.' He handed Karen the coffee and turned to leave.

She watched him exit the building and walk across the car park.

She could finish at a reasonable time this evening, have dinner with Mike, have a social life for once. But she wouldn't. Not with this case hanging over her head. She sipped the coffee and smiled at his thoughtfulness. Surprises weren't always a bad thing. She might not meet him for dinner tonight, but she'd make it up to him later.

She turned back to the desk sergeant. 'There haven't been any deliveries for me, have there?'

He lifted his eyebrows. 'Nothing this morning.' He looked under the desk. 'Doesn't look like anything was stashed under here yesterday. It could have been taken to the post room. What are you expecting?'

'A new mobile. Mine's gone on the blink. It was supposed to be here yesterday.'

He spread his hands. 'As far as I know, it hasn't arrived. I'll keep an eye out for it.'

'Cheers, Todd.'

On her way back to the office, Karen popped into the post room, but there was no sign of her new phone there either. She spotted PC Ray Watts at the end of the corridor, raised a hand and was about to say hello, but he blanked her. He seemed lost in thought, and he yanked the door to the stairwell open and disappeared.

Karen guessed she was no longer flavour of the month. What was the point in getting career advice from a detective sergeant when he could get it from a detective chief inspector? She'd been trumped by Churchill. She thought back to that odd exchange after the corruption meeting. She still felt uneasy about finding PC Watts lingering so close to the meeting room, when he had no real reason to be on that floor of the station. And Churchill had denied knowing who Watts was.

Arnie was at his desk, and when Karen walked past, he gave a dramatic groan. 'Save me.'

'What's up?'

'This CCTV.' He waved a hand at the computer screen. 'It's sending me to sleep. And it's making my eyes go funny.'

Karen looked at the footage on the screen. 'This is the outside of Laurel's apartment building?'

'Yes, I've watched hours and hours of it already.' He pulled a face. 'Tracked down the jogger the sister said let her into the apartment building. He's in the clear. Lives in the building but was staying in Leicester with his girlfriend when we believe the murder took place.'

'Anything else suspicious so far?'

'Nothing,' Arnie said, throwing up his hands dramatically. 'The only thing I've got from the recordings is a headache!'

Karen frowned at him. 'Maybe you need glasses?'

Arnie grunted. 'Maybe I need a break.' He paused, cocked his head. 'I don't suppose you'd take over for a few minutes? I missed breakfast, and there's a sausage sandwich in the canteen with my name on it.'

'Go on then.' Karen sat in Arnie's still-warm seat after he leapt up and swaggered off, whistling.

'You walked into that one, Sarge.' Rick was laughing. 'He won't be back for ages.'

Karen angled the screen so she could see better. 'I'm sure you have work to do, Rick.'

Rick lowered his head, still chuckling.

◆　◆　◆

Sparrow finished eating and dabbed his mouth with a napkin before glancing around the canteen. He was hiding in plain sight; no one bothered to look his way. Everything was coming together. Morgan was off the case and the team was divided. That should have put a smile on the boss's face, but Sparrow couldn't do a thing right in his eyes. He'd taken a call from Eagle earlier, who'd been spitting with rage. That was satisfying. Sparrow enjoyed getting under his skin, especially when Eagle knew he couldn't do anything to stop him – not yet, anyway. Sparrow held some power now, and that made a welcome change.

Sparrow stood and carried his tray over to the rack. There would come a time in the future when he would have to watch his back. Eagle was not someone you could upset and expect to get away with it or escape pushback. For now, Sparrow was safe, but that wouldn't last.

It didn't matter, though, because he had another plan.

◆　◆　◆

Rick was right. Arnie took forever to get back from the canteen and then spluttered excuses. 'It's not my fault, DCI Churchill collared me, asked me to do a job for him.'

'Really? What was that?' Karen pressed pause on the video and rubbed her eyes. Maybe she was the one who needed glasses.

Arnie tapped the side of his nose. 'I could tell you, but then I'd have to—'

'Yeah, very good. Well, you can take over now you're back.' She stood up. 'Any news on Laurel Monroe's computer yet?'

Arnie took his seat. 'Not as far as I know. I do know they're analysing her phone too. Might take a while.'

Karen stretched her arms over her head. Sitting hunched over in front of the computer screen had given her an ache between her shoulder blades. 'We could use some more comfortable chairs,' Karen said, thinking of the fancy padded chairs they had in the meeting room upstairs, reserved for the top brass.

Arnie turned, watched her stretch out the kink in her neck. 'You think you ache now. Wait until you get to my age.'

'Think I'll go and talk to Harinder. He might be able to give us preliminary findings on Laurel's phone and computer.'

'I can do that.' Sophie's head appeared over the top of her monitor. 'I'm free. I'll go now.'

'Ha! You sound a bit keen,' Arnie said, and Sophie's cheeks burned.

'All right,' Karen said, walking over to Sophie's desk. 'Ask him if they've uncovered any communications between Lloyd Nelson and Laurel Monroe, and if there's any evidence Laurel worked as a sex-cam girl.'

'If the evidence is there, Harinder will find it,' Sophie said confidently.

'Yes, but I'm wondering if the evidence exists.'

'What do you mean?' Sophie tucked her curly hair behind her ears.

'The allegations against Lloyd – violence towards his wife, embezzlement – have turned out to be dead ends so far. I'm wondering if we'll find the same is true of the allegations against Laurel.'

'You think the sex-cam stuff is made up?'

'Possibly.'

'But why?'

Karen shrugged. 'Smoke and mirrors. A distraction. An attempt to lead us away from the real motive behind their murders.'

Sophie's eyes widened. 'What *was* the real motive?'

Karen said, 'That's what we still need to find out.'

Sophie hurried down to the technical department. Many of the forensic tests were now carried out off-site, and some more unusual work was contracted out to private companies, but they relied on Harinder to analyse the results.

They really would be lost without him; he seemed to know everything about everything. Sophie admired his intelligence, but his best trait was his ability to explain things to his colleagues in plain English and not make them feel like fools.

She knocked on the half-open door and poked her head into the lab.

Harinder turned, spinning on his wheeled chair to face her. 'Sophie, what brings you down here?'

He was smiling. He did look pleased to see her, which gave her confidence a boost.

'Karen asked me to come down and see if you have anything for us on Laurel Monroe's computer yet. I know, the team haven't had it long, and I don't mean to put extra pressure on you. I'm sure you're very busy, but . . .' She hesitated. 'Well, we don't have much else to go on.'

Harinder wheeled over another chair. 'Have a seat.'

Sophie sat beside him and watched the scrolling data on his screen for a moment, mesmerised.

'It's just running a search.' Harinder ran a hand through his dark hair. 'I wish I could give you better news, but we've not found anything that would interest you yet.'

'Oh, so there's nothing to indicate that Laurel worked as a . . .' She swallowed. Her cheeks felt hot. *Just say it, Sophie. Don't be ridiculous. This is your job. Be professional.* 'A . . . er . . . sex-cam worker?'

'Nothing yet. Is it possible she had another computer?'

Sophie sighed. 'We haven't found one.'

'There's no videos stored on the laptop or her phone,' Harinder continued. 'Nothing in her browser history to suggest she visited sites that host the online stripper videos, or that she uploaded files.'

'Karen thought the allegations could be false.'

'Well, I can't say that for sure. Some more entrepreneurial online sex-cam workers take payments through websites they own and maintain themselves. But I can't find any evidence she visited any such site on her computer either. Sorry, Sophie.'

Sophie stood up with a sigh. 'Thanks for trying, Harry.'

'No problem.'

When she reached the doorway, she hesitated, tucked her hair behind her ears and turned back. 'Um, Harry, I just wondered . . . I mean . . . I hoped . . . What I wanted to ask is . . . would you be free for a drink sometime?'

CHAPTER TWENTY-THREE

At eight thirty, the office was quiet. Karen yawned and stretched. She'd been going through video footage, files and witness statements for hours, and her eyes were sore. Depressingly, she hadn't made much progress. There had been no breakthroughs, no links.

Morgan was still in his office, but the others had left. Rick needed to get home because his mother's carer left at six, and his sister was unable to help tonight. Sophie had left the station an hour ago to go for a drink with Harinder, after shrugging off some good-natured teasing from Arnie and Rick. Karen smiled. Sophie had been buzzing with energy and glowing with happiness.

Arnie and Leo had disappeared too, and she hadn't seen DCI Churchill for hours.

She needed a change of scenery. Perhaps fresh air would get her brain working. She grabbed her bag and coat and told Morgan she'd see him later.

The air outside was so cold it took her breath away. She clutched her coat closed and jogged over to her car. The drive to Lincoln Cathedral took her ten minutes. She parked uphill and walked the short distance to the cathedral's west front.

People were filing out through the large door below the Gallery of Kings. A service must have just finished, Karen thought as she walked against the tide, entered the building and looked up at the vaulted ceilings. A group of choir boys and girls stood to one side, dressed in formal white choral robes, talking excitedly.

Karen looked around furtively. She didn't want to run into Eunice and give the woman a chance to bring up the counselling group again. The thought of talking through her feelings with strangers made her skin crawl. Thankfully, there was no sign of Eunice.

Karen meandered, taking in the beautifully carved stonework, the elegant columns and hidden alcoves. Had the scene been important to the killer? Or had they simply taken advantage of the fact Lloyd had been here and alone in the Morning Chapel. *Cleansed of sin.* That certainly suggested a religious significance. Though Laurel had been killed at home, she lived alone, unlike Lloyd . . .

Karen turned in a slow circle, looking up at the galleried area and then across at the huge stained-glass rose window.

It was cold in the cathedral, but much more comfortable than being outside in the biting wind.

She carried on walking as she thought over the details of the case, then paused beside a pillar. She'd brought her daughter here a short time before Tilly died, and had pointed out the mischievous Lincoln Imp. The cross-legged stone grotesque looked down at Karen, a taunting grin on its face.

According to the legend, two mischievous imps were creating havoc in the cathedral when an angel threatened to turn them to stone. When one of the pair carried on misbehaving, the angel did so, and since that day the imp had looked over Lincoln Cathedral. The carving was centuries old.

Karen turned away from the memory and continued to walk. She headed back towards the huge west door and hesitated at the opening to the Morning Chapel. There was no sign any crime had been committed. The crime scene tape had been removed.

She entered the chapel, and it was like stepping back in time. She imagined the chapel looked much the same as it had five hundred years ago. She rummaged in her bag and pulled out some change. After dropping some coins into the collection pot, she selected a candle.

For Josh and Tilly.

She watched it burn brightly in the sandbox for a few minutes, alongside candles others had lit. If only . . .

She turned away, looked up at the high ceiling. There was no point thinking that way. The past couldn't be changed.

She sat in the nearest pew and closed her eyes. They just needed a break in the case, just a link – even a small one would help.

Minutes passed. Karen was lost in thought. Then the skin on the back of her neck prickled. She was the only one in the chapel, but she felt the definite sensation of being watched. Her eyes snapped open, but she didn't turn.

Her scalp tightened, and a frisson of fear rippled along her spine.

Someone was behind her.

She stood and turned in one smooth movement. Behind her stood PC Ray Watts.

He wore a scarf and a hat, so most of his face was hidden, but he was easy enough to recognise.

Karen couldn't hear anyone close by. There had to be other people around. The cathedral hadn't been closed for the night yet.

'What are you doing here?' Karen asked, looking over his shoulder towards the exit.

'Sorry, I thought I recognised you. I attended the service and spotted you as I was leaving, so I followed you in here.'

'Right.'

He put his hands up. 'That sounded creepy. I was only going to say hello, but when I saw you light a candle then sit there with your eyes closed.' He gestured at the pew where Karen had been sitting. 'I thought you were praying and didn't want to disturb you.'

Karen moved towards the exit. 'How was the service?'

'Great. I don't come often, but Christmas time is special.'

He stepped aside for her, and Karen managed a smile. This case had her on edge, and seeing him lingering close by after the corruption briefing update had made her wary.

She was overreacting. It was PC Ray Watts, a fresh-faced enthusiastic young constable who was probably about as much of a threat as Sophie, who didn't even like killing flies.

They walked out together, heading towards the Magna Carta. 'I've got my car. Do you need a lift?' Karen asked.

'No, I'm all right on the bus, thanks. Going to grab a bite to eat first. Don't suppose you fancy . . . ?'

Karen shook her head. 'No, I've got stuff to do tonight.'

She didn't. She had nothing planned but sitting with a glass of wine and going over and over the case in her mind.

Although . . . it would take her less than two minutes to walk to Mike's apartment from here. It was a tempting idea.

Her mobile vibrated in her coat pocket. She pulled it out as they walked over the slippery cobblestones. A voice message had been left on the answering service, but when she tried to tap the phone screen, it was unresponsive.

'I don't believe this.'

'What's wrong?' Ray craned his neck to look.

'My phone keeps playing up.'

'It is a bit old.'

Karen gave him a pointed look. He sounded just like Sophie. 'I've ordered a new one, but it hasn't arrived yet. I've got an answer-phone message but can't access it.'

'Don't you have a number you can dial from another phone to get your messages?'

Karen smiled. He was right. She did, though she hadn't used it for a while.

He offered his phone. 'Use mine.'

She dialled the messaging service, then took a step away from Ray. She was expecting the message to be from Morgan, telling her he was heading home and asking if she wanted dinner, but it wasn't. It was Anthony.

He sounded tense.

'Karen, can you give me a ring when you get this message? I really need to talk to you. It's about . . . Well, it concerns the matter we discussed on Monday. It's important. Call me.'

Karen turned to Ray, who was looking at the pub menu outside the Magna Carta. 'Can I make another call? I'll be quick.'

'Sure.'

She dialled Anthony's mobile number, but he didn't answer. The phone rang and rang. She tried again, but the same thing happened. She couldn't remember his landline number, and thanks to her stupid phone, she couldn't look it up in her contacts list either.

Her chest felt tight. Anthony had sounded worried. *Concerns the matter we discussed on Monday.*

What matter? They'd talked about Mike, Morgan, Christmas . . . and Churchill. Karen tightened her grip on the phone. Had Anthony uncovered some dirt on Churchill? He had lots of connections from his many years on the force.

She gave Ray back his phone. 'Thanks.'

'Any time.' He waved as Karen walked off, but she didn't look back.

◆　◆　◆

It took Karen less than ten minutes to reach her old boss's bungalow in Canwick. She parked up on the drive and was relieved to see the lights were on. Montagu Road was quiet and dark, and there was only one street light visible from Anthony's property.

As Karen locked the car, her relief gave way to a new creeping feeling of dread. She couldn't explain it.

She studied the quaint red-brick bungalow. It looked the same as always. Tidy, well kept. The light from the lounge illuminated the bare front flower beds with a yellow glow. If the lights were on and he was home, then why wasn't he answering his phone?

Her footsteps crunched across the gravel as she walked up to the front door. As she got closer, she saw the door was ajar. The feeling of dread multiplied a millionfold.

Scanning the area, she reached into her bag for her personal alarm. Should she go to the neighbours? Call for help from there? But maybe he'd left the door ajar himself. Perhaps Anthony had taken a bag out to the bin and . . .

She pushed the door wide. 'Anthony?'

Silence.

'Anthony. It's Karen.' She stepped into the hall.

The place felt still, unnaturally so. It was quiet – so quiet she could hear the gentle tick-tock of the carriage clock in the lounge. It had been part of Anthony's retirement gift, and he proudly displayed it on the mantelpiece.

She stepped into the lounge and felt some of the tension in her muscles ease. The lamp gave the room a cosy glow. Anthony's easy chair was beside the fire. His reading glasses were on top of the newspaper he'd put aside, on the footstool. The fire was burning cheerfully. The gold-coloured carriage clock sat, as usual, in the centre of the mantelpiece. A strip of green, frosted with fake snow and tied with Christmassy red ribbons, decorated the top of the fireplace. A small artificial tree stood in the corner of the room, its colourful lights twinkling.

Maybe Anthony was in the kitchen. Perhaps he had headphones on, and that was why he hadn't heard her calling him.

She turned to leave the room, and then stopped as her heart missed a beat. Behind the sofa, she saw his arm.

He must have fallen. Had a heart attack or a stroke. Karen fumbled for her phone as she darted forward, but when she reached the sofa, she stopped.

No. No. No.

This couldn't be real. It was a nightmare. It had to be. She curled her hands into fists, her fingernails digging hard into her palms, willing herself to wake up.

Though her eyes took in Anthony sprawled out on the floor, his forehead a bloody mess, her brain refused to process it.

She dropped to her knees beside him, and gently touched his face. 'Boss?'

She shuddered at the red line that encircled his neck. He was still warm. He could be alive. She needed to get her act together. She felt for a pulse. Nothing. He wasn't breathing.

His face was wet. Water, not blood. Why? Then she realised it was her tears. She was crying over him, contaminating the crime scene like a civilian, a rookie. What was wrong with her?

She grabbed her phone, but the stupid thing refused to work. With a sudden flood of rage, she threw it across the room. Then lunged for the landline phone on the windowsill.

Karen spoke to the emergency services operator in a rush, giving the details. Then left the phone connected as she tilted Anthony's chin, and tried to breathe air back into his lungs.

Deep down, she knew it was too late, but she couldn't give up if there were the smallest chance . . .

She fiercely wiped away the tears that refused to stop coming, then performed chest compressions. 'Please, boss. Please . . .' she said over and over again, as she tried desperately to bring him back to life.

His chest lifted and fell as she forced oxygen into his lungs. But it wasn't helping. She'd lost him.

Her mentor, her confidant, her stalwart supporter, her friend.

He had called her, and she hadn't reached him soon enough. She'd let him down.

CHAPTER TWENTY-FOUR

Karen didn't stop trying to revive Anthony until the first responders arrived. They guided her gently away from his lifeless body and took her into the kitchen. She wasn't sure how long she sat on the stool beside the breakfast bar. It could have been minutes or hours. The bungalow gradually filled with people.

One of the crime scene techs had come into the kitchen and asked for her clothes, giving her a white paper forensic suit to wear in exchange. She shivered. The suit was thin, and the front door was open, letting in the frigid night air.

'Karen?'

She turned and saw Morgan, who was wearing a similar suit but still had his clothes on underneath. He looked at her with concern.

'I'm sorry,' she said, shaking her head.

'Why are you sorry?' Morgan frowned as he came closer.

'I shouldn't have touched the body, other than to determine he was dead. But I so wanted to believe I could save him. I had to try.'

'DS Hart, are you ready?' This time they both turned and saw a short woman, one of the crime scene team. She held a test kit in her gloved right hand.

Karen said she was, and the woman proceeded to scrape under her nails. Then she took swabs from her skin. The swab from

Karen's cheek came away red. Blood. Anthony's blood. Karen felt a wave of pity mixed with fury. How could she have been so stupid?

Voices carried through from the living room. She recognised one of them as belonging to Raj, the pathologist.

Karen slid off the stool. 'I need to speak to Raj, to apologise.'

Morgan put a hand on her shoulder. 'No, you don't. I'm going to take you home.'

Karen tensed. 'I'm staying on this case.' She glared at him, daring him to try to convince her otherwise, but he didn't.

'We'll leave your car here, and I'll take you home. I'll ask one of the uniforms to drop your car off later.' He put an arm around her shoulders.

'I can handle this, Morgan.' She shrugged him off.

He looked at her for a long moment, not saying anything. 'You need to go home. Shower, get some sleep. Tomorrow, if you want to stay on the case, you'll need to impress the super, show her you can cope.'

'I'm fine.'

'Trust me. You're not.'

The fight deserted her. She didn't have the energy to argue.

They left the kitchen just as one of the crime scene technicians mentioned a letter. Karen stopped abruptly. 'The Cleanser left a letter here?' She hadn't seen it.

'You can look at it tomorrow,' Morgan said.

'What does it say?'

His face was blank.

'Morgan, please!'

He didn't reply. So Karen walked into the living room and up to the crime scene technician, who was holding the note in a plastic evidence bag.

She held out her hand. The technician shot a look at Morgan, who nodded. Karen read the note quickly.

I did warn you this one would be closer to home. DCI Anthony Shaw has been cleansed of sin. His guilt was a heavy burden. During his time in the police force, he took multiple bribes, purposefully left violent crimes unsolved, and destroyed evidence. He drank to try to ease his guilt, to free him of his demons, but it didn't work. But now, thanks to me, he is finally absolved, free of sin.

The Cleanser.

Karen felt sick. She pressed a hand to her stomach and handed the evidence bag back to the technician. 'It isn't true.'

'I know,' Morgan said, reaching for her arm. 'Let's go.'

They walked outside. Karen was trembling, partly due to the freezing temperature and partly from shock. Once inside Morgan's car, Karen buckled her seatbelt and Morgan put the heaters on high.

She couldn't stop shivering. 'I can't believe Anthony was killed by the same person who killed Lloyd Nelson and Laurel Monroe.'

'He was strangled, and his forehead was marked.'

'But he wasn't corrupt,' Karen said through chattering teeth. 'Not Anthony. I'd stake my life on it.'

'I know.' Morgan began to reverse, carefully manoeuvring the car past a marked vehicle.

'Are you just saying that to make me feel better because you think it's what I want to hear?'

'No, Karen. I'm saying it because I think all three of these letters are filled with lies. We haven't been able to verify any of the allegations.'

'But why?' She bowed her head, clutching her hands together in her lap, and tried to stop shivering. 'He was so proud of his career. Why would they try to destroy his memory?'

'I don't know,' Morgan said as he turned on to Lincoln Road.

Karen's head felt fuzzy. She pushed a hand through her hair. 'Why were you there tonight?'

'What?'

'Why were you at Anthony's? The super took you off the case.'

He shrugged. 'The duty sergeant called me. Told me you were there. I came for you.'

'Because you thought I'd fall to pieces?'

'Because I thought you'd need a friend.'

'Right. Sorry.' Karen turned her head and looked out of the window.

Morgan said, 'I acted as duty SIO. I wanted to get you out before Churchill arrived. It's his case, and he'll be throwing his weight around as soon as he gets there, and I thought you could probably do without that on top of everything else.'

'Thanks. I'll still have to talk to him tomorrow.'

'Yes, not much I can do about that. Unless . . .' He glanced at her. 'You could take a few days' leave.'

'No. I'm fine. I can handle Churchill.'

Morgan pulled on to Karen's drive, stopped the car and looked at her. 'Will you be all right?'

But Karen was focused on the black Lexus parked in front of her house. 'That's Mike's car. He's here?'

'I called him. I didn't think you should be alone tonight.'

'Right.' She fumbled for the door handle.

'Karen?' She turned. His face, usually so hard to read, reflected his concern. 'I'll see you in the morning.'

'Yes. Thanks for everything you did tonight.'

'You don't have to thank me.'

Her body felt stiff and heavy with exhaustion as she got out of the car. A fierce gust of wind swirled around the vehicle and hit her like a blast straight from the Arctic.

Her front door opened before she reached it. *Mike.* He'd been watching out for her. His dog, Sandy, sat obediently by his feet.

She turned and waved to Morgan before stepping inside. Mike shut the door and encircled her with his arms. She relaxed against his warm, solid chest as he held her tightly.

He didn't bother her with questions. He didn't ask how she was, which was good because she wasn't sure she'd be able to speak.

Sandy nuzzled against Karen's leg. She reached down to fuss over her.

After a few moments, they walked into the kitchen. There was a pot simmering on the hob, a smell of garlic in the air. Mike tore off some kitchen roll, wetted it and then dabbed at her cheek. 'Are you hurt?'

Karen shook her head. 'It's not my blood.'

He looked up at the ceiling, blew out a breath that puffed his cheeks. 'I'm so sorry this happened . . . I've made you dinner.'

'I'm not—'

'I know you're going to say you're not hungry, but you need to eat something.'

'What I need is a glass of wine.'

'I picked some up on my way over.' He gestured to the opposite counter where there were two bottles of red, next to the spare key Karen had given him a few weeks ago.

'Thanks.' She attempted a smile. 'I'm going to take a shower first, if that's okay?'

'Of course. I'll pour the wine, and dinner should be ready by the time you're finished.'

Upstairs, she stripped off the paper suit and turned on the taps. Leaning against the basin, she glanced at herself in the mirror. It wasn't as bad as she'd expected. Mike had wiped off most of the blood.

Her eyes were wide and staring and her skin was pale. If only she'd got Anthony's message sooner . . .

She shut her eyes. She was glad Morgan had called Mike, glad she hadn't come home to a cold, empty house.

Morgan wasn't keen on Mike, and yet he'd called him because he wanted what was best for Karen. He was a good friend. He'd also protected her from Churchill's inquisition tonight. She'd still have to face him tomorrow, but now she had time to prepare, to calm down, and would be able to handle him. She pushed away from the sink and got in the shower.

She turned the temperature up as hot as she could bear it, and gradually felt the heat push out the coldness that seemed to have settled in her bones.

As she reached for the shampoo, she thought about the contents of the letter. The accusation of corruption made her feel physically sick. The suggestion that Anthony was part of the network of shady officers operating within the force was a real kick in the teeth, as Karen had been so invested in tracking them down.

She didn't believe for a second that Anthony was involved.

Now she'd never know what he'd wanted to tell her tonight. She stopped lathering up the shampoo and thought back. She hadn't told Morgan about the message, and thanks to her ridiculous fit of temper, she didn't have her phone. It must still be on the floor of Anthony's living room, now evidence in the investigation, part of the crime scene.

A wave of sadness overwhelmed her, and as the water streamed over her head, washing away the suds, she let the tears come too. It was an indulgence. She would be sad tonight, cry for Anthony and drink too much wine, but tomorrow she needed to be back on it.

She needed to prove to the superintendent that she could handle the case, because she was determined to put this twisted criminal, who'd killed her friend, behind bars.

After her shower, she pulled on clothes, the first thing she found in the chest of drawers – a white T-shirt and yoga pants – then went downstairs to Mike. They sat at the kitchen table and drank wine and ate pasta.

When the food was gone, they took the second bottle of wine into the living room.

'Do you want to talk about it?' Mike asked.

'Not now.'

He sat on the sofa and lifted his arm so she could nestle in beside him. He smelled familiar and comforting. Christian Dior aftershave and soap.

Sandy settled on the floor close to them.

'Do you want to watch something. Maybe listen to music?' Mike asked as he topped up their glasses.

'TV, something mindless,' Karen said.

Mike grabbed the remote and selected a romcom movie on Netflix. She knew he'd picked it for her, thinking it was something she'd like, and though she wasn't a big fan of romcoms, she appreciated the thought.

Karen let the noise wash over her, and stared at the screen without really seeing. Her mind was in the past, focused on memories of DCI Anthony Shaw.

CHAPTER TWENTY-FIVE

The bedroom was dark when Karen woke. She reached for her phone, intending to check the time, and fumbled for it on the nightstand, nearly knocking over a glass of water, before remembering.

Memories of last night came flooding back.

Mike was sleeping soundly beside her, so she got out of bed quietly and headed to the bathroom. Sandy, who'd heard Karen moving about, bounded up the stairs to greet her.

She stopped to stroke Sandy and decided the unconditional affection was just what she needed right now. Karen's mouth was sour from too much wine, and her head ached, but Sandy's eager greeting eased some of the pain.

After getting showered and dressed, Karen headed downstairs and switched on the light in the kitchen. The illuminated digital display on the microwave told her it was a quarter to eight. Late. Too late to ask Morgan for a lift.

Her car had been dropped off last night, but she wasn't going to drive this morning. She'd had too much to drink last night.

She made a pot of coffee and stood by the kitchen counter, looking out at the dark garden. After staring out at the frost-covered trees for a few minutes, she made herself move. This was no time for moping and feeling sorry for herself.

She picked up the landline phone and then realised she hadn't memorised Rick's number. There were very few numbers she knew by heart – her parents' home telephone number and her dad's mobile number, which hadn't changed in over twenty years, and of course, Anthony's. She had to turn on her laptop to access her contacts to get Rick's number.

By the time Rick pulled up outside, Mike had surfaced. As he poured a mug of coffee, Karen kissed him on the cheek and said goodbye. She gave Sandy a final pat on the head and headed off to work.

Karen tried to tell herself this was just another day on the job, but her churning stomach was not solely due to the amount of wine she'd consumed last night.

'All right, Sarge?' Rick asked as she got in the car. 'I heard what happened last night. I'm so sorry.'

'Me too,' Karen said, putting her handbag in the footwell and then fastening the seatbelt.

'It must've been awful for you. Is there anything I can do?'

'You can help me find the evil sod who did it.'

Rick drove back to the main road. He was quieter than usual and a bit tentative around Karen. He was treating her with kid gloves, and she knew it would be the same when they got to the station. Furtive glances. Whispered comments. Pitying shakes of the head. But it wasn't their fault.

'This is personal. The Cleanser did this to hurt us,' Rick said. 'I heard there was a letter?'

Karen gave him a sideways glance. 'Where did you hear that? Were you at the scene last night?'

'No. Sophie told me. She texted me this morning. She wasn't gossiping . . . She was concerned about you, said you'd be upset.'

'Well, of course I'm upset, but I don't want you tiptoeing around me. That doesn't help.'

'Do you think the super will want more manpower on the case now? She might let me and Morgan transfer back on to the murders?' Rick asked, and he slowed the car to a crawl as they reached the traffic backed up before the new roundabout.

'I doubt she'll let Morgan transfer. Not after he was named in one of the letters.'

'Do you think she'll let you keep working on the case?'

Karen didn't know the answer to that. 'I hope so.' She desperately wanted to stay on the case and make sure they caught Anthony's killer, but the super would be cautious. She would want to stop the investigation becoming personal.

As soon as they got to the station, Karen went to find Superintendent Murray. She needed to get in there first and explain why she needed to stay on this case, before Churchill asked to have her taken off the investigation.

Pamela was sitting at her desk.

'Is she free?' Karen asked.

'She is.' Pamela got to her feet. 'I was very sorry to hear about DCI Shaw. I worked with him for a while.'

Karen hadn't known that. 'He was a good man.'

'He was.'

The superintendent's office door opened. 'Karen, I thought I heard your voice. Come in.'

The office smelled of fresh coffee, and there was a collection of Christmas cards lined up on her desk. Murray didn't sit down but walked over to the large windows and looked out at the patchy fields. The sky was a heavy, greyish white. The fields and sky met in a misty haze.

'I think we've got more snow on the way,' the super said.

'Yes.'

'There's a small get-together planned this evening. Just a few officers who worked with DCI Shaw over the years, gathering to honour his memory informally.'

'That's a nice idea.'

'Royal Oak, five p.m.' The superintendent turned back to face Karen. 'What happened last night was horrendous, and I can't imagine how distressing it must have been for you when you found his body.'

'It was incredibly difficult, ma'am, but I need to stay on this case.'

The super nodded slowly as she sat down, and then indicated for Karen to do the same. 'I'd be glad to keep you on the case with your knowledge and experience, but I'm not prepared to sacrifice your mental health.'

'I'm fine, ma'am.'

'I don't see how you can possibly be fine, Karen,' Murray said gently.

'No.' Karen looked down at the floor and took a deep breath. 'I can't pretend to be unaffected by Anthony's death. He was my boss for a long time. I had a great deal of respect for him, and we were still close. I'm going to miss him very much. But I need to stay on the case. I need to find the person who did this.'

Karen tried to judge the super's mood. Was she softening? Her blank expression made it difficult to tell. Was she taking inscrutability lessons from Morgan?

Finally, the superintendent said, 'All right, let's keep things as they are, if DCI Churchill is happy.'

Karen doubted that DCI Churchill would be happy, but at least she was still on the team for now.

'Thank you, ma'am.'

The superintendent smiled. 'How are things progressing on the case?'

'Haven't you spoken to DCI Churchill?'

'I have, but I'm asking for your opinion.' Murray rested her elbows on her desk and settled her direct gaze on Karen.

'Slowly. There was another letter found at the scene last night. Like the others, it contained allegations. In Anthony's case, I know they're not true. There's a pattern developing. Character smears. We've not been able to corroborate most of the claims in the letters. It seems as though The Cleanser is making things up.'

'To what purpose?'

'I'm not sure. Maybe to create a smokescreen. To lead us away from the true motive behind the killings. To justify the murders.'

'Interesting theory. The cleansing is simply an excuse to kill?'

'Perhaps The Cleanser truly believes the allegations, but we can't verify them.'

'You know people will be talking about the allegations against DCI Shaw?'

Karen tensed. 'About him taking bribes? Being corrupt?' She shook her head. 'It's ridiculous and untrue.'

'But people will still talk, and you need to be prepared for that.'

'He wasn't corrupt.'

'That won't stop people talking about it.'

The phone beeped on the superintendent's desk. 'Sorry, I won't be a moment,' she said, and took the call. It was Pamela saying her nine o'clock meeting was scheduled.

When Murray hung up, Karen said, 'If that's all, ma'am, I'll get back to work.'

The superintendent nodded, and then, as Karen was leaving the room, said, 'If things get too difficult, you'll let me know, won't you?'

Karen said she would, though she didn't see how things could get much more difficult than this.

Sophie sat at her desk, preparing for the morning briefing. She was dreading it.

After everything Karen had been through, she really didn't deserve this. Sophie knew how close Karen had been to DCI Anthony Shaw, and the fact that he'd been targeted because he was a police officer . . . Sophie shivered. The idea of a killer targeting officers made her skin crawl. She'd already told her mum and dad to be extra careful, make sure they double-locked the door even during the day, and she planned to stay at their house tonight. She'd had a brilliant time with Harinder last night, before she'd heard what had happened to Anthony.

She lifted her head as Karen walked into the open-plan office area. The DS looked tired.

'Sarge?' Sophie got up from her desk and walked over. 'Everything okay?'

'I've just been to see the super. We're still on the case.'

Sophie wasn't sure how she felt about that. Was it a good idea to stay on the investigation when Karen was so emotionally involved? If one of her friends had been killed, Sophie wasn't sure she'd be able to work the case – but she didn't voice her concerns. Karen needed her support right now, not her doubts.

'The superintendent said there's going to be drinks for DCI Shaw at a local pub this evening. The Royal Oak, five p.m. if you want to go. That goes for you too.' Karen raised her voice and looked at Rick, who was tapping away at his keyboard.

Sophie glanced at Karen's handbag. Had she forgotten they were supposed to be going to see the FBI expert from America tonight? Dr Michaels's talk started at seven, so maybe they'd have a drink for DCI Shaw and still have time to get to the presentation.

But then Karen would hardly be in the mood for a night out after what had just happened. Of course their plans had slipped her mind. It wasn't important in the big scheme of things, was it?

Sophie would go to the drinks for DCI Shaw and forget about going to see Dr Michaels. She could go another time. Okay, so the tickets weren't cheap, and he probably wouldn't be back in the UK for years, but . . .

'Are you okay, Sophie?' Karen asked, cutting through her thoughts.

'Yes, I'm fine. Five o'clock, drinks for DCI Shaw. I think that's a great idea. Maybe some of his old colleagues can share their memories of him.'

Karen smiled.

'DS Hart.' Churchill's voice carried across the room.

Sophie turned as he approached. He was an unappealing man. He was always smart, and Sophie generally admired that, but there was something smarmy about Churchill. And he always gave the best work to the men on his team, ignoring her and Karen.

Luckily, Leo and Arnie were easy to get along with.

Leo had always been considerate and polite to Sophie, and while no one would describe Arnie as polite, he had a kindness about him. He was an interesting person to work alongside, and the more Sophie got to know him, the more she liked him.

'I was told you were too upset to stick around and give a statement last night,' Churchill said, looking down on Karen. 'You seem to be holding up pretty well today.'

Sophie narrowed her eyes. That was an unfeeling thing to say. How could anyone blame Karen for not wanting to talk to him last night? She certainly couldn't.

'I'm all right, but it was a shock finding him like that last night,' Karen said.

'Let's go to my office now. You can talk me through it.'

Karen nodded.

Churchill turned to Sophie, surprising her by saying, 'You come too, DC Jones. Bring your notebook.'

She met Karen's gaze and gave her what she hoped was a supportive smile. They walked up to Churchill's office in silence.

He had to know he wasn't popular. Why didn't he make more of an effort? They all knew DI Morgan wasn't exactly a people person, but he was likeable. He was honest and trustworthy, and most of all, he was kind – pretty much the complete opposite of DCI Churchill.

'All right then, let's get started,' Churchill said, sitting down beside his desk. 'What happened when you got there?'

Karen and Sophie took seats on the other side of his desk.

'I received a voice message from Anthony last night. When I listened to the message, I was concerned. He wanted to talk to me. He said it concerned something we'd discussed on Monday. He didn't answer when I called him back, so I went to his house.'

'What had you discussed on Monday?' Churchill asked.

'Numerous things,' Karen said. 'We talked about Christmas, more specifically him spending Christmas with my family and me. And . . .' Karen paused, then fixed Churchill with a direct stare. 'We talked about the ongoing corruption case against DI Freeman.' Karen's gaze didn't leave Churchill's face as she spoke. Sophie noticed Churchill shift in his seat and look away.

'Do you think he wanted to tell you something about corruption?' Churchill asked.

'I think so. It sounded very serious, so I doubt he wanted to talk to me about Christmas.'

'Do you have any idea what he was going to tell you?'

'No, but it has crossed my mind that perhaps he was killed because he was going to tell me something.'

Churchill frowned. 'Are you linking his death to the corruption case? Suggesting our killer has done DI Freeman a favour by killing DCI Shaw before he could tell you something incriminating?'

'I'm simply considering all possibilities.'

'Right,' Churchill said, turning to look at Sophie. 'Are you taking all this down? I want your notes on this.'

Sophie wanted to ask why. But she decided she didn't fancy getting her head bitten off this early in the morning. If he wanted Karen's written statement, why didn't he ask her to write one? Sophie suspected he just liked to throw his weight around. He really was a piece of work.

'So, you turned up at his house. Then what?'

'The door was open, which made me think something had happened.'

'Why didn't you call for backup?'

'My phone wasn't working. I did consider going to a neighbour's house first, but thought I'd check to see if he was incapacitated. At the time, I thought he might have had a heart attack or a stroke and need medical assistance. I didn't even consider the possibility he'd been targeted like this.'

Churchill's face was blank. 'Then what happened?'

'I walked into the house and called out his name. He didn't reply, so I went into the lounge. At first, I didn't notice anything wrong, but then I saw him behind the sofa.'

'And you tried to resuscitate him. In your opinion, was he still alive at that point?'

Karen looked uncomfortable. She took a moment then said, 'Looking back, no, I don't think it was possible to save him at that point.'

'Did you detect a pulse? Was he breathing?'

'No, but I had to try. I couldn't just walk away.'

Sophie pressed her pen hard against the notebook. Was he being purposefully unkind?

'I didn't expect you to walk away, DS Hart. I expected you to follow procedure. But instead, you needlessly contaminated a crime scene.'

Sophie put down her pen and notebook and glared at DCI Churchill. He would never dare say any of this in front of the superintendent.

'Looking back,' Karen said again, 'I could have been more careful. Perhaps I shouldn't have tried to resuscitate him, but it was my first instinct.'

'And what happened to your phone? Why wasn't it working?' Churchill asked.

'It was frozen. It's been playing up for a while. I tossed it aside and reached for the landline to call for assistance.'

'And your phone is still at the scene.'

'Well, I suspect it's been collected and processed as evidence, but yes, I did leave it at the scene last night,' Karen said.

'Was there anything out of place when you arrived?'

'Everything looked as it always did.'

'And the allegations in the letter,' DCI Churchill said, leaning forward and narrowing his eyes. 'Do you believe any of them were true?'

'No, I do not,' Karen said. 'Anthony was a proud officer with an exemplary career. He was not corrupt, and he was not an alcoholic.'

Churchill turned, looked at Sophie. 'Did you get all that down?'

Sophie finished scrawling the last sentence. 'Yes.'

'I guess we'll soon find out whether or not DCI Shaw was corrupt, won't we?' Churchill looked directly at Karen. 'We'll go over his finances with a fine-tooth comb.'

Karen met his gaze steadily, refusing to look away. 'Of course. But you won't find anything.'

After a few more questions, Sophie and Karen left Churchill's office.

'Are you okay, Sarge?' Sophie asked as they headed along the corridor. 'He's awful, isn't he?'

'It wasn't the easiest thing I've ever done, but compared to last night, it was a cakewalk. We need to regroup, get the briefing done and start making some headway. I feel like we're stuck.'

'Leo was going over some CCTV footage this morning. Maybe something's turned up.'

Karen raised an eyebrow. 'Footage from where?'

'Outside Laurel Monroe's apartment building. I don't think he's got an ID yet, but it looks promising.'

They stopped in the corridor when Morgan approached, holding out a mobile phone. 'I thought you could do with this,' he said. 'It's a spare. My old phone. Pay-as-you-go, and it's still got some credit. You can use it until you get your phone back.'

'Thanks,' Karen said. 'I have ordered a new one, but it still hasn't arrived.'

'I've entered my number into the contacts,' Morgan said. 'Perhaps Sophie can do the same. Hopefully, you won't need it for long.'

'How old is it? Must be ancient. It's got actual buttons!' Sophie looked at the phone in amazement.

'About ten years. It's outlasted all my smartphones.'

Karen thanked him again and handed the phone to Sophie so that she could input her number. Sophie did so, and then dialled her own phone so she'd have Karen's temporary number.

'Any progress on the Sam Pickett case?' Karen asked.

Morgan sighed. 'Not yet. I'm heading to the superintendent's office to give her an update, but there's nothing to say. A twelve-year-old boy was knocked off his bike, and no one saw or heard anything.'

'It's hard to understand how anyone could cause an accident like that and then drive off,' Karen said.

Sophie agreed. How could a person live with that on their conscience? 'I can't believe anyone could be so heartless.'

They left Morgan and walked on to the office.

Arnie looked up from his desk near the coffee machine and waved Karen over. 'Come and have a look at this,' he said.

Sophie walked towards her desk, passing Leo. 'Found anything on the CCTV yet?'

'Yeah, and it looks good. We've got an ID. Going to bring him in later,' Leo said with a wide grin. Catching Sophie's expression, his smile lessened. 'Everything all right? You look a bit down.'

'I'm fine. It's just all this stuff with DCI Shaw. It's so sad.'

Leo nodded soberly. 'Yes, very sad and shocking. I wonder what made The Cleanser target him in particular.'

'It mentioned bribes and corruption in the letter,' Sophie said quietly, glancing across the room to make sure Karen hadn't heard. 'But Karen is adamant DCI Shaw was not corrupt.'

'It must be hard for her. No one wants to hear that sort of thing about a friend.'

'Especially when it isn't true.'

'Right,' Leo said. He turned away, then looked back. 'Anything else bothering you?'

'Well, not really. It's just I had plans tonight. I was going to listen to Dr Michaels. He's doing a presentation at the university.'

'Oh, and you can't go anymore?'

'There are drinks at The Royal Oak for DCI Shaw.'

'Did you know him?'

'No, I'd never worked with him, but I should be there to show support for Karen.'

'She'd understand if you couldn't make it, wouldn't she?'

Sophie thought for a moment. 'I'm sure she would, but some things are more important, aren't they.'

Then she shrugged, put her handbag in her desk drawer and locked it. Yes, it was disappointing, but she'd get over it.

CHAPTER TWENTY-SIX

Sparrow smiled. The new development had put a cat amongst the pigeons. It was exciting to see it all kicking off around him. They were oblivious to the fact they had a viper in the nest.

Last night, claiming the life of DCI Anthony Shaw had been harder than he'd expected. The others had been hard too, but they weren't innocent. He'd gritted his teeth and doled out their punishments.

But last night . . . He'd done the job, of course, and despatched the DCI as ordered, like a good little foot soldier. But he hadn't stopped shaking for hours afterwards.

Even if he hadn't enjoyed the act itself, he had to admit the result should keep Eagle off his back for a while. DS Hart had stumbled across his handiwork last night. He couldn't have planned it better.

The fact Karen had discovered the body had earned Sparrow a grunt of approval from Eagle. When he'd called the boss to tell him the job was done, there had been an edge to Eagle's voice, a grudging respect maybe? He'd been very quiet. Perhaps it wasn't respect. Perhaps it was fear.

Perhaps Eagle was scared of him.

Sparrow liked that idea. Eagle needed to understand that he wouldn't be controlled anymore. The threats against his family had been evil. Enough to cut himself off to protect them. Now, he had no one.

Fear for his family had kept Sparrow in line for a long time. The fear that his loved ones would be targeted had compelled him to follow orders without question.

But now the tables had turned, because Sparrow wasn't just doing the jobs asked of him. He might not enjoy his tasks, but he had discovered an unexpected talent for manipulation.

◆ ◆ ◆

On the way to the briefing, Karen asked Leo to put a note about drinks that afternoon in the diary. She didn't want to be told off by Churchill for being missing in action and no one knowing where she was.

'No problem,' Leo said. 'How are you doing after . . . last night?'

'I'm fine,' Karen said. 'Sophie said you'd found something on the CCTV.'

'Yes,' Leo said, opening the door to meeting room three and letting Karen walk ahead of him. 'I'm not sure whether it's our man, but it's the closest we've come so far.'

'That's excellent news. You've got an ID?'

'Yes. Brandon Ashworth, thirty-seven, married with two kids, from Wragby. He's not got a record, but he's shifty, hiding something. And as whoever killed Laurel Monroe had to come in and out of that building, and we've eliminated the other two people on the footage as suspects, it's got to be Ashworth.'

'Yeah,' Arnie said as he walked into the room. 'The trouble is there's also a fire door at the back that isn't alarmed and isn't covered by CCTV.'

Karen's hopes fell. 'So that means The Cleanser could have come in that way, and they wouldn't have been caught on camera.'

'Exactly.' Arnie pulled out a chair, plonked himself down, then loosened his tie.

'And the suspect you found on CCTV, Leo, does he know anyone in the apartment building? Did he give you a reason for being there?'

'Denied it was him. Denied everything. Very suspicious.' Leo sat beside Arnie. 'I've only spoken to him on the phone so far, but we'll bring him in after the briefing.'

Churchill walked in the room, looking jubilant. 'Great work, both of you,' he said, nodding to Leo and Arnie. 'Why don't you kick us off, Leo, and tell us about the suspect you've identified?'

Leo played the video footage on his tablet and gave them what he knew so far. 'Look, you can see him coming in the door here, but it's not a great picture of his face on the way in. But on the way out, he looks straight up at the camera. See.' He paused the video just at the point where a man in his late thirties to early forties with short brown hair and a receding hairline looked up at the camera. 'His name is Brandon Ashworth. He's an administrator at the university, thirty-seven years old.'

'Religious?' Karen asked, after Leo had finished giving the background he'd gathered on Ashworth.

'He's listed as Church of England, but I don't know whether he's a practising Christian. We don't know much about him at all, other than the basic facts. We were planning to go and pick him up after the briefing, sir,' Leo said, looking across at Churchill.

'Absolutely.' Churchill was clearly thrilled to be making some progress.

Karen felt she should be too, but she wasn't getting the streamers out just yet. There could be other reasons for Ashworth to have been in the apartment block.

'I'd be happy to go with you, Leo,' Karen offered, but Churchill shook his head.

'No, I think Arnie and Leo should go. After all, this is their result. Before you head off to collect him, let's just go over the letters one last time. We think that the claim about Laurel Monroe earning money running a sex-cam website was a lie, but she had a history of drug abuse. Correct?' All the officers in the room nodded, and Churchill went on. 'We believe that the claims against Lloyd Nelson regarding domestic violence and embezzlement were both false.'

'That's right,' Arnie said.

'And the final letter accusing DCI Shaw of corruption was a lie,' Karen interjected.

'And the alcohol problem?' Churchill raised an eyebrow.

'Another lie,' Karen said.

Churchill steepled his fingers beneath his chin. 'I have a report that states numerous bottles of alcohol, both full and empty, were discovered in and around the bungalow.'

'What do you mean *in and around the bungalow*?' Karen asked impatiently, leaning forward. She was growing defensive. She took a breath and waited for Churchill to answer.

'I mean there were lots of bottles in the house, and in the recycling bin, which suggests the contents were drunk recently.'

'That doesn't mean he was an alcoholic. I've known him for a long time, and yes, he liked to drink, but he didn't have a problem.'

'If you're too close to this to be objective . . .' DCI Churchill began, and then trailed off.

Karen put her hands up. 'I'm not.'

'Right. Well, we can speak to his doctor, I suppose, and we'll find out what state his liver was in after the post-mortem.'

Karen tensed and stared down at her notes. She hated the way Churchill was talking about DCI Shaw. She remembered her old boss as kind and supportive, quick to smile or, when deep in thought, frowning so deeply his bushy eyebrows met in the middle. Now he was just a dead body in the morgue waiting to be dissected.

She listened to Churchill discuss the plans for questioning Brandon Ashworth, and hoped this was the breakthrough they were all hoping for.

Then Arnie and Leo went to collect Ashworth to bring him back to the station for questioning, and Karen called Anthony's sister to offer her condolences.

The call was answered by Anthony's niece, who said her mother was too upset to come to the phone. Karen offered to help if there was anything the family needed, and told her to call anytime if the family had questions.

Using the computer, Karen downloaded her contacts stored on the cloud, but then groaned when she discovered Morgan's old phone had no way of uploading contacts in bulk. She'd have to add them manually, one at a time.

There was no time for that, so she just put in the most important numbers, then sent a text to her parents and sister just to make sure they were okay. Anthony's death had unnerved her. She worried that her family could be at risk too.

She made a strong black coffee, then sat at her desk and ploughed her way through the case files, trying to make sense of all the data they'd collected. There was a lot of it. The statements and background research felt overwhelming. The link between the victims could be hiding in the information they already had.

It all swirled around in her mind. There had to be a connection somewhere. Three random killings were so unlikely.

Karen flipped through the paperwork and stopped when she came to a printout of Anthony's call log. They'd managed to get hold of that fast. Leo and Arnie must have worked late last night. She scanned the numbers and saw her own at the bottom. Hers was the last number Anthony had called. She bit her lower lip. The number above her own looked familiar, though she couldn't place it. After logging onto the cloud and accessing her contacts again, she searched for the number.

She got a hit.

Alice Price.

Karen stared at the screen, thinking. Alice? Why had Anthony called Alice Price? They'd worked together in the past. But Anthony hadn't mentioned talking to Alice regularly, and Alice's husband didn't like her being in contact with her old colleagues. Had Anthony told Alice what he wanted to tell Karen?

She reached for her phone, then stopped. Protocol demanded she tell Churchill. If the investigation were headed up by Morgan, she'd go to him, but she didn't trust Churchill. What if he was involved? Alice had told Karen to look into Churchill once, after all.

Why Anthony? Had he been killed to stop him telling Karen something important? Perhaps it was an inside job, someone on the force who didn't want him revealing what he knew, so they'd decided to kill him and then cover up his death by making it look like he was the victim of the serial killer . . .

Her imagination had gone too far. She couldn't seriously think the corruption would go that deep.

A little voice whispered, *But they tried to run your car off the road . . . and killed Josh and Tilly.*

Karen glanced up and looked around the open-plan office at her colleagues. It all seemed so normal, so ordinary. People were sipping coffee, staring at their computer screens, tapping on keyboards or chatting away on the phone. Could one of these people have targeted Anthony?

But surely if they wanted Anthony gone, there were easier ways to do it. An accident, mow him down in a hit-and-run or . . .

Karen paused. The hit-and-run. Sam Pickett. Karen rubbed her hands over her face. She couldn't be emotional about this. She needed to think logically. That's what Anthony would tell her to do.

Think it through. Weigh up all the possibilities. Look at the case from every angle, and then you'll find what you're missing.

She remembered Anthony's oft-repeated advice and swallowed the lump in her throat.

Stomach rumbling, she checked her watch and was surprised to find that it was almost eleven. She hadn't eaten breakfast. Mike was right – if she wanted to work this case, then she needed to eat properly and sleep well to perform at her best.

She pushed up from her desk and headed out of the office, intending to go to the canteen. Halfway along the corridor, she slowed at the sound of raised voices and turned. The door to meeting room three was ajar, and Karen stood aside quickly as it was shoved wide open.

A tall man, broad-shouldered with a head of tousled brown hair, stalked out of the room, his whole body rigid with anger. 'You've got nothing. How is that possible in this day and age? We've got cameras everywhere, and still you don't have anything to go on. No witnesses. Nothing! My son got knocked off his bike, and no one saw a thing.'

DI Morgan stepped out of the room behind him and said, 'I wish I had more news for you, but—'

The man shrugged him off.

Karen knew it was Sam Pickett's father.

'Has it just been you investigating the accident? One officer looking into my son's death?'

'It's not only me. We've got people from the traffic division looking into the accident, and we've got officers going over all the cameras we have on roads leading to Waddington, but as you know there are no cameras on Hill Top itself, which means we have to go back to the larger roads and—'

'That doesn't help me, does it?' The man's voice was quieter. His fury had gone and was replaced by hopelessness.

'I really am sorry, Will,' Morgan said, but Sam's father just turned away and walked towards the exit with a uniformed officer.

Karen caught Morgan's eye. 'Difficult one?'

'Yeah, he's suffering. They both are, but I've got nothing else to go on. It's come down to us going through all the traffic camera footage, looking at every single vehicle heading in that general direction. I'm not sure we're going to get what we need, even if we do that.'

Morgan was upset. He was normally so stoic, calm and quiet, and although he wasn't raising his voice and ranting about the injustice of a twelve-year-old kid being hit by a car and then left for dead at the side of the road, she could tell he was finding this investigation incredibly hard.

'It's tough,' she said. 'The ones with the kids always are. Do you think there's a chance whoever knocked Sam off his bike thought they'd hit an animal?'

Morgan shrugged. 'He was cycling along Hill Top. It was dark, and the street lighting is poor. From the tire marks on the road, it looks like they were driving too fast, but we haven't had any witness statements from the houses nearby to suggest a car went roaring past. Though plenty of people complained that commuters use it as a cut-through.' Morgan sighed. 'Enough about my case. How are you holding up?' he asked.

'I'm okay,' Karen said. 'Look, I didn't mean for you to go home alone last night. I was supposed to be staying with you and monitoring the cameras. With everything that happened . . .' She shrugged. 'I forgot. I'm sorry.'

'No need to be sorry. You had a lot on your plate.'

'You should have asked Rick to stay.'

'He offered, but things are difficult for him at home with his mum.'

'Sophie then?'

Morgan mock-grimaced. 'I think I'd have preferred to come face-to-face with the killer than listen to Sophie explain the ins and outs of FBI protocol all evening.'

'You're not taking it seriously. Sophie's a good officer. She's interested in the academic side of crime. There's nothing wrong with that.'

'I know. She's a great asset, and I'm glad she's part of my team. But I like my own space.'

'You can have as much space as you like once The Cleanser is caught, but until then you'd better get used to company.'

Morgan put his hands up in defeat. 'All right.'

'Please be careful, Morgan. After Anthony . . .' Karen shook her head. 'If anything happened to you . . .' She looked away and swallowed the lump in her throat.

'I don't think The Cleanser is interested in me anymore.' Morgan squeezed her hand. 'I played my part.'

Karen shivered. She hoped he was right, but this killer enjoyed playing games. No one was safe until they'd been caught.

'I wanted to say thanks for calling Mike as well, and for getting me out of there before Churchill arrived. It was the right call.'

'Of course it was. I always make the right call.'

Karen managed a smile. 'I don't know about that. But I know you weren't working on the case, so you didn't have to show up like you did.'

Morgan's expression grew serious. 'Of course I did. I'm on your side, Karen. You know that.'

She met his gaze, then looked away. 'We've got a new suspect.'

'You have?' Morgan said, raising his eyebrows. 'Well, that's good news. Who?'

'A man called Brandon Ashworth. No record. He was caught on camera leaving Laurel Monroe's apartment building around the time we think she was killed.'

'Well, that's promising.'

'Yes, it is. Leo and Arnie are bringing him in. Don't you recognise the name? I wondered if he was someone you'd dealt with in the past. The Cleanser named you in the first note.'

'It doesn't ring any bells. Sorry,' Morgan said. 'Let me know how you get on.'

'Will do.'

Karen had every intention of getting something healthy for breakfast in the canteen, but ended up selecting an apple pastry and a cup of strong English Breakfast tea. She sat at one of the tables and polished off the sticky danish in about thirty seconds.

She sipped her tea, thinking about the case in the noisy surroundings. She allowed herself to go back over the possibility Anthony's murder was somehow tied into the corruption. Could it be a coincidence that he'd needed to tell her something and then that very night he was murdered?

Karen decided she needed to visit Alice Price, but she wouldn't go alone because that would open her up to criticism from Churchill. Alice's husband already had an axe to grind. He thought Karen had been hounding his wife, so she needed to do this by the book, and to do that she needed a partner.

She didn't dislike Arnie and Leo, and they seemed competent enough, but she needed someone she could trust. That was where Sophie came in. Karen stood up, put her plate on the tray rack and set off to find Sophie. They needed answers, and though Alice wasn't the most reliable witness, she might also be the only person to know what Anthony had been planning to tell Karen last night.

CHAPTER TWENTY-SEVEN

Karen was making a coffee when Arnie and Leo came back with Brandon Ashworth. Leo was beaming. Even Arnie was more enthusiastic, and they were both talking as though they'd cracked the case.

Karen hoped they had, but she wasn't convinced.

They'd left Ashworth in the interview room, giving him time to talk to the duty solicitor.

'Leo, what else did you uncover on this guy?' Karen asked, wondering what was behind their buoyant mood.

'I'll email you the file on him,' Leo said with a grin.

'I'd appreciate it.'

'He still denies he was there. I can't wait to show him the CCTV footage during the formal interview.'

Churchill strode into the open-plan office, clapped a hand on Leo's back and beamed at Arnie. 'Good job, lads. Let's hope he's the one. Dig deep. We need to unearth any connections between Ashworth and our victims, and also work out how he fits into the corruption angle. Find out what he's got on DCI Shaw.'

Leo and Arnie exchanged a glance and shifted awkwardly. Churchill hadn't realised Karen was sitting a short distance away. He turned, acknowledged her with a nod and carried on. 'If there's corruption in the force, it needs to be rooted out,' he said. 'If we're lucky, we could get a two-for-one result with this case.'

Karen's hand tightened around her coffee mug. The cheek of Churchill, accusing DCI Shaw of being corrupt! What a joke.

She turned her back as they paused beside the whiteboard to plan their questions and the direction of the upcoming interview. She lingered by the coffee machine, adding extra milk and stirring the contents of her mug. The suggestion Anthony had been corrupt got under her skin, but she couldn't let Churchill see that. He'd take her off the case faster than she could blink if she couldn't control her temper.

Finally, they moved away from the whiteboard, chatting as they walked.

'Which room will you be in? I might come and observe,' Karen said before they reached the door.

Leo checked his watch. 'We're in interview room three.'

Interview room three had an observation room next to it, so she'd be able to watch the interview live rather than on a recorded feed.

'We won't start for about half an hour though – we're giving him time with his solicitor.'

'Okay, thanks.'

Leo smiled and then turned to follow Churchill and Arnie into the corridor. Karen carried her coffee back to her desk and sat down with a sigh. She planned to use the next half an hour to try to make some sense of this case. She pulled the nearest file towards her.

Karen flipped over the cover and then froze. There was a bright yellow Post-it attached to the first page in the file. She didn't use Post-its, and these were her personal files that she'd collated. No one else had been using them.

Although the colour had caught her eye first and made her pause, it was what was written on the note that clouded her vision and made the world spin.

On the Post-it were the words *I'm closer than you think.*

She stared at them for a moment and then looked up sharply, scanning the room.

She'd been away from her desk. Anyone could have opened the file and attached the Post-it. But who? And why?

She read it again.

I'm closer than you think.

Karen shivered as the thought occurred to her that the note could have been left by The Cleanser. It was a taunt, a threat. Karen's mouth grew dry. Did it mean the killer had access to the station?

But maybe she was reading too much into it. Perhaps it was an old Post-it that had somehow found its way to Karen's desk . . . Could it mean something other than a threat? Was someone playing a joke?

But no one was looking at her. No one was trying to hide a smirk behind their computer screen. No one giggled.

And it wasn't funny.

The station had good security. A swipe card with security clearance was needed to leave the public area and access the staff-only sections. Did that mean whoever had stuck the Post-it on her file worked at the station?

She thought back. Churchill had been standing beside her desk earlier, talking to Arnie. He could have done it. Or maybe Arnie. And Leo had been there too.

But her suspicion focused on Churchill. Alice Price had said to look into Churchill when Karen had asked her about the network of corruption. And Anthony had called wanting to talk to her about something they'd discussed on Monday.

On Monday, they'd talked about Churchill.

Karen put her head in her hands. It all came back to him. DCI Churchill.

She looked again at the Post-it. Most of the letters were rounded, in neat handwriting. The *a* was written in a distinctive style. More like a typed *a* than handwritten. That could be important. She reached into her desk drawer and pulled out an evidence bag. She used the bag to pick up the note without touching it with her fingers, and carefully peeled it away from the paper.

As she sealed the bag, she wondered if she was overreacting. It could be a Post-it someone had used ages ago, and somehow it ended up stuck to this file.

Churchill was occupied. He was going through interview questions with Leo and Arnie. That meant his office would be empty.

Karen didn't hesitate. She left the evidence bag on her desk and moved quickly. Her heart was racing as she headed up the stairs.

It wasn't until she paused outside Churchill's office that she doubted her plan. If she was caught going through a senior officer's private paperwork, that would take some explaining.

She hesitated with her fingers on the door handle. Did she really want to do this? Was she sure Churchill was the bad guy? The truth was, she didn't know, and there was only one way to find out. She needed to get a look at his handwriting.

Karen pushed open the door, which thankfully was unlocked, and stepped inside. It smelled of printer ink and the sharp aftershave he wore. His jacket was hanging up on a hook next to the filing cabinet. His desk was clean and free of clutter. There was a picture of him and two children, a stationery organiser containing pens, pencils and paper clips, but no paperwork or notebook lying on the desk with a sample of his handwriting.

She gritted her teeth. Trust him to be so clean. She glanced over her shoulder, making sure she was still alone, then tried the desk drawers, but they were all locked.

She moved over to the filing cabinet. Again, locked.

Karen looked around. He must have written something somewhere! Then she froze at the sound of voices coming from the corridor. Churchill. He was coming back already. She rushed to the door. How was she going to get out of this?

She considered sitting down in front of his desk and pretending she was just waiting for him to return, but she wasn't sure she could pull that off. He wouldn't believe it.

Biting her lower lip, she peered out and saw Leo and Churchill walking towards her. She pulled back quickly. She was never going to talk her way out of this.

She heard Leo say, 'Actually, sir, there was something I wanted to ask you.'

Karen chanced another brief glance outside and saw Leo put a hand on Churchill's arm to stop him walking on.

'All right. What is it?' Churchill asked.

'Actually . . .' Leo touched Churchill's elbow and gently steered him around, so he wasn't able to see the open door.

Pulse racing, moving silently, Karen stepped out of the office.

'It's Arnie,' Leo said. 'I'm a bit worried about the sausage sandwiches, to be honest. He's not the healthiest chap, and he had that heart scare last year. I tried to talk to him about it, but he doesn't listen to me. I thought maybe you could have a word?'

Churchill pulled his arm away. 'Arnie's diet is no concern of ours. If he wants to eat sausages every day, it's his choice.' He turned and frowned when he saw Karen in the corridor. 'DS Hart, what can I do for you?'

Karen was still desperately trying to think of a way to get a sample of his writing. She needed an excuse, but her mind had gone blank. 'I thought I could run over the interview questions with you.'

'There's no need for that,' Churchill said. 'We've already finalised our interview strategy for Ashworth, but thank you for the offer.'

He moved past Karen and went into his office. He paused and looked around. Had she left something out of place? A sign she'd been in there? But after a moment, he sat down.

She needed to tell Churchill about the Post-it. Yes, she had her suspicions about him, but he was heading up the enquiry, and it could be crucial to the case. She stepped into the doorway and he looked up, but before she could say anything, his phone rang and he snatched it up.

'Churchill . . . Ah, thanks for getting back to me.' He swivelled his chair around, so his back faced Karen and Leo.

Karen exhaled a relieved breath and shot Leo a thankful look before rushing off. She probably owed Leo an explanation, but it could wait.

She had only been searching Churchill's office for a few minutes. They must have finished the interview plan very quickly.

Downstairs, she walked back to her desk. She was going about this the wrong way. She wasn't a vigilante. She was a police officer, part of a team.

She glanced around the office. Most of her colleagues were trustworthy and honest. Unfortunately, she wasn't sure which ones she could trust.

But she knew she could rely on Morgan. She wasn't alone. She could tell him about the Post-it note, and he'd know what to do.

Karen's gaze skimmed the desk, looking for the Post-it in the evidence bag. It wasn't there. She frowned, shuffling files and lifting the paperwork on her desk looking for it, but it had vanished. Karen put her hands on her hips and stared at the desk in disbelief. 'Someone must have taken it,' she muttered just as Leo strolled over.

'What was all that about upstairs, Karen?' he asked. 'What were you doing in Churchill's office?'

'It's a long story,' Karen said.

'I've got time,' Leo replied.

'No, you haven't. You need to do the interview.' She was still staring at her desk rather than looking at Leo.

'Are you sure everything's all right? I know you had a really difficult time last night.'

'I'm fine. There was something here on my desk a moment ago, but now it's gone.'

'Oh, what have you lost?'

Karen opened her mouth to tell him and then shut it again. She was going to sound crazy. *There was a threatening Post-it on my desk, and now it's disappeared.*

Why hadn't she put it in her desk drawer and locked it? She'd been in such a hurry to prove that Churchill had written it that she'd run up to his office to look for a sample of his handwriting without thinking things through. Unless someone else had picked it up? Maybe Sophie or Rick?

Karen walked away from a puzzled-looking Leo, and rapped on Morgan's office door.

He looked up and smiled. 'Everything okay?'

'Not really, no,' Karen said, walking in and sitting down. 'I had a note on my desk. Well, not a note. It was just a Post-it. Someone had written *I'm closer than you think* on it. I think someone left it there as a taunt. But now it's disappeared.'

'*I'm closer than you think.* I don't like the sound of that. You think it was left by the killer?'

'Well, if not from the killer, then somebody who thinks it's funny to play a practical joke like that.'

Morgan waited as Karen pulled out a chair and sat down, then said, 'How much sleep did you get last night?'

'Sleep?' Karen looked up. She met his concerned gaze with a shake of her head. 'I didn't dream it, if that's what you're implying.'

'All the other notes from The Cleanser were typed and printed by a laser printer,' he said.

'Yes, but the Post-it was handwritten.'

'And it's gone now?' Morgan said with a lift of his eyebrows.

'I know how that sounds,' Karen said, raising her hands, 'but it was there.'

'So, why did you leave it on your desk rather than bring it straight to the superintendent or me?'

That was a very good question.

Because she wasn't thinking straight. Because she was still devastated after yesterday. Because she was set on proving Churchill was the person behind Anthony's death. Or all of the above.

Karen sighed. 'Because I'm an idiot, all right? I put it in an evidence bag, left it on my desk and went to Churchill's office.'

Morgan's eyebrows lifted even higher, then he shrugged. 'You went to talk to Churchill. I suppose that makes sense. It is his case. I thought you might—'

'No, I went into his office to see if I could find a sample of his handwriting.'

Morgan didn't say anything for a beat. Then, 'You think Churchill wrote *I'm closer than you think* on a Post-it and left it on your desk.'

His face was expressionless, but Karen heard the scepticism in his voice. 'I thought it was possible, yes, so I wanted to find a sample of his writing. The way the letter *a* was written was very distinctive, and I knew he was busy with the interview questions, so I thought it was the perfect time to go and look.'

She knew it sounded bad.

'It was the perfect time to show me or the super the note, Karen. Not the perfect time to break into his office. What if he'd caught you?'

'It was unlocked. I didn't break in.'

Morgan didn't look impressed.

'I know, you're right. I shouldn't have done it, and he nearly did catch me. Thanks to Leo distracting him, I got out without him seeing but—'

'Karen,' Morgan said, and leaned back in his seat, shaking his head, looking disappointed.

'I know. It was a stupid thing to do, but I did it, and now the note is gone, and I don't know who sent it. I don't know if it was a joke or if . . .' She met Morgan's gaze. 'Or if The Cleanser is one of us.'

'One of us? Karen, these killings have been sick. They're the work of a serial killer. The Cleanser marks their victims.' He frowned. 'You think Anthony's death is somehow related to the corruption enquiry and the—'

Karen cut him off. 'I'm not sure what to think. All I know is that I got that Post-it on my desk, and it sounded like a threat to me.'

'All right. Let's think this through logically,' Morgan said. 'Could the Post-it have a completely innocent meaning? Or become stuck to your paperwork from a different case file?'

'I don't think so. The file has only been on my desk.' She shrugged. '*I'm closer than you think.* I can't see how that could be anything other than a taunt.'

'So the killer entered the station, bypassed the security, walked into the open-plan office, and while surrounded by police officers, they stuck a Post-it on your file, but it's not there now.'

'Exactly,' Karen said.

'You realise how that sounds.'

'I can't help how it sounds, Morgan. It's what happened.'

'Right. Well, let's look for this Post-it. I'll help you.'

They went back to Karen's desk and searched. They looked through every single sheet of paper, beneath the keyboard and under the computer, and Morgan even crawled around under the desk. They checked all of Karen's desk drawers, even though she insisted she hadn't put it in there. And her bag and her coat pockets.

'You're under a lot of stress,' Morgan said finally, when they'd given up the search and gone back to his office.

'Don't, Morgan. Just don't. I saw that note. I know it was real. I didn't imagine it. I haven't lost my mind.'

'Of course you haven't. I'm not suggesting that, but maybe you're tired. Maybe you misread it.'

'I didn't,' she said stubbornly. 'We can't ignore it.' Karen lowered her voice. 'What if it was from The Cleanser?'

'We won't ignore it. You're going to have to tell Churchill and the superintendent. Everyone working on the case, in fact.'

'But what if one of them left the Post-it on my desk?' Karen said. 'What if they're playing games? One of them could have killed DCI Shaw.'

'Do you really believe that?' Morgan folded his arms and leaned back in his chair.

'I know DCI Shaw wanted to tell me something, Morgan. I'm sure it was about Churchill. It's a pretty big coincidence that Anthony just happened to be killed the night he was planning to tell me something.'

Morgan nodded slowly. 'All right, I'll speak to the superintendent. But you have to tell Churchill.'

CHAPTER TWENTY-EIGHT

Telling Churchill about the note had been an uncomfortable experience. He'd been silent, jaw clenched, forehead creased in a frown. He was torn between disbelief and an urge to reprimand her for losing an important piece of evidence.

After a few sharp words, she was dismissed.

She went to join Morgan in the small viewing area behind interview room three, to watch Leo and Arnie question Brandon Ashworth.

Ashworth had a receding hairline and a large forehead. His heavy-lidded eyes gave him a sleepy appearance, though his constant fidgeting showed his agitation. He was smartly dressed in office attire, but his tie had been loosened and the top button of his shirt undone.

He had an air of respectability.

Could he have murdered and disfigured three victims? Was she now looking at the man who'd killed DCI Anthony Shaw? Karen wasn't sure.

The interview got off to a rocky start. Arnie led the questioning at first, but Ashworth and his solicitor were on the ball, declining to answer many of the queries. The solicitor looked smug, but Ashworth was uncomfortable. Arnie did his best to pry answers from the reluctant suspect, but Ashworth wasn't making it easy. He continued to insist he didn't know Laurel Monroe and had never been inside the apartment building.

The CCTV was their ace card, and Arnie didn't play it straight-away. He took his time, waiting for Ashworth to build his web of lies. After fifteen minutes of the back-and-forth, Arnie gestured to Leo, who opened the file in front of him and pushed the images of Ashworth leaving the building across the desk.

The solicitor's features tightened almost imperceptibly, but Ashworth's reaction was more dramatic. His mouth gaped. Then he put his head in his hands and groaned.

'Maybe we should start again,' Arnie said. 'Why were you visiting the Magnolia apartment block on Saturday? You said you don't know anyone in the building.'

Leo chimed in. 'I think it might be time to change your story, don't you?'

Ashworth gave his solicitor a desperate look. The solicitor gave a small nod and then said, 'I'd like to confer with my client.'

'You've had time to confer,' Arnie said. 'Now it's time to talk. We want answers.'

'I'm sure you do, Detective Sergeant, but I have a right to talk to my client in private.'

'I lied,' Ashworth said. 'I was there on Saturday.'

The solicitor gave him a sharp look. 'I don't think you should say any more until we've discussed the best way forward.'

'There's no point denying it. They've got me on camera,' he said, pointing at the image. 'Look, I denied being there because I wasn't supposed to be, but it's not what you think. I wasn't involved in any kind of a crime. I was just visiting my girlfriend.'

'Your girlfriend?' Leo clarified. 'But I thought you were married.'

Ashworth grimaced.

'Oh, I see,' Leo said. 'And so you lied to the police because you didn't want your wife to find out where you were. Is that it?'

'I just didn't want anyone getting hurt.'

'So you wasted police time.'

'No. You brought me here. I haven't wasted anyone's time. I didn't ask to be interviewed.'

They continued questioning but now Ashworth was very open, answering everything they put to him, as he was eager to dissociate himself from the crime. They'd check with his girlfriend, but Karen felt Ashworth was now telling the truth. He wasn't The Cleanser.

A few minutes later, Arnie slapped his pen down on the table and snapped, 'Interview terminated at one fifteen.' Then he got up to leave the room.

Karen left the viewing area with Morgan as Arnie stalked past them in the corridor.

'He didn't look too happy,' Morgan commented.

'I'm not surprised,' Karen said. 'Ashworth was our main suspect.' She folded her arms and looked up at the ceiling. 'I don't know what to do, Morgan. We need to find this killer. I don't think they're going to stop until we do.'

'I need to check in with Rick, see how he's getting on with the CCTV regarding the traffic for the hit-and-run Friday night. But after I've done that, why don't we get together, brainstorm a bit and see if we can come up with something.'

'Thanks, I'd appreciate that,' Karen said. 'Churchill isn't keen on my input at the moment. He implied I imagined finding the note on my desk.'

'I've told the superintendent, and she wants me to look through all the entry logs to see if anyone entered the station who isn't authorised to be here.'

'Good idea,' Karen said. She forced a smile.

The entry logs were a start, but her deepest fear was that the person who'd left the note was authorised to be at the station because they worked there. If the note-writer had killed Lloyd, Laurel and Anthony, they could be working side by side with a killer.

Karen walked back to the open-plan office to ask Sophie to go with her to Alice Price's house in Washingborough. She needed a partner, and she thought another woman would be less threatening than if Arnie or Leo accompanied her.

Karen passed Arnie's empty desk, then stopped and stared. There, beside the keyboard, was an almost-new packet of yellow Post-it notes.

It didn't mean anything. Lots of people used them, and they were freely available from the stationery stock cupboard. Post-it notes were everywhere, and even if they had been Arnie's, who's to say someone couldn't have just plucked one from the top and used it.

She moved closer and ran her finger over the top of the Post-it notes, feeling the bumpy indentation of letters. She grabbed a blunt pencil from the stationery pot on Arnie's desk, and angled it to rub the soft graphite gently over the top of the note. It showed up the dips in the paper left from the previous note.

Holding a breath, she read: *Bread, milk, tea, potatoes, beef mince.*

She smiled and shook her head. A shopping list. Whoever had written the note hadn't done so on top of this stack of Post-it notes. She peeled off the top Post-it and put it in the bin.

◆ ◆ ◆

Outside, Sophie and Karen moved quickly across the car park as sleet started to fall.

'Did you get your car back last night?' Sophie asked.

'Yes, they dropped it off, but I had a fair bit of wine last night and didn't think driving would be a good idea this morning, so I asked Rick to pick me up.'

'How are you feeling now?' Sophie asked as they reached her car.

'Not bad.'

They both got into the car.

'It must have been a horrendous experience. I can't believe you're at work today.'

'Where else would I be?'

'I don't know. Maybe at home, feeling sad and sorry for yourself. I think that's what I'd be doing.'

'I just want to find who did this.'

Sophie started the engine. 'Hopefully Alice Price will give us something to go on.'

As Sophie drove towards Washingborough, Karen filled her in. She told her about the Post-it note and that Alice had previously suggested that Churchill should be investigated.

'So Alice thinks Churchill was working with DI Freeman?'

'She didn't say that exactly, but she suggested DCI Churchill was someone I should look into, because she said he'd acted suspiciously in the past.'

'She didn't say what he'd done to make her think he could be corrupt?'

'Alice is . . . She's a troubled woman,' Karen said. 'Sometimes I think she knows more than she's letting on, and on other occasions, she just seems confused. But DCI Shaw spoke to her the day he died. She might know what he wanted to tell me.'

'What if DCI Shaw just wanted to talk to you about something mundane?' Sophie asked tentatively, shooting Karen a nervous sideways glance.

Karen hesitated. They had spoken about Christmas. That could have explained the call. Maybe it was nothing more than him wanting to let her down gently, and tell her he was going to spend Christmas with his sister after all.

He wouldn't want to hurt her feelings, which would explain his serious manner. But then she dismissed the idea. She knew him too well. His voice had taken on a very grave tone when he'd left the message. He'd sounded preoccupied, worried.

'Maybe he was.' She looked out of the passenger window as the sleet blurred the landscape. Not knowing what Anthony had wanted to tell her was going to drive her mad.

◆ ◆ ◆

'You again.' Alice Price's husband Declan stood at the door, his arm across the doorway, blocking their entrance. 'I'm pretty sure I made it clear you aren't welcome here anymore, DS Hart.'

'We're here on an official matter,' Sophie said, holding up her ID. 'We need to speak to your wife, Alice Price, please.'

'Official matter?' He squinted at her warrant card, looked at Sophie and then back to Karen. 'What do you mean *official*?'

'It's your wife we need to speak to, please, sir,' Sophie said.

Declan Price gritted his teeth, but he let them in and led them through to the kitchen, where Alice was sitting at the breakfast bar. Alice gave Karen a quick, nervous smile, her gaze flickering up and then quickly back down to the counter.

'Is it all right if we sit down, Alice?' Karen asked, pointing to the two empty stools on the other side of the breakfast bar.

Alice smiled tentatively. 'Of course. Can we get you a cup of coffee?'

'No, they're not staying long,' Declan said, standing behind his wife.

'We'd like to talk to you about a phone call you received from DCI Anthony Shaw yesterday, Alice,' Sophie said.

The woman glanced up. 'Why?'

'I'm afraid I've got some bad news,' Karen said. 'Anthony was murdered last night.'

Alice's pale, elfin features slackened in shock. Her lower lip trembled. 'Anthony?'

'Yes, and we're trying to find out who did it.' Karen put her hand over Alice's and squeezed gently. It was instinct. They weren't supposed to touch. No physical contact. It was drummed into them during training. But the woman looked so lost, so sad, that Karen couldn't help reaching out. 'We know you spoke to him yesterday, and we thought you might be able to help by telling us what you talked about. Did he mention any worries or concerns?'

Suddenly the shutters came down. Alice's face was blank.

Declan put a hand on her shoulder. 'Alice doesn't know anything about his murder.'

'I'm not suggesting for one moment that Alice was involved,' Karen said. 'I just want to find out what they talked about yesterday.'

Alice shivered. 'I can't really remember.'

'It could be really important, Alice. Please try. Yesterday he left me a message asking me to go and see him because he had something to tell me. Did he tell you about that?'

Alice looked terrified. 'I don't know what he was going to say.'

But Karen wasn't sure that was true. Alice looked like she wanted to say something. It was almost as though she was scared to speak.

Karen glanced at Declan. 'Do you think we could have a few minutes alone with Alice, please?'

Declan shook his head stubbornly.

'It's your choice. Either you let us talk to your wife alone, or we're going to have to take Alice to the station.'

He glowered at Karen, but then finally let out an angry huff of air and stalked out of the room.

'Sorry, Alice,' Karen said, leaning her forearm on the countertop. 'You're not in any trouble. If you want to tell me something in confidence, you can. I'm not here to pressure you. I just need to find out what happened to Anthony, okay?'

'Okay.'

'You want to know what happened to him as well, don't you? You want whoever killed him brought to justice,' Sophie said.

Alice brushed away a tear. 'Of course. He was a really good man. He was so kind. Even after I had to leave the force, he kept in touch.'

'So what did you talk about yesterday?' Karen prompted gently.

Alice took a deep breath. 'I'm in a good place at the moment. I'm on a new medication. The doctor says I'm doing well, and I don't want to get sucked back into that paranoia again.' She looked at Karen beseechingly. 'Please don't ask me to get involved in this.'

'I don't need you to get involved in anything, Alice,' Karen said. 'I just need you to tell me what Anthony said to you yesterday.'

Alice looked up at the circular LED lights in the ceiling and blinked. 'He said he was concerned. He knew you were working with a new team headed up by DCI Churchill. And he wanted any information I could give him.'

'And what did you say?'

'I told him I didn't have any information. I said at one time I thought Churchill, or someone working with him, was accepting bribes, but I had no evidence. I overheard a conversation but it was just before my breakdown, and it's likely paranoia skewed my reaction. I had to leave the force because my allegations weren't true, and I can't make that same mistake again, Karen.'

Karen gave Alice what she hoped was a reassuring smile.

Churchill. Everything seemed to circle back to him.

'Can you tell us about the conversation you overheard?'

'I was walking by his office, and I heard two men joking about taking payment in kind. When I asked DCI Churchill about it, he said it hadn't been him.'

'Did you recognise his voice?'

'At the time, I thought so, but maybe I assumed it was him because they were talking in his office.'

'You didn't see who was in there?'

'No.'

'Who was in his team at the time?' Karen asked.

'I'm sorry, I don't remember. I tried to put all this behind me after the breakdown.'

The pressure Alice had been under had been too much for her. She'd accused two senior officers of corruption, but an internal investigation cleared them of wrongdoing. They were exonerated, and Alice had been forced out.

They asked Alice some more questions, keeping the language informal and reassuring. Sophie made notes on her tablet, then a few minutes later Declan came back into the kitchen.

'I think you've had enough time. I don't want you upsetting Alice.'

Karen stood up. 'Thank you for your help, Alice. If you think of anything else, give me a ring.'

Alice said she would.

Karen turned to Declan, who stood near the kitchen door with his arms folded, scowling at them. 'It's okay. We got what we came for.'

CHAPTER TWENTY-NINE

Sparrow stepped outside the police station and took a breath of freezing air.

He stopped just by the entrance, where there was some shelter from the heavy sleet. His lungs felt like they were going to burst. Nervous laughter bubbled up in his chest, but he managed to suppress it.

He'd been so close to getting caught. The adrenaline rush he'd experienced after putting that note on Karen's desk made his head swim. And then taking the note back before she'd shown anyone so that no one believed her – that had been a stroke of genius. The look on her face! He'd made her doubt her own eyes.

He remembered Morgan digging around under the desk and Karen frowning as she sifted through every sheet of paperwork. Somehow, he'd managed to keep calm and play innocent.

Improvisation was exciting, but the boss was getting angsty. Eagle was ordering him to tone it down, and as much as Sparrow hated to admit it, the man was probably right. He needed to keep things under control. His overconfidence increased the chance they'd catch him soon.

Capture was inevitable. Maybe it was the only way. He didn't consider himself an evil killer. Not really. It was a job, just like being a soldier.

Over time, he'd trained himself to numb his mind during the physical act of murder, but afterwards the shakes still hit him hard. He didn't want to kill anyone. It wasn't his choice. But this week, something had shifted inside him. He was taking back control.

He turned to go inside. He had to go back to work and try to keep up his act. It wouldn't be easy, but he would do it because he was a professional.

◆　◆　◆

Outside the Prices' house on Barn Owl Way, Sophie put the key in the ignition and glanced at Karen. 'You told Declan we got what we came for. Did we?'

'Yes. We know why Anthony wanted to talk to me. Churchill.'

'You think Churchill is corrupt. But do you think he's connected to DCI Shaw's murder?'

'I don't know,' Karen said honestly. 'I've been trying to work it out, but we're looking for a serial killer. I can imagine Churchill taking bribes to cover up more minor crimes, or giving a local yob the nod when there's a raid due, but Anthony was killed in the same way as Lloyd Nelson and Laurel Monroe. I did consider the possibility his murder was designed to look like the work of The Cleanser. A way to get rid of Anthony without raising suspicions. But we haven't released details about the markings on the victim's foreheads – the only people who know about that are officers involved in the case.'

'And scenes of crime officers, the pathologist's office, admin support staff . . .'

'That's true,' Karen said. 'I suppose there could be a leak.'

'So DCI Shaw was killed by The Cleanser. Was his death completely unrelated to the fact he was digging up dirt on Churchill? Is that our working theory?'

Karen stared out of the fogged-up windscreen as Sophie angled the hot air vent to clear it. 'I'm not sure I have a working theory.'

Karen's gut feeling told her Churchill couldn't be trusted. That didn't necessarily mean he was corrupt, and it didn't suggest he was involved in Anthony's death either. It could be a personality clash. It wouldn't be the first time. Churchill was an unlikeable character, and she wasn't alone in that opinion. Morgan, Sophie and Rick all had their reservations about him, and even Leo and Arnie – members of his own team – admitted his shortcomings.

The windscreen was slowly clearing. Karen sighed. She had to look at it logically – the way Anthony would have told her to approach the case.

Look at the facts, and the links will appear.

If only, Karen thought. She'd looked at the facts until she was blue in the face, and come up with nothing.

'You don't really think the Post-it note was from The Cleanser, do you?' Sophie looked sceptical. 'It's hard to believe.'

'I know.'

'The idea a serial killer would risk getting caught by walking into a police station in the first place . . . I mean, it would be a huge risk.'

'It would.' Karen was well aware of how far-fetched it sounded.

'And no one else saw the note?'

'No,' Karen said, 'but before you ask, I didn't imagine it.'

'I think it's more likely to be a joke, Sarge. Someone probably put it on your desk, then thought better of it and took it back. They're not going to admit to it because they'd get in trouble.'

'If it was a joke, it's not very funny.'

'I know, but some of the officers have a really odd sense of humour,' Sophie said. 'I mean Rick, for example. He finds the strangest things hilarious.'

'Rick would never—'

249

'No, you're right. He wouldn't,' Sophie said hurriedly.

She was quiet as they drove across Pelham Bridge, but when she stopped at the traffic lights, she turned to Karen with a concerned expression. 'If it wasn't a joke, then the killer was in the station. That's a terrifying thought.'

Karen pulled a pen and small notepad out of her handbag and scrawled down the lower-case *a* in the same style as the one on the Post-it note. 'Have you seen anyone write their *a*'s like this?' Karen asked, holding the notebook up.

Sophie glanced at it and said, 'Sure,' and then pulled away from the lights as they turned green.

'Who?' Karen asked.

'My secondary school form tutor, Mrs Hush. She—'

'No, I mean people you know now. People who work at the station.'

'Oh, I don't think so. Not that I can recall. Why?'

'The *a* was written like that on the Post-it note I found on my desk.'

Sophie shivered. 'You think the note was written by The Cleanser, don't you?'

'It's possible.' Karen was starting to think that not only had The Cleanser got into the station, but the killer was probably one of their own. 'Sophie, you've done a lot of research into serial killers. How often do they turn out to be police officers?'

Sophie blew out a breath. 'It happens more than you think – in America anyway. They enjoy positions of power, and often try to involve themselves in investigations. They admire other killers, often idolise them. There have been murders involving psychologists, expert witnesses, that sort of thing. So . . . I suppose it's not beyond the realms of possibility that our serial killer could be a police officer,' Sophie said, glancing sideways at Karen. 'But it does seem very bizarre.'

Karen agreed. 'What does Dr Michaels say on the subject?' she asked, and then suddenly stopped. 'Oh, that talk was tonight, wasn't it?'

'Yeah, but it doesn't matter.'

'I'm sorry,' Karen said. 'I don't feel up to going tonight. You don't mind, do you?'

'No, of course not,' Sophie said, shaking her head as she stopped at another red light. 'I'm sure he'll visit Lincoln again soon. But funny you should ask, because in his most recent book he does describe a case where a serial killer in California turned out to be an ex-police officer. It took a while to track him down.'

'How did they catch him in the end?'

'DNA at the scene,' Sophie said. 'He got careless, left a knife behind on his final murder.'

'How many people did he kill before he got caught?'

'Seventeen.'

Karen's eyes widened. 'Let's hope we don't get to seventeen deaths before we capture The Cleanser.'

◆ ◆ ◆

Morgan sat in his office watching security footage. There were four exits and entrances at Nettleham HQ: the main entrance, along with the custody door and two fire exits. There were cameras on every one.

He checked the fire doors first. No one had entered or left the building using those doors today. The custody suite entrance had been used by three officers he recognised, bringing in two arrests.

The main entrance would take more time.

He watched the video on 3x speed, and checked the time-stamped logged IDs from the swipe cards against the footage.

Morgan knew most of the people he saw coming into the station, but not all of them. Every time he saw someone he didn't recognise, he made a note of the time they entered and put a question mark next to it on his notepad, intending to go back to them later.

He was worried about Karen. She'd seemed so convinced the Post-it note was a message from The Cleanser. But no one else had seen it. It was very concerning.

It meant either someone had stuck the Post-it note inside the file and then taken it back when Karen left her desk, or Karen had imagined the whole thing.

He trusted Karen implicitly, but she'd been through a very difficult time. The past few years had been a trial that would test even the strongest character, and last night . . . well, that would have shaken anyone, even Karen.

Perhaps she hadn't slept last night. She could have fallen asleep at her desk and dreamt the note.

But there was no evidence that had happened.

So, as unlikely as it seemed, he believed Karen was telling the truth. There had been a note.

His first instinct made him think someone was playing a sick practical joke, but just in case, he needed to review all the footage. If it was an outsider, Morgan was determined to track them down.

'All right, boss?' Rick said, poking his head into Morgan's office.

'Yes. I'm going through this footage.' He gestured at his computer screen. 'There's a few people I don't recognise. You've been here longer than me. Perhaps you could take a copy of the footage, look up the times I've noted down here, and see if you recognise them?'

'Oh, great.' Rick's shoulders slumped. 'More CCTV footage. Fabulous.'

Morgan leaned back in his chair. Rick looked tired. He had been overwhelmed with video footage over the past few days. 'Yes, sorry. You've been a bit loaded down with recordings. How's it going with the traffic cameras?'

'It's never-ending. We may as well send Forensics to look at every car in Lincoln. It feels like I'm up against insurmountable odds. I haven't been able to narrow it down much.'

'I know it seems like we're not making progress, Rick, but we can't give up. Sam's parents . . .'

'I know, boss,' Rick said. 'They need a result. Whoever hit Sam left him to die at the side of the road. That's sick.'

Morgan gave a grim nod.

Rick sighed. 'I'll keep at it. It just feels a bit frustrating at the moment.'

'Yes.' Morgan understood exactly how Rick felt.

CHAPTER THIRTY

When Karen and Sophie got back to the station, DCI Churchill was in the open-plan office, giving Arnie and Leo a pep talk. They were all standing around Leo's desk, looking thoroughly discouraged.

'We don't give up that easily,' Churchill said, tapping the top of the desk for emphasis. 'Follow up on Ashworth. Talk to his boss, his friends and his wife.'

'You want us to ask his wife whether or not he was having an affair, boss?' Leo said.

'That's going to cause a bit of marital strife,' Arnie said, folding his arms and chuckling.

'I'm not interested in their marital situation. I'm interested in catching a killer,' Churchill said.

Karen and Sophie paused by Leo's desk.

'Ashworth was in the vicinity when Laurel was killed, but he's got an alibi for the time Lloyd was killed. And he doesn't have a motive,' Arnie said with a shrug. 'I reckon we're barking up the wrong tree with Ashworth.'

'I agree,' Karen said. 'I think we need to start looking elsewhere.'

'It's very easy to criticise, Karen, but I don't see you uncovering any further evidence or suspects.' Churchill turned away with a shake of his head. 'Apart from disappearing Post-it notes of course.' He muttered the last sentence under his breath.

Leo's eyes widened, and even Arnie looked shocked.

Churchill flushed, then waved a hand. 'Sorry, that was uncalled for.'

Karen didn't respond. She walked over to her desk in silence. Sophie walked away too, after giving the three men a scathing look.

After Churchill had left, Leo and Arnie approached Karen cautiously.

'He was bang out of order,' Arnie said. 'You okay?'

'Fine.'

'You don't look okay,' Leo said, pulling over a chair and sitting down. 'We're all on the same side, you know? We all want to bring whoever's done this to justice.'

Karen raised an eyebrow. 'But you think I'm lying about the note. You think I made it up.'

'No, of course not,' Leo said. He paused. 'It's just that no one else saw the note.'

'You've got to admit it's a bit weird,' Arnie said, perching his ample backside on the corner of Karen's desk. 'Look, you've had a terrible twenty-four hours. No one can blame you if you misread a Post-it and assumed the worst. We're all jumpy. We've had police officers getting notes sent to their homes, and now one of our own has been murdered by this killer.'

Karen took a long, deep breath. 'I didn't imagine it. I saw the note, and it said *I'm closer than you think.*'

'But it could have been an old Post-it that had come unstuck from some paperwork and got attached to one of your files,' Arnie suggested. 'It might be harmless. Maybe a quote, or something some-one wrote down ages ago, and just by chance it stuck to your file.'

Karen looked at him doubtfully.

He shrugged. 'All right, so I'm clutching at straws, but the alternative . . . well, it means someone who works here is messing with our heads.'

'Or The Cleanser's one of us,' Leo said in a quiet voice.

They all looked around the room nervously, and then Arnie snorted. 'Don't be daft. You're going soft. It's just someone with a bad sense of humour, having a laugh.'

'Could be,' Karen said. 'It's a pretty sick form of humour, though.'

'Agreed,' Arnie said. He stretched, his shirt tightening around his large stomach. 'Right. I'm going to get something to eat. Can I get anyone else anything?'

Karen shook her head, but Leo asked him to bring back a ham sandwich from the canteen.

Alone at her desk, Karen pulled the files towards her. Was this case related to a grudge against the police? Was it personal? Had Anthony been targeted because of his close connection to Karen?

The first letter from The Cleanser had mentioned Morgan. They'd been through Morgan's old cases, looking for possible suspects, but perhaps it was time for Karen to look through Anthony's past cases.

She sighed. That would take a very long time.

Then again, it could be unrelated to Anthony's previous cases. He could have been killed because of what he knew. Her thoughts returned to DCI Churchill.

They couldn't discount the possibility that Anthony had been murdered to stop him talking. Whatever he'd been about to tell her would now never be said.

Frustrated, Karen tapped a pen against her notepad. The letters The Cleanser had sent were filled with nonsense. They hadn't been able to verify all the claims in any of the messages, and she was certain that the corruption allegations against Anthony were false.

A little voice in the back of her mind whispered, *But you thought you could trust DI Freeman.*

She slammed the pen down on her desk. She wouldn't give in to paranoia. Yes, she'd trusted Freeman, and yes, he'd betrayed her in the worst possible way, but that didn't mean she could never trust anyone again.

She was part of a team, and there were honest, hard-working police officers all around her. They believed in the job just as she did, and she needed to trust them.

Karen decided to talk to DS Grace again about Churchill. It was Grace's job to investigate the corruption, and if Anthony had known something about the officers involved, then perhaps DS Grace could find out what it was.

Karen sighed. She had to admit Morgan was right about the holes in her theory. If Anthony's death was related to the corruption, why was he killed by the same person who'd murdered Lloyd Nelson and Laurel Monroe?

It was possible that it was smoke and mirrors, like the letters. Perhaps Anthony had been killed in a copycat murder. The Cleanser's crimes may have been used as a way to mask the true motive for Anthony's death. Maybe the perpetrator just wanted the police to believe Anthony was killed by The Cleanser.

Anyone working at the station would know the case details. They'd know about the marking of the body after death. The board was up in the briefing room, which meant the details of the crime were on display to anyone with access to Nettleham HQ.

Karen tapped her pen on her pad again, thinking. The alternative was that all three cases were related.

Were Lloyd and Laurel's murders also linked to corruption? Had they witnessed a crime? A crime that someone powerful wanted to cover up?

What if The Cleanser was simply a cover for the assassination of people who were a threat to the corrupt officers? The Cleanser could be a tool to confuse and misdirect the police.

But they hadn't come across any evidence that Lloyd or Laurel had crossed anyone rich or powerful, or anyone in the police service. Karen mulled it over and then rejected the idea.

She had no evidence, and that was the problem. All she had were fanciful ideas.

Karen rubbed her hands over her face, then reached for the landline phone on her desk and dialled DS Grace's number.

'DS Grace.'

'It's Karen. I hoped we could meet up? There are some ideas I want to discuss if you have time.'

'Sure, though I'm busy this afternoon. Does it have to be today?'

'Preferably. It concerns DCI Shaw's murder.'

'All right. I could call into Nettleham when I finish my last interview – about six thirty, if you'll still be there?'

'Perfect,' Karen said.

'Right. See you later.'

After she hung up, Karen turned to her computer and logged on to the system before filing a request to access Anthony's old case files. She'd need the application to be approved by the superintendent, but she could fill in the form so all the superintendent had to do was sign.

The drinks scheduled tonight in Anthony's memory started at five. She'd have time to stay for an hour and then get back for her meeting with DS Grace. An hour was enough to pay her respects. And besides, solving the case was a better way to honour his memory than getting drunk.

After she'd submitted the request for the superintendent's digital signature, Karen took her notepad and pen down to the lab to see Harinder.

She knocked on the open door of the lab before walking inside. He turned away from the microscope bench and smiled.

'Hope I'm not disturbing you. You look busy,' she said, nodding at the array of slides beside the microscope.

'I'm always busy,' Harinder said with a dramatic sigh, 'but now and again it's nice to see someone who doesn't wear a lab coat. How can I help?'

'Just a quick question about handwriting.'

He looked thoughtful. 'That's not my area of expertise, but I could probably find out anything you need to know. What is it?'

'It's about a handwritten lower-case *a*. On a note I received, it's written unusually, more like a typeset *a* with the arc over the top.' Karen put her notepad down on the bench beside Harinder and showed him what she meant. 'Do you know how common that is?'

'I think it's more common to write them the other way, without the arc,' Harinder said, 'but I don't think it's that unusual. Does this have something to do with the Cleanser case?'

'Someone left a note on my desk. It could have been a joke, but if it was, it was in pretty bad taste. They wrote the *a* like that. Don't suppose you know anyone at the station who writes that way?'

Harinder shook his head slowly. 'Can't say I do. What did the note say?'

Karen hesitated, and Harinder quickly followed up by saying, 'Sorry, you don't have to tell me.'

'No, that's okay. It was a single line written on a Post-it, and it said, *I'm closer than you think*. Then I left my desk after putting it in an evidence bag, and when I came back, about fifteen minutes later, it was gone.'

Harinder's eyebrows lifted.

'I know it was stupid to leave it on my desk. Whoever wrote it must have come back and removed it. Maybe they had second thoughts and realised it wasn't very funny after all.'

'I hope that's the case,' Harinder said, 'because the alternative is not good. Not good at all.'

'No,' Karen said, putting her hands in her pockets and frowning at the notepad.

'Because you know what it could mean, don't you?' Harinder asked gently.

Karen nodded. 'If it was written by The Cleanser, then they have access to the station.'

'Yes.'

'One possibility I was mulling over,' Karen said, 'is that the killer and the letter-writer might not be the same person. That's possible, isn't it?'

'I suppose it is, yes.'

'Someone trying to distract us.'

Harinder rubbed his chin thoughtfully. 'Why would they want to do that?'

'I don't know. This case is baffling.'

Karen glanced at the clock on the wall, and Harinder did the same. 'Are you going to the drinks for DCI Shaw tonight?' he asked.

'Yes, at five. I need to get back here to talk to DS Grace afterwards, but I'll go for one. You?'

'Yes,' Harinder said. 'For once, I'm going to leave work at five o'clock.'

'You know . . .' Karen hesitated. 'All those things in the letter weren't true. He wasn't corrupt. He never took bribes.'

Harinder gave Karen a sympathetic smile. 'He'd be the last person I'd suspect of corruption.'

'We'll get the financial reports soon, and we'll be able to prove it, but I don't need to see those because I know he was innocent.'

Harinder put his hand on Karen's shoulder. 'I'm sure you're right. DCI Shaw was a good man, and he didn't deserve this.'

No, Karen thought, *he didn't*. He didn't deserve to die in such a way. No one did. And as an insult to his memory, now his old colleagues were digging around in his private life, going through bank statements and savings looking for evidence of corruption. He deserved so much better than that.

CHAPTER THIRTY-ONE

At a quarter to five, Karen was still sitting at her desk. She'd worked her way through some of Anthony's most recent cases, after getting the superintendent's approval. His older files hadn't been digitised, so tomorrow Karen planned to go to the document storage facility to access the old paper files as well.

An hour earlier, Morgan and Rick had gone to Waddington to talk to the Picketts, and were planning to drive straight to the pub from there.

Karen logged off her computer, stood up and stretched, and looked over at Sophie's desk. 'Is it all right if I get a lift to the pub with you?'

'Oh,' Sophie said, looking up. 'Sure. Harry is driving, but you can come with us. I'm sure he won't mind.'

'I can give you a lift,' Leo called over as he grabbed his coat from the back of his chair. 'We're just about to leave.'

Arnie stood beside him. He chuckled. 'Yes, you should give the lovebirds their privacy.' He waved a hand at Sophie, who blushed furiously.

'We're not lovebirds,' Sophie muttered, tidying away the things on her desk. 'I'm just getting a lift.'

'Whatever you say.' Arnie smirked and shrugged on his padded jacket.

They all walked downstairs together. Sophie headed off to the lab to find Harinder, and Arnie, Leo and Karen walked across the freezing car park to Leo's car. The sleet had turned to light, fluffy snow.

'They got the forecast right for once,' Arnie said, looking up at the sky. 'I reckon it'll settle overnight.'

The drive to the pub usually took two minutes, but Leo drove cautiously as the snow got heavier. Slush had been pushed to the side of the road by passing vehicles on the main road, but the smaller lanes were white and slippery.

The journey took twice as long as usual, and when they pulled into the car park Arnie said, 'Did you hear about Assistant Chief Constable Fry's car?'

'It was stolen, wasn't it?' Karen asked.

'That's right. But it's been found.'

'Where?'

'Burnt to a crisp in a farmer's field just outside Newark. Apparently he was spitting with rage. I'd have loved to be a fly on the wall when he found out.'

'Not a big fan of his, then?' Karen commented dryly.

'He's a pompous old fool.'

Karen didn't think Fry was much older than Arnie, but decided not to mention that. 'He likes to throw his weight around, a bit like Churchill,' she muttered.

Leo grinned, catching Karen's eye in the rear-view mirror. 'You've got a point there. They are similar in some ways. Though I don't think Churchill's as bad as Fry.'

They entered the pub, which was dimly lit and busy. A fire burned brightly at the back of the main seating area. The ceiling was low with dark wooden beams. It felt cosy and warm.

The bar was packed, but there were plenty of free tables and seats. There were already a few officers and civilian staff from Nettleham sitting at two large tables.

DCI Moorland spotted Karen and lifted his pint.

'Can I get you another?' she asked.

'No, I'm fine,' Moorland said, getting up from his seat. 'I thought once everyone's here, I'd say a few words about Anthony, unless you'd like to?'

'No, I'm happy for you to do it,' Karen said.

There would be a funeral and a remembrance service for Anthony. His family would organise that, and Karen would attend, but tonight was a way of paying their respects to one of their own.

Moorland had worked with DCI Shaw even longer than Karen had, and had known him well.

'What are you having, Karen?' Leo asked.

'Just an orange juice, thanks.'

'Sit down. I'll bring it over,' Arnie said.

She left them at the bar and sat at DCI Moorland's table.

'How are you?' Moorland asked. 'It's been a tough year, hasn't it?'

'It has. I'm doing okay.'

He gave a *what else can you do?* shrug.

Moorland took a sip of his pint, sighed and said, 'And then this on top of everything else. Are you any closer to catching who did it?'

'It doesn't feel like it,' Karen said, 'but we'll get there. Whoever killed him won't get away with it.'

Sophie and Harinder arrived. Sophie said hello to Karen, then said she was going to the bar to inform Arnie he was dripping beer on his shoes, while Harinder stayed by Karen's table.

'Here you go,' he said, handing Karen back her cracked phone in an evidence bag, along with a release form to sign. 'I could have waited until tomorrow, but I thought if you're anything like me, you'd feel lost without your mobile.'

'Thanks, Harry,' she said, scribbling her signature on the form and handing it back.

Harinder folded the paper in half and stuck it in the back pocket of his trousers. 'I had to wipe it.' He spoke quietly.

'Oh, why?'

'I found spyware installed on the phone's operating system.'

Karen stared at him. 'Spyware? Someone's been spying on me?'

'It's more common than you think. Though it's more sophisticated than the programs I've come across before. I've made a backup copy so I can look into it tomorrow.'

She looked around the bar, but no one was listening to them. They were all caught up in their own conversations. 'What information could have been stolen?'

'Actually, it looks like it was installed so someone could listen in to your conversations by activating the phone microphone.'

'Someone was *listening* to my conversations? For how long? I've always got my phone with me. In meetings. During interviews.'

'Looks like it was only installed a week ago. Did you click any suspicious links in text messages or emails?'

'No.' Karen shook her head and thought back. She usually spotted spam messages easily, although some could be very convincing. Last month, she'd had a text from her mobile company, telling her to update her payment details. She'd ignored the text and checked her account online instead. 'I'm sure I didn't click any links. Does that mean someone physically installed the software?'

'Perhaps. We'll look into it tomorrow. I had to put a report in because it's a security breach.'

'Of course. The phone has been playing up – freezing at odd times. I didn't even consider spyware or the possibility I'd been hacked.' She pressed a hand to her forehead. 'I should have realised.'

'Don't be too hard on yourself. The software is designed to hide in plain sight. Come and see me tomorrow afternoon, and we'll try to work out how it was installed.'

Karen nodded. That meant a well-meaning lecture on the danger of clicking on links in text messages or emails. She'd been planning to ask Harinder if they'd extracted any more information from the evidence gathered at the scene, but now she was distracted by the idea someone had been spying on her. Was it a simple scam, or something more sinister? Could it be related to the Cleanser case? Corruption? The thought made her chest tighten.

She tried to put it out of her mind. She would deal with it tomorrow. Tonight was supposed to be a remembrance of DCI Anthony Shaw. Not of the way he died, but the way he lived.

Harinder went to get drinks at the bar, and Sophie sat beside Karen. They listened to the officers at the next table recalling an incident where Anthony had shoved open a door during a raid only to find a shocked elderly couple in their bed, rather than the drug dealer he'd been expecting.

It hadn't been his fault, and Karen was sure the story had been embellished, but she laughed with the others. It felt good to listen to stories of Anthony's life rather than remember the last time she'd seen him.

Soon the pub was full of people talking about Anthony, sharing memories.

Karen had almost finished her drink when DCI Moorland got to his feet.

'Just a few words,' he said. 'I'm not one for long speeches.'

He was jeered. DCI Moorland was known for his incredibly long briefings.

He laughed with them, then grew serious as the cheeky comments faded and the room fell silent. 'We're all here this evening to remember a fine upstanding officer, Anthony Shaw. I was fortunate to be taken under his wing as a young DC, and he promised to teach me all he knew. First things first, how to make a good cup of tea.'

Everyone laughed.

'Goodness help you if you added too much milk!' Moorland shook his head. 'It's impossible for me to stand here and tell you all the kind and courageous things he did over the course of his career, so I won't even try. But on behalf of all those he trained, all those he backed and all those he helped – thank you, DCI Shaw.'

Moorland raised his glass and said, 'To Anthony, DCI Shaw.'

Everyone else did the same. There were a few moments of sub-dued conversation, and then the noise picked up to the same level as before, as people began sharing stories, laughing and joking.

Ten minutes later, DCI Churchill walked in. Karen thought it might be time to leave. She had to get back for her meeting with DS Grace anyway.

'Ah, Churchill. Good to see you. I didn't know you knew DCI Shaw,' Moorland said, standing and offering to buy Churchill a drink.

'I didn't know him well, but thought I'd come and pay my respects. No, you sit down. I'll get these,' he said, patting DCI Moorland on the shoulder. 'Anyone else need a refill?'

'I wouldn't say no, boss,' Arnie said, holding up his half-empty pint glass. Everyone else said they were fine.

When Churchill turned and walked to the bar, Leo leaned across to Karen. 'Do you want to leave? I need to get back home anyway. My wife asked me to pick up something for dinner tonight.'

Karen didn't need asking twice. 'Do you mind dropping me at the station?'

'No trouble at all,' Leo said, grabbing his jacket and then shrugging it on.

Karen turned to Sophie and winked. 'I'll see you tomorrow. Have fun.' She looked meaningfully at Harinder, and Sophie's cheeks turned scarlet.

'Don't you worry, Karen. I'll keep an eye on them,' Arnie said, much to Sophie's horror.

◆ ◆ ◆

Sophie's cheeks burned. Honestly, they were all so embarrassing. What must Harinder think?

She avoided eye contact and took a gulp of her rosé wine. Arnie was making smooching noises now. They were determined to humiliate her. She glared at Arnie. 'That won't be necessary.'

She glanced at Harinder and smiled, trying to cover her embarrassment.

Arnie chuckled and drained the rest of his pint before thanking DCI Churchill, who put a fresh one in front of him.

Sophie sat with her handbag on her lap. She hadn't taken her coat off either, because she still felt a bit chilly.

Through the small diamond-latticed window, she could see the snow coming down heavily. That was a bit of a worry. She hoped she'd be able to get a taxi home later.

She took another sip of wine and wondered whether she should ask Harinder if he wanted to go and see Dr Michaels tonight. He might find the presentation interesting. Then again, he might think she was too keen.

'Everything all right?' Harinder asked.

'Oh yes,' Sophie said, reaching for her glass again. 'Sorry about that,' she said, nodding at Arnie, who was now grinning at them, raising his drink.

Harinder laughed. 'He's winding you up because you're reacting to his teasing.'

'I'm not reacting,' Sophie said. Then she shrugged. 'It's like water off a duck's back to me.'

She shifted in her seat so Arnie was out of her eyeline. It could be worse. At least Rick wasn't here to join in. Sophie glanced at the door. Where was Rick, anyway? He and Morgan were supposed to be meeting them at the pub. She guessed their visit to the Picketts' house must have taken longer than expected.

Harinder grinned, and tilted his glass to chink it against Sophie's.

She decided she would ask him after all. If they left in the next few minutes, they'd get there in time for the start, and she really did want to hear what Dr Michaels had to say.

She'd just gathered up the courage to ask Harinder if he wanted to go with her when they were interrupted by a young PC. Sophie couldn't remember his name, but she'd seen him around the station a lot recently, once talking to Karen and once talking to Churchill.

'Sorry to bother you,' he said. 'Do you know where Karen is?'

'She's gone back to the station. She has a meeting.'

He looked through the window at the snow-covered car park. 'I didn't think she'd brought her car.'

'She didn't. She's gone with DC Clinton. He had to go home anyway. He promised his wife he'd pick something up for dinner.'

'What?' Arnie said, suddenly tuning in to the conversation. 'I think you must have misheard, Sophie.'

'What do you mean?'

'Leo's wife left him months ago. She lives abroad now – Spain, I think.'

'Maybe she's come back,' Sophie said. 'Didn't you hear him?'

She turned to Harinder, who shrugged. 'Sorry, I wasn't really listening.'

'So you're sure Karen's gone back to the station?' the PC asked urgently.

269

There was something about his manner, the tension in his expression, that set off alarm bells. Sophie looked at her handbag, imagined the beautiful, crisp white tickets tucked inside the inner pocket, and then looked at Harinder. 'I'm sorry. I'm going to have to go back to the station too.'

'Oh, okay. I'll take you,' Harinder said, putting down his lemonade.

'No, it's fine. You stay here.' Sophie studied the young, fair-haired PC. 'Are you going back now?'

She remembered his name: PC Ray Watts. He'd been working when they found the first body. She remembered seeing his name on the witness reports.

Ray licked his lips nervously. 'Yes, I need to find Karen.'

'Then I'll come with you.'

CHAPTER THIRTY-TWO

Leo had just pulled out of the pub car park when Karen dropped her wallet in the footwell. She lifted her bag and shifted her legs to the side, looking for it in the dark space.

Leo switched on the light between the two sun visors, and as he did so, he dislodged a yellow Post-it note, which fluttered down and landed on Karen's knee.

She picked it up, and her whole world shifted on its axis.

'Have you found it?' Leo said, craning his neck to look for oncoming traffic before pulling on to the main road.

But Karen couldn't reply. Her gaze was fixed on the Post-it note.

'Leo,' Karen said slowly, 'why do you have Anthony's address written down?'

She ran a finger over the writing, feeling the indentations in the surface of the paper.

Leo glanced at the Post-it. 'Oh, it came off one of the files, so I stuck it behind the visor, planning to take it back later.'

But Karen didn't believe him. She stared down at the word *Montagu* in the address. DC Leo Clinton wrote his *a*'s with the arc above the letter. The same way as the person who'd left the Post-it note on her desk.

'I'm closer than you think,' Karen said.

'What?' Leo looked in the rear-view mirror and then glanced at Karen. 'What are you talking about?'

'It's you, Leo. You left the Post-it on my desk.'

◆ ◆ ◆

Leo gripped the steering wheel. She knew. There was no point denying it now.

He didn't say anything straightaway, staying silent, eyes on the road as he tried to work out his next move.

He'd underestimated her. That much was obvious. The note on her desk had been a step too far. He wasn't ready yet.

He glanced across and saw realisation dawning on her face. She looked pale, haunted.

She'd never understand. He wasn't a monster. The murders had been a job, nothing more. His hand had been forced. If he hadn't been trapped, forced to commit those crimes . . .

Could he try and talk her round? Tell her the Post-it had been an ill-considered joke, and he'd regretted it, taken it back? No, he could grovel, lie and twist the facts, but she was on to him now.

The first act was over. It was time for Sparrow to step out of the shadows.

He raked a hand through his hair. It might be hopeless, but he had to try.

'Look, Karen. I know it looks bad.'

'You admit you wrote the note and left it on my desk.'

'Yes,' Leo said. Would she fall for it? He wasn't ready for it all to end yet. 'It was a stupid thing to do. I'm sorry. I just thought it would be funny, but now I know it was a really, really horrible thing to do, and I'm very sorry.'

She turned – her expression serious, her eyes hard – and said, 'I don't believe you.'

'What don't you believe? That I wrote the note? I know it's out of character. It was nasty. I didn't mean to hurt you.'

She shook her head. 'The person who killed Anthony . . . there's hardly any evidence at the scenes. All the murders were well planned and immaculately clean. They were carried out in places where there isn't good CCTV coverage. The killer managed to get in and out of buildings without being seen. They left minimal forensic evidence. They knew how we work. Leo . . .' She stared at him. 'Did you kill them?'

He laughed as he wiped away the sweat from his forehead with the back of his hand. 'Me? I don't even like squashing spiders.'

But he knew she didn't believe him. The game was up. He put his foot down on the accelerator, and they sped along Welton Road, past the turning for Nettleham.

'What are you doing, Leo? Where are you going?'

'I think we need time to talk.'

◆ ◆ ◆

Outside the pub, Sophie put her hand on Ray Watts's elbow. 'What's going on? Why are you following Karen? Why do you have such an interest in what she's doing?'

'I don't know what you mean,' Ray said. 'I just wanted to talk to her.'

'About what?'

'About work, something private.'

'Don't play me for a fool. Something's going on. I've seen you hanging around the station like a bad smell.'

'That's not very nice.'

She stared up at him. 'You're as subtle as a brick. Now, tell me why you're so interested in Karen and why you're looking for her.'

He said nothing.

'Did you know DCI Shaw?' Sophie asked, putting her hands on her hips and narrowing her eyes.

'No, not personally.'

'Then what are you doing here?'

'A couple of the people at the station mentioned it. I thought it would be nice to pay my respects. I might not have worked with him, but he was a colleague all the same.'

'You're up to something, Ray. I'm going to find out what it is.'

'You're overreacting,' he said. 'Can we talk about this at the station?' he asked, hunching his shoulders against the cold wind as the snow swirled around them. 'It's freezing out here. Let's just get in the car, all right?'

'No, it's not all right. Why are you looking for Karen?'

'I'm worried about her.'

'Why?'

'After everything she's been through, I just want to make sure she's all right,' he said.

'Have you got a crush on her?' Sophie asked.

His cheeks pinkened. 'No.'

His phone rang, and as he pulled it out of his pocket, Sophie got a glimpse at the screen. DS Grace.

He walked away from her, talking quietly so she couldn't hear.

DS Grace was the officer in charge of the corruption enquiry. Was Ray somehow involved in the corruption? She'd seen him talking to Churchill. Was he reporting back? Was Grace somehow tied up in this too?

The possibility that the officer meant to be looking into the corruption was corrupt herself made Sophie's head spin.

She needed to get to Karen and warn her. She wished Morgan or Rick were here, but she could ask Harinder to help. She turned, ready to run back into the pub, when Ray called, 'Wait!'

He grabbed Sophie by the arm and hung up.

274

She snatched her arm away and glared up at him. 'What are you caught up in?'

'It's not what you think.'

'Then tell me.'

He sighed. 'I can't tell you. It's more than my life's worth.'

'Then I'm going inside, and I'm going to tell everyone in the bar that you're up to no good.'

'No, wait, please.' He put his hands up and then gave an exaggerated sigh. 'All right, fine. Look, DS Grace asked me to keep an eye on Karen.'

'Why?'

'Because she's worried about her.'

'You and DS Grace are in cahoots. You're part of this corrupt network of officers,' Sophie said.

Ray shook his head. 'No, you've got it all wrong. We're the good guys. We're trying to protect Karen.'

◆ ◆ ◆

'I have to take your phone,' Leo said, holding out a hand.

'No,' Karen said, rummaging around in her bag for the phone Harinder had returned to her less than an hour ago, planning to call for help.

But Leo leaned forward and pulled something from beneath the seat. When Karen turned to look, her breath caught in her throat. She was staring down the barrel of a gun.

'Where did you get that?'

'A raid a couple of years ago. Didn't submit it as evidence. I thought it might come in handy at some point.'

'You're working for Churchill, aren't you? You're corrupt. Just like Freeman.'

Leo didn't answer. 'Give me your phone. I'm serious, Karen, give it to me.'

With shaking hands, she held out the phone Harinder had just returned.

She was acutely aware of the other phone she had in her coat pocket – the phone Morgan had given her. Leo didn't know she had it.

He took his hand off the wheel to grab it and then pulled his own phone from his jacket, keeping the gun trained on Karen. He nudged the steering wheel with his knees as the car strayed towards the middle of the road. As they passed the junction to Heath Lane, he lowered the window. Icy wind blew snow into the car, and he slowed and threw both phones on to the snowy verge.

'That's better,' he said.

'You put the spyware on my phone,' Karen said. 'You've been listening to my conversations.'

'I had to.'

'How long have you been spying on me?'

'Not long. A couple of days. Wasn't hard. You shouldn't leave your phone on your desk.'

'It's locked with a passcode.'

'Which is the year of your daughter's birth. Not very hard to guess.'

He kept the gun pointed at Karen, but focused on the road as the snow tumbled down around the car. It was impossible to see more than a couple of metres ahead.

'Where are we going?' Karen asked.

'Nowhere,' he said. 'I'm just driving to give us a chance to talk.'

'What is there to talk about?'

'A lot. You need to understand.'

Was he going to try to turn her? Did he think she wouldn't run to report him as soon as the gun wasn't pointed her way?

Whatever he said, she would go along with it. Whatever it took, she would try to stay alive. She would deal with the aftermath later.

'I had no idea it was you,' Karen said. 'I mean Churchill, yeah. I had him pegged from the start, but not you, Leo. Why?'

'No choice,' he said. 'I did something stupid when I was a young constable. Helped myself to a bag of coke during a house raid. My partner found out and threatened to report me. But *he* stepped in. I thought he was trying to help me at first. My career would have been destroyed, and I'd have probably ended up going to prison, and you know how fellow prisoners love cops in jail.' His upper lip curled. 'I'd have done anything to stay out of prison. And they threatened my family. That's always a popular one. Just when you think you don't care anymore, that you're going to turn yourself in, that's when the new threat comes, targeting the people you love. And then what do you do? They've got you then, haven't they?'

'They threatened your wife?'

He nodded. 'Yeah, and my daughter. I ended up telling my wife that I didn't love her anymore, that they were both holding me back. I told her I didn't want to see my daughter again. I did all that to keep them safe. Can you imagine having to do the things I did just to keep them safe?'

'No, I can't,' Karen said softly. 'So it wasn't your fault, Leo. I mean, if you explained how you were coerced, how you were put under unfair pressure, and your family was threatened. That's going to help you if you come forward. If you talk—'

Leo smiled. 'That's not going to happen, Karen.'

'Why not? Come on. You know they're after the big guns. All right, you'll probably serve a couple of years, but they'll want the ringleader. They want the killer. They want Churchill.' Leo said nothing. The silence weighed heavily in the car, and then Karen said quietly, 'Unless . . . you killed them.'

'Yes, I killed them.'

'You killed Anthony?' Karen's mouth was so dry she could barely get the words out.

'Yes, I killed all three of them.'

'But why? What did he ever do to you? What did any of them do?'

'It wasn't what they did to me personally,' Leo said. 'None of it was personal. I just did what I was told.'

'Who told you to do it?'

Leo shook his head and said nothing.

'Hang on, wait.' Karen looked at him in disbelief. 'Are you telling me that you slaughtered three people and then mutilated their bodies because someone told you to?'

Still, he said nothing.

'How did anyone make you do that? How could you be *forced* to mutilate a body?'

'To be honest, that part was my idea.'

Karen looked at the gun and then up at him. She was shaking with a mixture of fear and rage.

'It was a distraction. A serial killer was guaranteed to attract a lot of attention, but that wasn't the aim. I just wanted something that would cover my tracks.'

Karen stared at him, struggling to take it in. 'You're The Cleanser?'

Her eyes were wide as the truth dawned on her. She was trapped in a car with a serial killer.

A wide smile stretched across Leo's face.

At Welton Hill, he turned left on to Eastfield Lane and then pulled up at the side of the road. It was dark, and the snow was heavy.

He pointed at Karen with the gun. 'Come on. Get out.'

'Why? Where are we going?'

'A walk. Down there.' He pointed past a ditch to the fields beyond. It was a steep bit of land. The fields ended in a small copse.

Karen wasn't familiar with the fields here. Everything was white. She looked around for landmarks. There were lights, but it was hard to judge how far away they were.

Why did he want to go down there? A cold shiver of dread ran along her spine that had nothing to do with the freezing cold, and everything to do with absolute terror.

He was going to kill her.

He planned to hide her body among the trees, so it wasn't found for a while. It could be days before a dog walker came across it. Bile rose, stinging the back of her throat.

'You don't have to do this, Leo. We can find a way out. They'll want the kingpin, the big man behind it. You give us Churchill, and I promise I'll fight to make sure you get minimal jail time.'

He grinned, his teeth as white as snow. 'You expect me to believe that?'

'Yes, I'm telling the truth. You have my word.'

He chuckled. 'It's a shame it has to end like this. I enjoyed working with you. We'd have made a good team. Come on, let's go.'

They set off down the hill, slipping and sliding on the snow-covered grass.

Karen's teeth chattered. 'All I want is Churchill! Just give me something on him, Leo, and you can go.'

'You're not in a strong bargaining position,' he said, and then slipped, falling hard on his side.

The gun went off and Karen ducked, scrunching into a ball, making herself as small a target as possible against the ground.

Leo swore and got to his feet, wiping the snow from his coat and looking around. 'Good job there was no one around to hear that, wasn't it?' He gestured with the gun. 'Get up.'

Karen gingerly got to her feet. 'You can just run off. I won't follow. I promise.'

He laughed. 'You will. It's in your nature. You can't help yourself.'

'Please, Leo, don't do this.'

She was bargaining with someone who'd shown no mercy to three other victims. Her eyes swam with tears. She sniffed as the cold, biting wind battered them, and hugged her coat tightly around her body. 'If you're going to kill me, then at least tell me I was right about Churchill. At least give me that before I die.'

He paused for a moment, then reached out to grab her arm, pulling her close and looking directly into her eyes.

He said, 'I could do better than that. I could tell you who's behind everything.'

CHAPTER THIRTY-THREE

'I think you'd better start explaining,' Sophie said as she fastened her seatbelt.

Ray started the engine and sighed. 'I'm not supposed to say anything. It's more than my job's worth.'

'She's with DC Leo Clinton. What do you know about him? Is he a danger to Karen?'

Ray shrugged.

'If she's in danger, I need to know.'

Ray didn't reply. He reversed out of the parking bay, left the car park and drove along the winding road.

They didn't see any other vehicles. The lack of traffic was understandable due to the weather. The snow was coming down heavily.

Sophie yanked her seatbelt so she could turn and face Ray. 'I'm serious. I need to know.'

She studied Ray's profile. Had she made a mistake getting in the car with him? Was he part of the network of corrupt officers that Karen was so sure existed? How deep did all this go?

'Ray?' Her voice was calmer now, but firm.

'I was asked to keep an eye on Karen. Just a bit of surveillance, that's all.' Ray kept his gaze on the road.

Sophie's mind filled with possibilities.

DS Grace was monitoring Karen. Did she suspect *Karen* could be corrupt? After everything that had happened to her, how she'd suffered at the hands of corrupt officers?

'But why are you following Karen? It doesn't make sense,' Sophie said. 'Does DS Grace think she's involved in the corruption somehow?'

Ray pushed a hand through his hair. 'I'm not very good at this undercover stuff. It's harder than I'd expected.'

'You poor thing,' Sophie snapped. 'Just tell me why you've been watching Karen.'

'It was to ensure her safety. DS Grace was concerned. She wanted to know who Karen was talking to. I think she was worried Karen might try to bring down the head guy herself.'

'Who's the head guy?'

'That's the trouble,' Ray said. 'No one knows.'

'And Leo is involved somehow?' Sophie murmured.

Leo Clinton. Sophie thought back. Leo had seemed harmless, especially compared to Arnie. He was so . . . normal.

'I don't know. I know he's worked for DCI Churchill for a long time.'

'Karen thought Churchill could be on the take,' Sophie said. 'She didn't trust him. Do you think his whole team is in on it?'

Ray shrugged as he braked for a corner. 'I really don't know. DS Grace only asked me to keep an eye on Karen, and report on who she'd been talking to and meeting with. That's it. It wasn't like I was on twenty-four-hour surveillance. I'm pretty new to this.'

Sophie could tell. She sat back in the passenger seat and thought hard as Ray slowed the car again. The snow reflected the beams from the headlights and visibility was terrible.

Maybe she'd jumped to the wrong conclusion. Perhaps they'd get back to the station and both Leo and Karen would be there. She imagined Rick laughing at her for overreacting.

But then why had Leo said his wife wanted him to pick up something for dinner if she'd left him? Sophie had never spoken to Leo about his wife. Never asked him anything about his personal life. She knew nothing about him other than he liked ham sandwiches and had worked for DCI Churchill for a few years.

Arnie didn't have all the answers. Maybe he'd got it wrong about Leo's wife, or they could have reconciled.

In a few minutes, they'd be back at Nettleham station, and then Sophie would have her answer.

She tried Karen's number again, but it went straight to voicemail. Then she tried the number of the phone Morgan had given Karen earlier that day. It just rang out. Maybe it was on silent? Perhaps, right now, Karen was back at the station having an important conversation with DS Grace and didn't want to be disturbed.

That was the most likely explanation. Sophie smoothed her skirt down over her knees. Her palms felt sweaty. She hoped Karen was safe in her meeting, but she couldn't deny the situation was very concerning.

◆ ◆ ◆

Karen's feet skidded from under her, and she fell hard on her back then tumbled a few feet down the incline. She managed to slow her fall by digging her heels in and clawing the snow with her fingers. Winded, grazed and dazed, she came to a stop at the bottom of the slope.

Leo rushed over to her. He held out a hand, but Karen ignored it and struggled to her feet without his assistance.

'So, who's this person you're going to give me?' she panted. 'Churchill is involved, isn't he?'

Leo grinned. 'No, that's the funny thing. Churchill doesn't have anything to do with it. You were wide of the mark there.'

She stared at him. 'But I was so sure.'

He grinned again. 'Nope. Churchill's just an obnoxious character. But they wouldn't involve him. He's too independent. Thinks too highly of himself. They like to get people who are vulnerable, powerless to resist.' He shrugged.

'And that's how they got you?' Karen said. 'Look, Leo, why don't we just go back to the station? You can explain it all, and we'll listen. You'll get a deal.'

'I don't think so,' Leo said.

'What's the alternative?' Karen asked, spreading her palms and looking up at the swirling snow. 'You're not going to get away with this. You're going to be remembered as a two-time cop killer.'

'That might cut me a bit of slack in prison,' he said with a wry smile.

Karen felt numb. He was going to kill her. She was defenceless. The only thing she could do was stall for time.

She put her hand in her coat pocket, feeling for the phone. Trying to dial without looking at the screen was ridiculously difficult, and she had no idea if she was pressing the right buttons, but she had to keep trying.

'Where are we going?' she asked as Leo waved her forward with the gun.

He gestured in the direction of the copse. Karen had known he was leading her there. He wasn't going to shoot her in the open, leaving a bloody mess in the snow. He'd make her walk to a secluded spot before shooting her.

She looked around at the wide-open space, nothing but white fields and a few sparse hedgerows in the distance. The shelter the bare, stumpy branches would offer was negligible. If she made a run for it, she was as good as dead.

He'd shoot her in the back. Then it would all be over. The only thing she could do was delay, and hope he let his guard down enough for her to risk grabbing the gun.

Or perhaps if she delayed long enough, they'd be discovered. Someone would be looking for her by now, wouldn't they? When she didn't turn up to the meeting with DS Grace, she'd be missed.

She thought about Mike. He'd be waiting for her tonight. When would he be concerned enough to call to ask the others where she was? Would Morgan have noticed, or would he now be at the pub, drinking and toasting memories of Anthony?

A lump formed in Karen's throat as she was overwhelmed with self-pity. How had it come to this? Why had she never suspected Leo?

They trudged slowly towards the trees. Muscles slow and awkward from the cold.

'Why did you kill Laurel Monroe and Lloyd Nelson, Leo? What did they ever do to you?'

'They didn't do anything to me. I told you, I was ordered to get rid of them.'

'But why?' Karen said. 'What did they know? Did they witness a crime? Or had they angered a criminal gang?'

Leo squinted back up the hill. 'Stop delaying. Less talking, more walking.'

He nudged her in the back with the gun, and Karen walked on towards the dark trees in the distance.

She wouldn't make it easy for him. She wouldn't kneel, close her eyes and surrender as he pressed the gun against her temple.

When they got close enough to the trees, she would try to grab the gun. Or if grabbing the weapon wasn't an option, she would run. Under cover of the trees, she'd have a chance – more chance than out in the open, anyway.

'You said you'd give me a name.' Karen rubbed her hands together, trying to get some feeling back into her cold fingers. 'Who's behind this, Leo? Who ordered you to kill them?'

◆ ◆ ◆

Sophie's heart sank as she walked into the open-plan office area. DS Grace sat at Karen's desk, her red hair falling forward as she looked down at her phone, but there was no sign of Karen.

DS Grace looked up, smiled at Sophie, but her expression changed when she saw Ray walking through the door.

'Have you seen DS Hart?' she asked, getting to her feet.

'We hoped she'd be here with you,' Sophie said, stopping beside the desk, putting her bag down and shrugging off her coat.

'She's supposed to be. We had a meeting. She wanted to tell me something.'

'Related to the corruption case?' Sophie asked.

'I can't discuss that.'

Sophie tucked her hair behind her ears. 'I realise some details will be confidential, but I'm worried about Karen. Ray's been following her.'

Grace looked at Ray sharply.

'I had to tell her something,' he said, shifting awkwardly under Grace's gaze. 'She'd figured it out, and said she'd tell the whole pub if I didn't.'

'So, where is Karen?' DS Grace asked, looking at Sophie and then at Ray. 'You're starting to worry me.'

'She left the pub with DC Leo Clinton a few minutes before we did. She should be here by now, but Leo's car isn't in the car park.'

'DC Leo Clinton?' Grace said. 'He's part of DCI Churchill's team, isn't he? Is there any reason to suspect that he's a danger to Karen?'

'If you'd asked me that a few hours ago, I would have said no, but right now, I'm not sure,' said Sophie. 'All I know is that Karen should be here, and she isn't. You've had Ray following her. I don't understand what's going on, and I'm not going to be happy until I speak to Karen and find out she's okay.'

'You've called her?'

'Yes, multiple times. She's not picking up, and neither is Leo.'

DS Grace glanced over at the window. It was dark, and the snow was falling fast. 'The weather is pretty bad. They could have had an accident. Have you checked?'

'No, but I can do that now,' Sophie said. 'And then I'm going to put a trace on Karen's phone.'

'Okay.'

Sophie got to work filling out the forms needed for the trace and contacting the officers required for approval, all the while muttering under her breath at the frustrating paperwork.

Who'd have believed it? Sophie loved paperwork. Usually, nothing made her happier than keeping her records in perfect order. Rick would laugh if he could see her now.

Where *were* Rick and Morgan? They'd probably be at the pub by now. She decided to call them as soon as she'd finished with the trace.

She checked the time. The superintendent often worked late. She might still be in her office.

Maybe Sophie would be teased for overreacting tomorrow, but it was a chance she had to take.

'I'll be back soon.' She stood up. 'I've put requests in for both phones.'

'Both phones?' Grace queried, raising her eyebrows.

'Yes, Karen's phone hasn't been working properly, then she left it behind at a crime scene, so DI Morgan lent her an old one. I think she's got both of them on her, so I traced them both.'

'Okay, good.'

Sophie left DS Grace and Ray and raced up the stairs, taking the steps two at a time. Pamela, the superintendent's assistant, was not at her desk. Sophie felt deflated when she saw the lights were off in the superintendent's office too.

Did she dare phone the super at home? No, she was better off trying Morgan again first. She turned away and walked straight into Assistant Chief Constable Fry, who'd just exited the gents' toilets.

'Oh, sorry, sir,' Sophie said.

'No trouble. Were you looking for the superintendent?'

'Yes, I was. She doesn't seem to be in her office, though.'

'No, you just missed her. We were finishing up a meeting when she had a call to say her son had been injured at his karate club. Dislocated his shoulder. Can I help?'

Sophie hesitated. Could she tell the assistant chief constable? She'd look ridiculous if Karen walked in the station safe and sound in the next few minutes.

She pushed her curly hair back from her face and looked up at Fry. He was offering to help, and her gut told her Karen was in trouble. So what if she was the butt of the station jokes tomorrow? It was better than not doing anything now and regretting it later.

'Actually, sir, I think you might be able to help,' Sophie said, and began to fill him in. It took her a couple of minutes to explain everything to Fry's satisfaction.

Finally, he looked at her with a grave expression and said, 'Let's go downstairs and talk to DS Grace. As you may know, I've been supervising the corruption investigation under Chief Constable Grayson.'

'I do, sir.'

'Karen hasn't been out of contact for long.'

'No, sir. It's just we can't get in touch with her, and she was supposed to meet DS Grace half an hour ago.'

How could she make him understand? She couldn't explain it was just a sense something was wrong – small things that didn't feel right, which on their own could be explained away, but together . . .

Why would Leo lie about his wife unless it was a way to make him blend in, seem harmless? Picking up groceries on his way home from work was a perfectly normal reason to leave the pub and offer Karen a lift.

Maybe Leo had left the note on Karen's desk. Was he gaslighting them? Trying to make people think Karen was losing it, that she couldn't be trusted?

But Leo? Could he be responsible? He was so affable, so pleasant, so normal. If Karen was right and DCI Shaw was killed because he knew something about the corruption network, then Karen's life might be in danger too.

But why would Leo be involved? Money, she supposed. It always came down to money and power.

'I've initiated a trace on Karen's phone, sir. I'm still waiting for authorisation, but hopefully we can locate her from her phone signal.'

'Right. Has anyone called in at her house?'

'Not yet, sir. I could ask a uniform to do so.'

'Yes, that's a good idea. Have you spoken to her boyfriend? Mike, is it?'

'Not yet. I didn't want to worry him.'

'Call him. Do you have his number?'

'I do.'

'Don't let on that we're concerned, just ask if he's seen or spoken to Karen. Now, let's go and talk to DS Grace.'

As she walked back downstairs, this time with ACC Fry, Sophie called Mike. Trying not to give him a reason to panic, she infused her voice with a cheerful tone, explaining that Karen's phone had been playing up so it was nothing to worry about, but had he spoken to Karen recently?

He hadn't.

Feeling guilty, Sophie made an excuse and hung up before he asked too many questions.

Fry and Sophie walked into the open-plan office area. DS Grace was pacing beside Karen's desk, and Ray sat on one of the wheeled padded chairs, pushing with his feet so he turned in a slow semicircle.

Assistant Chief Constable Fry took charge. He nodded at DS Gray and Ray, and said, 'I understand you were supposed to be meeting DS Hart here this evening.'

'I was, sir,' DS Grace said as she stopped pacing. 'But she hasn't shown up. Her colleague, DC Jones, is worried about her. She left the drinks for DCI Anthony Shaw in the company of DC Leo Clinton. He was supposed to be driving her back here.'

'We've checked, and no accidents have been reported in the vicinity,' Ray said. 'And we didn't pass them on the way back. They should have travelled the same route we did back to the station.'

'Right. Well, let's get these phone traces organised.'

It seemed to take forever for the authorisations to come through, so Fry made a call to fast-track the process, and after that, they managed to get locations for the phones.

'I've got two different locations,' Sophie said, frowning at the screen. 'Karen's phone was last detected on Welton Road, near the Heath Lane turning. But the phone DI Morgan gave Karen is on Eastfield Lane. No, hang on. It's not exactly Eastfield Lane. It looks like she's in the middle of some fields . . . or at least the phone is.' Sophie looked over her shoulder at ACC Fry. 'Something is seriously wrong, sir.'

'I agree. Did you trace Leo Clinton's phone?'

Sophie frowned. 'No, I didn't think to do that.'

'Okay, I'll authorise it directly, and then I think you and I should go to the locations and check them out.'

'Absolutely.' Sophie tapped away furiously on the keyboard, setting up the trace for Leo's phone as ACC Fry discussed Karen's possible whereabouts with DS Grace.

Just as Sophie was finishing up, she heard Ray say, 'I think Karen knew I was following her. She saw me at the cathedral, and she saw me lingering outside after the meeting you had with the chief constable. I was waiting to talk to you, but of course I couldn't tell her that. I made up a stupid excuse about wanting to see DCI Churchill.' He shot a sheepish glance at DS Grace. 'Sorry.'

'We'll talk about it later, PC Watts,' Grace said. 'I'm more concerned with the fact that you blabbed as soon as DC Jones started asking you questions.'

He grimaced and apologised again.

'The last signal from Leo's and Karen's phones are at the same location,' Sophie said. 'Welton Road.'

'And you're still getting a signal from the phone DI Morgan gave to Karen?'

'Yes – according to this, the signal is coming from farmland,' Sophie said, shaking her head again. 'I don't understand it, but that's what the data is telling me.'

'Right,' ACC Fry said. 'I'm going to collect my jacket, and I'll meet you downstairs in reception, DC Jones.'

Sophie nodded and began to log out of the system. A moment later, she grabbed her coat and bag, said a hurried goodbye to Ray and DS Grace, and hurtled out of the open-plan office.

On her way downstairs she dialled Rick's number. This time he answered. 'Rick! Where have you been?'

'Waddington. At the Picketts' house. I've been there with DI Morgan. We're on our way back now. Took longer than we expected. Why? Have you lot drunk the pub dry?'

'No, listen, this is serious. I'm really worried about Karen.'

'Why? What's happened?'

'I don't know where she is, Rick. I can't get a hold of her. She was supposed to meet DS Grace, and she didn't turn up. Leo offered to drive her back to the station.'

'Do you think they've had an accident?'

'We've checked. There have been no accidents reported, and I took the route they should have done from the pub to the station and didn't see the car or evidence of an RTA. I've traced Karen's phones, both of them, and they're in two different locations. That's where we're going now.'

'Right. Okay, hang on a minute.' She heard a muffled noise and guessed that Rick was talking to Morgan. A moment later, his voice came back on, loud and clear. 'We're heading to the station now.'

'Okay. I'm going to the locations we got from Karen's phones with ACC Fry.'

'Assistant Chief Constable Fry? What's he doing there?'

'He was having a meeting with the superintendent when she got called away. Her son's hurt his shoulder or something. Anyway, I'll call you later. I've got to go.'

She hung up and burst into the reception area, where ACC Fry was waiting by the door.

CHAPTER THIRTY-FOUR

Before getting into Fry's Qashqai, Sophie picked up a child's toy from the passenger seat.

'Sorry,' he said. 'This is my wife's car. She's always ferrying the grandchildren about.' He took the toy from her and put it on the back seat.

'Did they find your car, sir? It was stolen, wasn't it?' Sophie asked.

He glowered, and Sophie winced. She probably shouldn't have mentioned it.

'Yes, it was found, burnt out in a field. Hooligans,' he muttered, and pulled out of the station car park.

The windscreen wipers were on full speed, but the snow was coming down at a tremendous rate, making it very difficult to make out the road ahead. Fry drove infuriatingly slowly. Sophie clutched her hands together in her lap and tapped her foot.

It seemed to take forever to get there, and when they finally arrived at the spot, there was nothing to be seen except snow-covered verges, bare hedgerows, and dirty grey snow churned up on the road.

There was no sign of Karen or Leo – or Leo's car.

As soon as Fry brought the Qashqai to a halt, Sophie got out to look around. There were no streetlights, but the snow made the landscape seem brighter than it otherwise would have been on a cloudy night. It was quiet and still. No sounds from approaching traffic.

Maybe the car had broken down, and they'd had to walk – but then where was the car? They hadn't passed it on their way back from the pub.

She pulled out her mobile and dialled Karen's number. Nearby, a phone rang, a cheerful tinkling sound that seemed out of place in the snowy silence.

Sophie looked around and saw a glowing light coming from the snow at the side of the road. The phone was already half covered by a blanket of white. She pulled a pair of thin nitrile gloves from her pocket, tugged them on and snatched up the phone. The screen was cracked. She noticed another phone a short distance away. That had to be Leo's. Holding both, she turned to look at ACC Fry.

'Maybe they were stolen?' he suggested.

'But why would their phones be thrown away like this?' Sophie asked. 'It doesn't make sense.'

She scanned the area. There was no sign of a crash, no footprints in the snow except their own. Unless the recently fallen snow had covered them.

There was no damage to the verges or to the hedgerow. It didn't look like the scene of a recent accident.

The air was so cold her breath came out in steamy plumes. She tucked her hair behind her ears and tried to think what could have happened here. The phones had been discarded. Why? Had Leo wanted to make sure they couldn't be followed? Had he thrown away the phones so he was untraceable? Maybe he didn't know Karen still had the phone Morgan had given her.

Sophie looked around again, then went back to the car to get her bag and rummage around for evidence bags. She put the phones in separate bags. Hopefully, that was overkill, but she couldn't be too sure. She put them on the back seat.

'Sir, I think we should put out a local alert for Leo's car.'

'Do you know the registration number?'

'I do.' Sophie had made a note of it while waiting for the phone trace requests to be processed.

'Let's not jump the gun. Let's see if we can find them at the second location.'

Sophie agreed and got back into the car.

It took them five minutes to get to the next location. Despite Fry driving at a snail's pace, the tyres lost traction, sliding over the snow as they took the final turn into Eastfield Lane. Sophie's stomach lurched as the car began to spin. Leo's car was parked in the lay-by just ahead, and their out-of-control Qashqai was heading straight for it. She held her breath as Fry wrestled with the steering wheel, possibly doing more harm than good, but somehow he managed to keep control.

He exhaled and pushed back in his seat as the car came to a stop a short distance from Leo's. 'That was a close one.'

After Fry edged the vehicle closer to the side of the road, they both got out of the car. Leo's vehicle was empty.

Sophie stared out at the white landscape.

It was hard to see through the swirling snow. The stark whiteness covered everything. Nothing but fields and a copse of trees in the distance.

She looked for footsteps around Leo's car and spotted a disturbance on the grass verge. It looked like someone had recently travelled over it, but where had they gone? Through the gap in the hedge and into the fields. That was the only way they could have gone.

Sophie pointed it out to ACC Fry, who nodded grimly.

The snow flurries made it hard to see, and the cold made it hard to concentrate. Sophie zipped up her coat, scanning the field. How would they find them in this? They needed backup. She needed to call Rick and Morgan. Get more people down here. Start a proper search.

Then, suddenly, Sophie's gaze stopped moving across the landscape as she spotted something.

'Wait, is that them, over there?' She pointed.

ACC Fry stepped beside her. 'Where?'

'I saw something moving over there by the trees. Do you see them?'

'Yes, I think I do. Yes, that's them.'

'Karen!' Sophie shouted, but ACC Fry shushed her.

'No. Don't shout. We don't know what's going on. She could be in trouble. Let's go after them.'

'I'll call for backup,' Sophie said.

'No, I'll do it. They'll act quickly if it's the assistant chief constable on the phone.' Fry pulled out his mobile and began to issue orders, asking for more officers on the scene.

Sophie stared at the distant figures, dark against the snow. They needed to act now. They couldn't wait for backup. If Karen and Leo disappeared into the trees, they'd lose sight of them.

'We'd better follow them, sir,' Sophie said as he continued to talk on the phone.

He nodded his agreement, and Sophie moved towards the gap in the hedgerow. She tried to jump over the ditch but landed awkwardly with one foot in ice-cold water. She sucked in a breath of frigid air and then swore under her breath.

With one sodden foot, she pushed her way through the prickly hawthorn hedge. ACC Fry managed to follow with his mobile still clamped to his ear, and they set off down the slippery slope. Twice, Sophie fell hard on her backside, but she pushed herself up and carried on. Her right foot was so cold, she couldn't feel her toes, but she kept moving.

ACC Fry muttered orders into his phone as they walked.

Then Sophie's phone rang.

Karen.

◆ ◆ ◆

Karen ran the tips of her fingers along the front of the old-fashioned phone. It was a good job it *was* old. She had no idea how she'd have been able to dial on a touchscreen phone while it was in her pocket.

She could try 999. Was nine at the bottom right, or was that the asterisk? She couldn't remember, but then a thought occurred to her. The last number redial. If she pressed the large rectangular button on the left, which was the green dial button, that should eventually connect her to the previous number she'd called.

Who had that been? Sophie. Karen pressed the button three times. There was no indication that the call had connected, or been answered, but she had to hope it had worked.

Somehow they had to find out where she was, and get to her before Leo put a bullet in her brain.

'You're just full of talk, Leo,' Karen said. 'I bet you don't know who's behind it all. You've probably been following an anonymous set of instructions like a complete idiot.'

'I know what you're trying to do, Karen. It won't work.'

'What exactly am I trying to do?'

'You're trying to turn me against them. Make me feel like they don't care about me.' He laughed.

'Well, they don't. They won't show you any loyalty. Think about Freeman. They just left him to rot.'

'Freeman knows to keep quiet. If he doesn't, an unfortunate accident will occur involving a member of his family. Look,

297

whatever you say now, it's not going to help. We're not some kind of brotherhood. We're not friends. I don't expect them to save me.'

'Then talk to me, Leo,' she said. 'Give me the ringleader's name. Maybe I can help. Maybe we can swing this, so you don't get the blame. Why should you go down for Churchill?'

'I told you, it's not Churchill. He's not involved.'

'Right. So who is?'

'Do you really want to know?' Leo laughed. He was enjoying stringing her along.

'Yes. You said you'd give me a name. So stop playing games.'

He cocked his head to the side, eyes narrowed, cheeks red from cold. 'You want to know who issued the order to despatch your dear friend, DCI Shaw.'

Karen swallowed back the bitterness. 'Yes.'

'It was ACC Fry. Of course, I'm not allowed to refer to him like that. I have to call him Eagle. Can you believe it?' He snorted. 'Eagle. The ego of the man is unbelievable. My code name is Sparrow. He picked that too . . . What's the matter, Karen? Cat got your tongue?'

◆　◆　◆

Sophie had the phone pressed hard against her ear. She hadn't heard every word clearly, but she'd certainly got the gist.

She turned and looked in horror at the man standing beside her. Assistant Chief Constable Fry.

'What's wrong?' he said, slightly out of breath from walking in the deep snow.

For a moment, Sophie couldn't speak. Words caught in her throat, but eventually she managed to squeak out, 'N . . . nothing.'

'Who was on the phone?'

'Wrong number.'

He snatched it from her and looked at the screen. 'Is it still connected?'

'I—'

He shouted down the phone, 'Sparrow!' Then he threw Sophie's phone on the ground. 'Come on.'

They struggled. Sophie snatched her phone back, but he grabbed at her elbow and yanked her along, pulling her down the slope.

Sophie tried to pull away, but he was much stronger than her. 'No, wait! I think we should wait for backup.' Sophie tried to stop their momentum. 'It's not safe—'

'Stupid, stupid Sparrow.' Fry spat the words out as they continued down. His face was flushed with rage.

'Who's Sparrow? I don't know what you're talking about,' Sophie said, looking around desperately for a way to escape.

ACC Fry gave her a sharp look. 'I think you do, DC Jones. That's the trouble.'

Sophie shook her head, staring at him as their steps grew faster until they were running down the hill. How could this be happening?

The assistant chief constable. He was so high up. How could he possibly be involved in this?

'How could you, sir?' Sophie said quietly. 'How could you betray the police service and the officers you've worked alongside for so long?'

'Oh, do shut up, you self-righteous little fool,' Fry said. 'Keep moving. We need to find them.'

'Why are you so bothered? You don't care about Karen.'

He shot her a look then, and understanding dawned. Sophie realised he didn't want to find Karen to save her. He wanted to kill her, and Sophie was now expendable too.

She knew too much. She couldn't possibly get out of this alive.

She'd wanted to help, but she'd messed up. She'd brought Fry, a wolf in sheep's clothing, straight to Karen.

Sophie shouted out to warn her.

The two figures were moving near the trees. Had they heard? She couldn't tell. But before she could shout again, ACC Fry raised his fist, and the blow that hit the side of her head knocked Sophie off her feet.

Her body crumpled. Her face hit the snow, hard. She tasted the metallic tang of blood, and then everything went black.

CHAPTER THIRTY-FIVE

'Sparrow!'

Karen's spirits sank even lower when she saw ACC Fry striding towards them, his long legs wading through the snow.

Karen felt a wave of helplessness wash over her. Her chances had been small before, but now . . . She might have managed to catch Leo off guard and grab the gun. But against two of them, she didn't stand a chance.

Leo looked irritated at the interruption. His face was pinched and angry as Fry approached.

She didn't have long to think it through or plan a route of escape, but she knew this distraction was her best chance. Her only chance. She set off at a sprint, darting into the trees, hoping they'd provide protection. If he shot her now, then at least she'd die trying to escape.

The snow slowed her progress. Branches scratched at her clothing. She tripped over a fallen tree and went sprawling, hitting the ground with a thud. The fall made her head spin, but she got up and kept moving, sucking icy air into her lungs.

'Shoot her, you fool!' Fry yelled, but she didn't stop. She didn't slow down.

There were footsteps behind her and heavy breathing, and then suddenly she felt hands on her shoulders, forcing her to the floor.

She tried to stay upright, but her legs buckled and she fell – landing on something hard, buried beneath the snow, the air forced from her lungs.

'Got you,' she heard Leo snarl. 'Don't try that again.'

His voice was strong, but he was shaking from the effort of chasing her down.

Karen's hands touched the painful spot on her ribs. A broken branch lay under her.

As he tried to haul her up, she grabbed the branch, raised it and brought it down on his head. Leo released a string of swear words but didn't loosen his grip.

He pushed her hard against the rough bark of a bare oak tree. It scratched against her cheek. She was too out of breath to speak.

He wiped away the blood from his forehead as Fry reached them, short of breath and panting.

Fry bent at the waist, hands on his knees as he recovered from the exertion.

Leo had Karen's arm secured behind her back, making it painful to move. She begged, 'Please, Leo, don't do this. You're not a killer. Not really.'

He leaned closer to whisper in her ear. 'I am, though, Karen. I killed DCI Shaw, Lloyd Nelson and Laurel Monroe.'

'Why?' Karen tried to push away from the tree, but Leo pinned her firmly.

'Because he did as he was told,' ACC Fry said as he reached them. 'Now, follow orders, Sparrow. Shoot her. It's the only way. She won't keep quiet.'

'You ordered him to kill Anthony?' Karen asked, turning her head to look him in the eye, the man who had ordered the death of her friend.

'Yes,' Fry said. 'Although I had nothing to do with the ridiculous cleansing serial-killer idea. That was all him.' He gestured in Leo's direction. 'Absurd. It was almost as if he wanted to get caught.'

Karen felt Leo tense. She twisted until she could see his face. 'You did, didn't you? You wanted to get caught?'

Leo's face slackened. 'I—'

'Enough! Stop wasting time. Shoot her!' Fry roared.

'I don't know if it's escaped your attention, but I'm the one holding the gun,' Leo said through gritted teeth. 'I'll decide what we do next.'

'You don't have to listen to him anymore, Leo,' Karen said. 'He's treating you like a puppet, pulling your strings, manipulating you.'

'I said shoot her!' ACC Fry shouted. 'If you don't do it, I will.' He made a move to grab the gun from Leo, but Leo stepped back, raising it, pointing it menacingly at the assistant chief constable.

'Get back,' he snarled.

Fry took a step back. 'Calm down. What's got into you?'

'Don't listen to him, Leo. He's wrecked your life. He's ruined so many people's lives.'

'Shut up!' Fry snarled. 'If you don't shoot her, then we'll all get caught. You'll go down for this, Sparrow, and I'll make sure I find your wife – even if she is in Spain, she's not out of my reach.'

Leo hesitated.

'The only way out of this,' Fry continued, 'is to shoot them both.'

'Both?' Karen asked, trying to slow her breathing.

'You and the unfortunate DC Jones. She's been looking for you. She wanted to tell the superintendent you were missing. Fortunately, I intercepted her.' He scowled at Leo. 'I had to clean up your mess.'

'Where is she now?' Leo asked.

'What?' Fry asked.

'DC Jones, Sophie. Where is she?'

'Back there.' He waved a hand. 'At the edge of the woods.'

'You left her there alone,' Leo said incredulously. 'And you say I'm the fool?'

'It's fine. She's unconscious. Out cold.'

Karen fought the urge to be sick. This couldn't be happening. Not Sophie.

'Please.' Karen struggled to turn around. 'Sophie doesn't know anything. She's no threat to you. Please just let her go. I'll do anything you want, just let her go.'

'Unfortunately, she is a threat, thanks to your phone call.'

Leo looked at Karen and then back at Fry. 'What phone call? She hasn't got a phone. I took it. Got rid of both of our phones.'

'DI Morgan gave Karen a spare phone today. You obviously didn't search her, and threw away only one of her phones. She called Sophie just a few minutes ago. I saw Sophie's reaction. You must have mentioned my name because, after the phone call, she looked at me as though I'd grown two heads.'

Leo gave a frustrated grunt and kicked the tree. 'Come on,' he said, yanking Karen away from the trunk and pushing her forward. 'Don't try to run away again. I will shoot you in the back if you so much as look in the wrong direction.' Then he turned. 'Show us where Sophie is,' he instructed Fry, who nodded and set off.

◆ ◆ ◆

Sophie was dreaming. She was at home in bed, but for some reason, she was freezing. So, so cold. She reached for the duvet, but her hand touched something else. Snow. Her eyes blinked open, and she looked around. She remembered where she was and what had happened with a sickening jolt.

Her lip was swollen and sore. She sat up quickly, which made her head spin. He'd left her. Would he be coming back?

She frantically patted down her coat pockets. Had he taken her mobile? She felt the reassuring solid rectangle of the phone and yanked it out of her pocket. Then, looking around wildly, expecting Fry to return at any moment, she dialled Morgan's number.

◆ ◆ ◆

Karen's chest tightened when she saw Sophie. She looked dazed and disorientated, but she was conscious and sitting up.

How could Karen get them both out of this mess? All she could do was try to pry Fry and Leo apart, divide their loyalties and make them realise they weren't on the same side. She needed them to turn on each other if they were to have any chance of getting out of this situation.

'You have to kill them,' Fry said, and turned around to face Leo. 'There's no other way. We'll make up a story. Maybe you stopped to help a man whose car had broken down, but it was a trick. It was The Cleanser. The serial killer overpowered you at the side of the road. We'll come up with a description, keep our stories straight. Say he had a gun. Maybe I could shoot you in the leg, just a graze. It would lend weight to the story. I'll say when I arrived with Sophie, we all tackled the killer, but sadly two officers lost their lives in the process.' Fry looked at Karen.

He'd really thought it through. But surely the story wouldn't be believed. The timings wouldn't match up, for a start.

Leo prodded Karen in the back, warning her to keep walking.

When Sophie spotted them, she tried to get up and run, but she took two steps and then fell, her hand clutching her head.

'Stay there, or he'll shoot!' Fry yelled, and Sophie froze.

When they reached Sophie, Karen fell to her knees.

'I'm so sorry,' she said. 'Are you injured?' Karen took in Sophie's cut lip, the blossoming bruise on her cheekbone, and put her arm around the young officer's shoulders.

'I'm sorry, Sarge. I knew you were in trouble. I thought I could help. I didn't realise I was bringing that monster out here, leading him to you.' She looked at Leo. 'How could you?'

Leo rolled his eyes. 'All right. Enough talking. Get up and give me your phone.'

'You don't have time to get away,' Sophie said, holding out her mobile. 'He's already phoned for backup. They'll be here within minutes.' She looked at Fry, who chuckled.

'Don't be ridiculous. I was only pretending to call. Honestly, if you're representative of the state of detectives in the force these days, it's surprising cases get solved at all.'

'You're the assistant chief constable! And you couldn't even prevent your own car from getting stolen, let alone find out who did it!' Sophie said bitterly.

Sophie's words hit Karen like a bolt of energy. Why hadn't she made the connection earlier? It was Fry. He was the missing piece of the puzzle.

Karen pushed up from the floor. 'It was you. You're the person who links all of the victims – Laurel Monroe, Lloyd Nelson. It was your car.'

Fry scoffed. 'I don't know what you're ranting about. Are you deranged?'

'You know exactly what I'm talking about,' Karen said. 'What were you doing on Friday night? What time did your car get stolen?'

He glared down at Karen, and for a moment she thought he was going to deny everything, but then he just laughed. 'I suppose it doesn't matter since you won't be alive to tell anyone. It's been an entertaining few months, Karen, watching you running around trying to integrate yourself in the corruption case. So brave,' he said mockingly. 'And there I was, supervising the whole thing, and you had no idea.'

'I don't understand.' Sophie shakily got to her feet, and Karen reached out to steady her. 'You're The Cleanser. You killed Laurel, and Lloyd, and DCI Shaw?'

'No,' Fry said with a sigh. 'Leo did that.'

Sophie's eyes widened, and she clutched Karen's arm. 'What?'

'Walk,' Leo said, waving the gun. 'Back to the car.'

'Why?' Fry scowled. 'Shoot them here. We don't want to be seen. Do it now.'

'I've got the gun. I'm in charge now.'

Fry muttered under his breath, 'You're a fool.'

'Can somebody just . . . tell me what is going on?' Sophie said.

'ACC Fry knocked Sam Pickett off his bike,' Karen said, rubbing her sore ribs. 'He left him to die at the side of the road. But it wasn't a hit-and-run with no witnesses as we thought. I'd bet there were at least two. Lloyd Nelson and Laurel Monroe. They didn't tell anyone. Perhaps because they were worried they'd be in trouble. Lloyd was driving without a licence. Maybe Laurel was under the influence of cocaine. Whatever their reasons, they didn't come forward. But what they didn't know was that ACC Fry didn't want any witnesses who might suffer a pang of conscience. Isn't that right, *Assistant Chief Constable*?' Karen gave him a scathing look.

Leo laughed. 'You've got to be impressed, *Eagle*. She worked it out. I didn't tell her about the accident.'

Fry narrowed his eyes.

Karen turned to Leo. 'And then you cleaned up his mess. You killed the witnesses, made it look like a deranged serial killer was responsible. You probably took Fry's car and set it alight to destroy the evidence for him, but the one part of all this I don't understand is Anthony. He didn't witness the accident, did he?'

Leo shook his head. 'He was on to me. Well, at least, it was looking that way. I overheard him on the phone to Alice Price. He wanted to ask Alice about the other officers on Churchill's team. Seems he wasn't as convinced as you that Churchill was behind it all.'

'So Anthony suspected you were involved, and you killed him so he couldn't tell me?'

'That's about the size of it. Though I was happy to wait to find out how much he really knew, Eagle wanted him eliminated,' Leo said, meeting Karen's gaze. His face was devoid of expression. No regret. No pity. Nothing. His eyes never left hers. 'So, now you can see I'm well and truly evil.'

Karen was shaking with rage. After butchering Laurel Monroe, Leo had interviewed Laurel's sister, offering false sympathy for her loss. He'd produced a letter, supposedly from The Cleanser, and pretended to be concerned for his own safety. He'd sent a letter to *Morgan*. She wanted to snatch the gun from him, press it to his head and hear him beg for his life. Would she show him mercy? He hadn't shown any to Anthony.

Karen screwed her eyes shut, trying to push away images of Anthony lying dead on the floor of his home, his forehead cut and bloody. 'Why did you send a letter to Morgan asking about his sins? We thought he was in danger.'

'Fry didn't want the same team working on the hit-and-run and the murders,' Leo said. 'He thought if Morgan's team worked both cases, you'd be more likely to pick up on a connection. I had nothing on Morgan. The man's as clean as a whistle, but the letter was enough to make the superintendent take him off the case.'

'None of that matters now,' Fry said, dismissing Leo with a wave of his hand and focusing on Karen. 'Tonight, you and Sophie are going to be victims of The Cleanser – his *final* victims.' He turned to Leo. 'You've been pushing your luck. This nonsense ends now.'

'Wait! Tell me about Charlie Cook. Did you authorise it?'

'I have no idea what you're talking about,' Fry said.

'Charlie Cook forced my husband off the road. Did you give him the go-ahead? Did you try to have me killed?'

'That was all down to the Cooks. Nothing to do with me.'

'But you helped cover it up? You ordered Freeman to pay off the traffic officers and cover up the fact Charlie Cook murdered my husband and daughter?'

He said nothing.

'I hope you rot in hell.'

Fry raised a fist, breathing heavily. 'If you don't shoot them, Sparrow, I will.'

'But it won't be the same,' Sophie said. 'The Cleanser's victims weren't shot.'

'No,' Leo said, pulling out a rope from his pocket. 'They were strangled.'

Karen's stomach lurched. Her mouth was dry as she stepped in front of Sophie. 'Don't do this, Leo. This is your last chance. You could blame it all on Fry. Let's do that. We'll all say it was ACC Fry. We'll be your witnesses, your defence.'

'That won't work,' Leo said calmly. 'I was careful, but there's always something left behind. Forensics might not be good enough at the moment to put me away, but techniques will improve. Eventually, they'll come for me. And you . . .' His mouth lifted in a smile. 'You don't have it in you to lie.'

'Please, Leo,' she said, desperate to get through to him. She had to save Sophie, if nothing else.

Leo held the thin white rope out to Fry. 'You do it.'

Fry studied the rope in horror but made no move to take it. 'This is what you used to strangle them?'

'Yes.' Leo tossed the rope at Fry.

He caught it, stared down at the rope and then wrapped the end around his fist and looked at Sophie.

Karen imagined Morgan and Rick standing in the field beside their bodies, staring down at the crosses on their foreheads. She thought of Josh and Tilly. Of how this all started. It seemed such a long time ago. She pictured Mike sitting by the phone, wondering where she was and why she wasn't answering.

Then she turned and shouted, 'Sophie, run!'

But Fry's legs were longer, and he reached Sophie in a few strides, wrapping his arms around her so hers were pinned to her sides.

'Enough of this,' he growled as he tried to stop Sophie kicking his legs. 'Just shoot them. We'll just say The Cleanser changed his MO because we attacked him, but he managed to escape.'

Leo lifted his gun, and Karen shut her eyes.

The gunshot was so loud. The sound echoed in her ears, and she waited for the bloom of pain but felt nothing. Had he shot Sophie? She opened her eyes, but Sophie was standing beside her. Then she saw ACC Fry lying on the floor, a bullet hole in the middle of his forehead, his blood seeping into the snow.

'Leo, you've done the right thing,' Karen said. Her voice trembled. 'You can put the gun down now. Let's go back to the station, all right?'

But Leo laughed. 'Sorry, but that's not how this ends. Come on.' He gestured for them to walk back to the road.

They slipped and slid up the snowy slope. Karen's hands and feet were numb. Pale and trembling, Sophie climbed the hill in front of them.

Karen had to get Leo talking. She needed to make a connection. Now that Fry was out of the picture, perhaps she and Sophie could work together to get the gun. But what if it went off during a struggle? How would she live with herself if Sophie was shot?

'What are you g . . . going to do?' Sophie asked when they got back to Leo's car.

'I'm going to handcuff you to the doors,' he said, opening the boot and pulling out handcuffs. He ordered them both to sit in the back of the car and attached Karen's left hand to one of the rear passenger doors. Then did the same with Sophie on the other side.

He slammed the doors on them and then got in the front and began to drive. Sophie looked over her shoulder, back at the quiet road behind them. She leaned across, rested her head on Karen's shoulder and whispered, 'I called Morgan.'

'Stop talking,' Leo barked as he indicated right and turned on to a larger road. The snow had been cleared, and he accelerated away from the murder scene.

'What are you doing, Leo? What's your plan?'

'My plans have never mattered. I was sick and tired of being a tool for Fry, but there's no way back for me now.'

'It doesn't have to end this way.'

'No?' He smiled. 'Maybe I'll drive to the coast and get a boat. I could go to Spain and see my daughter,' he said.

He was dreaming if he thought he'd be able to get out of the country. 'They're going to be looking for you, Leo. Just put the gun down, take us back to the station. We'll find a way through this together.'

'You don't mean that. I killed your boss, Karen. That was me. Yes, I might have been pressured into it. I might have been blackmailed, but I did it.'

'Are you going to kill us?' Sophie's voice was so quiet it was almost a whisper.

'I didn't plan for this,' Leo muttered. 'I never wanted any of it.' He glanced in the rear-view mirror, looking at Karen. 'You should know that I wasn't going to kill you in the woods. I was heading to an old barn on the other side of the copse. I was going to use the rope to tie you up, so I'd have enough time to get away, then I was going to call it in, let them know where you were. I wouldn't have hurt you.'

Karen turned to look out of the window. Pain was radiating around her ribcage. He *had* hurt her. And as for his victims . . . He may have been coerced, but he was still a killer.

His face crumpled. 'I don't know what to do. I'm out of options.'

'What was your original plan, Leo?' Karen asked. 'You wanted to get caught?'

'I couldn't see any other way. I've been living with Fry's threats for years, doing his dirty work. Handling his bribes, disposing of people who got in his way.' He met Karen's gaze in the rear-view mirror again. 'Alice Price was wrong about Churchill. It was me she heard. I was in Churchill's office, putting pressure on some poor sod to cough up the money he owed Fry.'

Karen thought of Alice. Her accusations of corruption in the force had been ignored. She'd been broken by the fallout, her career ruined.

Fry had hit upon the truth when he'd said Leo took on the role of serial killer because he wanted to get caught, though the assistant chief constable hadn't been perceptive enough to realise it. The scheme had been Leo's way of ending his involvement with Fry. He couldn't hand himself in and come clean, because that would have put his family at risk. Instead, he wanted to be put away for murder. As long as he stayed quiet while he served his time, his wife and daughter would be safe. Though, as a cop, Leo's time in prison wouldn't be easy.

Leo was a desperate man, looking for a way out.

He had been ordered to kill Anthony, Laurel and Lloyd. If he'd refused, his wife and daughter would have been in danger. But he hadn't just killed them. He'd mutilated their corpses, carved crosses into their flesh. Could a sane person do that? Perhaps if they'd been used as a contract killer for years, if they were desensitised to the act enough to—

Karen's thoughts were interrupted by Sophie asking, 'How many deaths were there?'

Leo shook his head. His hands tightened on the wheel. 'I didn't want to kill anyone.'

'Can't you just stop the car and let us go?' Sophie asked, her voice shaking.

'Quiet,' Leo snapped. 'I'm trying to think.'

After five minutes, he indicated as they approached a service station. 'We need petrol,' he said.

But as he rounded the corner, flashing blue lights appeared in the rear-view mirror. Sirens blared.

Leo pressed the brakes hard, twisting around to look at the approaching vehicles.

Within seconds, they were surrounded by police cars. Leo sat still, one hand on the steering wheel, his other hand on the gun.

'Let us go, Leo,' Karen pleaded. 'You won't be hurt if you do.'

'I'll go to prison.'

Yes, Karen wanted to say, *and you'll deserve it for what you've done.*

She needed to de-escalate the situation, fast.

He lifted the gun, and Karen held her breath. But instead of angling it at them, he placed it against his temple.

Shouts came from outside the vehicle, ordering them all to get out of the car with their hands raised.

'I know you don't owe me anything,' he said, turning to face Karen as the blue lights lit up the interior of the car, 'but if you could tell my daughter that, despite all this, I loved her, I'd appreciate it. I'm sorry how things worked out.'

'Leo—' Karen started to say, but it was too late. He squeezed the trigger.

The sound of the gun going off in the small, enclosed space was deafening. Karen and Sophie both recoiled at the shock.

Blood splattered the windows, and Karen felt some hit her cheek. She fumbled with the door handle, desperate to get it open. She couldn't raise her arms, so instead screamed out, 'Police!'

The lights and the swarming officers made a confusing sight. Marksmen approached the vehicle, weapons trained on the car and its occupants.

Within seconds, they were surrounded by armed police, who soon realised Leo was no longer a threat. A senior officer began to bark orders, telling them to release the handcuffs.

After her arm was free, Karen managed to stand, but her legs were trembling. She looked behind her to make sure Sophie was okay and saw Rick beside her.

He wrapped his arms around Sophie and squeezed. 'That was the worst hour of my life.'

'It wouldn't make my top-ten best moments either,' Sophie said, her teeth chattering.

Karen jumped when a hand touched her shoulder. She turned to see Morgan. Her chest tightened. 'It's over.'

'Yes,' he said, looking more stressed than she'd ever seen him. 'It's over now.'

'Sophie managed to call you?'

'Yes, we found Fry's body. We had an all-units alert on Leo Clinton's car. Got word it was on the A46.'

Karen looked around at the vast number of officers and vehicles. 'Nice to know we were missed.'

'You'll be pleased to know the superintendent threw everything we had at tracking you down. The budget went out of the window.' He pointed at an ambulance that had just come to a stop behind the police vehicles. 'Come on, you'd better get checked out.'

'I'm fine,' Karen said, though the pain in her ribs forced her to take shallow breaths.

'You say that a lot. You know that it's okay to admit you're not fine?'

'Now you sound like my mum.' She pulled a face.

He grinned. 'You're still getting checked out by the paramedics.'

As they walked towards the ambulance, Morgan said quietly, 'I had no idea.'

Karen shook her head. 'Me neither. He had all of us fooled.'

CHAPTER THIRTY-SIX

It had taken two weeks for the bruises on Karen's ribs to turn from purple to a faded yellow. She looked in the mirror and lifted her shirt. The damage had almost healed.

She pulled down her shirt and reached for her hairbrush. All in all, bruised ribs had not been a bad outcome. Sophie had come off worse. She'd had to stay in the hospital for two nights, suffering from a concussion.

Now they were both back at work, as the aftermath of what had happened sent shockwaves around the station. The press had delighted in the scoop, describing Fry as *the rogue assistant chief constable*. One of the local rags had taken to calling Fry a *wolf in sheep's clothing*. Karen thought that was apt.

She had spoken briefly to Chief Constable Grayson after the incident. Then there had been endless rounds of questions, as DS Grace, the superintendent and Internal Affairs tried to figure out if the corruption ended with Fry. In Karen's opinion, it did. He'd been a narcissistic bully and the mastermind behind it all.

The full story hadn't been revealed to the media. Karen and Sophie hadn't been named in the details that had been released, but that hadn't stopped journalists identifying them. A crowd of reporters had hung around Karen's house for the past ten days, hoping to get a quote when she left for work in the morning and returned in the evening.

When she went downstairs, Mike was standing at the living room window, holding a mug of coffee and glaring at the group standing at the entrance to the drive.

'One of the photographers is taking photos of the house,' he said. 'Shall I have a word?'

'No, leave them. They'll get bored eventually.'

The snow had gone, but the weather had turned even colder. The early-morning sky was still dark, and frost covered the trees and bushes in the front garden. Christmas was just a few days away.

After she said goodbye to Mike, Karen left the house, head down, ignoring the questions shouted by the journalists and the flashes from the cameras. She gently edged the car out of the drive, worried she'd be on the receiving end of a lawsuit if any of the pests had their feet crushed by her tyres.

When she finally got to Nettleham, she stopped by Sophie's desk. 'You doing all right?' she asked.

'Yes, I've got another counselling session at lunchtime.'

'Is it helping?'

'A bit, I think. I'm still jumping at the slightest noise, though.'

'That's understandable,' Karen said. 'I think we're both going to do that for a while.'

'It's hard. I never for a moment thought . . .' Sophie trailed off.

'No, neither did I,' Karen said, and then slid something on to Sophie's desk.

Sophie looked up, surprised, then opened the white envelope. Her jaw dropped, and then her face broke into a wide grin. 'I thought it was sold out. How did you manage to get these?'

'I pulled a few strings,' Karen said. 'It's still a month away. It's at the end of his UK tour, but it's in Norfolk, so not too far to travel.'

Sophie stood up and hugged Karen. 'Thank you. I've wanted to see him for so long.' She looked down at the tickets to Dr Michaels's talk. 'Two?' she said, holding them up. 'You're coming with me?'

'If you want me to,' Karen said. 'But if you want to take Harinder instead—'

'I'd like you to come, Sarge. If you don't mind?'

'I don't mind at all,' Karen said. 'I'll look forward to it.'

'It's DCI Shaw's funeral tomorrow, isn't it?'

Karen nodded.

Sophie sat down again. 'It's infuriating Fry can't be held to account for killing Sam Pickett.'

Morgan and Rick had been working relentlessly, trying to find physical evidence to prove Fry had killed the young boy. The burnt-out car had been useless so far, and the traffic cameras, though they indicated he'd been near the scene at the time of the accident, didn't prove Fry had knocked Sam Pickett from his bike. They had a statement from a waitress that confirmed Fry had consumed a bottle of wine before leaving the restaurant and driving home. The friend he'd been dining with conveniently couldn't remember how much alcohol they'd consumed with their meal.

Arnie and Churchill had been pretty quiet since Leo's involvement in the corruption had been revealed. They'd worked side by side with him for eight years and had never suspected he was capable of murder.

Karen left Sophie and went to sit at her desk, then opened up her email and checked her messages. There was one that made her hold her breath. Not because of the subject, which just said *Information*, but the email address of the sender.

LeoClinton98765.

Karen's hand hovered over the mouse. How could it be from Leo Clinton when he'd been dead for two weeks? Karen had seen him die.

She clicked on the email.

Karen, if you're receiving this message, it's likely I didn't make it. I'm not going to pretend to be a good guy. There's no point. You probably know everything I've done by now.

If I'm dead, then I think it's very likely that ACC Fry killed me. He's been blackmailing, extorting and killing anyone who stands in his way for a long time. He's the one you've been looking for, the head of the corruption ring.

I've scheduled this email to send in fourteen days, unless I cancel it.

I'm giving you the evidence you need to put Fry away for a very long time.

Watch and listen to the attached files. I think you'll find them very interesting.

Leo.

At the bottom of the email were multiple attachments: a text document, a video and two audio files.

She opened the document first. It was all there. Names, dates, locations and payment records. Fry was top dog, and seven police officers were named as Fry's henchmen. Leo's written confession listed nineteen previously unsolved murders. Leo believed Fry had first associated with the Cook family back in 2004. But it didn't stop with the Cooks. Fry had been taking bribes from councillors and local business owners to bury cases for years. It was all there in black and white. Freeman's involvement was listed too. There was no way those responsible could escape justice with this evidence against them.

Karen reached for her mobile and typed out a text message to DS Grace: *We've got them. Leo's left us all the evidence we need.*

Then she double-clicked the file.

The video appeared on the screen. It was a recording of someone travelling on a dark road. The camera jumped as the vehicle hit potholes and dips in the road.

At first, she wasn't sure what she was looking at, and stared at the screen in confusion.

Karen put her hand over her mouth. It was a dashcam video, and the car the footage had been recorded from was travelling along Hill Top, going far too fast for the winding route. There was no lighting except the bouncing headlights. Before Leo had torched Fry's car, he must have made a copy of the dashcam footage for insurance.

She knew what was going to happen next. She spotted him long before the driver.

Twelve-year-old Sam Pickett, in his red jacket, was cycling on the left side of the road. The driver didn't react until it was too late. The car was travelling too fast to stop.

There was a horrifying split second when Sam looked over his shoulder, saw the car coming, and his face contorted with fear. Karen would never forget the expression on the child's face.

The car hit Sam and sent the boy on to the bonnet. The bike spun away. Sam's head crashed against the windscreen, and then, as the vehicle slowed, he tumbled to the side of the road.

The vehicle slowly reversed.

Another car was coming up behind. Karen could see the headlights. The vehicle pulled up alongside. The driver got out and stared at the scene in front of them. It was Laurel Monroe.

More headlights from the opposite direction. Another car stopped. A Volvo. Karen recognised the number plate. Lloyd Nelson.

He stopped the car and got out.

She saw them both inspect the body. They looked down at Sam sprawled at the side of the road, but they didn't touch him. Not once did they even check he was breathing. They didn't reach for their phones to call for help.

Karen leaned forward. She knew how this ended, but that didn't stop her screaming internally for them to do something, to help him.

The camera lifted slightly as though the driver had got out. Karen held her breath as ACC Fry walked around the front of the car, his face illuminated in the headlights.

Now, they had the evidence they needed. It was ACC Fry who'd knocked Sam Pickett from his bike.

A couple of minutes passed, and they all just stood around doing nothing. Even though it had happened in the past, and Karen couldn't change the situation, she found herself willing them to pull out their phones and call for an ambulance, but none of them did.

Laurel was the first to leave. She ran back to her car and drove off. Lloyd ran a hand through his hair multiple times, he flung his arms around, shouting at Fry, but ultimately he did nothing to help Sam.

He went back to his car as well, performed a three-point turn and left the scene.

ACC Fry walked back to his own car, inspected the damage and then disappeared from view. The camera dipped again – Fry getting back into the driver's seat.

Then he drove away, passing the smashed bicycle and leaving Sam Pickett to die alone.

Karen exhaled a shaky breath and pushed back from the desk. In death, Leo would have his full revenge on ACC Fry. Now they had something to tell the Pickett family. They couldn't bring Sam back from the dead, but justice was the next best thing.

She clicked on the first audio file. It was a recorded conversation between Leo and Fry. Fry ordered him to despatch the witnesses and destroy his car. The second file was Fry sentencing

Anthony to die. Leo objected and said it was an overreaction, but Fry overruled him. DCI Shaw knew too much.

Karen lifted her head. She'd been so involved that she hadn't noticed the open-plan office had fallen silent. Officers had moved closer to hear the recordings. They gathered around her desk.

'We've got the evidence now, Sarge,' Sophie said gently.

Karen couldn't speak. She only managed to nod.

◆ ◆ ◆

The crematorium was packed full of people of all ages for Anthony's funeral. Some Karen knew, most she didn't. Mike stood beside her. He hadn't known DCI Shaw, but he was there for her, and she appreciated his solid presence and support.

Her hand gripped his as the curtains shut on the coffin.

Afterwards, they walked outside and looked at the flowers. They'd donated money to the British Heart Foundation at the family's request, but the area outside the crematorium was filled with flowers and wreaths.

The cold air was sharp with the scent of cut flowers. As they stopped by a bouquet of white roses and peonies, Karen saw DS Grace, smartly dressed, talking to Anthony's niece. Though Karen hadn't been permitted to work with the team who'd brought in the corrupt officers, DS Grace was doing a sterling job – sorting through the evidence, liaising with Internal Affairs and the CPS to make sure appropriate charges would be brought against every person involved.

She had considered pressing the matter with the superintendent, asking to be present to witness DI Freeman's face as the charges were levelled against him, thinking it would help her move on from the betrayal. But it was enough to know that justice would be served. She didn't need to be there to gloat.

Karen shivered as they walked back to the car. The sky was bright blue, but the air was bitterly cold. 'You know,' she said, turning to Mike, 'I might give that group thing a try.'

Mike turned, lifting his eyebrows in surprise. 'The group counselling? But you said you weren't the type for cups of tea and sympathy.'

'I won't know until I try, will I?' Karen said, throwing his own words back at him.

He smiled. 'True enough.'

◆ ◆ ◆

Two weeks after Christmas, Karen sat on a moulded plastic chair in a small room at the back of the cathedral. Eunice had beamed when she saw Karen arrive. There was a big tea urn on a long trestle table, along with two plates of biscuits.

Karen had helped herself to two chocolate hobnobs because she felt like she deserved them for sitting through the upcoming meeting. She'd spent months resisting, but now here she was, ready for a miracle, hoping for help to move on. Her palms were sweaty, and her mouth felt dry. She was starting to regret being there already, but how bad could it be? It was only an hour, and if it didn't suit her, she didn't have to come back.

She'd been in touch with Leo's widow yesterday and passed on Leo's message to his daughter. It had been a long conversation. She couldn't answer all their questions, but tried to be honest.

Last weekend, she'd gone to the cemetery, to stand for a while at Josh and Tilly's memorial stones. No one else had been around, so she'd talked aloud, telling them what had happened, telling them how much she missed them and how sorry she was.

Tilly would have been eleven this year. Karen tried to imagine what she'd have looked like if she'd lived. She pictured Tilly in a secondary school uniform.

'Do you mind if I sit here?'

Karen turned and saw a woman with curly white hair, dressed in a long pink coat and a bright yellow scarf.

'Not at all,' Karen said, shifting aside slightly.

'Hobnobs,' the woman said, peering at Karen's biscuit. 'Good choice. You've not been here before, have you?'

'No, first time.'

'It's not so bad when you get used to it. Nice bunch,' she said, as the man at the front of the room called the meeting to order.

They were an eclectic group, and despite her instinct to hold back, Karen couldn't help feeling interested in their stories, their backgrounds and what had brought them here.

'Why don't we make a start?' the group leader said with a wide smile. 'We've got some new faces here tonight. Would you like to kick us off?' he said, looking directly at Karen.

No, she thought, *I wouldn't*. But she forced a smile and said, 'Sure.'

'Why don't you tell us a little bit about yourself, and what help you hope to get from the group?'

Karen looked around the room at all the faces. There were a lot of them, but they all seemed friendly.

She took a deep breath, and began to talk.

ACKNOWLEDGMENTS

My fantastic editor, Jack Butler, deserves a massive thank you for the hard work he has put into the Karen Hart series. It's been a pleasure to work with such a talented group of people at Amazon Publishing.

Special thanks must also go to the insightful Russel McLean for his input and invaluable attention to detail over the series.

Much gratitude to Jane, Lesa and all the people at Branston Community Library for generously spreading the word about my books.

To my family, a special thank you – and as always, thanks to Chris for his belief in me.

And finally, most importantly, thank you to my readers who have read and recommended my books. The support keeps me going even on those days I have a negative word count! Your kind words and encouragement mean the world to me.

ABOUT THE AUTHOR

 Born in Kent, D. S. Butler grew up as an avid reader with a love for crime fiction and mysteries. She has worked as a scientific officer in a hospital pathology laboratory and as a research scientist. After obtaining a PhD in biochemistry, she worked at the University of Oxford for four years before moving to the Middle East. While living in Bahrain, she wrote her first novel and hasn't stopped writing since. She now lives in Lincolnshire with her husband.